The Quarantine Station

MICHELLE MONTEBELLO

The Quarantine Station

Michelle Montebello is an Australian author and British English spelling is used in this novel.

ISBN: 978-0-9876416-0-1

Editing by Lynne Stringer and Marcia Batton
Cover Design by Kris Dallas Design

To Joanne.
My sister and friend.
This book is for you.

Blurb

**The rules were crystal clear.
She broke them all.**

1918 ... When Rose Porter arrives on the shores of Sydney with little money, she must take a job as a parlourmaid at the mysterious North Head Quarantine Station. It's a place of turmoil for passengers and strict rules for employees.

But Rose quickly discovers some rules were made to be broken.

2019 ... Over a century later, Emma Wilcott is struggling to help her dementia-suffering grandmother from wandering at night. Her long-term memories are leading her somewhere, and Emma realises she is searching for someone from her past.

Emma's investigation takes her to the Quarantine Station where she meets Matt, the station carpenter, and together they unravel a mystery so compelling it has the power to change lives, to change everything Emma ever knew about herself.

Grief is the price we pay for love.

~ Queen Elizabeth II

From the Author

While this story is largely based at the Quarantine Station, a site located on Sydney's North Head, the characters, storyline, some events in time and certain aspects of the station are fictitious and drawn from imagination.

Chapter One

The call came after midnight.

Its ring pierced the quiet, rousing Emma from sleep. Her fingers fumbled in the dark, finding her phone on the nightstand next to her and closing around it. When she glanced at the screen, a number flashed that she recognised instantly.

It was the call she always dreaded.

'Hello?'

'Is this Mrs Wilcott?'

'*Ms Wilcott*,' Emma corrected.

'My apologies, Ms Wilcott. It's Anastasia Thornbury from Eastgardens Aged Care. I'm sorry to ring you so late.'

'Is my grandmother all right?'

There was a pause. 'Mrs Wilcott, she's gone wandering again.'

'Again?'

'Yes.'

'How is that possible?'

'My staff were doing their rounds at eleven-thirty and when they checked on her, they found her bed empty. We've notified the Mascot Police Station. They're assembling a search team now.'

Emma closed her eyes. *Not again.*

'Mrs Wilcott, are you still there?'

1

'I'm here.'

'If you would like to come down to the facility, I can sit with you while they search for your grandmother. I'm sure she hasn't gone far.'

'Yes, of course. I'll be right there.'

'I'll see you soon, Mrs Wilcott.'

'*Ms Wilcott,*' Emma said, but the line had already gone dead.

* * *

Emma climbed out of bed and changed into jeans and a jumper, pulling uncombed hair into a ponytail. The night was cold and she felt it on her face the moment she stepped out of her apartment block. The road was slick with water and a veil of rain floated from the sky to blanket everything below.

As her car grumbled to life, she tried not to think of Gwendoline roaming the dark, wet streets alone. This wasn't the first time her grandmother had gone wandering. She was prone to it. It was often at night and right under the noses of the staff whose duty it was to care for her.

'For someone with dementia, she can be as cunning as a spy,' Anastasia Thornbury, the facility director, often remarked, as though Gwendoline made the conscious decision to purposely sneak off. Emma never knew how to take the forthright Ms Thornbury. She had wanted to say numerous times that it wasn't Gwendoline's cunning ability that outsmarted her carers, but perhaps their own inability to do their job properly. But she always bit her tongue.

Emma navigated her small, protesting VW away from her Kensington apartment block and onto ANZAC Parade. Traffic was light and she was carried easily to Bunnerong Road, then to Wentworth Avenue, where she turned into a quiet tree-lined street in Eastgardens. The rain was still falling, light drops fluttering onto her eyelashes as she stepped out of her car.

She locked the car door and crossed the road to Eastgardens Aged Care, a small complex of beige buildings with grey-tiled roofs and neatly trimmed hedges. It was the place she'd made the heartbreaking decision to admit her grandmother two years earlier when she'd been diagnosed with moderate cognitive decline.

It was a decision she'd struggled with ever since. Gwendoline was all that Emma had in the world. Placing her into permanent care had felt like a betrayal, a failure on her part to care for the one person who had cared for her when her world had fallen to pieces.

But simple moments of forgetfulness had developed into larger gaps in Gwendoline's memory. Numerous times she'd left the gas stove burning when Emma was at work, or the bathtub running, which almost flooded the apartment.

When Gwendoline had disappeared for an entire day, finally tracked down in bushland in La Perouse, Emma knew something had to be done. Quitting her job was not an option. She had to support them and full-time carers—even part-time—were expensive and not something she could afford. It was with a heavy heart that she decided to relocate Gwendoline to the nursing home.

But Gwendoline had started wandering frequently from there too and Emma worried that one day, she wouldn't come back to her. One day she would slip and fall, hit her head or drown in the nearby bays. One day, it would happen—the unthinkable—and panic seized Emma the way it always did when she was called to the facility in the middle of the night.

She shrugged off the dark thoughts and hurried through the main doors. Anastasia Thornbury was waiting in the foyer and came quickly to greet her. She was dressed impeccably in a navy blue suit and heels. Her dark hair was sleek and short, her face perfectly painted on as though she hadn't too, been fast asleep when the nurse raised the alarm.

She shook Emma's hand. 'Mrs Wilcott, thank you for coming.'

'It's *Ms Wilcott*,' Emma said, smoothing down her messy ponytail.

'Of course. I was just about to call you.'

'Have they found her?'

'Yes. Come into my office and we'll talk.'

Emma scrawled her signature in the visitors' book and followed Anastasia into her office. She took a seat in front of the large oak desk. 'How is she? Where is she?'

Anastasia sat too, in a dark brown leather chair. She leant backwards, pressing her fingertips together. 'I've been told she's fine. The

3

ambulance is at the scene now, assessing her. If she's okay, they'll transport her back here.'

The sweetest feeling of relief washed over Emma. 'Where did they find her?'

'Remarkably, she was all the way over on Foreshore Road. It's quite a hike from here, about an hour's walk. She was just wandering, which is a dangerous thing to do on a busy road like Foreshore. She could have been hit by a car. She seems to be drawn to the water each time.'

'How did this happen? Why weren't your staff watching her?'

Anastasia Thornbury's back stiffened. 'Mrs Wilcott, our nurses are extremely busy. We're not paid by you to provide dedicated care. It really is up to the patient to remain in her bed at night. It appears that Gwendoline takes advantage of our trust and slips out the door when no one is watching.'

'How can a one-hundred-year-old woman with dementia take advantage of that?' Emma asked pointedly.

Anastasia's eyebrows lifted before she quickly set them back in place. 'I apologise, Mrs Wilcott. I didn't mean to suggest...' She pursed her lips and waved her hand. 'In any case, when Gwendoline wanders from the facility, it is deeply upsetting for my staff. We're terribly saddened that this has happened again.'

Emma sighed at the response she'd heard countless times before. Anastasia was an expert at shifting blame and Emma felt helpless to challenge her. She needed this facility. Aged care was expensive in Sydney and Emma managed the expenses solely from her dwindling inheritance and Gwendoline's meagre pension fund. The facility in Eastgardens was affordable, close to home and Gwendoline was settled there. She had few other options at her disposal.

The director cleared her throat, seemingly eager to steer the conversation back into neutral territory. 'Mrs Wilcott, your grandmother has been unsettled of late. That's not uncommon in patients with moderate cognitive decline. The syndrome targets short-term memory first and can leave them confused with simple daily tasks. But in some cases, if the long-term memory is still unaffected, sufferers will go in search of those memories for comfort. These wanderings, in particular, seem to be related to Gwendoline's childhood. I think she's revisiting something.'

4

Emma sat forward, intrigued. 'Okay.'

'Sometimes we ask Gwendoline after these incidents what she was looking for. The response is always the same.'

'Which is?'

'That she's going to the wharf to look for the boat.'

'The boat?'

'Yes. Does that make any sense to you?'

'My grandmother was born on the Quarantine Station in Manly in 1919. Her mother worked there and Gwendoline lived there until she was seven. Perhaps she's looking for the boats that used to come ashore with the sick.'

'It's possible, though it's never *boats* as in plural. She seems to be looking for a particular boat.'

'I'm sorry, I'm really not too sure.'

'I have a suggestion,' Anastasia said.

'Please.'

'Does Gwendoline have any old photographs, letters or diaries from her time at the Quarantine Station that you could bring here? I feel that if you could show her these items or read to her from them, she may feel comforted and less inclined to go wandering.'

Despite Emma's feelings towards Anastasia Thornbury and the level of security offered at the facility, she had to admit it was a good idea. She was willing to try anything at that point. 'I've lived with my grand-mother since I was fifteen. I don't recall seeing anything like that from the Quarantine Station. All her belongings are in storage now, but I can go through them again.'

'I think it's worth a try.'

'I'll do it first thing in the morning.'

Anastasia's phone tinged and she glanced at it. 'Great news, the ambulance has arrived. Your grandmother is here.'

They both stood and Anastasia walked around the desk to shake Emma's hand. 'I'm glad we could have this chat. I do hope we can resolve this matter once and for all.'

Emma shook her hand and followed Anastasia and her tremen-dously tall heels back out to the foyer.

'They'll transport Gwendoline through the back doors so you can wait in her room if you like. I'll bring her to you.'

Emma thanked her and walked down the north corridor of the facility to Gwendoline's room. The door was open and she let herself in, turning a lamp on.

It was small and minimalistic; the same room Gwendoline had been in since she was admitted two years before. The carpet was thin and blue, the walls sterile white. A window overlooked the carpark at the back of the complex and Emma could see the ambulance lights bouncing off the buildings in the dark.

Over the years she had tried to make the room homely, bringing familiar items from Gwendoline's life to fill it with—paintings from her walls, her own reading lamp and frilly doilies to dress the surfaces. Still, that little room in the north wing of that nursing facility would never be Gwendoline's home. She belonged with Emma and she felt a familiar twinge of guilt over it.

As she waited for Gwendoline to arrive she tidied up the room, sorting laundry and preparing a clean nightgown for her. She straightened the items on the bedside table—a vase of red roses—Gwendoline's favourite flower—and a framed photograph of Emma's family. She picked it up and gave the glass a fond wipe with her sleeve before setting it back down front and centre on the table.

The bed was unmade, Gwendoline's indent still visible on the sheets. There was a tattered old book on her pillow, one that Emma had seen many times before—Jane Austen's *Pride and Prejudice*.

Emma picked up the book and turned it over in her hands. Her grandmother had been reading the same story for years, further evidence of her gradual mental decline. Emma swallowed back a sob.

Gwendoline was a hundred years old. She had made it to a century; a worthy milestone, but there wasn't much time left. Her condition would eventually deteriorate, developing into Alzheimer's, and she would forget how to speak, how to eat. Her psychomotor skills would be lost and she would die. There was no cure and little treatment available. Gwendoline would be gone and Emma would be alone in the world.

There was a knock on the door and she turned.

'Look who we have here,' trilled Anastasia proudly, as though she had found Gwendoline herself.

Gwendoline, small and curved in the back, lifted herself from the wheelchair. Her white hair looked like a compact nest and she had on a wet nightgown and a pair of muddy slippers.

'Grandma,' Emma said, dropping *Pride and Prejudice* onto the bedside table and reaching for her, wrapping her arms gently around her. 'Where have you been?'

'Catherine, dear, you came to see me.'

The statement gave Emma pause. 'No Grandma, it's Emma. Catherine's... not here.'

Gwendoline squinted at her. 'Oh Emma, it is you. How silly of me.'

'Come sit down, Grandma.' Emma helped Gwendoline to the bed. She looked exhausted from an hour of walking in the rain.

'They gave her an IV for fluids in the ambulance,' Anastasia explained, 'but otherwise she's fine. She'll need a good night sleep and the doctor will examine her in the morning.'

'Thank you. Can I stay with her a while?'

'Just sign out when you're done.' Anastasia closed the door to Gwendoline's room and Emma could hear the sound of her heels retreating down the corridor.

'Grandma.' Emma sat on the bed beside her and held her hand. It felt frail and bony in Emma's youthful grip. 'Why did you leave the facility again? You know you can't go walking away like that.'

'I was trying to find it,' Gwendoline said.

'Find what?'

Emma watched her grandmother closely, but a veil of confusion had settled between them. On one side, there was Emma and Eastgardens Aged Care and on the other, there was Gwendoline, stuck somewhere in the vast well of her memories.

'I wanted him to come back. I had to ask him...' Her words trailed off into mutters and Emma couldn't understand who or what Gwendoline had been trying to find. She wasn't sure she knew either.

'Grandma, do you have any old photographs or letters from your time at the Quarantine Station? Is there something I can bring to you that we could read together?'

Gwendoline looked at her with refocusing eyes. 'I don't think so, dear. We left the station in a hurry with one small suitcase between the three of us. Most things we left behind.' Her eyes strayed to the Jane Austen book then she slipped again from the present, muttering something about a boat.

'You're tired, Grandma. Let me help you into bed.' Emma removed Gwendoline's wet slippers and nightgown, changed her into a clean one and helped her under the covers. She sat and stroked her hand until Gwendoline drifted to sleep.

The sky was turning pink outside; a new day was upon them. As Emma watched over her grandmother, tucked safely away in peaceful slumber, her heart ached for a woman who was finding it increasingly difficult to tell memory from reality, whose body was at the end of its time.

'I'm not ready for you to leave me too,' she whispered as her grandmother slept. 'Please stay a little longer. Stay until I can find out what you're searching for.'

Chapter Two

The rain eased overnight, sweeping out to sea. A clear autumn day dawned.

Emma dozed uncomfortably in a chair by Gwendoline's bedside, waking at six am when the doctor stuck his head in with a jolly 'good morning!' He examined Gwendoline, gave her a clean bill of health, then breakfast was wheeled in.

As Gwendoline drank tea, Emma prodded her curiously about the previous night's walk and who she might have been looking for, but her grandmother was evidently sceptical that such a walk had even taken place. 'I don't think I did that, dear.'

Emma stole a slice of toast from her grandmother's tray, kissed her cheek goodbye and stepped out into the morning sunshine. She had an afternoon shift at The Coffee Bean and probably should have gone home to shower and sleep, but thoughts of Gwendoline searching the dark, wet streets for a mystery boat fuelled her interest.

She drove to Mascot, stopping along the way for coffee, and spent the morning in the storage facility where she had relocated her grandmother's possessions years earlier. She rifled through bags and boxes, old plastic tubs and photo albums, but she was sure finding anything related to her grandmother's time at the Quarantine Station would be a futile exercise. She was positive she hadn't seen anything like that when she'd packed it all up and she was certain she wasn't going to come across it now. The key to settling Gwendoline's night-time wanderings was not going to be found in that storage container.

Eyes heavy and back aching, Emma locked the roller door and went home to change for work.

The lunch rush was over at The Coffee Bean when she arrived at two. She pushed through the door and felt cool afternoon air follow her inside.

Her boss, Chloe, was behind the coffee machine on tiptoes, filling the grinder with beans. 'Hey, hey,' she sang out as Emma dropped her bag behind the counter and shrugged out of her jacket.

'Need a hand with that?'

Chloe was just over five foot and her petite arms were trembling under the load of the bag. 'It's okay,' she said cheerily, copper curls bouncing. 'I've got it.'

The café had almost cleared except for a few patrons sipping the last of their coffees. Emma stepped out from behind the counter and cleared the tables. She carried plates and glasses into the kitchen and began stacking the dishwasher. Her body was tired, her thoughts sluggish and she hoped for a busy afternoon to keep her eyes from closing.

'How was your night?' Chloe asked, walking into the kitchen.

Emma closed the dishwasher, setting it to a heavy-duty cycle. It gurgled to life. 'I spent it at the nursing home.'

Chloe leant against the stainless steel bench and flicked a tea towel over her shoulder. 'Is everything all right?'

'My grandmother went wandering again.'

'Oh, Em, that's like the third time in three months.'

'I know.'

'What's the nursing home doing about it?'

Emma sighed. 'The usual. They won't accept responsibility. They blame my grandmother for it, like she's purposely sneaking out.'

'Move her out of there.'

Emma stifled a yawn. 'I can't afford to move her. For the money I pay, the facility is pretty good. They just can't seem to keep an eye on her.'

'Have you slept yet?' Chloe didn't wait for an answer. 'Let me make you a coffee.'

Emma wiped down the bench and began preparing for the afternoon rush. She pulled a cheesecake and quiche from the refrigerator, slipped on disposable gloves and began to slice equal portions.

The Coffee Bean was a small establishment two blocks from Emma's apartment and next door to the local cinema. The patronage was a mix of office workers, university students and moviegoers, a constant flow of diners keeping the café busy until doors closed at ten.

It had been a scribbled job advertisement taped to the café window that had led Emma there three years earlier. She'd had no waitressing experience and was floundering around at rock bottom when Chloe had taken a gamble on her, offering the position. Emma had been there ever since.

Chloe returned with a latte and placed it down on the bench. 'Here you go; three shots of espresso. That will wake you up.'

Emma sipped, making a face. 'And keep me awake for days.'

'I've got two new university students starting at five. If it's shaping up to be a slow night, you can go home early.'

'Thanks. I should be fine after this.' Emma set the coffee down and went back to slicing the quiche.

Chloe leant against the bench again and studied her. 'So, what are you going to do? Obviously something has to change.'

'Yes, something has to change,' Emma agreed.

'You need to be more forceful with that director. She keeps slithering her way out of any responsibility. At the end of the day, you pay her a lot of money to care for your grandmother.'

'I guess I don't want to be a bother in case she asks me to leave. I don't have any alternatives and I can't care for Gwendoline full-time.'

'I doubt she'll ask you to leave,' Chloe said.

'She suggested that when my grandmother wanders, she could be chasing old memories. It's like they're leading her somewhere. She grew up on the Quarantine Station in the early 1900s. She lived there until she was seven. Did I ever tell you that?'

'The Quarantine Station in Manly? No kidding.'

'Yes. And when she wanders, she talks about going down to the wharf to find the boat.'

'Boats would have been in and out of that place all the time to drop off the sick.'

'Yes, but I think it's more specific than that.' Emma set down the knife. 'She's looking for a particular boat. I'm completely baffled. I don't know what it could mean. The director said I should find some old photographs or letters from Gwendoline's time there. If I could find something like that, it might give her comfort and she'll stop wandering.' Emma finished slicing the quiche and cheesecake and placed them both back in the refrigerator for later. She started on the salads.

'Does your grandmother have anything stored away that you could use?'

'No. I went through all of her belongings in storage this morning but couldn't find anything. And I don't remember seeing items like that when I packed it all up years ago.'

'Why don't you go to the Quarantine Station and ask around? Someone might know something.'

Emma stopped slicing tomatoes. 'I hadn't thought of that. I've never been out there, to be honest.'

'It's scary as hell at night. The ghost tours are good.'

Emma chuckled. 'I'll take your word for it.' But as Chloe left to serve a customer at the counter and Emma finished preparing the salads, her words continued to sound in Emma's mind. *Why don't you go to the Quarantine Station and ask around?*

The shift picked up and diners came and went. After helping to train the new staff, Emma left at nine and walked two blocks home, under a row of street lamps, to her Kensington apartment.

The air was cool and a bright moon balanced in the sky. She let herself into her apartment, dropped her bag on the lounge and kicked off her shoes.

Home was on the small side but she didn't need much space. The apartment comprised of a single bedroom, living room, kitchen and bathroom with windows that overlooked a street lined with pubs that never failed to remind her of how lacking her social life was. The walls were plain, the carpet a once-pretty cream and the furniture mostly

Gwendoline's because Emma had been thrust back into single life with barely more than a suitcase of clothes.

She flicked on a lamp. Exhaustion had crept in on the walk home and she wasn't sure if she was hungry or tired or both. Chloe had fixed her a container of quiche and salad for dinner. She placed it on the coffee table for later and ran a hot shower, scrubbing food and coffee from her skin.

Settled on the lounge with her plastic container of dinner, she switched on the television. This was her usual nightly routine—sitting alone in her pyjamas on the lounge, eating leftovers from the café, watching bad TV and listening to the frivolities of east Sydney life beneath her windows.

Friday nights were lonely, Saturday nights lonelier. She thought of her time with Drew and the challenges they'd had, and she wasn't sure if she desperately missed him or desperately hated him, though she suspected both.

The universe had thrown some curveballs in the past, life-altering ones, and Emma had clung on as best she could, adapting to each hurdle, picking up the pieces and trying to move on.

She didn't want to think what life would be like after Gwendoline was gone. There would be no trips to the aged care home, no frail little hand to hold or soft papery skin to kiss. It would be the end of all that she had left in this world.

Emma rested the quiche and salad on the arm of the lounge and reached for her laptop. The conversation she'd had earlier with Chloe still rang in her ears and her curiosity began to outweigh her exhaustion.

She typed 'Quarantine Station Manly' into the Google search field and hit enter.

The link to the official Q Station page popped up and she clicked on it, scrolling through the photo galleries and tours available. It was a different place now from when Gwendoline had been there a century before, having closed its doors as a working quarantine station in 1984.

In 2006, the Mawland Group had taken over the lease of the site and began an eighteen million dollar conservation and restoration project. The name was changed from the Quarantine Station to the modernistic Q Station, and it was now used for weddings, conferences, historical education programs and ghost tours. It was heritage-listed, significant in Aboriginal history and part of the Sydney Harbour National Park, located on North Head.

Emma browsed the website, read all the information, and it was after midnight when she finally closed the laptop and yawned. Her mind was made up and as she crawled into bed, her brain began to formulate a plan.

Chapter Three

T wo days later, Emma climbed into her humble VW on her quiet Kensington street and turned the ignition.

It was Sunday and she wasn't rostered to work at The Coffee Bean. Usually, she liked to make herself available for Chloe, picking up extra shifts when the university students called in sick after a night out. It helped with the rent but that day she was determined to make use of her time off.

The Q Station was located forty minutes from Emma's apartment, in Manly on Sydney's Northern Beaches. Emma navigated her grumbling car over the Sydney Harbour Bridge, up through Military Road and across Spit Bridge, the autumn sun bouncing off glassy water in Middle Harbour.

She felt light all of a sudden, as though bestowed with a sense of purpose. Rarely did she do anything outside visiting Eastgardens Aged Care or working at The Coffee Bean and certainly never anything as adventurous or spontaneous as this.

She knew very little about Gwendoline's childhood, only that she'd been born and raised at the old Quarantine Station in 1919. In 1926, at the age of seven, Gwendoline had left with her mother and father. She hadn't shared many details about her young life, or perhaps, disappointingly, Emma hadn't bothered to ask. Understanding who her grand-mother was and where she'd come from felt long overdue.

Emma turned her VW onto Sydney Road and ground to a halt in the weekend traffic. When she eventually crawled into Manly, she was greeted with a stretch of turquoise ocean that nudged up against the horizon. The sky was peppered with wheeling seagulls, tourists swarmed the esplanade and she heard a ferry toot its horn as it pulled away from the wharf.

She turned onto Darley Road and travelled up the hill past the Manly Hospital. Following the signage to North Head, she drove beneath an arch with the words 'Parkhill' engraved in the sandstone and followed the road to the Q Station. The view was lovely to her right; Sydney Harbour sparkling around the headland. With a view like that, there could have been worse places in the world to be quarantined.

In the Q Station carpark she found an empty spot and turned her car off, the engine ticking down. A few metres away stood a small building with the sign 'Reception' on the front. Emma shrugged out of her jacket, throwing it back into the car. The day had grown warm and she grabbed a bottle of water, her backpack and started walking.

The reception area was empty when she pushed through the doors and she approached the counter where a woman sat, glancing over a computer screen.

'Welcome to the Q Station,' she said, looking up with a smile. Her name tag read 'Joan'.

'Hi,' Emma said. 'I'm wondering if I could speak to someone about locating some historical information, specifically old photographs or letters from 1919 through to 1926.'

'Are you conducting research for a project?'

'Actually, my grandmother was born here in 1919 and lived on the station until she was seven.'

'How wonderful!'

'Yes, and I'd love to learn more about her time here. She's in a nursing home now with early dementia and we think it could help her.'

Joan looked thoughtful. 'We have a small museum on site. But I'm not sure if anyone is available down there right now to take you through. You would have to call ahead and book an appointment with the visitors' centre.'

'How about tours running today? I haven't pre-booked anything, but I'm happy to join if you have a spot available.'

'I'm sorry, dear. We have a daily history tour called the Wharf Wanderer, but it's already started, and the Quarantine Station Story tour only runs on Saturdays.'

'Oh, that's a shame,' Emma said, trying to mask her disappointment. 'I should have been more organised.'

'You're still welcome to walk around the grounds. Most buildings are open to the public and you can roam as you please. If you catch up to the Wharf Wanderer tour, I'm sure no one will mind if you tag along,' Joan said with a smile.

'That's very kind of you. I'll do that.'

'The shuttle bus is due to leave in a few minutes. It can drop you near the Former First Class Precinct and you can start there. You can board it again anytime from anywhere. Just wave Ted down as he passes.'

Emma thanked Joan and stepped back out into the sunshine. She boarded the shuttle and a few minutes later the driver, Ted, pulled away from the reception building.

The bus bounced down Wharf Road with a handful of passengers, the scenery beyond the windows an intriguing mix of steeped bushland and old weatherboard buildings propped up on sandstone piers. The verandahs, surprisingly spacious, had been restored with freshly-painted timber balustrades.

Ted dropped Emma on Main Axial Road at the beginning of the Former First Class Precinct and she stepped down into a light breeze. The shuttle continued on, disappearing around a bend. The sun was warm and there were a few people out strolling, but the expanse of land was so great it hardly seemed bustling.

Emma wandered down Main Axial Road, trying to grasp what life may have been like in the nineteenth and twentieth centuries if one were a first-class citizen forced into quarantine. She passed the former men's smoking room and women's sewing room and read from a large information board about a former liquor bar, barbershop, croquet lawn and tennis court. If you were in good health and good class, quarantine didn't seem like a bad place to be.

She passed a white building with the signs 'painter' and 'carpenter' over the top of two separate doors. She passed the former kitchen and first-class dining room, then a row of cabins, interconnected by walkways that were once the first-class passenger sleeping quarters, now refurbished guest accommodation.

Across the road was the Former Second Class Precinct, with a similar layout and beyond that, thirty hectares of heritage buildings and Australian native bush that sprawled across the headland. The sheer size of it was immense.

Emma reached the end of the Former First Class Precinct and stopped at a junction, feeling small in that vast place. She scratched her head, not sure which direction to go. A sense of disorientation set in and she wished she'd asked Ted for directions or Joan for a map.

She had no idea where Gwendoline had stayed with her family when she'd lived there and no idea where to start looking. Surely there must have been staff quarters somewhere on the station, but where they were and how she would get there, she hadn't figured out.

Perhaps the museum was a better place to start or she could try to find the Wharf Wanderer tour. At the very least, she wanted to find the wharf where Gwendoline's memories seemed to stem from, the mystery boat that so often drew her from her bed at night.

Deciding on the wharf as a focal point, Emma crossed over the junction, sticking to Main Axial Road. She reached a fork in the path and crossed over to Asiatics Road. After ten minutes of walking, an information board alerted her that she was now in the Former Third Class Precinct. With no wharf or water in sight, she feared she'd gone too far in the wrong direction.

She doubled back, but Asiatics Road somehow led her to Isolation Road and, with her sense of direction deserting her, she became hopelessly lost. She gave up somewhere near an old freestanding weatherboard building, which, according to another information board, was the former Gravedigger's Cottage.

Frustrated and hot, she sat on a grassy knoll next to it and pulled her drink bottle from her backpack. The sun was beating down, the day too warm for autumn, and she gulped back her water. In the bushland behind her, animals scurried around in the undergrowth and birds trilled.

There were no other tourists around. This area of the station was empty and Emma glanced up and down the road for Ted and his shuttle bus, wondering just how far she'd strayed off course.

She took another gulp of water and screwed the lid back on her bottle, tossing it into her backpack. She stood and headed back down the grassy slope, continuing along Isolation Road, embarrassingly relieved when she finally happened across a man perched over a set of timber steps, inspecting them. He was wearing work boots, shorts and a polo shirt and had a tool belt around his waist.

Emma walked quickly to him and he glanced up at her approach. 'Hello,' she said. 'Can you help me?'

He smiled warmly. 'I can try.'

'I'm think I'm lost. I'm trying to get down to the wharf, but I seem to have taken a wrong turn somewhere.'

'I'll say you have,' he said with a chuckle. 'You're nowhere near the wharf.'

She rolled her eyes at her own incompetence. 'I figured as much. Do you think you could point me in the right direction?'

'I can do one better. I can walk you there.'

'Oh, you don't have to do that. I don't want to interrupt your work.'

'You're not interrupting. I was heading down there anyway.' He smiled that warm smile again, exposing rows of perfect white teeth and Emma felt her stomach flip strangely in a way it hadn't in years.

'I'm Matt,' he said as he led them down Isolation Road.

'Emma. That's what most people call me anyway.'

'Emma,' he repeated, and she blushed at the sound of her name on his lips.

'So you work here?'

'Yes,' he replied. 'I'm from a long line of carpenters. My father, grandfather and great-grandfather all worked at this station at one time or another.'

'That's impressive. My grandmother was born here in 1919,' she explained as they walked, her sneakers and his work boots kicking up small rocks along the road. 'She lived here until she was seven, and then moved away with her parents. She's in a nursing home now. She suffers dementia.'

'I'm sorry to hear that. If she was born in 1919 that would make her...'

'A hundred years old.'

'What an achievement. Good for her!'

'Yes, though she has a tendency to wander from the home at night. It's starting to occur more frequently and I'm worried that one day something will happen to her, that maybe she won't come back.'

Matt was quiet as he listened and Emma wasn't sure why she was telling this stranger her woes, only that she felt oddly at ease in his presence.

'The aged care director said that introducing some items from my grandmother's past might stop her wandering, perhaps something from her days at the Quarantine Station; letters, photographs, that sort of thing. Unfortunately, she doesn't have anything like that in her possession, and I get the impression her parents packed up and left this place suddenly in 1926 with little more than a suitcase between them.'

'So you came to see if you could find something that will help her?'

'Yes, though I'm embarrassingly unprepared. This place is enormous,' she said. 'I don't even have a map or a clue where to start.'

He laughed. 'I remember the first day I started working here. I got lost a bunch of times. The station is huge. I've worked here for eight years and I'm sure there are still hidden pockets that I've never seen before. It's an incredible place.'

He spoke about it with such passion that Emma was able to glimpse past the disorienting presence of it and into the beauty. They were high up on the headland when they arrived at a cluster of buildings, interconnected with walkways, similar to those in first class. The view of the harbour was one of the most impressive Emma had seen so far.

Matt explained that it was the Former Isolation Precinct. 'This was the place you were brought to if you'd been in contact with a sick person but had yet to present symptoms yourself. It wasn't a great place to be in but the views were nice.'

'Almost worth going to isolation for?'

He laughed. 'Almost.'

They continued down Isolation Road, reaching the Former Hospital Precinct where two hospitals sat opposite each other.

'The original first-class hospital burnt down in May 1919 and they had to rebuild it.' He pointed to one of the buildings that looked slightly more modern than the other.

Emma turned and stared out at the view across the harbour to South Head. White sailboats bobbed calmly on the water and Sydney city glistened beneath a pale azure sky. 'It's hard to imagine there was so much death and illness in such a lovely place.'

'There were a couple of reasons why they built the hospitals up here,' Matt explained. 'Being high up, the wind blew away the stench of death. Can you imagine how awful the smell would have been otherwise?'

'It would have been horrible.'

'They also thought all the fresh air would blow disease away. Their thinking was a little backward, but you have to give them points for trying.' He touched her arm. 'Come, we're nearly at the wharf. The rest is downhill from here.'

He led them to a narrow path carved through sandstone that declined sharply. They followed it down, Emma holding onto the railing, sunshine wattle and bottlebrush on either side.

When they reached the bottom, Matt pointed to a long, wide jetty that extended out into clear water. 'And there's the wharf.'

He explained that most of the original wharf timber had been infested with white ants and extensive work had been undertaken to restore it to its former glory. The tracks from the funicular railway were still visible.

The buildings that made up the rest of the Wharf Precinct were brown brick and some had been refurbished and transformed into eateries. There were more tourists down here than in the other precincts, gathered around the café tables or sitting on the beach.

'Over there, near the restaurants, are the old shower blocks and the autoclaves. Arriving passengers were treated to showers with carbolic acid to remove lice and eggs from their hair and skin. Their luggage was fumigated in the autoclaves to kill anything that would spread disease.'

'Sounds awful.'

'Yes but it was necessary. Those treatments were effective, stopping typhus in its tracks.'

'I see. I was hoping to catch up to the Wharf Wanderer tour, but perhaps I won't have to,' Emma said smiling. 'You know so much about this place.'

'I guess it's in my blood. I find it fascinating. And when you love something like that, you just soak it up.' He led her to a long brick building closest to the wharf. 'Then you babble about it to complete strangers.'

They came to rest outside a doorway and Emma was able to glimpse Matt properly for the first time. His hair was dark, though sun had lightened the ends and his eyes were hazel with flecks of green and gold. He had long lashes and light stubble on his face that Emma found attractive. He was rugged and tanned, strong yet gentle, and she felt her cheeks flush at the thought of him.

'This is the museum,' he said, indicating the doorway and if he had noticed her sudden colour, he didn't acknowledge it. 'There could be something in here for your grandmother. You could take a few photos and show her.'

'That would be great.'

'I have a spare ten minutes,' he said. 'Want me to show you around? It's only small but—'

'Yes please,' Emma said quickly, and it was Matt's turn to blush.

He led the way through the door and they stepped into a large room with glass cabinets and displays that had been erected to form a winding path. There were old suitcases and tombstones, medical implements, framed maps and a yellowing book titled *Quarantine Deaths 1881–1962*.

Emma wasn't sure where to cast her eye. There were many things to look at—clothes and shoes, chinaware, teacups and teapots, items from a time so long ago that it hardly seemed possible they could still be here.

She followed the path around the museum, taking time to read the stories behind glass frames and to study dishes of medical instruments—

syringes, scales, jars and vials. The tombstones saddened her, for behind the intrigue were stories of disease and death, of families that had arrived whole but left parentless or childless.

Matt was a knowledgeable guide. He led her around the exhibits while she took photos on her phone, describing the use of certain implements and telling her stories about the staff and passengers who had been thrown together by circumstance. He answered her questions in detail and at times, her focus strayed from what he was saying to how he was saying it, with strong hands, that incredible smile and eyes that crinkled beneath long lashes.

'That was fantastic,' Emma said when they reached the end of the trail and arrived again at the doorway. 'Almost like stepping back in time.'

'I'm sure there are still hundreds of items hidden away in rooms and buildings that no one has come across yet. The place is just too big to have collected it all.'

'Well, thank you for walking me down here and for your impromptu tour. I enjoyed it immensely.'

'No problem. I enjoyed it too.'

'I better let you get back to work,' she said.

'Yes, I suppose.'

A moment passed between them, then Emma made the first move, slipping through the doorway and back out into the sunshine. 'Goodbye, then.' She started up towards the shower blocks where she hoped to catch the shuttle back to her car.

Matt called out after her. 'Do you still want to search for something for your grandmother?'

Emma turned and squinted into the sun. 'Yes!'

'Come back soon. I'll unlock the archive room. There's a lot of stuff in there.'

'Really?'

'Yes.'

'That would be great!'

His eyes lingered on her then he slipped back into the museum. Emma continued up to the shower blocks to wait for the shuttle, wearing a smile the entire way.

Chapter Four

ROSE 1918

Rose Porter squinted over the advert again, the sun's glare bouncing off the newspaper. It was unseasonably hot for May and she was sweating beneath her hat, gloves and the unforgiving fabric of her corset.

She smoothed her brow and dabbed the shine above her lip, clutching the railing for support as the ferry to Manly tumbled over rough water in the harbour. Foam sprayed up and wet her face but she didn't mind. It was some respite from the heat.

She glanced down at the advert again in her lap. *Parlourmaid Wanted. North Head Quarantine Station. First-Class Precinct. Board and Meals Provided.*

Rose folded the newspaper and set it in her lap. She wasn't a qualified parlourmaid nor had she served in a great house before. She had arrived from London only days before. Her home had been under air siege by the Germans, and Rose's family, her mother, father and six siblings, had decided upon refuge in the English countryside when Rose declared she would not be joining them.

Instead, she boarded the troopship *Ormonde* for Sydney, securing passage as a seamstress, making and mending troop's uniforms and helping in the galley. It had been a treacherous journey across unsafe waters, the transportation of civilians having ceased years earlier when

24

the Great War exploded. Nevertheless, after months at sea, she'd planted her feet safely on Australian soil. With little more than a handful of coins in her purse, she was eager to secure work.

Just like England, employment opportunities in Sydney were scarce. Seamstress roles had dried up, so too had jobs in munition factories and great houses, for with all the men sent to the Front, thousands of women had been forced into the workplace.

So when Rose had glanced at the newspaper over breakfast the day before and saw the advertisement for a parlourmaid at the Quarantine Station, she'd been intrigued. She had heard stories of the Quarantine Station, that it was the kind of place to make a grown man quiver should he find his boat docking at its wharf. Thankfully, the *Ormonde* had entered Australian waters disease-free.

To be willing to apply for a role in such a place was testament to Rose's desperation. She was far from home, in a foreign land and her money was dwindling. She had barely enough left for another two nights in her squalid shared room at the boarding house in Surry Hills. She had to find work soon if she didn't want to become a lady of the night like the other girls in her room.

The ocean splashed up as the ferry dipped and Rose smoothed the back of her pinned hair. The sun was fierce. Sweat trickled down the inside of her dress, though she refused to remove her hat and gloves. There would be hundreds of applicants vying for this role, if the women of Sydney were half as desperate as she was. She wanted to look the part of a skilled parlourmaid and hoped the interviewing officer could forgive her lack of experience.

The ferry docked at Manly Wharf and Rose disembarked with her handbag and a suitcase of clothes. Seagulls squawked and flapped near her ankles but she paid them no mind.

She walked purposefully towards the esplanade, bustling with people. She stopped to tuck the newspaper beneath her arm. Opening her handbag, she retrieved a map of the area she had collected at the Circular Quay terminal. She calculated the distance from Manly to North Head where the Quarantine Station was located, hidden away from civilisation. It was too far to walk, especially in the heat.

Rose looked around, considering her options. She didn't have enough money on her person to hire a ride in a new taxi cab; a luxury reserved for the rich, but she did have enough to spare for one of the few remaining horse-drawn carriages still in operation.

She approached a bearded man in a dirty shirt and suspenders. He reeked of tobacco, even from his position high on the carriage.

'Excuse me, sir. I'm looking for transportation,' Rose called up to him.

He spat tobacco out his mouth. 'Where are you going?'

'To North Head.'

'The Quarantine Station?'

'Yes.'

He peered down at her, his mouth moving beneath his yellowed beard. 'It'll cost you one shilling.'

Rose was outraged. '*One shilling*!'

'One shilling. And I won't take you all the way up. I'll stop at the quarantine arch. You'll have to walk the rest of the way.'

Rose didn't know where the 'quarantine arch' was, but it didn't sound close to where she needed to go. 'I need you to take me all the way into the First Class Precinct.'

'I value my life thank you, ma'am. I ain't going anywhere near the place.'

'Fine. Five pence and you can take me to the arch.'

'Ten pence. My final offer.'

Rose sighed in frustration. The only other horse-drawn carriage was pulling away from the curb with a passenger, leaving her with no bargaining power. She was conscious of time. 'Settled then. Ten pence it is.'

He hopped down from the carriage, took her suitcase from her and offered his yellow fingers for support. She placed one foot on the footplate and he helped her up onto the seat.

Rose sat with her hands clasped tightly in her lap while the driver stored her suitcase in the trunk, then climbed aboard the front perch. He requested she pay the ten pence in advance and she retrieved the beloved coins from her purse and begrudgingly handed them over. She had only a little left for the ferry ride home and didn't want to think about the long walk back to the esplanade she'd have to endure if she didn't get the position.

The driver snapped the reins and the horse surged forward. He clomped heavily along the road, pulling the carriage up enormous hills and along coastal streets where the ocean stretched endlessly to the horizon.

The landscape began to change and Rose sensed they were heading deep into bushland as they approached the station. A feeling of isolation settled over her as the trees grew thicker, the headland higher and the road emptier. There were fewer houses and then civilisation disappeared altogether. At the top of a hill, they arrived at a large sandstone wall with an arch.

The driver pulled on the reins, halting the horse and carriage. 'This is as far as I go,' he said, turning to her. 'The quarantine arch.'

'Surely you can spare a young lady a walk in this searing heat and go forth a little further.'

'This is as far as I go,' he repeated and turned away from her. 'If you had any sense, you'd hitch a ride back down with me.'

The challenge made her jut out her chin, hoist up her skirts and climb down from the carriage unassisted. She didn't wait for him to join her. She retrieved her own suitcase from the trunk and stood on the side of the road watching him. He snapped the reins and muttered good day without meeting her eyes. Turning the carriage around, he accelerated back down the hill, around the bend and out of sight.

Rose looked around. She was alone and the sound of the horse's hooves had died away. The only noise left was the thud of her own heartbeat in her chest. With her suitcase in hand, she concentrated on placing one foot in front of the other, forcing herself on. She didn't dare allow her thoughts to roam should her courage desert her and she turn and sprint back after the driver.

At the sandstone arch, she pushed through a set of double wooden gates and continued on the deserted road. She was incredibly parched, with her corset laced far too tightly for the heat. Her hands were clammy in her gloves and her hair was damp beneath her hat.

She noticed the landscape was different from that of London— thick and rugged bushland, and there was a sharp scent of something medicinal in the air that she couldn't place. The wildlife was different too. She heard the raucous laugh of a bird and glimpsed the strangest little critters with long snouts in the undergrowth.

After some time on the road, she reached a security post where an officer sat sleepily in a small guard house. He sat up when she approached and stepped out to greet her. 'Good day, ma'am. Can I help you?'

Rose stopped and tried to force saliva into her dry mouth. It felt like cotton wool. 'Yes, I'm here to meet Miss Dalton. I have an appointment for an interview.'

The officer was young and in full naval uniform. He seemed stunned that she was standing there. 'Did you arrive on foot, ma'am?'

'I had a carriage bring me up from Manly, but he dropped me at the quarantine arch. I walked the rest of the way.'

The officer whistled in disbelief. 'That's some walk. I'm sorry, this is a restricted area. We're not allowed to let the public enter.'

'Can you let Miss Dalton know I'm here?'

The officer scratched his head. 'Miss Dalton. Now, which one is she?'

Rose furrowed her brow.

'I apologise, ma'am. It's my first day and I don't have the radio with me. I can't call anyone to bring her down.' He chewed his lip at the dilemma. 'I suppose it wouldn't hurt to let you go in just this once. But please go straight to her. Don't deviate.'

'Of course.'

'If you continue down the hill and to the right, you'll find the first and second class precincts. They're across from each other. You can't miss them. I guess Miss Dalton's office is in there somewhere.'

'You are terribly kind.'

'And be sure to stay on the path at all times. We have brown snakes in these parts.'

'Are they dangerous?'

'One bite will finish you, ma'am.'

Rose suppressed a gasp. 'I will keep an eye out. Thank you, sir.'

She was off again. Her shoes were starting to pinch and sweat was running down her back. For all the effort she'd put into dressing for her interview, she would be a dripping mess by the time she found Miss Dalton. And she still had a walk back to Manly to endure if she didn't get the position.

A further thirty minutes on foot and Rose arrived at the Second Class Precinct. It was at odds with all that she'd perceived of the place. The disease and death had either been grossly exaggerated or was confined to another part of the station. Here groups of adults sat on the grass, smoking and eating oranges, with relaxed faces turned up to the sky. Children with glowing cheeks chased each other or played quoits, their peals of laughter ringing through the air.

She asked a young lad to point her in the direction of first class and Miss Dalton's office, and he gave her petite waist an admiring glance before directing her across the road. Within minutes she was standing outside a wooden door with a brass plaque that left little doubt as to whose office it was.

There were no other applicants in sight and Rose's heart sank. She was extremely late and the others must have already had their interviews. The position was likely filled and she would have to find her way back to her boarding room jobless and penniless.

She straightened her hat, dabbed at her brow and gave the door a reluctant knock.

It opened and a tall, thin woman in a white blouse and high-waisted ankle-length skirt greeted her. She had short brown hair pinned at the sides. 'Hello, can I help you?'

'I'm Rose Porter,' Rose said. 'I'm here for the parlourmaid position. I have an appointment for an interview.'

The woman's eyebrows lifted. 'How did you get in here?'

'The guard at the post gave me directions.'

'I asked those guards to send for me if anyone arrived for the position. This is a quarantine station, not a park. The public can't walk in and out as they please.'

'The officer was new and didn't have a radio.'

The woman huffed. 'I suppose you're here now. Best you come in.' She stepped aside and Rose entered.

The office was small with dark oak floors and a thin Persian rug. An uncluttered oak desk stood in the middle of the room and a carriage clock on a mantelpiece ticked loudly.

The woman gestured for Rose to take a seat opposite her. 'I'm Miss Dalton,' she said, sitting behind her desk. 'I'm head of housekeeping here at the Quarantine Station. I manage all passenger accommodation —first, second, third and Asiatics.'

Rose set her suitcase down and sat in a high-backed chair, trying to persuade her body to stop sweating. She longed to take her hat and gloves off, to fan herself. The room was stuffy and the only window was closed.

Miss Dalton shuffled papers around on her desk and looked at Rose. 'So, you're applying for the parlourmaid position in first class.'

'Yes. Am I too late? Has the position been filled?'

'Filled?' Miss Dalton's eyebrows went up again. 'Hardly. You're the only one to have applied.'

'The only one?'

'I've advertised the position twice. It's been running in the paper for weeks. There's been not a single enquiry.'

'You mean—'

'That's right, nobody else has applied. You're the only one.'

Rose opened her mouth to speak but no words came out.

'Don't look so surprised. Most people are fearful of this place.' Miss Dalton reached for a jug of water on her desk and poured Rose a glass. Rose accepted it gratefully and while she sipped, Miss Dalton spoke. 'You're English.'

'From Bethnal Green in London.'

'The war must be terrible there.'

'My family have relocated to the countryside to escape it.'

'And you decided to move yourself across the other side of the world?'

'I'm looking for opportunities.'

Miss Dalton nodded appreciatively. 'Well, I must say, I admire your tenacity. It's something you will need here. The Quarantine Station is not for the fainthearted.' She gave a wry smile. 'The station has been in operation since 1830. Ships entering Sydney are subject to mandatory health inspections. Any passenger suspected of carrying an infectious disease will force the ship into immediate quarantine. This includes passenger ships as well as troopships. No one is exempt from the process.'

Rose nodded. This much she had deduced.

'Once all passengers and crew have been assessed on board, the infected are moved off the ship and into our hospitals. The uninfected passengers are moved into appropriate accommodation to wait out the duration of their quarantine.'

Miss Dalton stood and smoothed down her skirt. She walked to the window and opened it, cool salty air rushing in. Rose felt it instantly on her face.

'It's terribly warm for this time of year,' Miss Dalton said to no one in particular. 'Warm air is good though. It keeps disease at bay.'

Rose remained silent as Miss Dalton continued to stare out the window.

'We cater for all illnesses here—cholera, typhus, bubonic plague, smallpox,' she said. 'Without a quarantine system like ours, the population would perish. The stories out of Europe are disturbing. They say there's a deadly flu circulating. They're calling it Spanish Influenza. We pray it never reaches our shores.' She shook her head grimly and returned to her seat once more.

'The logic behind quarantine is simple, Rose. The average passenger remains here for forty days. If they do not present symptoms, they are free to leave. If the passenger is ill, they remain until they recover or until such time as they die.'

Rose suppressed a shudder. Tenacity. She had to exhibit tenacity.

'Our burial grounds are filling up. We have two on the station.' She indicated somewhere behind her with a wave of her hand. 'We'll need a third one soon. Many people die here—men, women, children, soldiers, the rich and poor. It's something you'll have to get used to. Refrain from making friends with the children. No good can come of it.'

Rose nodded again, battling the voice inside her head that was telling her to stand up and run.

'The key to living, working and surviving here on the station is to remain vigilant to the spread of infection. If in proximity of the hospital

31

or isolation precincts, wear a mask at all times and scrub your hands upon leaving the area. Scrub them until they bleed, if you must.'

'I understand.'

'So with all that in mind, are you still interested in the position?'

Rose didn't pause, lest her courage dissolve. 'Yes,' she said determinedly. 'I'm still interested.'

Miss Dalton gave a small smile. 'There's that tenacity again. Very good. The position of parlourmaid is right here in the First Class Precinct. The role will consist of three shifts a day in the dining room and kitchen with breaks in between. You may or may not get a day off. Board, meals and a wage of two shillings a week are included, as well as uniforms. Female housekeeping reside in the female staff cottages just up the hill. No males allowed. All housekeeping report directly to me.'

'Yes, Miss Dalton.'

'We have strict rules about engaging in inappropriate relations with the male staff and especially with the male passengers. If anyone is caught doing this, it will result in their immediate dismissal without pay or references. The rules are in place for a reason. We don't have a schooling system here nor the budget to fund your babies.'

'Understood.'

'Well, that concludes the formalities. Do you have references?'

Rose reached into her handbag and produced two pages of references from London.

Miss Dalton ran her eyes over the details. 'Your references are good, but I see no experience as a parlourmaid. Have you worked in a great house?'

'No, but I'm a fast learner. I pick things up quickly.'

Miss Dalton spent an age considering her. Finally, she sighed. 'It's not like I have any other applicants to consider. And I do need to fill this position.' She shrugged. 'Very well Miss Porter. It's yours if you want it.'

Rose, despite all she'd heard, smiled broadly. 'I want it very much.'

Miss Dalton stood and Rose did the same. 'It's settled then. Your first shift will start at six o'clock tomorrow morning. And I see you've already brought your suitcase. Excellent. I'll show you to your room.'

Chapter Five

'This is all of first and second class,' Miss Dalton explained as they walked down Main Axial Road, separating the two precincts. 'As you can see, they're quite close to each other. We keep third class and Asiatics on the other side of the station, well away from here.'

They sidestepped a cricket ball that had come to rest at their feet. Rose looked up and saw a game in progress, the men turning to throw them appreciative glances.

'Most of the station has electricity now. Certainly the hospitals, isolation and the autoclaves do, as well as the morgue and laboratory. The only places that still require oil lamps or candles are the staff cottages, Third Class Precinct and Asiatics.'

Rose nodded.

'Your job will be to serve meals in the first-class dining room. You will take plates of food from the kitchen,' she pointed to a brick building they were passing on one side of the road, 'and transfer them across the road to the passengers.' She pointed to the other side where Rose glimpsed a dining room filled with chandeliers, elegant chairs and tables dressed in white cloths.

'Will that be all?'

'That will be your primary role, though we take on many roles here, chipping in wherever we are needed.'

'I understand.'

'We have the women's sewing room here and men's smoking room over there,' Miss Dalton continued, pointing. 'The first-class sleeping quarters occupy this whole section with the painter's and carpenter's workshops just here.'

They navigated around a potato sack race as children squealed. They left first and second class behind as the road inclined and they turned left at a junction.

'Now that you are employed by the Quarantine Station, you are not permitted to leave the grounds at any time without permission from me,' Miss Dalton said.

Rose quickened her step in order to keep up, the sudden incline and her suitcase causing her to lag.

'I must then request permission from the superintendent. You should be aware that he usually says no. We don't want our staff to potentially carry infectious diseases into the population.

'You are also not allowed visitors. You are allowed to receive letters and parcels, after fumigation in the autoclaves, of course. We have a post office that you can collect them from. The postmaster can assist you with all of that.'

They turned left onto Wharf Road then right onto Cottage, the lovely views of the water sliding away behind them. The bushland grew dense, tall gums rattling in the breeze. A cluster of weatherboard cottages with corrugated iron roofs appeared amidst the trees.

Rose guessed they had reached the female staff quarters. Some of the women were hurrying off to their shift in uniform or smoking on veran-dahs, others were hanging washing out to dry on makeshift lines. They were respectful when Miss Dalton passed, stopping to straighten their dresses and flick their cigarettes away.

Miss Dalton led Rose up a set of wooden steps onto a verandah, pausing in front of a door. She fished around in her pocket, extracting a set of keys and turning one of them in the lock.

Rose followed her into the room and saw a large girl clamber to her feet, a cigarette dangling from her mouth, which she quickly snatched away.

'Bessie Briar!' Miss Dalton said sternly. The room was heavy with cigarette smoke and she waved it away with her hand. 'Goodness, open a window.'

Bessie turned, opened the window behind her bed and tossed the cigarette out.

'This is Rose Porter,' Miss Dalton said. 'She's new. You'll be sharing a room.'

'Nice to meet you,' Bessie said.

'And you,' Rose answered.

'Bessie is a scullery maid in the first-class kitchen,' Miss Dalton explained. 'She's been here for two years.'

Bessie was a plump girl with pale, dimply skin and rosy cheeks. She had a tumble of golden curls and Rose noticed her hands were covered with open sores.

'A nurse from the hospital will be here soon to give you your inoculations; six in total. I do hope you're not squeamish around needles.'

'I'm not sure,' Rose said, grimacing.

Miss Dalton pursed her lips. 'We will soon see. After that, I will have your uniform sent up. Some of the ladies think they can be a little free around here, but not my girls. You are to wear your corset always.' She held up her finger for emphasis. 'Shape is important.'

'Yes, Miss Dalton.'

'Your first shift starts tomorrow morning. We meet at the first class kitchen at six o'clock sharp. Be prompt. I do not tolerate tardiness.' She gave them a curt nod and exited the room, her heels clomping on the wooden verandah.

Bessie flopped back onto the bed, which groaned heavily beneath her weight. She extracted another cigarette from a packet of Lucky Strikes in her draw and held it up to Rose. 'Do you want one?'

'No, thank you.'

Bessie struck a match, lit the cigarette and exhaled, blowing a stream of smoke into the air. 'Are you English?'

'Yes, from London.' Rose looked around the room. Across from

Bessie's bed were two others side by side, each with a sheet, blanket and pillow at the foot of the mattress.

'I've always wanted to go to England,' Bessie said dreamily, inhaling on her cigarette. 'I want to meet the royal family and marry a prince.'

'Princes don't marry commoners,' Rose said.

'Oh but he would love me so that he would change the law.'

Rose chuckled. 'Did you grow up in Sydney?'

'I'm from Leura in the Blue Mountains.'

'Is that far from here?'

'Three hours west by automobile or a day's trip by carriage.'

Rose eyed the beds again. 'Can I choose any one of these?'

'I wouldn't choose that one,' Bessie said, pointing to the one Rose almost sat on. 'Agnes, my former roommate, had a promiscuous way about her. Fifteen times on that bed!'

'Oh!'

'She was caught with some of the sailors from the troopship *Canberra*. Now she's with child. Miss Dalton made her leave the station without pay or references.'

'That's terrible. The poor girl.'

'The isolation can make people go a little crazy.'

Rose moved to the bed that wasn't Agnes' and sat on the mattress. She heard a crack and one side of the mattress collapsed. She slid, almost falling off the edge.

Bessie dissolved into laughter. 'And that one's broken! The leg keeps snapping off.'

'So a soiled bed and a broken one.' Rose stood and straightened her dress.

'You can go in search of the carpenter. He'll be able to fix it for you.'

'Where can I find him?'

'His workshop is in first class next to the painter's.'

'I recall seeing it.'

'If he's not there, he could be somewhere else on the station. You can leave a note for him.' Bessie flicked her cigarette butt out the window and climbed to her feet. She clutched at her dress and wriggled it up over her head, tossing it onto the bed. She was standing in little more than her petticoat, rolls of pale flesh exposed.

Rose blushed and turned away as Bessie squeezed into a brown uniform and apron.

'I have to get back to the kitchen to warm the ovens for the dinner service,' she said, tying a bonnet over her head to tame her curls. 'I'll see you later for staff supper. We eat at nine o'clock in the kitchen.'

Bessie left the room and Rose was alone. After a moment collecting her thoughts, she removed her hat and gloves and placed them down on her bedside table.

Next, she pulled her suitcase up onto the broken bed and opened it. She had brought only a few items from England—some clothes and her small sewing kit, which she rested on the floor by her bed. She placed three tunics and a skirt and blouse neatly into one of the empty drawers in the bedside table, followed by undergarments, two pairs of stockings and two petticoats. Then she set a pair of shoes at the foot of her bed and hung her coat over a chair.

Aside from the beds and bedside tables, the room was mostly bare. There was a single window near Bessie's bed, a table that held a wash basin and ewer and plain hardwood floors. There was no closet or mirror nor a cast iron radiator for heating, and Miss Dalton had been right about the electricity in the staff cottages. There were no electric light fixtures, just a small oil lamp and a lantern with a cluster of candles on the floor beside Bessie's bed.

Returning to her suitcase, Rose collected her hairbrush, pins and peony perfume and placed them down next to her gloves and hat. She arranged them meticulously, eager to dispel her fears and make this place feel like home.

The fact that she had managed to secure the position at all was of some relief. Instead of finding her way back to Surry Hills to spend another night in the squalid boarding house, she was moving into the staff cottages at the Quarantine Station. It hadn't been the position she had expected to fill; not quite seamstress work or a maid in a great house. Nevertheless, it was a job with a wage, food and board. All she had to do was work hard and avoid the cumulative cycle of disease.

The nurse arrived an hour later, just as Rose finished unpacking her suitcase. Sister Clark was old and dour with a severe face and bun to match. She ran dark beady eyes over Rose and sniffed as if to disapprove of her youth and beauty.

'You will need to remove both arms from your sleeves and push your bodice down.'

Rose removed the sash at her waist and unclipped the two pearl buttons at the nape of her neck. She wriggled both arms free and slid her dress and petticoat down midway, exposing her corset.

Sister Clarke produced a steel tray with six brass syringes, the cylinders filled with liquid. Rose turned away, staring out the window as she heard the sister preparing the injections. There was a sharp scent of alcohol then something wet hit her skin as it was disinfected. Rose winced when the first thick needle plunged into her muscle.

'That was tetanus. It always hurts,' Sister Clark said dispassionately and Rose felt the plunge of a second needle, then a third. Sister Clark taped a patch of gauze over her arm.

Before Rose could catch her breath, the sister was reaching for her other arm, disinfecting the skin and jabbing it hard with vaccine after vaccine—typhoid, tuberculosis, cholera, smallpox and plague.

'You're going to be sore around the injection points for a few days,' she said as Rose pulled her dress agonisingly back over her arms, fastened the buttons at her nape and tied the sash around her waist. 'You might feel unwell too. If there's anything severe, come down to the hospital.'

She piled the syringes back into the steel dish and left the cottage.

Rose moved to the bowl and filled it with water from the ewer. She splashed water on her face and neck, washed her hands and took a deep breath, feeling the colour return to her face.

Patting her skin dry with the towel, she reset the pins in her hair and went in search of the carpenter.

* * *

Rose found Main Axial Road easily this time. She located the white building that housed the painter and carpenter's workshops and entered through the carpenter's door.

Inside, his workshop was dim. There were no windows and she

flicked on a switch that gave her a spluttering burst of light before fizzing out.

She left the door open and looked around. There was a workbench along one wall with all the woodworking tools she might expect to find on it—hammers, nails, wood, dirty rags, hand drills and chisels. Hanging from nails in the wall above were more tools.

Unfortunately, there was no carpenter. He could be elsewhere on the station, Bessie had said and Rose decided she would leave him a note.

She searched around the mess on the bench for a pen and scrap of paper. She lifted boxes of nails and moved aside oil cans. She bent low to inspect the bottom shelf, rustling around amidst the tools when she heard a voice behind her.

'Can I help you?'

Rose jumped and hit her head on the underside of the bench. There was a chuckle as she extracted herself and rubbed her head. When she turned, a man stood in the doorway. She was unable to see his features, his silhouette backlit by the light outside, but she detected a slight grin on his face as he leant against the doorframe, watching her.

'I beg your pardon for the intrusion,' she said blushing.

He remained there, arms crossed, watching her.

'I was looking for the carpenter.'

The man pushed off from the doorframe and took a step forward. 'You found him.'

He moved past her into the room and Rose squeezed out of the way, sidestepping to the door. From there, she was able to glimpse him better. She noticed a strong jaw, brown ruffled hair and a smear of dirt across one cheek. He had eyes that were humble and kind.

'The bed in my cottage is broken,' she said as he turned to his bench and rummaged through the items. 'I was searching for a pen and paper to let you know.'

He looked up at her. 'Do you work here?'

'Yes.'

'I've never seen you before.'

'I'm new. I started today, well tomorrow. I start tomorrow.'

'What's your name?'

'Rose Porter.'

'Nice to meet you, Miss Porter.' He extended his hand, 'I'm Thomas Van Cleeve, the station carpenter.'

'It's nice to meet you, Mr Van Cleeve.' She shook his hand politely.

'Are you one of Miss Dalton's girls?'

'I am.'

'I like Miss Dalton. She's strict but fair.' He returned his attention to the bench. 'So you have a broken bed?'

'Yes. One of the legs has snapped off.'

He collected his leather tool bag, handsaw and a piece of wood. 'Well, Miss Porter, I suppose we had better take a look.'

* * *

She accompanied Thomas up to the female staff quarters, making small talk along the way. He pointed out the local wildlife—koalas and possums high up in the trees; animals she had never seen or heard of before—and she told him about her journey from Manly in the horse and carriage, then the impossibly long walk to Miss Dalton's office. He seemed to like it when she spoke, smiling all the way.

She opened the cottage door for him and showed him the broken leg on her bed.

'I can fix it, but did you know there's a perfectly good one next to it?'

'That was Agnes' bed,' Rose said.

A smile formed on Thomas's lips and his ears reddened. 'Ah yes, Agnes. We all heard.' He scratched his head. 'Well, I just need to remove the old leg, cut a new leg to fit, then nail it in place.'

'That would be wonderful.'

'It could take me a while,' he said. 'Best you wait outside. We're not supposed to be alone in your lodgings together.'

Rose went to sit outside on the verandah steps for Thomas to finish. She could hear him whistling as he worked and at one point, he joined her at the front of the cottage to cut a new piece for the leg.

Rose watched his powerful arms move the saw back and forth, cutting the wood, realising she had never taken the time to admire a man before. She had come of age in London as the war broke out, at a time when she should have been courting but when all the boys had been sent to the Front. She'd had many advances from drunken sailors on the *Ormonde* but had fought them off, staying close to the cook; a burly man with a fatherly nature and a good aim with a meat mallet.

Watching the carpenter now from her position on the verandah, she noticed how rugged he was in his trousers and shirt, how the muscles in his arms flexed and relaxed. She liked the smear of dirt on his cheek, the dirt on his hands, the boyish way he flicked hair from his eyes.

As she watched, she found herself wondering who Thomas Van Cleeve was and where he had come from. When he looked up and caught her staring, she blushed and turned away.

He went back inside and the sun began to dip below the trees. Rose rested her chin on her knees and settled into the quiet. Birdsong trilled from the trees and animals rustled in the undergrowth; such tranquillity when compared with the noise and grit of London's streets. Still, she was overcome with a sense of displacement in this strange land where everything looked and felt perplexingly foreign.

Thomas emerged later onto the verandah with his satchel of tools. 'All fixed. It's as good as new now.'

Rose stood. 'Thank you. I'm most appreciative.'

'It was nothing.'

They stood on the verandah as a moment passed between them, neither moving nor speaking. Their eyes met and held then Thomas broke away. 'I should go.'

'Of course. I've kept you too long.'

'Actually, I'm finished for the day,' he said, trotting down the steps and turning back to her. 'I was thinking I might stroll down to the wharf. The sunset is lovely on the water.'

'That would be a sight indeed.'

'Would you care to join me?' he asked.

She hesitated.

'We could stop by and see Bessie. She might have something in the larder for us.'

Rose brightened. She hadn't eaten anything since breakfast at the boarding house. 'I am quite famished.'

Thomas smiled. Rose slipped into step beside him and they walked back down the hill to first class. They visited Bessie in the kitchen and she passed them two oranges from behind the cook's back with a sly grin.

Next, they stopped at Thomas's workshop and he dropped off his tool bag. Rose waited outside and when he emerged again, he had on a clean shirt and the smear of dirt from his cheek was gone.

He led the way to the wharf, guiding Rose down winding paths flanked by thick brush. He pointed out the funicular railway to her, where luggage was transported from the wharf, through the luggage shed and fumigation chambers of the autoclaves, curving around the shower blocks before it was hauled up the steep sandstone incline to healthy ground. They turned at Quarantine Creek Junction and Rose caught sight of the Hospital Precinct high on the hill; a place she had no desire to visit.

They talked and peeled their oranges, and when Rose bit into hers, it was wonderfully sweet and juicy, like nothing she'd tasted before. Her fingers and lips were sticky as she sucked on the flesh.

'So what has brought a young English lady like you all the way across the world, Miss Porter?' Thomas asked as they continued along the path.

'Please, you may call me Rose.'

'All right, Rose.'

'The war has been hard on England, Mr Van Cleeve, particularly London. My family are from Bethnal Green. They decided some time ago to pack up and move to the country and when they did, I decided to come here.'

'So you boarded a vessel, crossed seas filled with your enemy's ships and sailed across the world to a foreign country on your own? I've never met a person like you before.'

She smiled. 'I'm not sure if that makes me sound terribly brave or terribly silly, but yes, that's what I did.'

'Certainly not silly,' he said with admiration. 'In fact, you are so brave that you accepted a position as a parlourmaid in a quarantine station where people are dying and the odds are against you every day.'

'Now that decision I may have to rethink,' she said laughing.

'You are braver than most, Miss Porter.'

They reached a small cove where the ground grew flat and Thomas pointed out the buildings of the Wharf Precinct—the autoclaves, boiler room, luggage shed and disinfecting shower blocks.

They stepped down onto the sand as water lapped gently at the shore. Thomas bent to wash his sticky hands in the sea and Rose followed. When he sat down to take his shoes off and sink his feet into the sand, Rose hesitated.

'Go on,' he said. 'When was the last time you felt sand as soft as this between your toes?'

'I've never felt sand before, Mr Van Cleeve.'

Thomas patted a spot next to him. 'Then I insist.'

Rose sat beside him and unlaced one shoe. She slipped it off then unlaced her second. She had them both off in minutes and sat with her stockinged toes sinking into the sand.

'Isn't it something?'

'It's beautiful,' she said, grasping a mound of it in her hands and letting it fall through her fingers.

'It's peaceful here. Sometimes I like to come down to the cove on my own and just sit. Down here it's easy to forget all the sad things that are happening back up there.'

Rose stared out at the heavily-treed escarpments across the water. Everywhere she looked, the Australian bush stared back—quiet, unassuming. It was so unlike the noisy, over-crowded streets of home. She wasn't sure whether to feel calmed or unsettled by it.

'Across the bay you can see Middle Head, Smedley's Point and Little Manly Point,' Thomas explained.

'Have people ever tried to escape across the water to avoid quarantine?' Rose asked.

'A few,' Thomas said. 'But they don't usually get far. Sometimes they drown or the bush kills them. If they're sick, they succumb to their illness.'

They sat in silence for a time with the station behind them a hive of activity. Rose breathed in the smell of driftwood and the sharp tang of the sea. She heard the bird with the raucous laugh again, deep in the trees.

Thomas nodded towards the wharf, jutting out into the water like a long planked arm. 'Boats are inspected by health officials as soon as they come through the Heads and into Port Jackson. If illness is suspected among the passengers, the ship is anchored out here in this bay and the passengers are transferred to the wharf.'

Rose squinted at the wharf in the dying sunlight. A group of young men sat with their feet dangling over the edge, their toes skimming high tide. She could hear their laughter and smell their cigarette smoke.

'They're the boys from the autoclaves and luggage transfer,' Thomas explained. 'They're a good bunch.'

'How long have you worked here, Mr Van Cleeve?'

'Please, Thomas,' he said with a smile. 'I've worked here for five years.'

'And you've managed to escape illness yourself. That's an achievement.'

'I mostly keep to myself. I don't socialise much,' he said, drawing his knees up and leaning his elbows on them. He offered nothing more and Rose sensed that he was a contemplative man. She didn't want to disturb his solitude and sat silently beside him as the sun finally dipped, casting the beach into shadow.

After dusting the sand from their feet and slipping on their shoes, Thomas walked Rose back to first class where he bid her good evening and disappeared into his workshop. Rose walked the rest of the way up the hill to the staff cottages. She washed and changed her clothes and at nine o'clock, she stepped out for the staff supper.

As she walked, she tried to picture what her first day as a first-class parlourmaid might be like but instead, inexplicably, all she could think about was the carpenter.

Chapter Six

At six o'clock the following morning, Rose reported for work in the first-class kitchen. Bessie was already there, boiling large copper pots of water and heating the ovens. Rose had heard her leave the cottage sometime before dawn, when the sky was still black and the birds soundless. Rose had risen not long after, washing her face, setting her hair and pulling on her new uniform and apron.

Miss Dalton was waiting in the kitchen, dressed in a smart plum jacket and skirt with a silver watch necklace. Standing in a small circle were five other parlourmaids and the cook, Mrs March, a plump woman with ginger hair and beady eyes.

Miss Dalton introduced Rose to Mrs March and ran through her duties for the morning. Rose listened, trying to grasp the many instructions—manage your section of the dining room, lay the toast and spreads, tend to the tea and coffee, serve the hot breakfast, be polite and attentive, do not engage in conversation, do not drop anything on the floor or on the passengers and clear the dining tables afterwards.

'After service, all dishes and cutlery can be stacked on this bench for Bessie to scrub,' Miss Dalton said.

Rose glanced over at Bessie who was already up to her elbows in steaming water.

'Staff breakfast is at nine-thirty after the dining room has been cleared, followed by lunch at two and supper at nine in the evening.'

'And might I add,' Mrs March said, crossing her arms over her ample bosom, 'if I catch you stealing food from my larder, you'll leave this kitchen with no hands.'

Rose swallowed and Bessie giggled from her spot by the sink.

Miss Dalton consulted the watch on the end of her necklace. 'Guests will be arriving in the dining room in thirty minutes. Rose, follow the lead of the other parlourmaids. They can show you the ropes. I have to get up to third class to ensure all is in order there. I'll be back shortly.'

Miss Dalton stepped out of the kitchen, and Mrs March and the parlourmaids burst into a torrent of activity. Rose was given a pile of plates and cutlery to push across the road to the dining room on a serving trolley, and was shown how to set the breakfast tables properly.

She slipped on a pair of white gloves and placed down cutlery and side plates, taking care to position them exactly an inch from the edge of the table. She laid out salt and pepper with accompanying salt spoons, along with butter dishes and knives. Following that was the marmalade, honey, sugar cubes and napkins.

She had barely caught her breath when Miss Dalton arrived back, whirring through the dining room to inspect each table. 'Those spoons need buffing,' she pointed out. 'There's no marmalade on this table. Where are the napkins for this setting? My goodness girls, are we still asleep?'

Rose and the other parlourmaids ran frantically to make the corrections as the doors swung open and first-class passengers began to pour in.

Rose had never before seen such aristocracy gathered in the one room. There were men in smart suits and polished shoes, their moustaches trimmed and combed. Women wore dresses of fine silk, their throats garnished with pearls. The children had clean skin and neat hair, and were dressed in tailored shorts and pretty frocks. They took their seats and waited to be served and, despite being healthy but stranded in quarantine for forty days, Rose hardly felt their circumstance was a poor one.

They were served bacon, sausages and eggs with hot toast and beans. The parlourmaids were attentive with the tea and coffee. Rose felt she must have poured a thousand cups by the end of service, moving through a heady haze of aftershave and perfume.

She wasn't quite sure how Bessie and Mrs March were keeping up in the kitchen, only that they were, for the food continued to flow as she ran from the dining room, across the road to the kitchen and back again with serving trolleys full of plates.

When service was finished and the passengers began to idle out of the dining room—men donning their smoking jackets for the smoking room and women fussing over the children—they cleared the tables.

Rose piled the empty plates, teacups, cutlery and butter dishes back onto the trolley and pushed them across the road to the kitchen where Bessie was madly scrubbing, her plump cheeks bright with sweat.

Miss Dalton appeared in the kitchen looking flustered. 'Gather round please, everyone. I have an important announcement to make before we sit down to breakfast. You too, Mrs March.'

They gathered in the middle of the kitchen to listen to Miss Dalton speak.

'A passenger boat came through the Heads early this morning and was inspected by health officials. They discovered a suspected outbreak of Spanish Influenza.'

There were gasps and murmurs.

'Yes, yes, I know,' Miss Dalton said. 'I fear the pneumonic flu has made it to our shores. Let us pray it is the only case we see. But that's not all.' She pursed her lips. 'Passengers on board include the Duke of Northbury and his wife, the Duchess of Northbury. The duke is the first cousin to His Majesty, the King.'

'Cousin to the king? What's he doing all the way out here?' Mrs March asked.

'I am told the duke is here in an official capacity. I do not know any more than that. His business is his own.'

Bessie squealed. 'A visit from royalty!'

'Those plates won't wash themselves, Bessie Briar,' Miss Dalton snapped. 'We have lunch service in a few hours.'

Bessie returned to the sink, plunging her raw hands back into the scalding water.

'So who caught the influenza then?' Mrs March asked.

'I understand that the duke is well, but the duchess has taken ill. So too, have a number of their crew. There was a stop at a port in Papua New Guinea where one of them is believed to have contracted it. And, of course, it spread from there.'

'Where are they now?'

'The duchess and infected crew have been taken to the Hospital Precinct. The other crew members are in isolation. But the duke has absolutely refused to go there. He wishes to be brought straight here to first class.'

'The duke won't go to isolation?' Mrs March looked outraged. 'But he has to. He's been on an infected ship, sleeping next to his infected wife. He's going to make us all sick by coming straight here.'

'He has yet to present any symptoms and as we believe is the case with Spanish Influenza, it is extremely fast moving. So let's hope he hasn't contracted it. In any case, we will set up a room for him here in first class where he can carry out his isolation in comfort. He will not visit the dining room for the next two weeks and I will tend to him personally.'

'Will the duchess recover?' Rose asked.

Miss Dalton looked grim. 'That answer I cannot give you.'

Mrs March harrumphed and went back to sorting the staff breakfast. The small table in the kitchen was cleared and reset with cutlery and plates, and Mrs March served eggs and sausages with toast and jam. Bessie poured tea for Miss Dalton and the parlourmaids, and Rose pushed out a chair for her to join them.

Bessie coloured at the gesture. 'I'm the last one to eat, Rose. Only after all the dishes are done.'

'Oh.' Rose coloured too. 'I'm sorry, I didn't realise.'

'That's all right. I'm used to it.'

The parlourmaids and Miss Dalton ate while Bessie went back to scrubbing the dishes, and Mrs March prepared a plate of breakfast for the duke.

When the meal was over, Miss Dalton dismissed them and Rose

pushed in her chair, feeling guilty for leaving Bessie behind, who was still cleaning up. With two hours to spare before she had to return for the lunch service, Rose went back to the cottage to change out of her uniform and wash her face and hands.

She slipped the stockings off her feet and contemplated unlacing her corset. There was something terribly freeing about being on the station, where daily life was more about survival than the rigid dress code of society. She untied the corset, her waist crying out in relief and tossed it into her suitcase with her stockings, remembering that she would have to put both back on before next service, otherwise risk the wrath of Miss Dalton. Then she slipped a blue tunic straight over her petticoat.

It was a warm morning when she stepped back out and she wandered again down to first class. She wasn't sure what to do or where to go. There was time to spare and she wanted to explore, but the station was vast and she didn't want to become lost or end up somewhere she wasn't supposed to, like the unhealthy ground where the hospitals and isolation were.

Rose thought about returning to the cove to run her fingers through the sand. She walked down Main Axial Road and hesitated out the front of Thomas's workshop. It was unlikely he would be there, his work taking him all around the station. She wasn't even sure why she had stopped there, only that going to the cove had reminded her of him.

She shook her head and decided to keep walking when he stepped out of his workshop and almost collided with her.

'Rose!'

'Thomas.'

'I'm sorry, I didn't see you there.'

'I apologise. I was just out for a walk and...'

He was watching her so intently that her breath caught.

'Well, I thought to stop by and say good morning and then I decided you might be busy and so I was going to keep walking...' She was rambling, her cheeks burning.

'It's a lovely morning for a walk,' he said.

She breathed. 'Indeed.'

'Are you going somewhere in particular?'

'I was thinking the cove.'

He nodded. 'The cove. Lovely.'

'Yes.'

'If you would like some company, perhaps I could join you.'

'I would like that very much,' she said.

He smiled. 'Okay. I just have to check on something for Mrs March and then I'll be right back. Would you mind waiting a few minutes?'

'Not at all.'

Rose watched Thomas hurry across the street to the first-class kitchen. She heard Mrs March's booming voice as she explained of a mishap with one of the larder shelves. She barely heard Thomas at all, so softly-spoken.

He emerged from the kitchen and trotted back to her. Bright sunlight had turned his hair auburn and his eyes were hazel with flecks of green and gold. He smiled at her and for a moment she thought he was going to take her hand, but he swung into step beside her and they strolled down the street towards the wharf.

Soon they were on flat ground by the shower blocks and autoclaves. On the beach they sat and untied their shoes and Rose, in the absence of stockings, felt the warm, soft sand between her toes.

'It's just marvellous,' she said, dragging her fingertips through it.

'The cove is one of my favourite spots on the station.'

'I can see why.'

They stared out across the water, sunlight twinkling off the surface. A large vessel painted with the royal coat of arms was anchored and bobbing in the bay.

'Did you hear?' Rose asked.

'About the king's cousin?'

'Yes. His ship was quarantined because of Spanish Flu. His wife, the duchess, has taken ill.'

'I'd heard. It's not often we get royalty coming through the station. In fact, I can't remember it ever happening before. And it's our first case of Spanish Flu. That can't be a good sign.'

'I do hope the duchess will recover.'

They sat quietly as the water broke gently against the sand. Rose heard the raucous laugh of that bird again and turned to Thomas.

'Tell me, what animal makes that maniacal sound?'

Thomas laughed heartily. 'That's a kookaburra.'

'*A what?*'

'A kookaburra. It's a bird native to Australia. We call him the Laughing Kookaburra or sometimes the Bushman's Clock. He's a happy fellow and yes, he does have a crazy laugh.'

'A kookaburra,' she said, trying out the word. 'He has an equally crazy name.'

Thomas laughed again and placed his hand over hers. Rose felt something pulse through her like electricity. For a moment, she thought he might leave it there, but he pulled it away and traced it through the sand.

'So tell me, Rose Porter, you've travelled a long way from home. That much I know. What made you embark on such a journey?'

'I wanted a new life.'

'But why? What makes a young lady decide to leave her home and take on the world?'

Rose looked up to the sky, feeling the sun on her face. She felt it warm her muscles and bones, melting away the England damp. She felt it invade every fibre of her in such a way that she wanted to open up to Thomas, to tell him everything about her and learn all that she could about him. Suddenly, it felt as if they were the only two people for miles.

'When my parents decided to move us from Bethnal Green to the country to escape the war, my father also decided I should marry. The butcher's son in the country town we were moving to was his choice.'

Thomas let out a low whistle.

'Perhaps I was impulsive and childish, even a little ungrateful, but that wasn't the life I wanted. I didn't want to marry the butcher's son, to have his babies and run his household. I wanted to see new things, to learn and be educated. That's not to say I don't wish for marriage and children, for certainly I do, but perhaps with someone of my own choosing. Someone I actually like.'

'You're a sensible girl, Rose, though I suspect not one who conforms so easily.'

'Time will tell if I've made the right decision.'

'You could have just moved to Scotland. It would have been a lot closer and you still would have made your point.'

Rose laughed out loud. 'Yes, you're probably right. In hindsight, Australia was a bit far.'

'I'm not complaining. In fact, I'm glad for it,' he said.

Rose's heart flipped.

'So what do you like to do when you're not marrying butcher's sons and settling in the English countryside?'

'I'm good with a needle and thread and can get by as a seamstress.'

'But is that what you love to do? Is that what excites you and makes your heart want to burst?'

'I like to write,' Rose said. It was something she had never admitted to anyone before. Her father would have thought it silly. 'I enjoy writing. I'm not terribly gifted at it nor do I have a preference; stories over poems for example. I just like words. I like to learn new ones and see how they look on a page. I love the way the meaning of a sentence can change entirely just by tinkering with a few words.'

'*Tinkering*. I like that word.'

'What about you, Thomas Van Cleeve? What do you love to do? What makes your heart burst?'

'I love carpentry. I love wood. I love to build and fix things. I love *tinkering*, as you say.'

'So you're already doing what you love?'

'I believe I am.'

They sat on the sand for the next hour, talking of life and dreams. It was with heavy regret that she took Thomas's hand and he helped her to her feet. The lunch shift was due to start and she had to return to her cottage to change.

Thomas walked her back up to first class and she said goodbye to him at his workshop. He disappeared inside and she continued up to the female staff quarters to change back into her corset and uniform.

She passed a large cottage on her way; still part of the First Class Precinct but separate from the other buildings in that it wasn't connected by walkways or close to any of the first-class amenities. It was freestanding and nestled among the blue gums. *Accommodation perfect for isolation.*

There was a man standing on the verandah, staring at her as she passed. He was smoking a pipe and wore a crisp white shirt and brown tweed pants. He looked only slightly older than Miss Dalton, with dark hair and eyes so deep and blue they seemed to pierce a hole straight through her.

He gave her a half wave as she walked by and she quickly averted her gaze, continuing up the hill to her quarters.

She felt the duke's eyes on her the entire way.

Chapter Seven

EMMA 2019

E mma scrawled her signature in the visitors' book and started down the north corridor of Eastgardens Aged Care towards Gwendoline's room. She visited her grandmother twice a week, on Tuesday and Saturday mornings and she always brought with her a bunch of Gwendoline's favourite flowers—red roses.

She found her grandmother sitting up in bed staring blankly out the window. Emma leant forward, kissed her soft cheek and went in search of the vase she regularly used, locating it on the top shelf of the narrow wardrobe.

'How are you feeling today, Gran?' Emma called out from the bathroom where she filled the vase with water from the tap.

'I'm lovely, Catherine. How are you?'

Emma forgave the slip. 'I'm good.' She placed the vase on the bedside table and sat the roses in it, arranging them neatly, noticing that Jane Austen's *Pride and Prejudice* was out again. 'I see you've been doing some reading. Would you like me to get you a different book? There are plenty in storage I could dig out for you.'

'No thank you, dear. I like the one I've got,' Gwendoline said, leaning across to tuck the book safely away in her bedside drawer.

Emma finished arranging the roses and cleared a spot at the back of the table to place the vase. The framed photograph of her family caught her eye, as it always did, and she picked it up.

It had been taken when she was fourteen, a photo of the five of them on a boat on the Hawkesbury River—her mother, father and twin brothers, Max and Liam.

She remembered that day like it was yesterday. It had been sweltering hot, everyone eager to swim and water ski, a moment of captured conviviality.

She placed the frame down and sat on the edge of the bed. Gwendoline was watching her closely.

'You brought me roses,' she said.

'I always bring you roses, Gran.'

'That's because you're a good girl.'

Emma gave her a sad smile. 'I haven't always been.'

Gwendoline reached forward to pat her hand understandingly. Emma studied the frail fingers on her own, the translucent skin and the ridges of blue veins. It was old age at play, when the body wilted and the mind failed. When a person was no longer the powerhouse they once were, reduced to something feeble and childlike.

Panic tugged at Emma's heart. *I can't lose you too.*

'How's work?' her grandmother asked.

'Good. Busy.'

'Are you getting out much and meeting new friends?'

'I don't have time for things like that, Gran.'

'You don't have time or you're not making time?'

Emma looked down at her jeans and ignored the remark. Her grandmother could be forgetful sometimes. At other times she could express an irritating degree of lucidity.

'Well?'

'You don't need to worry about me. I'm fine.'

'Oh but I do worry. Ever since...' She trailed off, her eyes growing shiny.

Emma squeezed Gwendoline's hand. 'I know. I miss them too.'

'Life hasn't been easy for you, Emma.'

'No, but I get on with things.'

'Yes, I suppose. You're much like Catherine in that way. She was the strong one.'

Emma's heart tightened at the sound of her mother's name. Her eyes stung as she swallowed back her emotion. 'So, guess where I went on Sunday.'

'Tell me.'

'To the Quarantine Station.'

'The *Quarantine Station*?' Gwendoline's eyes brightened. 'How wonderful! I lived there when I was a little girl, did you know that?'

'I did and I want to hear more about your time there, Gran. I've never really asked you about it before.'

'Probably because it would bore you terribly. It was a long time ago.'

Emma tucked her legs up onto the bed to get comfortable. 'When I visited on Sunday, I saw the Former First Class Precinct as well as third class and Asiatics. I also visited isolation and the hospitals. Then I went down to the wharf. Where the boats came in.' Emma said this last part carefully and watched Gwendoline for a response.

Gwendoline's eyes glazed over and Emma sensed she was no longer seeing the room before her, with its single bed and sterile white walls. She'd retreated somewhere else.

'Gran?'

'Those places do bring back memories, lots of them.'

'So you were born on the station?'

'Yes, in 1919, the year of the hospital fire.'

'The hospital fire? Yes, I heard about that. The first-class hospital burnt down.'

'That's right. It was also the time of the Spanish Flu pandemic.'

'The station must have been busy.'

'The busiest it ever was. The staff weren't always allowed to have children on site. I recall my mother saying once that there was a strict rule in place preventing staff from fraternising with each other because the station didn't want to raise everyone's babies. But after the pandemic was over, they changed the rules.'

'What was your life like? Did you go to school? Were there other children to play with?'

'Yes there were other children there while I was there. There was no school or governess on site so we were homeschooled each morning. And after that, we were free to wander.' She sighed. 'Oh and what a marvellous playground it was! Of course, it was still a working station and there were areas that were out of bounds, like the hospital and isolation, but we were allowed access to the rest of it.

'We'd chase each other through the accommodation, down among the graveyards, around the Gravedigger's Cottage. Oh, how we tormented that poor man.' She chuckled at some private thought.

'So both your parents worked at the station?'

'Yes, your great-grandparents were both employed there.'

'Why did they leave with you suddenly in 1926?'

Gwendoline's eyes clouded over again.

'Gran?'

'I waited every day at the wharf,' she muttered. 'Every day.'

'Who did you wait for?'

'I used to sit on the edge at high tide and dangle my toes in the water. Every time a new boat came, I'd hold my breath and wait, hoping it would be him. Then one night, my parents said we had to leave.'

Emma watched her grandmother, wondering who she could have been waiting for. *Him.* She'd been waiting for a male. Was it her father? Or a boy who'd left and she'd been waiting his return? Every time Emma tried to reach in to coax the answers out, all it seemed to stir up was a puddle of displaced memories.

Still, she pressed on. 'Is that where you go when you wander at night from the nursing home? Are you looking for a man or a boy on a boat?'

Gwendoline released a shaky breath.

'Who were you looking for? Who *are* you looking for?'

The veil lifted and Gwendoline blinked rapidly. 'What is it you're saying?'

'The boat, Gran.'

'The boat?'

Emma sighed and squeezed her grandmother's hand gently. 'Never mind. You must be tired. I've kept you talking long enough.'

'Is Catherine coming?'

Emma smiled sadly. 'Not today. It's time for your nap though.'

Gwendoline slid down onto her pillow and Emma tucked the blankets securely around her. She sat and gently stroked her grandmother's hair until Gwendoline's eyes began to close. 'Don't forget my roses on Saturday, Emma.'

Emma leant forward and kissed Gwendoline's cheek. 'I'll never forget your roses, Gran.'

* * *

Emma's next day off was on Thursday and she wasted no time climbing into her VW and driving across the city to the Q Station. Morning peak hour had subsided and the traffic was moderate all the way to Manly and up to North Head.

She parked her car by reception and Joan recognised her instantly when Emma called in to say hello. She boarded the shuttle bus and chatted with Ted as they bounced down Wharf Road, but this time she didn't disembark at the Former First Class Precinct. She stayed on, watching the sights from the window with a renewed sense of purpose that had been sparked by her latest visit with Gwendoline, when her grandmother had announced she'd been waiting for a *male* on a boat. It was a crumb, really, but Emma had swept it up eagerly.

She disembarked the shuttle at the shower blocks. Rocks crunched under her shoes as she walked past the autoclave and onto the wharf.

She waited there for five minutes, hoping he'd received the message she'd left on the visitors' centre's answering machine, and praying that he was at work that day.

It had been a risk going down there again, not knowing if he would want to help her or if she were being a nuisance. He was obviously busy, but when he stepped out of the museum with a wide grin that seemed just for her, Emma released the breath she'd been holding and walked to meet him.

'Emma.'

'Matt.'

'It's good to see you again.' He smiled at her, warm air ruffling his hair. He had on cargo shorts, a Q Station polo shirt and work boots.

'Thank you for meeting me. I wasn't sure if you'd gotten my message.'

'The tour ladies passed it on. I was glad you called.'

They stood on the wharf in a pleasant silence until Matt spoke. 'So did you want to check out the archive room today?'

'I'd love to. If you have time,' Emma said.

'I do. I'm here all day, so I've moved my jobs to the afternoon.' He bit his lip, like he was hesitating. 'Do you want to grab a coffee first?'

'A coffee?'

'Yeah. I just figured, it's a nice day...'

'Coffee would be great.'

He looked relieved and they fell into step beside each other, circling back towards the shower blocks. They continued past them to the restaurant and café where the boiler room had once operated.

They ordered lattes and went to sit outside in the sun. The warmth was gentle, the breeze off the water soft. They made small talk about the weather and Matt's work on the station until their coffees arrived, then they stirred in sugar and took silent sips.

'So,' Matt said, sitting back in his seat. 'Where does Emma live and what does Emma do?'

'Well, Emma lives in an apartment in Kensington.'

'Ah, a city girl.'

'Yes and she works at a café nearby called The Coffee Bean.'

'A café?' He raised an eyebrow. 'Okay, so a tough critic! How is our coffee stacking up?'

'It's stacking up well,' she said, realising he might be flirting and she might be flirting back.

He feigned relief. 'Phew.'

They sipped their coffees again and Emma chose the lapse in conversation to study him. His unexpected interest was a little disconcerting. She couldn't remember the last time a man had shown her attention, talking, flirting, if that's what they were even doing. She didn't want to misread the signs, found the whole thing baffling and was probably reading far too much into it.

God, she was out of practice!

Matt was staring at her and she realised she'd gone quiet for a few minutes. 'And how about you, Matt? I already know what you do, so where do you come from?'

He leant forward and crossed his arms on the edge of the table. 'Well, I'm a local boy. I grew up in Fairlight, just around the corner. My parents and grandparents are also local. My great-grandparents were from Mount Sheridan in Queensland, though my great-grandfather worked here at the station before that.'

'Yes, you mentioned that last time, that your great-grandfather worked here.'

'For many years, in fact.'

'I wonder if he knew Gwendoline or her parents. Their stay must have overlapped at some point. It can be a small world like that.'

'How is your grandmother doing?'

'She's doing well,' Emma said. 'She still gets confused, usually when her childhood memories muddle with her recent ones.'

'Is she your mother's mum or your father's?'

'My mother's.'

'She must admire what you're doing for her.'

Emma hesitated. They were entering ground she wasn't sure she wanted to tread. 'I guess. I haven't seen my parents in a long time.'

'Oh, how come?'

She shifted around in her seat. This wasn't the direction she was hoping their coffee date would take. It felt like too much too soon.

'My family died in a plane crash when I was fifteen,' she said.

Matt looked horrified. 'Oh Emma, I'm so sorry.'

'My parents and my twin seven-year-old brothers were holidaying in France. They took a light plane over the Champagne region and it...' She looked down at the table, the words stalling on her lips.

Matt reached for her hand. She saw it there, folded around her own.

'The plane came down. There were no survivors.'

'Shit.'

Emma closed her eyes and breathed. When she opened them again, she searched his face for signs of panic, for signs that he might like to bolt from the table. *Too much too soon.* She wouldn't have blamed him.

But he wasn't panicking. Instead, he was watching her carefully. 'I'm sorry, Emma. I didn't mean to...'

'It's fine.'

'No, I feel terrible. I shouldn't have pushed.'

Emma gave him a sad smile. 'Don't feel bad. It is what it is. I'm thirty-two now. I've had a long time to get used to them being gone.'

'Does anyone ever get used to that?' His hand was still on hers.

'No. I guess not.'

'What were their names?'

'My mother was Catherine and my father was John. My brothers were Max and Liam. They were the funniest little things. Mostly they just drove me nuts. Now I wish I'd taken the time to appreciate them more. I can't imagine how scared they would have been when that plane...' She faltered.

'It probably happened quickly.'

'After we were told the news, I went to live with my grandmother. The loss hit her hard too. We had each other, but she had the tough job,' Emma smiled sheepishly, 'raising a wild, grieving teenager.'

'I can understand why she's so important to you. Why you feel the need to protect her.'

'She's all I have left. I can't imagine life without her in it.'

Matt nodded in understanding.

'About two years ago, her health began to fail and she was diagnosed with stage four mild cognitive decline. She was living with me, but caring for her became difficult. She'd forget to turn the stove off, almost burning the house down, or forget to turn the bathroom taps off, flooding the place. And it was around that time that she began to wander. Placing her in permanent care was one of the hardest decisions I've had to make.'

'But probably one of the best.'

'I still need to hear that sometimes.'

'Well, if it helps, I think it's a wonderful thing you're doing for her now.'

'Thank you. Tracing her history is important. Her wanderings are leading her somewhere. I want to find out where. I need to understand them because one day she'll wander and she won't come back.'

Matt gave her an encouraging smile and gulped down the rest of his coffee. 'Let's get to the archive room then. With any luck, it will have a few stories to tell.'

Chapter Eight

Matt led the way, guiding Emma through the museum.

'When I was researching my family history, the archive room came in handy,' he said as he headed towards the back, past the glass cabinets, old suitcases and gravestones. 'The museum is ideal for displays and tourist information, but all the good stuff is in archive. Thousands of documents and photographs are stored there, dating back to when the station first opened in 1830. It was all rounded up after its closure in 1984.'

They paused by a door and Matt fished out a set of keys from his pocket. He turned one in the lock and let them into the room. It was dark and cool inside. Emma felt the blast from the air conditioner hit her cheeks.

Matt flicked on the light and closed the door behind them. 'I just need to sign us in. Everyone who comes in here has to record their visit.' He paused by a clipboard hanging on the wall and signed and dated the form.

A small sink and towel stood beside the doorway. A sign above it instructed all visitors to wash and dry their hands thoroughly before touching the items.

'We no longer use gloves when handling old documents,' Matt explained, turning the tap on and pumping soap from the dispenser. 'A few years ago, it was confirmed that it might do more harm than good, so now we just wash our hands.'

Emma followed suit, scrubbing her hands with soap under the water then drying them on the towel. She placed the towel back on the rack and followed Matt into the centre of the room. Against the walls were rows of tall filing cabinets and piles of brown, acid-free boxes stacked on top of one another. At the back of the room was another closed door.

'Where do we even begin?' she asked, unsure where to cast her eye.

'I've been in here a few times,' he said, 'but I haven't gone through everything.'

'Where did you find information relating to your family?'

Matt rubbed his jaw. 'It was a while ago, but I recall starting with the filing cabinets. They're categorised by year, so it made sense to start there. I found a lot of old carpentry order forms and one or two photographs of my great-grandfather and his workshop, but that was it. I get the feeling he was a quiet man who kept to himself.'

'Not a bad way to be,' she said.

Matt moved to one of the tall filing cabinets and opened the top drawer. He walked his fingers along the tabs of the folders, his face set in concentration. 'What year did you say your grandmother was born?' he asked, looking up.

'1919.'

'This one is 1850 to 1880. It's too early for her.' He pushed the top drawer back in and rolled open the drawer beneath it.

Emma stood close beside him. He smelt fresh and clean like soap and shampoo, and she tried not to inhale him so obviously. It was followed by an overwhelming sense of gratitude for the time he was taking out of his workday to help her, all the jobs he'd pushed to the afternoon to walk her through the archive room, and which he'd have to finish later.

'Thank you, Matt,' she said.

He looked up in surprise. 'For what?'

'For helping me with all this. I know you're busy.'

'It's no problem.'

They smiled, held each other's gaze, then he went back to the folders.

'Well, this one's no good either,' he said, pushing the drawer back in. '1880 to 1915. It must be this one.' He pulled open the bottom drawer and they both sank to their knees to peer inside. Matt flicked through the folders; 1916, 1917, 1918, then, with a triumphant 'Ah ha!' he pulled two folders for 1919 out.

They settled on their bottoms and crossed their legs. Matt handed her one of the folders and Emma opened it. Inside were hundreds of documents separated by acid-free sheets of paper. She extracted each one carefully, perusing it before placing it back between the sheets. Matt did the same next to her, their movements slow and deliberate with the delicate paper.

There was information on passenger arrivals and departures, employee timesheets and the various occupations of staff. Emma found a proposal for a new road in third class, a rabbit infestation report and hundreds and hundreds of supply order forms, everything from tools to food, medical supplies, coal and wood.

'How are you going over there?' Matt asked after ten minutes.

Emma let out a slow breath. 'There's a lot of interesting information here, but nothing that relates to Gwendoline directly. How about you?'

'My folder mostly contains log entries for jobs carried out on the station.' He picked up a sheet. 'This one's for the cleaning and washing-out of individual rooms by housekeeping. I've got another one here for electrical and mechanical repair of the funicular railway, another here for water preparation for the shower blocks and how much coal was consumed by the autoclave for fumigation. Not much to go on either.'

Emma set down an order form for smallpox vaccines. 'Gwendoline talks often of a boat. Not boats in general, but *a boat*. She said that she waited every day at the wharf for the boat to come.'

'That could mean anything. There were boats in and out of here all the time. Perhaps her mother or father had to leave and she was waiting for them to come back. Maybe it was a child she'd befriended and they had to leave.'

'I think the person she was waiting for was male. But yes, you're right, it could have been anyone. That's what makes it hard. It's like looking for a needle in a haystack.' Emma glanced futilely down at the documents and protective sheets of paper in her lap. 'Still, it's the reason she wanders.'

'This is probably a stupid question, but have you asked her who she's waiting for?'

'I asked her just yesterday but she became confused. I can't get a straight answer out of her.'

'There's got to be a trail of her somewhere. Do you know what her parents' names were?'

'I'm not sure who her father was, but her mother's name was Rose. She started working here in 1918 and was a housekeeper in first class.'

'If Gwendoline was born in 1919, Rose must have fallen pregnant relatively soon after starting.'

'Yes, she must have. And I know that Gwendoline's father worked on the station also, because they packed up hurriedly and left in 1926.'

'Maybe 1919 isn't the place to start. Maybe we need to look through the entire seven years Gwendoline was on the station.'

Emma cast her eye over the remaining filing cabinets and the hundreds of documents they contained within them. 'I'm conscious of time. I don't want to hold you up too much.'

He grinned. 'Don't worry about me. I'm enjoying this.'

She smiled back and they packed up the documents, returning them neatly to the acid-free sleeves and back into the folders. Matt stood and stored them away in the bottom drawer.

He moved to the next filing cabinet along and retrieved another set of folders, and he and Emma sat for the next two hours perusing order forms, maintenance logs and passenger manifests, until Emma's back ached.

They went through the entire contents from 1919 to 1926. They opened boxes and trawled through the many documents and photographs stored in archival albums, but there was nothing they could relate to Gwendoline or Rose, why they left suddenly in 1926 and who Gwendoline could have been waiting for by the wharf as a child.

Matt slid the last album back into its box and fastened the lid. He returned to his spot on the floor beside Emma while she stretched her legs out.

'This floor can be unforgiving,' he said.

'Or I'm just getting old.'

He laughed.

'Thank you for helping me today.'

'I'm sorry we couldn't find anything. What's the nursing home doing to stop your grandmother walking out the door? Surely they can keep an eye on her.'

'That's a whole other story.'

'And this time, I'm not going to make you tell me.'

Emma chuckled. 'The facility is reasonably priced and mostly they're great. It's just this one thing they can't seem to get right.'

'It's a huge thing.'

'Yes. It's dangerous for her and I don't know what to do about it. I've tried talking to the director but she always seems to shift the blame, like it's Gran's fault that she goes walkabouts.'

Matt looked thoughtfully at the filing cabinets. 'And you're sure you don't know who Gwendoline's father was?'

Emma shook her head. 'I don't recall her ever mentioning his name. And I wasn't the attentive grandchild that I should have been.'

'You had a lot going on.'

'Yes, but before my family passed away, I could have asked the questions. I could have taken the time to sit with her and learn about her childhood. Then when everything changed, I became too lost in my own misery to even be nice. Now I'm worried this is all too little too late.'

Matt reached out and placed his hand on Emma's arm. It was warm on her skin in the cold room. 'Don't be so hard on yourself. I didn't start researching my family's history until I was an adult. As a kid and a teenager, it was the last thing I wanted to do.'

'I just wish I'd done things differently. I wish I'd paid more attention and asked more questions. I wish I'd hugged my mum and dad and brothers a little tighter before they left.'

'Why didn't you go to France?'

'Because I was selfish. Because going to my best friend's sixteenth birthday party was more important. I didn't want to miss out. Everyone from school was going to be there.'

She looked down at her hands, embarrassed at the sound of her own appalling actions. 'I kicked up such a fuss about it when my parents booked the trip. Instead of being grateful for the opportunity, I argued and slammed doors and wouldn't talk to either of them until they finally relented and let me stay.'

'But if you had gone...'

She nodded. 'I know. If I'd gone I wouldn't be here now. But for a long time, I wished I had gone with them. Sometimes I still do.'

Matt was quiet.

'I feel guilty that I dodged the bullet. Through being a selfish brat, I managed to avoid the same fate. I should have been there with them.'

'That's a lot of guilt to carry around. You didn't know how it would play out. You were only fifteen. No one can ever predict these things.'

Emma saw the logic in what he was saying, but guilt had a funny way of being all-consuming. While she heard the words, she didn't feel assuaged.

They sat that way for a time in the cool room, surrounded by history, Matt's hand still on Emma's arm, and she realised how nice it was to feel a man's touch. It had been too long.

He broke the reverie with a gentle squeeze of her arm before releasing it. 'Well, I'm not entirely sure we're going to find much in here. All these documents seem to be related to day-to-day activity on the station.'

Emma nodded her agreement.

'And without 1919 birth records from the hospital or your great-grandfather's name, we can't say for sure who fathered Gwendoline.'

'Correct.'

Matt chewed his lip. 'There's another room.'

Emma inclined her head. 'Another room?'

'Yes. Behind us.' He pointed to the back wall and Emma saw the closed door she had noticed earlier. 'People rarely go in there. It's full of odd pieces, nothing worth putting on display, but no one ever had the heart to throw it out.'

'Another room?' Emma said again, her smile widening.

'It's worth a try.'

Chapter Nine

Matt unlocked the door, flicked the light on and they stepped inside. It was smaller than the archive room and not as cold. The air was thick with age and Emma noticed all around a clutter of old sheets, blankets and suitcases.

'This room has a different feel,' she said.

'Yeah, it's the old bedding that gives it that musty smell. Many people died on the station and left behind suitcases full of clothes and shoes. Mostly they were disposed of, but sometimes they piled up.'

Emma walked slowly around the room, glancing at the old suitcases stacked against the walls or high on top of each other. Some had inscriptions stamped into the leather—*Percy Bowden 1875, Elizabeth Plimsoll 1898, George Raymond RMS Lusitania 1906.* If their luggage was still on the station over a hundred years later, Emma could only guess as to the fate of each of those souls.

Matt gently dragged one of the suitcases into the middle of the room and they both sat on the floor, cross-legged once again. The case was mustard-coloured with metal studs lining the edges and a strong smell of old leather.

'I've only been in here a couple of times and haven't gone through everything. There's no order in here. We'll just have to take a stab in the dark.' Matt snapped back the luggage locks and opened the lid.

Emma peered forward. The suitcase was filled with stiff dresses, corsets, old lace-up boots with pointy toes and yellowing petticoats that had undoubtedly been a creamy satin once. The clothes smelt pungently stale like the room and she was almost grateful when Matt closed the lid again.

'Those clothes look like they're from the 1800s. We need something more recent.' He fastened the locks and pushed the suitcase back to its original position. He dragged over another. 'Let's try this one.'

The next suitcase was full of melted pairs of shoes.

'These must have gone through the old fumigation system, before the autoclave was built. The old system used to burn and melt things.' He closed the lid, snapping the locks, and returned the case to the corner where it had come from.

He looked around the room, his face set in determination, and Emma felt a small rush of affection for this stranger who had become so intent on helping her. She would still be lost at the Gravedigger's Cottage if it hadn't been for Matt.

He moved across the room and pulled a thick grey blanket away, revealing several suitcases beneath it. He folded the blanket and placed it to one side.

'I've never had a look in these.' He gently tugged one of the suitcases out and Emma caught another strong whiff of old leather. The suitcase was faded bottle green with tanned straps and he set it down between them on the floor.

With some effort, he flipped the stiff locks and pried open the lid. The top layer of items contained a black dress and white apron that looked like a housekeeping or maid's uniform. There was a pair of black laced boots, a handheld mirror, a hairbrush, a strange-looking corset with a wide, flexible front, two satin petticoats and an old glass perfume bottle that no longer held any scent or liquid.

Matt removed the top layer of items and set them to the side. It revealed another layer, this time of small brown books with three silver fountain pens. He picked up one of the books and handed it to Emma while he reached for another.

Emma ran her palm over it. All the books looked the same—a tan hardcover with a small tarnished clasp that was firmly locked. They appeared to be diaries, but where were the keys?

'Can you see them anywhere?' Matt said.

'No.'

He hunted around in the suitcase, pulling out another pair of shoes, a coat and three tunics and setting them aside, anticipation growing on his face.

'They would only be little, so they could have fallen to the bottom,' Emma said.

He pulled out stockings, undergarments, two baby dresses with matching bonnets and a pink crochet blanket. He reached the bottom of the suitcase, but there were no keys. He straightened his back and sighed. 'They're not here.'

'They have to be somewhere,' Emma said, returning to the pile of items on the floor. She shook out the crochet blanket and dresses and overturned the shoes. She stretched out the corset and stockings, but the keys weren't there. 'We just have to think like the owner of these diaries. Clearly it was a woman. Where would a woman hide a set of tiny keys that she wouldn't want anyone else to find?'

'I have no idea.'

'Think like a female, Matt.'

'Um...'

They both laughed.

'If it were my diary,' Emma said, 'I would hide the keys in a place no one would think to look.'

'Like where?'

'Like the *inside* of the diary.'

Matt gave a slow smile. With the diary still in her hands, Emma turned it upside down, spreading the outer covers as far as they would extend, which wasn't far. She shook, gently first then more vigorously. Nothing.

Then *plonk!* A small brass key slipped out of the pages and onto her lap.

Matt looked up with surprise. 'No way!' He picked up the diary in his lap, turned it upside down, spread the outer covers like Emma had done and shook. He shook and shook, then *plonk*. Out fell another key.

There were five diaries in total and Emma and Matt shook each one, and out of each fell the small brass key to unlock it with. Emma opened her diary first, inserting the key into the hole in the clasp and turning it. The clasp sprang free and she opened the cover.

A thrill charged up her spine. Scrawled in neat black curves on the first page were the words '*This diary belongs to Rose Porter, 1918*'. Gwendoline had never mentioned her mother's maiden name before and Emma couldn't be certain this was the same Rose, but the diary had been written in 1918 and it was too great a coincidence not to be.

Matt shuffled across the space to sit close to Emma and she set the diary down in front of them so they could both see. She turned to the first page and read aloud.

18th June, 1918

The gift was unexpected, though spoke volumes. He had listened to me speak in a way that no one has before. When he gave me the gift, my heart soared and I was unprepared for that. I have never felt anything so intoxicating and yet, I know I shouldn't. I know I should lock away my feelings like I do these words, but I cannot help it. I do not want to help it.

Life on the station can be a bewildering concept. The people arrive, either terribly sick or perfectly healthy, and they survive and move on or they die. Looking at the people in first class, it is hard to imagine that others are suffering just nearby. They eat, drink and wile away their quarantine in merriment. Sickness has not visited their doorstep. They are the lucky ones.

While I have been inoculated now against many of the diseases, I have not yet traversed the unhealthy ground near isolation and the hospitals, but I have sat on the sand and watched the boats come; an endless stream of people offloaded, their eyes sunken and skin pale from days at sea. It is hardest to watch the children suffer.

And yet, life seems to go on in first class, mostly unaffected. I work hard in the kitchen and dining room, I complete my shifts to the best of my ability, I cherish the time between those shifts when I can run my fingers through the sand and just be. The weather is cold now with the turn of

season, but it does not stop me wanting to go to him, a weakness I shouldn't indulge, but I cannot help myself. Forgive me.
Rose

Emma looked over at Matt and found his eyes on her.

'Rose was in love.'

'Yes,' she said. 'With someone she wasn't meant to fall in love with.'

'Probably another staff member or a passenger.'

'When I spoke to my grandmother, she told me about some rules on the station, that staff weren't allowed to fraternise for fear of pregnancies. Rose indicates the same constraints. *A weakness I shouldn't indulge.*'

'Your grandmother was right. They had strict rules about relationships back then. And Rose seemed smart enough not to mention his name. If the diary had been found, she could have gotten into a lot of trouble.'

Emma chewed her lip. 'I wonder if this mystery man was Gwendoline's father. It would make sense, considering how quickly Rose fell pregnant.'

'Whoever it was bought her a gift of some kind. If we could trace the gift, we might be able to trace the person. If we trace the person, we might be able to work out who Gwendoline's father was and possibly who she was waiting for by the wharf.'

'That makes sense.' Emma turned to the next entry, dated a few days later. Rose's neat cursive hand filled the page.

21st June, 1918

Everyone is talking of the duke and duchess. She continues to recover from Spanish Flu. We have been told her progress is hampered by complications of the lungs. She still resides in the hospital while the duke resides in first class. Although his isolation is officially over, he remains a recluse, preferring meals in his room where he continues to conduct official business for the king. Miss Dalton takes him his meals and tends to his housekeeping, though I get the impression she thinks him bothersome.

My dear friend, Bessie Briar, almost self-combusts whenever we speak of them! She loves the royals. I find her terribly funny, like a breath of fresh air. She is my dearest companion, sweet and young at heart, and I consider her family. I couldn't imagine sharing lodgings with anyone else.

The station continues to beat its usual rhythm. Boats arrive daily, the people pour in, graveyards fill up. A third cemetery was opened last week and already headstones dot the hill like needlepoints on canvas.

I have watched the passengers disembark from the boats, covered in pustules or racked with fever, their bodies limp and their eyes sunken. I do not mean to turn away, but I loathe seeing such suffering.

I wrote to my father three weeks ago to inform him of my safe arrival in Sydney and my job on the station. He was furious when I turned down the butcher's son's proposal, furious still when I packed my bags and left Bethnal Green for Australia. I do not anticipate a reply. Perhaps he will surprise me, though I fear his disappointment is so great it will span oceans.

I so enjoy writing to you, dear diary. You are a vessel for my thoughts, for things that are in my head but I cannot say aloud. You know especially whom I speak of. I long for the breaks in my shift when I can see him, speak to him, feel his eyes on me. He is handsome and gentle and so very kind.

The need to see him is powerful and that scares me. I know it is forbidden. The rules are clear. I do not mean to be insubordinate, but I fear my attraction is stronger than me.

Rose

On and on they read, page after page of Rose Porter's most private thoughts and desires. The young maid spoke of day-to-day life on the station and of the contrast between first class and the rest of quarantine. She spoke of the duke and duchess, Miss Dalton and Bessie Briar, and she always spoke of the mysterious man she had come to revere, though never did she name him.

The end of the first diary took them to the fifteenth of July, 1918. Emma set it down and straightened her back. Beside her, Matt uncrossed his legs and stretched them. She tried not to glance down at his powerful legs, the closeness of his body next to hers and how they had been like that for well over two hours as they'd read through the diary. Back there, in the tiny room behind the archives, she felt oddly suspended in time.

'Shall we work out which diary comes next?' he asked.

Emma locked the diary they'd been reading, slipped the key back between the pages and glimpsed her watch. 'It's already four pm. I've kept you here the entire day.'

Matt glanced down at his watch too. 'Wow, that went fast.'

'I should let you get back to work.'

'I suppose.'

They carefully folded and placed Rose's clothing and other items back into the suitcase. They laid the diaries on top with the keys securely tucked between the pages, with every intention of coming back to read the rest later.

Matt closed the lid and fastened the luggage locks, sliding the suitcase back to its original position and throwing the blanket over it.

They stepped out into the fading afternoon light as the sun sank below the station. It was still bright enough for Emma to squint after the dimness of the previous two rooms. 'That was incredible, Matt. I can't thank you enough.'

'No problem. I'm just glad we have a lead now.'

'We found Rose's diaries. I mean, we actually found them. Gran will be so pleased.'

'And there's still plenty more to go through, so whenever you're ready, come back and find me.'

Emma's breath caught on an invitation that brimmed with promise. Another day to read Rose's diaries and spend time with Matt. She couldn't help the lopsided grin forming on her face. 'I'd better let you get back to work. You'll still be here till midnight otherwise.'

'Okay.' He touched her wrist lightly and something pleasant tingled up her arm. 'Goodbye, Emma.' Smiling, he turned back into the museum.

Emma started up the path to the shower blocks to wait for the shuttle. It had only taken her a few steps to realise what was happening.

She liked this guy. She liked him, probably more than she ought to at this stage. It was the butterflies, the way she felt around him, the strange, thrilling, heart-warming anticipation she'd experienced that morning at the thought of his company.

It was all the things she hadn't felt in a long time.

Not since Drew.

Chapter Ten

'Do you think they're much like us?'

'Who?'

'The royals.'

'What do you mean "much like us"?'

'You know, like normal people.'

Rose threw the piece of bark she'd been playing with down the steps of the verandah and leant back. A pale sun cut through the trees that surrounded the female staff cottages. The breakfast shift was over and lunch was still an hour away. Bessie had just returned from the kitchen and was smoking a cigarette beside her on the verandah.

'I suppose. They are human after all. They live and love and make mistakes like the rest of us.'

'Yes but their lives are grander than ours. I mean, could you imagine marrying a prince or a duke? You could have anything your heart desired. You would never have to plunge your hands in filthy hot water again to scrub someone else's dishes.'

Rose gave Bessie a sympathetic smile.

'I wonder if the duke will marry again after the duchess dies.'

'Bessie Briar!'

'What? She's not getting any better. She's been ill for weeks. Everybody knows it.'

'It's not for us to discuss.'

'Do you the think the duke would take one of us for his new wife?'

'Have you even met the duke?'

Bessie drew back on her cigarette and blew out a stream of smoke. 'No, I've only glimpsed him from afar like everyone else. He never comes down from his verandah.'

'Well, people like the duke do not marry commoners like us.'

'It could happen.'

'You're being far too dreamy, Bessie Briar.'

'Yes, you're probably right.' She flicked her cigarette down the steps to join Rose's piece of bark. Then she scratched and picked at her raw hands.

'Are they terribly sore?' Rose asked.

Bessie shrugged. 'I'm used to it. No chance of them being any different with my hands in water all day.'

'Can you ask Miss Dalton or Mrs March for some ointment?'

Bessie gave her a dubious look. 'People like me don't get ointment, Rose.'

Rose averted her eyes.

'Don't feel embarrassed. I chose this job. I can leave anytime I want. Truth is, I like it here. I like the free board and food and I'm not afraid of a little hard work. There aren't too many prospects out there for women like me. I'm not pretty or educated like most.'

'I think you're pretty.'

'That's because you're far too kind,' Bessie said.

Rose caught sight of movement in the trees. Thomas materialised and walked towards their verandah. The sun caught flecks of auburn in his hair and his eyes were green and gold as he smiled at them both. He had a small package wrapped in brown paper under his arm.

'Good morning, ladies.'

'Hello Mr Van Cleeve,' Bessie said. 'What brings you all the way up here?'

'Just checking to see if anything needs repairing.'

Rose caught his playful smile and dipped her head to hide her own.

Bessie looked back towards their open front door. 'No, I don't think so. We're all fine here, Mr Van Cleeve.'

'Very well.'

'Anyway, I better get back to work. Mrs March will have my head on a plate if I'm late.' She stood, tugged at the tight uniform that strained around her hips and stepped down off the verandah. She gave them a final wave before disappearing through the trees.

'Are you well, Miss Porter?' Thomas asked when they were alone.

'I am thank you. And you, Mr Van Cleeve?'

'Yes. I had a busy morning up at third class fixing the dumbwaiter, but I have an hour free now. Would you like to walk with me?'

Rose smiled. 'I would like that very much.'

She climbed to her feet, trotted down the steps and together they headed towards first class, bypassing it and continuing on down Wharf Road.

'You have a package beneath your arm,' she said as they walked.

'Indeed. You are most observant.'

'I do try.'

'You're very good at it.'

It was the kind of playful banter they shared on their regular walks down to the cove. Rose had come to appreciate Thomas's light humour, something he intermingled with his serious side, when they spent long hours talking on the sand. He was quiet, intelligent and did not seem to mind that she, as a woman, had an opinion. In fact, he encouraged it.

And Rose, unable to temper what she knew was an attraction to him, felt the full weight of the rules bearing down on her. She knew she shouldn't spend time with him, knew that to encourage it was wrong, but she didn't know how to stop herself. She didn't *want* to stop herself.

They reached the sand and Rose took a seat beside Thomas, unlacing her shoes. A large ship was anchored in the bay and two rowboats ferried passengers across to the wharf where doctors and nurses waited, along with the luggage boys from the autoclaves.

'Poor souls,' Thomas said, dusting sand from his hands as they watched the infected disembark and walk, hunched and weak, towards the shower blocks with the aid of nurses. 'They don't stand much of a chance.'

'What will they do with the infected ship?'

'The decks will be scrubbed with lime and they'll burn or disinfect cargo that might carry lice eggs. A lot of it will go through the autoclaves.'

When the children were carried off, Rose had to look away. She couldn't bear to watch. No matter how many times she'd witnessed the boats come in, the children were a sight that still affected her. Instead, she glanced down at the package in Thomas's hand.

He caught her gaze. 'I have a surprise for you.'

'For me?'

'Yes. I got the idea when we spoke about it some weeks back.'

Rose drew a blank. They'd spoken about many things on this patch of sand. 'I'm intrigued.'

He smiled and handed the package to her. She accepted it and tore open the paper.

'I worked with the postmaster to place the order. It wasn't difficult. If you include the trip to the autoclave for fumigation, the whole process took about two weeks.'

A hard tan corner poked out from one side of the packaging and when she had torn all the paper away, she was left holding a book with a small brass clasp and a velvet pouch that stored a key. A silver fountain pen slipped from the package and into her lap.

'Do you like it?' he asked, his eyes hopeful.

'Is it what I think it is, Thomas?'

'That depends on what you think it is.'

She breathed the words. 'A lock-up diary and pen?'

He nodded, a big grin on his face.

'Oh, Thomas!' She was ecstatic and breathless and humbled all at once.

'You love to write, Rose. And because you aren't sure what you love to write yet, I thought a diary would be a good place to start.'

She stared down at the gift in awe. She had a sudden urge to wrap her arms around him and say thank you in ways that she knew were not allowed. She settled for brushing her fingers against his in the sand and he responded in kind.

'I love it, Thomas,' she said.

'I'm so glad you do.'

'You really listened to me.'

'I will always listen to you.'

Rose's breath caught in her lungs. A longing invaded her body, shooting into the pit of her stomach like a physical ache; a longing for someone she wanted. How cruel the universe was to thrust Thomas into her path knowing she could never have him.

Rose wrapped the diary, key pouch and pen away in the brown paper and tucked it in her lap where prying eyes couldn't see it.

'Where do you sleep, Thomas?' she asked as waves gently lapped the shore.

'In a bed, like most people.'

She nudged him. 'No I mean, where are the male staff quarters?'

'They're up near third class.'

'So is that where you sleep? In the male quarters?'

He stared at the water as it sighed in and out. 'I'm a quiet man, Rose. I don't care for the antics of the other lads. I don't sleep in the male quarters.'

'Where do you sleep?'

He looked at her as though considering something. 'When is your next shift?'

'In about thirty minutes.'

'Would you like to see where I sleep?'

Rose nodded slowly. 'Okay.'

'Come then. I will show you, but we must be quick.'

She laced her boots and he helped her to her feet. She tucked the diary under her arm, careful to ensure no part of it was exposed.

'Are you cold?' he asked her as they climbed the hill towards third class.

'I'm all right.'

'We can stop by your cottage and collect your coat if you like.'

Rose shook her head. The breeze had grown chilly, reaching through her dress and into her bones, but she didn't want to waste a precious second going via her cottage first.

They passed by the humble, weathered accommodation of third class and the freezing outdoor dining areas of Asiatics, with little Orientals in funny pointed hats eating bowls of rice around a wood fire.

Rose didn't go up there often. There was no reason to. Her work was in first class and she alternated between there, the female staff quarters and the Wharf Precinct. The conditions in third class and Asiatics were vastly different and it was not lost on her that had she been a passenger coming through quarantine, third class was probably where she would have ended up.

Thomas led her to the male staff cottages that were not unlike the female ones, clumped together, out of sight and surrounded by trees. All was quiet, for the luggage and autoclave boys were busy down at the wharf.

He guided Rose towards the rear of the quarters and through to a narrow trail that curved away into bushland. With no one around to see, he reached for her hand and she gave it to him. With her other hand, she hitched up her tunic and they walked along the path, their bodies side by side as they headed towards the station's outer perimeter.

Rose smelt a medicinal smell in the air that she could now associate with tea tree and eucalyptus, and she heard the friendly call of the kookaburra high in the trees. She saw a fat furry animal waddle into the undergrowth, which Thomas explained was a wombat. The path they walked was flanked with native Australian flora that she could easily name by sight—sunshine wattle, banksia, waratahs and carpets of flannel flowers.

She had Thomas to thank for the knowledge; he had taught her much about the local landscape.

They had been on the track for a few minutes when the bushland cleared to an opening on a large cliff with a small cottage set back from the edge. Only metres away was an enormous drop, a view of Port Jackson and a sea of deep blue extending across to the next headland.

'This is where the boats first come in,' Thomas explained, still holding her hand. Rose stood close to him, the wind ruffling her dress and hair. 'They sail in through the Heads, where they're stopped by health officials. If all passengers look healthy, the boat is allowed to continue on to Sydney, but it takes just one unhealthy passenger and... well, you know the rest.'

'And the cottage?' she said, looking behind her.

'In the 1800s, the coastal officer used to live up here. He would monitor the boats coming in. If he saw one, he would alert the health officials by way of a light signal. He would then walk down the track to the station and inform the hospital staff that a boat was potentially incoming.

'We've advanced a bit since then and there isn't a need for a coastal watch up here. When the cottage became vacant, I made some repairs and moved in.'

'The view is breathtaking.'

'It's the best of the whole station. Come, I'll show you inside.'

He led her to a brown painted door and opened it. Rose stepped across the threshold. It was a simple room that looked much like her own—plain hardwood floors, a single bed, neatly made, and a table with a basin, ewer and a towel.

But the windows were different. There wasn't just one but a whole row of glass panels that drank in the view and filled the room with light. The windows were open and curtains fluttered in a salty breeze.

'It falls woefully short compared with first-class accommodation, but it's clean and quiet and I like it up here.'

'It's lovely,' she said, looking around.

He turned to her and reached out, gently removing a strand of hair from her eyes and tucking it behind her ear. '*You* are lovely, Rose.'

Rose's heart skipped a beat as his fingertips moved down her cheek and caressed her chin, the softest touch she had ever felt. She was breaking a thousand rules just by being there and so was he. They were being reckless and indulgent, and while she knew all this, while her brain screamed for caution, she couldn't stop. She couldn't move. Her feet were weighted to the floor as if by cement.

'Thomas.'

'I don't want to get you into trouble. But I can't help myself.'

'I feel the same.'

'When I'm with you, I...'

'Me too.'

He smiled at her, letting his hand drop slowly from her face. He took a composing breath as though sense were prevailing. 'Come, my sweet Rose. I'd better get you back.'

'I don't want to leave.'

'But you'll be late for your shift. And that will surely make Miss Dalton wary.'

She conceded and, slightly giddy, stepped back out into the sunshine with him. They held hands and followed the path, returning to the male staff quarters. Once there, they glanced around to ensure no one was watching before giving each other's hand a final squeeze.

Rose said goodbye, thanking Thomas again for the diary, and hurrying back to her cottage.

It wasn't long after they parted that Rose was counting down the minutes until she could see him again. She reached her room and placed her diary, key pouch and pen beneath the petticoats in her drawer. She changed out of her tunic and back into her corset, stockings and uniform. She washed the flush from her cheeks, reset her hair and tried to still the untamed happiness coursing through her.

She still had a lunch service to get through.

* * *

'Rose Porter, you are *late*,' Miss Dalton declared as Rose dashed into the kitchen where the parlourmaids, Mrs March and Bessie were gathered in a circle.

'I apologise, Miss Dalton. Time got away from me.'

'Indeed! See that it doesn't happen again.'

Rose found an opening in the circle, smoothed down her uniform and tucked loose strands of her hair away. Bessie eyed her curiously.

'As I was saying,' Miss Dalton said, 'The duchess remains unwell. She has recovered from Spanish Influenza but has developed a secondary bronchial infection and is receiving treatment in the hospital. The duke will continue to await her recovery here in first class.'

'His isolation period is finished. Is he going to make an appearance in the dining room or are we expected to wait on him hand and foot?' Mrs March asked with her hands on her round hips.

'It's an unusual circumstance. I don't think we have had royalty come through the station before.'

'I don't care if the king himself is here,' Mrs March argued. 'We're not a luxury hotel. We're a quarantine station. The duke can come to the dining room like everyone else.'

'I don't disagree with you, Mrs March. I'm far too busy to be taking him meals and tending to his housekeeping. But,' she said when Mrs March opened her mouth to interject, 'I will tolerate it just a little longer in the hope that the duchess recovers soon and they will be on their way.'

Mrs March harrumphed.

'The duke's impression of us will no doubt reach the king. We must demonstrate our hospitality.'

'*Hospitality*,' Mrs March muttered, leaving the circle.

'Now, to other business,' Miss Dalton said. 'We've had another boat arrive with several suspected cases of Spanish Flu. The hospital, understandably, is in a flap about it. Apparently, there is a new vaccine available in Great Britain, but it will be some time before we receive a batch of it here and probably only limited vials. Please stay away from the unhealthy ground. We do not need an outbreak in first class on top of everything else.'

There was a compliant murmur.

'Very well, that will be all.'

Bessie returned to the sink to scrub pots as the parlourmaids made their way across to the dining room to set the tables for lunch.

Rose hung back to collect plates.

'Why were you so late?' Bessie whispered once Miss Dalton and Mrs March were out of earshot. 'Did you take a nap?'

'No, I went for a walk.'

'Where to?'

'Just down to the cove to watch the boats come in.'

'Who with?'

The lie came so smoothly it made Rose cringe on the inside. 'No one.'

Chapter Eleven

The next morning at six o'clock, Miss Dalton arrived to the kitchen flustered. Her usually sleek brown bob was sticking out at odd angles and not even her pins could hold it in place.

'I've just come from Asiatics,' she said. 'Last night they cooked rice in their rooms and almost burnt down the dormitory.'

'What do you mean they almost burnt down the dormitory?' Mrs March asked.

'Exactly what I said. Curtains, beds, a wall and part of the floor went up in flames. They claim it's too cold to cook outside so last night they cooked inside.'

'Well, that will have to come out of their rice rations!' Mrs March said.

'Perhaps it is too cold,' Rose said from her spot by the table polishing cutlery. 'Perhaps they could eat in the third-class dining room until the weather warms again.'

'Orientals eating in the third-class dining room?' Mrs March looked outraged. 'Has this whole place gone mad? Next thing we know third class will be asking to eat with first class.'

Miss Dalton wrung her hands.

'What are you going to do about it?' Mrs March asked, looking warily at her.

'I'm going to have to inform the superintendent. He'll be livid. The last thing we need is to be pouring funds into repairing a dormitory when we have a deadly flu on our doorstep.'

'Let me brew you some tea.' Mrs March pulled out a chair.

Miss Dalton shook her head. 'Thank you, Alice, but not right now. It would only give me indigestion. I'll tend to this first then I'll come back. Rose?'

Rose looked up. 'Yes, Miss Dalton?'

'You will take care of the duke today. See to it that he receives three meals, with morning and afternoon tea in between. You will also need to tend to his room. I'm afraid you won't get much of a break between shifts.'

'Yes, Miss Dalton.'

'Thank you. That will be all, everyone.'

The kitchen resumed its early morning activity. Rose placed the cutlery into a tub and heaved it onto a serving trolley to take across to the dining room.

Miss Dalton appeared beside her. 'Rose, finish setting the tables then come straight back and take the duke his breakfast. Mrs March will have the tray ready for you.'

'Yes, Miss Dalton.'

'And a reminder not to engage in conversation with him. Not that he's a chatty fellow anyway, but refrain from being a nuisance. He's a busy man and you must mind your place.'

'I won't bother the duke.'

'Address him as Your Grace. And curtsey. That's very important.'

Rose nodded.

'Thank you, Rose. I feel a migraine coming on and it's only six-thirty in the morning.'

She pinched the spot between her eyebrows then swished out of the kitchen.

While Mrs March was bent over in the larder, her huge bottom filling the doorway, Bessie dried her hands on a dish towel and came to stand beside Rose at the table. 'You lucky thing!' she whispered.

'I wouldn't call it lucky. I feel rather like I've drawn the short straw.'

'Don't be ridiculous. We're all dying with jealousy. You'll have to tell me everything tonight—what he looks like, what he sounds like, what he smells like.'

Rose made a face.

'I want to know what he eats and how he likes his tea. I bet it's with milk and two cubes.'

'I'll be sure to give you all the details,' she said, placing a pile of plates on the trolley before wheeling it towards the door.

Bessie threw her one last envious look before Rose pushed the trolley across the road to the dining room, wheels clattering on the concrete.

* * *

Rose finished setting the tables with the other parlourmaids, then returned to the kitchen to collect the duke's breakfast. Taking care not to spill a drop, she pushed a serving trolley past the laundry for fresh bed linen, then up the hill to the duke's accommodation, set back amidst a cluster of blue gums.

When she reached the verandah, she collected the breakfast tray from the trolley and climbed the steps to the front door. It was ajar and she gave a knock while balancing the tray.

'Come in, Miss Dalton,' said a crisp male voice from inside.

Rose pushed open the door and saw the Duke of Northbury standing by a polished walnut bureau, looking down at a piece of paper in his hand. He glanced up and frowned. 'You're not Miss Dalton. Where is she?'

Rose curtseyed. 'I apologise, Your Grace. She has another matter to attend to. I will look after you today.'

The duke studied her. He struck an imposing figure in a tweed suit and vest, dark tie and white collared shirt. There was something compelling about him, from his head of thick brown hair to his penetrating cobalt blue stare. 'What's your name?'

'I'm Rose Porter.'

He gestured to the dining table. 'Very well. You may set up.'

Rose set the tray down on a small round table draped in a lace tablecloth. The living area was generous, with dark oak floors, a Persian rug similar to the one in Miss Dalton's office, the bureau and a small floral settee. At the back of the cottage were two doors that Rose presumed led to a bedroom and separate dressing room.

She busied herself at the table, removing cloches from the plates of bacon, eggs and sausages, and measuring an inch from the edge of the table for the cutlery, as she'd been taught to do in the dining room. Next, she laid out a rack of toast with a butter dish, jam and honey.

'I heard commotion outside my window late last night. It woke me up,' said the duke brusquely as Rose worked. 'Is that the reason Miss Dalton is absent?'

'Yes, Your Grace. There was an incident.'

'What kind of incident?'

Rose hesitated as she set up the teapot. 'The passengers in Asiatics almost burnt their dormitory down.'

'Savages!' the duke said.

'I wouldn't call them savages, Your Grace. They were just trying to keep warm.'

The duke gave her a double look. 'What did you say?'

'I said, they were just trying to—'

'They're Orientals and they nearly burnt their dormitory down. If not savages, then what *would* you call them?'

Rose met his eye this time. 'I would call them people, just like everyone else.'

The duke narrowed his eyes, and Rose bit down on her lip. She had spoken out of turn, exactly what Miss Dalton had warned her against doing but which she'd gone and done anyway.

'That's an interesting opinion for a parlourmaid.'

'I apologise, Your Grace.'

'Really?'

'Well, you did ask.'

She heard a small harrumph then he said, 'So am *I* just like everyone else?'

Rose wasn't sure if he was testing her, but there seemed only one appropriate answer to give. 'No, Your Grace. You're different, of course.'

His vanity came beaming across the room and she knew she had given the correct response. She finished setting the table then pulled the chair out for him to sit. 'Would you like me to serve your breakfast now?'

The tension in the air cleared. 'Yes, Rose. Thank you.'

He walked to the table and sat. Rose laid a white napkin across his lap and he reached for a piece of toast.

'Tea, Your Grace?'

'Please. With milk and two cubes.'

Rose smiled. Bessie would be pleased. She poured his tea, added the sugar and he took a sip, making an 'ah' sound.

'You pour a magnificent cup, Rose. Better than Miss Dalton, I dare say.'

'That's very kind.'

'You're from England,' he said, looking directly into her eyes.

Rose nodded. *Not a chatty fellow, hey?* 'I am, Your Grace.'

'I do miss England. Where are you from? It sounds like you're from the south.'

'My family are from London. Bethnal Green.'

'I see.'

'The houses there aren't quite like Buckingham Palace. A place is what you make of it, I suppose.'

'Buckingham Palace is overrated,' he said waving his hand. 'I live in the north.'

'You sound southern though,' Rose said, placing the newspaper on the table by his elbow.

'You don't miss a beat, Rose,' he said, smiling. 'I was born and raised in Knightsbridge. The king granted me land titles in the north so that's where I reside now, in Somersby Castle.'

'The north is lovely.'

'Oh, but I do miss London. Your voice reminds me of home,' he said wistfully.

He held her gaze a moment and she thought she had never seen eyes as blue as his. She turned away, her cheeks flushing.

'This quarantine business is ghastly, Rose. I have no time for it,' the duke said, staring absentmindedly into his tea.

'You must be terribly worried for the duchess. I do hope she will recover soon.'

'It just makes it difficult to carry out my duties from here.'

'We will do everything to make your stay comfortable.'

He looked up at her again. 'Thank you, Rose. I do hope you will.'

Rose curtseyed and extricated herself from the room, leaving the duke to stare into his tea again. The bedroom was located at the back of the cottage; well-sized with a large bed, radiator heater, closet and a tall Victorian lamp by sash windows. There was a dresser with a basin and towel for washing, and fresh lace curtains hung in an open window, cool salty air rushing in.

The room smelt of lemon from Miss Dalton's previous cleaning efforts and ammonia from the duke's chamber pot. Rose gathered up the bed linen and slipped back through the living room as silently as she could while the duke ate and read from the paper.

She beat the pillows quietly on the verandah and, with fresh linen from the trolley, she remade his bed. She washed out the chamber pot, laid clean towels and dusted the room down.

When she returned to the living room, the duke had finished eating and was back at the bureau sorting papers. After piling the breakfast items onto the tray, she carried it out to the trolley.

'Will you need anything else, Your Grace?' she asked from the front door.

'Not for now, Rose. I will see you at morning tea.'

She bid him good day and closed the door behind her.

* * *

Rose returned the breakfast trolley to Mrs March and took the bed linen to the laundry. She helped the washhouse girls load the sheets into large copper tubs, fires blazing underneath to heat the water. Sharp fumes of disinfectant burnt her throat as she stirred the sheets with a pole, steam rising and wetting her face.

With twenty minutes to spare before she had to return to the kitchen to prepare the duke's morning tea, she left the girls to fish the sheets out and put them through the wringer. She stopped by Thomas's workshop on the way back and found him inside measuring cuts of wood.

'Rose,' he said, placing down the tape measure with a smile. He walked to the doorway to greet her. 'What a nice surprise. I was looking for you earlier. I thought you might like to take a walk down to the cove before lunch.'

'I'm sorry. I can't today. Miss Dalton has me tending to the duke. I'll have little time, I'm afraid.'

He leant against the doorframe. His hazel eyes were lovely in the morning sun. 'Ah, the duke. I see. You must be the envy of all the parlourmaids.'

'I doubt that.'

'I heard them talking about him. They think him very handsome.'

Rose shrugged. 'I don't think any of them have seen him up close to tell for sure.'

He laughed. 'As long as *you* don't find him too handsome, Rose. That's all I care about.'

She smiled at the possessive way his words sounded; as though she were his. She wanted to stay in that doorway forever, with his eyes on her, like fingertips on her skin.

'I'd better go.' She stepped back. 'Can we take our walk tomorrow?'

'I'd like nothing more.'

She left the workshop and headed back to the kitchen, unable to wipe the smile from her face.

* * *

'The duke's morning tea is over there,' Mrs March said, jabbing a plump finger at a tray on the table. 'Scones, jam, clotted cream and peaches. Don't spill the tea on the way up.'

'Yes, Mrs March.' Rose loaded the tray onto the serving trolley and headed for the kitchen door.

'When you're finished with the duke, come back here and help the girls set up for lunch in the dining room. Miss Dalton's orders.'

'Yes, Mrs March.'

Rose pushed the trolley onto the road and up the hill towards the duke's cottage. When she reached the door, she knocked.

'Come in, Rose,' he called.

Rose ventured in and curtseyed. 'Good morning, Your Grace. I have your morning tea.'

'Thank you. Set it down on the table.' The duke was seated at the bureau again, writing a letter, pen scratching against paper. 'I won't be a moment.'

Rose set the tray on the table and removed the cloches. As the duke worked, she laid out the scones and fruit and poured the tea, stirring in milk and two cubes of sugar.

When he arrived to take his seat, she pulled out the chair for him and laid a napkin in his lap.

'This is a lovely setting, Rose,' he said.

'Thank you. Will that be all, Your Grace?'

The duke looked up at her. 'What do you think of the war?'

Rose was taken aback. 'I beg your pardon, Your Grace?'

'The war. What do you think of it?'

It was as an odd question. Rose hadn't been in service long but she was fairly certain parlourmaids were not asked their opinion on such matters. 'I don't think anything of it.'

His eyebrows lifted. 'I find that hard to believe.'

She shifted uncomfortably.

'Go on. You won't get into trouble. There's no right or wrong answer.'

'Well, Your Grace,' she said carefully, 'I believe the war is an unnecessary waste of human life.'

'Is that so?'

'Yes. For one, I do not believe it was Great Britain's war in the first place. The Russians and the Austro-Hungarians should have settled their differences over Franz Ferdinand and the Balkans without involving everyone else.

'Secondly, how many people have already died because of this useless fight? Millions, not to mention it triggering a Spanish Influenza outbreak. Then Australia and New Zealand became involved in Turkey, losing plenty of lives there. At what point does everybody just stop?'

The duke looked amused. 'That is quite an opinion for someone who didn't have one.'

Rose grimaced.

He sipped his tea and placed the cup on the saucer. 'Do you think the king was wrong to encourage Britain's involvement?'

'I would not presume to tell the king what is right or wrong.'

'But you think it is a useless fight?'

Rose remained silent.

'I'm in Australia to urge the government here to send us more fleet. Do you think that is a wise move?'

'I think peace is always better than war.'

He smiled, blue eyes crinkling. 'Your opinion intrigues me, as do you, Rose.'

Rose's stomach flipped unpleasantly. 'I hope I have not spoken out of turn.'

'Quite the contrary.'

'Will that be all, Your Grace?'

He nodded. 'Yes. Thank you, Rose. I will see you at lunch.'

* * *

'Tell me everything!'

Rose slipped her shift over her head and dropped down onto her bed, exhausted. 'There isn't much to tell.'

'Do not be coy with me, Rose Porter. I have been dying all day to get back to this room and see you.' Bessie lit a cigarette and sat on the edge of her bed, dragging back on it hungrily. 'I need to know everything that happened. What is he like? Did he talk much? Did he eat all his food, drink his tea, read the paper?'

Rose chuckled at the questioning. 'He's nice, surprisingly chatty. He drinks his tea with milk and two cubes, you will be pleased to know. He ate the bacon and some of the eggs but mostly he liked the toast.'

'He liked the toast,' Bessie repeated with relish. 'What else?'

'For lunch I served him roast beef and chutney sandwiches, which he seemed to like. For dinner, he picked at the chicken. He said he prefers salmon.'

'I prefer salmon too. What else?'

'There isn't much else to tell. I served him his meals and poured his

93

tea. I changed his bed linen and I was on my way. It's been an exhausting day.'

'Miss Dalton must think highly of you to give you this task. I heard the other parlourmaids talking about it. They're all terribly envious of you.'

'Well, it was only for one day. Miss Dalton will take over again tomorrow and I can go back to the dining room.'

'The duchess is still unwell. She has that persistent bronchial cough. I bet the duke is beside himself with worry, though they say he hasn't visited her once in the hospital.'

'It's probably for the best,' Rose said. 'The unhealthy ground is not a place to visit right now. You heard Miss Dalton, we should all keep away. We don't want an outbreak in first class.'

'Yes, I suppose.' Bessie tossed her cigarette out the window and climbed beneath the covers, yawning. 'You're right, Rose. It *has* been an exhausting day.'

'And tomorrow is a new one, Bessie Briar.'

Bessie blew out the candles in the lantern beside her bed. 'Goodnight.'

'Goodnight.' Rose climbed beneath her covers too, her head sinking into the pillow.

'Rose?'

'Yes.'

'I just wanted to say, you are the best friend I've ever had. I hope we're friends forever, no matter where life takes us.'

Rose smiled in the darkness. 'We will be, I promise.'

'And when I marry a prince or a duke, I will have you come to visit as our special guest in our castle. You can even come live with us if you like.'

'I couldn't think of a nicer invitation.'

Silence, then Bessie's gentle snores rumbled across the room.

Rose lay for a while staring up at the ceiling with a chattering brain not ready to slow. She thought of Thomas and wondered if he were in his bed too. Was he thinking of her as she was of him, as she thought of him every night; the kind of thoughts that made her cheeks warm and her body hum? Was he longing to feel her next to him? Was his desire for her just as strong?

Giving up on sleep, she rolled over and opened her drawer, retrieving the diary he'd given her from beneath her petticoats. She slipped out of bed, collected the lantern from the floor and brought it back with her. Placing it on the bedside table, she relit the candles inside and they crackled softly to life.

She settled back against her pillow and spread the covers of her diary as far as they would extend. Out dropped the little key to unlock it; a hiding place she had thought of to prevent inquisitive eyes from accessing her most private thoughts.

She unlocked her diary and, with the silver fountain pen in hand, she wrote everything that she often thought but could not say, everything she felt for a man she was falling in love with.

There she sat, writing until dawn coloured the sky.

Chapter Twelve

Rose was laying out the cutlery in the dining room for breakfast the following morning when Miss Dalton appeared.

'Rose, I need to see you, please.'

Rose looked up, surprised and, with the eyes of the other maids following her, she stepped aside with Miss Dalton. 'Yes?'

'A troopship arrived this morning with six more suspected cases of Spanish Influenza on board. The soldiers were thought to have contracted it when they took on new passengers at Newcastle.'

'It's coming.'

'Indeed. I doubt there will be any stopping it now. I have an emergency meeting this morning with Matron Cromwell from the hospital, the superintendent and the Minister for Health. Then I will have my hands full dealing with this for the rest of the week. I will need you to tend to the duke.'

'For how long?'

'The next five days.'

Rose's heart sank. The next five days! She'd been looking forward to seeing Thomas after breakfast. She'd planned a whole morning at the cove with him.

Miss Dalton must have caught her look of angst for her back straightened. 'Will that be a problem, Rose?'

Rose's shoulders slumped. 'No, Miss Dalton.'

'Good. I knew I could count on you. Finish setting the tables then you can take the duke his breakfast.'

* * *

After the dining tables were set, Rose snuck away to Thomas's workshop. She poked her head in the doorway but he wasn't there.

After a quick glance around to ensure no one was watching, she slipped inside and searched for a pen and paper. When she couldn't find one she used one of his carpenter's pencils to scratch out a message on the wooden benchtop.

She told him there would be no walks to the cove for the next week. Just writing the words made her heart ache, but she had little time to dwell on it. She covered her message with his measuring tape where he was sure to find it, then darted out of the workshop and back to the kitchen.

Mrs March was waiting for her with her hands on her hips. 'Where did you scamper off to? The other parlourmaids are already serving breakfast.'

'Ladies' business,' Rose mumbled under her breath.

Mrs March gave her a dubious look. 'The duke's tray is ready. Off you go.'

Rose collected the tray and loaded it onto the serving trolley along with the morning paper. Bessie was elbow deep in greasy water, scrubbing a cast iron pot. She managed a quick smile before Mrs March ordered her to scrub faster.

Rose pushed the trolley along Main Axial Road, stopping by the laundry to collect clean linen before starting up the hill towards the duke's cottage.

The door was ajar when she reached it and she gave it a knock.

'Is that you, Miss Dalton?' came the duke's voice from inside.

'It's Rose, Your Grace.'

'Rose?' There was a pause then he was at the door, thrusting it open with a smile. 'Rose! How marvellous to see you! Do come in.'

Rose carried in the breakfast tray, setting it down on the table.

'This is a pleasant surprise.' The duke stood beside her, inspecting the plates as she lifted the cloches. 'I thought Miss Dalton was back today.'

'She sends her apologies. She has some urgent business to attend to for the rest of the week. I'll be serving you.'

'Is that so?' He looked chipper at the thought. 'Wonderful! Well, I'm quite famished this morning. Everything looks delicious.'

Rose pulled the chair out for him and he sat. She laid the napkin across his lap and set the table. He watched her with an almost curious avidity as she laid out the cutlery and condiments. When she poured his tea and he took a sip, he made an exaggerated 'ah' sound again, as though it were the best tea he had ever tasted.

She sat the paper by his elbow and curtseyed. 'Enjoy your breakfast, Your Grace. I will see to your room now.'

'Do you miss home, Rose?' he asked.

She turned back to him. 'Excuse me, Your Grace?'

'Do you miss home?'

'Sometimes I do.'

'I do too. All the time. This place feels foreign to me. It's so different from everything I know.' He gave her a sorrowful look.

She smiled encouragingly at him. 'I felt a bit like that when I first got here.'

'Did you now?' he said, leaning forward.

'Yes. The trees and the smells and the weather, it was all different, but you get used to it.'

'I'm not sure I ever will.'

'Once the duchess recovers and she is back with you, you will feel less homesick.'

He ignored the comment and pushed out the chair next to him, motioning for her to take it. 'Sit with me, Rose.'

'Oh... I shouldn't.'

'I just want to speak to you for a minute.'

'I'm really not allowed.'

'Just for a minute.'

'Miss Dalton would be—'

'Miss Dalton will never know.' He gave her a wink. 'It will be our little secret.'

Rose opened her mouth to protest, but the duke gestured at the chair again. She sank slowly into it and folded her hands in her lap, her spine rigid as a rod.

'There we go. Now, would you like some tea?' he asked.

Rose shook her head firmly.

'Toast? Bacon?'

'Please, Your Grace. I can't...'

'Very well,' he said. 'I don't want you to feel uncomfortable. I only want to enjoy your company.'

Rose avoided his eyes and stared down at her hands.

He cleared his throat. 'What brought you all the way out here? Are you married? Did you come with your husband?'

'No, Your Grace. I sailed alone.'

'Alone?' He sat back and crossed his legs.

'Yes, on a troopship. I earned passage making and mending sailor's clothes. I'm a decent seamstress.'

'But why would a young girl like you make a journey out here alone?'

'My father was going to marry me off to the butcher's son in the country town we were moving to, so I ran away.'

The duke fell silent for a moment then he slapped his knee and roared with laughter. It was a full minute before he stopped. 'Oh, Rose! I can see you doing that too, putting your foot down in defiance.' He laughed again. 'What a marvellous story.'

Rose, in spite of herself, laughed too. 'My father wasn't happy.'

'I imagine not. Oh, but Rose, that is who you are. You're not to be trapped like a caged bird. You're a modern woman with modern thoughts. Why, I bet you believe in a woman's right to vote, don't you? I can see you out there, being a menace with all the other suffragettes.' He roared again with laughter.

'I wouldn't partake in anything illegal, Your Grace, but yes, I do believe in a woman's right to equality.'

'Equality! Ha! Marvellous. Just marvellous! I've never met a woman like you. So proper on the outside and yet, on the inside, you're wildly untamed.'

Rose wasn't sure if that was a compliment. 'Will that be all, Your Grace?'

The duke smiled. 'That will be all for now. Thank you for sitting with me.'

She climbed to her feet, curtseyed and left him at the table, still chuckling to himself.

* * *

The next five days crawled by. Between caring for the duke and helping the parlourmaids in the dining room, it was a full week since Rose had seen Thomas. Their separation had left her feeling strangely disjointed, as though maybe, this whole time, he'd been a figment of her imagination.

If she found a minute to spare, she strolled past his workshop in the hope of bringing him to life again, but disappointingly, he was never inside, his job taking him to other places on the station.

The duke did not invite Rose to sit at the dining table again, much to her relief, though he still engaged her in conversation. They talked of everything from the war, to working at the station, to her life back home in London. He always seemed cheerful upon her arrival and announced his joy at everything she served him as though she had cooked it herself.

The duchess remained in the hospital fighting a bronchial infection, though if the duke was worried for her, he never said so out loud. In fact, he never mentioned her at all.

On the fifth day, Rose served a lunch of roast beef and Yorkshire pudding with iced tea and Victoria sponge for dessert. The duke was in a pleasant mood and so was Rose, the idea of being back in the dining room and back with Thomas making her hum all the way to the kitchen.

She pushed the trolley up the ramp as the parlourmaids across the road began to clear the dining room after lunch. The day had been blessed with a beautiful winter sun. Passengers were strolling past with faces turned up to the sky and a cricket game had commenced on a grassy patch near second class.

Bessie was by the sink, hands deep in scalding water, when Rose walked in.

'What are you looking so perky about?' Mrs March barked, pulling pots off the stove and dumping them near Bessie.

'The duke enjoyed his lunch immensely, Mrs March.'

Mrs March wiped her hands on her apron. 'Is that so?'

'Yes.'

'Well so he should. Miss Dalton wants to see you in her office. Finish unloading the trolley and go.'

Rose carried the plates, cutlery and cloches to Bessie, adding them to a pile that never seemed to shrink. When she left the kitchen, enthusiastic shouts from the cricket game followed her up Main Axial Road towards Miss Dalton's office.

When she reached the door, she gave it a knock.

'Come in.'

Rose turned the handle and let herself in.

'Close the door behind you Rose and sit.'

There was a tone to her voice that Rose couldn't interpret but as she closed the door and took a seat at the oak desk, the expression on Miss Dalton's face left little doubt. She was displeased.

She leant forward and rested her elbows on the desk. 'The Duke of Northbury came to see me this morning.'

'He did? What for?'

'I think you already know the answer to that.'

'Excuse me?'

'Did something happen this past week while you were serving him?'

'I'm not sure what you mean.'

'Did anything improper take place?'

Rose thought of the morning she'd sat at the table with the duke. He'd offered her tea and breakfast and had wanted to talk. She'd resisted but he'd encouraged it. Had he informed Miss Dalton that Rose had accepted his invitation? That she, a parlourmaid, had been brazen enough to sit at the table with a member of the monarchy.

Miss Dalton drummed her nails on the desktop. 'Now is the time to tell me, Rose.'

Rose squirmed. The carriage clock ticked loudly on the mantelpiece.

'Maybe you'd like to explain then, why the duke came to request your service for the remainder of his stay. Why he has asked for you and you only.'

The line of questioning was so unexpected that Rose was still trying to grasp what she was being accused of. 'He asked for me only?'

'Yes, so you must tell me, did you engage in inappropriate activities with him this past week? He has obviously become fond of you.'

Rose shook her head firmly. 'No, Miss Dalton. I mean, he likes to talk, but nothing untoward has occurred.'

'He's a lonely man, Rose. It would not surprise me if he desired a young, healthy maid like you. And maybe the thought of bedding a member of the royal family has made you forget your place as well.'

'I promise, Miss Dalton. I have not been improper with him.'

Miss Dalton studied her for a long time.

'Are you going to fire me?'

She sighed. 'No, Rose. I'm not going to fire you.'

Rose let out a trapped breath.

'I admit I was surprised when he made his request. I wondered what you could have done to become so highly sought.'

'I haven't done anything.'

'I believe you.' Miss Dalton looked at her in earnest. 'I didn't at first. In fact, I was highly sceptical. But you obviously have the patience for him, something I don't have. And he seems to have noticed that.'

Rose's relief at not being fired was quickly negated by the realisation she was to remain in service to him. Time with Thomas was slipping through her fingers again. 'Perhaps now we should ask him to visit the dining room for meals,' she said. 'I see no reason why he can't socialise with the other passengers.'

Miss Dalton held up her hand. 'I did suggest it, but he would have none of it. He wants the current arrangement—you serving him in his quarters until he leaves. You can understand why this had me concerned.'

Rose nodded dejectedly. 'Of course.'

'Well, I'm glad we had this little talk. The duke will be most pleased when I inform him that you will continue in the role.'

'Yes, Miss Dalton.'

'Thank you, Rose. That will be all.'

* * *

'Go on, you can tell me.'

'There's nothing to tell,' Rose said.

'He must want you for a reason.'

'I don't know why. Nothing's happened.'

'Not even one little kiss?'

Rose threw her pillow at Bessie, hitting her squarely in the face, causing her to fall back onto her bed with a squeal of laughter.

'Not even one little kiss,' Rose said. 'The duke has been a perfect gentleman.'

'I bet his thoughts are not gentlemanly.'

'We're fellow compatriots and he's homesick. That's all it is.'

'I bet he wants to slide his hand right up your dress and have a feel.'

'Bessie Briar, you are revolting.'

Bessie collapsed into giggles again.

'He doesn't think like that,' Rose said as she sat on her bed, her hair separated into three sections while she roped them into a plait. 'He just likes to talk.'

'Well if you ever get bored with him, I will happily swap with you. I will take the duke his meals and you can scrub the pots in the kitchen with Mrs March,' Bessie said, scratching her hands.

'Your skin needs ointment. Let me ask Miss Dalton in the morning.'

'It doesn't bother me.'

'You scratch them until they bleed. That must bother you.' Rose secured the end of her plait with a piece of ribbon.

Bessie yawned and climbed under her covers, tossing Rose back her pillow. 'Don't worry about me. I'm tough.'

Rose caught the pillow, slid beneath her covers and turned the oil lamp down low.

'Do you wish for marriage, Rose?' Bessie's sleepy voice spoke from the shadows.

'I do, Bessie.'

'With a husband who is rich and handsome?'

'With a husband who is humble and kind.'

'What about children?'

'I would like them too, someday.'

There was silence across the room. Then, 'Do you think a man could ever love someone like me?'

Rose climbed up on one elbow. 'That's a silly question. Of course I do. There are lots of good men out there who would fall over themselves to marry you.'

'I'm just a lowly scullery maid.'

'You're not *just* a scullery maid.'

'I'm not beautiful like you. My body is fat and my hands are hideous. I didn't even finish school. I'm an uneducated lump.'

'Bessie Briar.'

'It's the truth.'

'It's not the truth.'

'Those are the first things a man notices.'

'They're not and I truly believe there is someone for everyone.'

Bessie sighed. 'You really are the kindest person I know, Rose Porter. And my dearest friend.'

'And you are mine.'

A few minutes later, Rose heard the soft snores of her companion as she drifted to sleep.

Rose lay back down and closed her eyes, but sleep wouldn't come. Bessie's words of self-loathing tumbled over in her brain and tugged at her heart. Unable to relax, she rolled onto her side and reached across to her bedside table, opening the drawer. Beneath the layers of undergarments and petticoats, her fingers closed around her diary but as she was about to retrieve it, she heard a soft clatter outside, like small pebbles being thrown against glass.

She quickly closed the drawer and threw back the covers. The air was frosty as she moved to the window by Bessie's bed to investigate.

When she leant forward to peer out the glass, she saw Thomas outside, hand raised, about to throw another pebble.

Rose smiled brightly. *Thomas!*

She ran to the front door and, with a slight creak, opened it and stepped out onto the verandah. Thomas walked around the side of the cottage and met her at the stairs.

'What are you doing here?' Rose whispered, wrapping her arms around herself. The night was freezing. 'It's almost eleven o'clock.'

'I wanted to see you.'

She blushed, sure that he would notice in the darkness.

'Would you like to walk with me, Rose? I want to show you something.'

'Now? I'm in my nightgown.'

'Put your coat and shoes on.'

Rose considered the conversation she'd had back in Miss Dalton's office only hours earlier, the fear of almost losing her job still fresh in her mind, but it took her less than a second to realise that she'd missed Thomas. That she couldn't turn him away, even though her head was telling her she should. Already she could feel her hand in his, their bodies close, so close it made her heart quicken at the thought.

She crept back inside, pulled her stockings, boots and coat on, sprayed herself with her peony perfume and stepped back out onto the verandah, closing the door softly behind her.

Thomas reached for her hand and she took it as he led her out of the trees and onto Cottage Road.

'I've missed you,' he said, smiling down at her. His fingers tightened around her hand and she squeezed his back.

'Did you get my message?'

'Yes. Underneath my measuring tape.'

'I'm sorry I haven't been able to see you this week. Working with the duke has taken up all my time.'

'You don't have to apologise. I understand. But I'm glad the week is over and Miss Dalton can look after him again.'

They cut through third class and past Asiatics where the outdoor ovens were cooling and the Orientals had moved inside. One end of the dormitory still bore the scars of their indoor cooking attempt the week earlier.

'About that, Thomas,' she said. 'I've been asked to tend to him indefinitely.'

Thomas gave her a sideways glance. 'Indefinitely?'

'Yes. Until he leaves. Miss Dalton spoke to me about it today.'

There was an uneasy pause. 'Well, she must think highly of you to give you such an important role like that.'

'It wasn't her idea. The duke asked for me.' She regretted the words as soon as they were out.

Thomas lapsed into silence.

'He's homesick,' she said, trying to brush it off. 'And I'm English. We have that in common. That's all it is.'

He stared ahead, not meeting her eyes, the air heavy beneath the weight of all that was unsaid.

'I'm sorry,' she said after some time. 'I didn't mean for this to happen.'

'Don't be sorry. You're just doing your job.'

'Yes, but you think poorly of me. Everyone assumes I've done something to encourage him.'

Thomas's face softened. 'I don't think that at all.'

'He's just lonely and likes to talk.'

'Okay.'

'You're not happy.'

'I'm not happy because I was looking forward to spending time with you again. And I also suspect the duke likes you and that makes me uneasy. I don't want anyone else to like you the way I do.'

His words picked apart the awkwardness, sending Rose's heart soaring. She was relieved at how he wore his emotions on his sleeve and how much she needed that after days spent apart from him.

'Anyway, let us not speak of him. I don't want to waste our precious time together discussing the duke.'

She happily conceded. She didn't want to speak of him either. She wanted to disappear into that invisible bubble she always seemed to exist in whenever she was with Thomas, where nothing from the outside world could penetrate. She concentrated all her thoughts on the way her hand was tucked in his and the way their hips brushed as they walked.

A swarm of bats beat their wings overhead as Thomas led her away from third class and into the trees past the male staff quarters. Windows all around were black or illuminated by weak lantern light. The station was quiet; a rare moment of peace.

He guided them behind the cottages and onto the path that led through the bush.

'Where are we going?' Rose asked.

'I want to show you something.'

'Near your cottage?'

'Yes.'

He held fast to her hand as the station faded behind them and they picked their way along the path. The wildlife was different at night. Thomas pointed out bilbies and bandicoots, their bright beady eyes glowing in the dark, and he asked her to train her ears for the unusual squeak of the sugar gliders.

He led her from the brush and out onto the clearing where his little weathered cottage stood. The breeze instantly took her hair and night-gown and ruffled it with belligerence.

He guided her closer to the edge so that she could hear the crashing of the waves against the escarpment below, the moon balancing high in the sky, casting silver light across the harbour.

'Look up at the sky,' Thomas whispered in her ear.

Rose lifted her head and saw billions of tiny stars above her, splattered against the night. It was more than she had ever seen in her lifetime; certainly more than she'd ever seen in London or down at the station.

'There are so many of them. How is it possible?'

'I don't know. But when I'm out here at night, away from all the lights, there seems to be a million more.'

'It's beautiful, Thomas.'

'I thought you would like it.'

He shrugged out of his jacket and laid it down on the rocks for her to sit.

'No, it's too cold. Put it back on,' she said.

'I'm not cold. Please sit.'

She reluctantly accepted and sat down on it. He sat beside her and they stared out at the water. It looked like black syrup gently rippled by the current.

Thomas pointed. 'Can you see all the way across to the next headland?'

'Yes.'

'That's South Head and The Gap.'

Across the water, Rose could see the shadowy outline of South Head and the swooping beam of a lighthouse that carved through the darkness like a sword, guiding vessels to safety.

'Can you see the lights of the ships?'

She counted three anchored in the harbour. 'Yes, I see them.'

'They're waiting to be moved into quarantine tomorrow. They must have failed a health inspection.'

'Spanish Influenza?'

'It's likely. They're talking of a new law, one that will see every ship quarantined, regardless if symptoms are present.'

'Every ship? But that will cripple us.'

'They've started erecting tents in the Hospital Precinct. The wards are already full. There isn't enough space.'

Rose shivered in the cool air, the breeze whipping through her coat. Thomas moved closer and placed an arm around her shoulder. Warmth crept from his body to hers as she nestled into him.

'Are you enjoying your diary?'

'Oh, I am. You were correct. When one doesn't know what to write, they should write in a diary.'

'I'm glad.'

'You're too good to me, Thomas,' she said, looking up at him. His face was close; inches from hers.

'You deserve all of it and more. So much more than I could ever hope to give you.'

'I don't need much.'

His lips moved closer.

'Thomas...'

'I wake every morning thinking of you, Rose. There are things I've wanted to say to you.'

'Like what?'

'Like how much I'd like to kiss you.'

Rose's breath caught in her lungs.

'Can I kiss you?'

Her voice was a whisper. 'Yes.'

His lips brushed hers softly, yet it was enough to make her heart race and her blood pulse. She parted her lips and kissed him back, and although she had never kissed a man before, with Thomas it felt as natural as if she had been doing it for years.

They sat on the clifftop, beneath the star-splashed sky, high above a sea that rippled like ink. They remained that way and kissed until Rose began to shiver again.

'It's getting cold, my love,' he said.

'I'm not cold.'

'I should get you back to your cottage.'

'I want to stay here with you.'

He smiled and tucked a strand of hair behind her ear that had come loose from her plait. 'Not tonight, my Rose. We've broken enough rules.'

She looked out across the sea, disappointed. Thomas cupped his hand under her chin and turned her face towards his. His eyes were so bright and green in the dark, she felt transfixed, swallowed by them.

'Don't be sad. If we can't spend time together during the day, would you like to see each other here at night?'

She nodded. 'I would like that very much.'

'Not every night, for I don't want you to grow tired, but some nights.'

'As many nights as we can.'

Thomas climbed to his feet and helped Rose to hers. 'Come. Let me get you back to your warm bed.'

They left the whistling breeze behind on the clifftop and Thomas led Rose carefully back through the bush, along the path surrounded by night creatures. They crept through the male staff quarters, the station a silent, sleeping giant around them.

Back at her cottage, Rose was reluctant to let Thomas go. She waved at him from the front door and watched as he disappeared into the darkness.

Inside, she shrugged out of her coat and slipped off her stockings and boots. Bessie was fast asleep, her body rising and falling with each breath. Rose had an overwhelming urge to wake her to tell her the news. She'd kissed a boy! And it had been everything she could have hoped for. She was so giddy with happiness that she wanted to shout it from the rooftops.

But of course she couldn't, for this was not a love to be indulged. Strictly forbidden, it broke all the rules and if anyone ever found out what they'd been doing, they'd both be fired. Still, despite this, Rose was helpless to fight it, helpless to control it.

And after that kiss, she didn't want to.

* * *

Rose had barely opened her eyes the next morning when a pleasant feeling washed over her and she remembered the night before and the kiss outside Thomas's cottage.

She dressed quickly and left the room, skipping down the hill to first class. The air was cold, the sun too weak to thaw the frost and she rubbed her hands together against the chill.

She entered the kitchen just as Bessie was receiving a berating from Mrs March for not scrubbing the skillets properly.

'Good morning,' she said, far too cheerfully.

Mrs March whipped her head around and narrowed her eyes suspiciously. 'What's got you so merry?'

'Nothing. Just happy.'

'She has the duke indefinitely,' Bessie said, grinning from the sink.

'I'd heard as much,' Mrs March said, hands on her hips. 'He's asking for you and you only.'

Rose shook her head. 'That's not the reason I'm—'

'Stop gloating over it then and take him his breakfast. The eggs are getting cold.'

'Yes, Mrs March.' Rose collected the duke's breakfast, loaded it onto the serving trolley and pushed it along the road. She stopped at the laundry for fresh linen and continued up the hill towards his cottage.

At the verandah, she parked the trolley and climbed the steps to the front door, giving it a light knock.

The duke appeared in the doorway with a wooden smile.

'Good morning, Your Grace.' She curtseyed. 'I have your breakfast.'

'Do come in,' he said flatly.

Rose collected the tray from the trolley and stepped into the cottage. The duke watched her as she set the tray down on the table, clasping then unclasping his hands as though he couldn't work out what to do with them.

She laid out the cutlery and spreads as he hovered over her shoulder. She wasn't sure what had gotten into him. He was usually so buoyant.

Then, from behind his closed bedroom door, Rose heard the murmur of voices.

'My wife is here,' he said dully. 'The doctor and nurse are with her in the bedroom.'

Rose set down the teapot she was holding. 'Your Grace, that's wonderful news. Has she recovered?'

'Not quite. She still has a bronchial infection, but they need to free up the bed in the hospital for the more critical, and so it was decided she would relocate here for the remainder of her recovery.' He said this with a surprising amount of displeasure.

'I'm pleased to hear she is stable enough to be moved. She'll be more comfortable here. And once she recovers, you will be on your way and that must be some consolation to you.'

Apparently not, for the duke looked crestfallen. 'You will still come, won't you?'

'I'm sorry?'

'Nothing has to change. I still need you. You will come to me each day?'

'Of course, Your Grace. I will still come.'

His shoulders slumped with relief. 'That makes me happy indeed. Thank you, Rose.' He watched her with a strange longing and, as she finished laying out breakfast, his gaze never faltered.

Chapter Thirteen

EMMA 2019

20th July, 1918

The weather has grown cold in Sydney, though I must say, not as bitterly cold as London.

My days are long and full. I care solely for the duke now. He is a curious man, with an exterior that exudes (if I may) a certain narcissism, yet on the inside he can be surprisingly vulnerable. We talk at length about all matters—England and politics, the war and women's rights. He doesn't seem bothered that I am a woman in service and have an opinion. Rather, he seems amused by it.

The duchess has been relocated to the duke's cottage in first class. She remains ill, fighting a bronchial infection of the lungs. I hear her coughing and gasping for air through the walls, though I have yet to see her. The duke has moved to the dressing room and the duchess now occupies the main bedroom.

I do not serve the duchess her meals nor tend to her room. She has a nurse who sits with her around the clock, and Doctor Holland visits each morning at nine.

The duchess has become somewhat of an enigma. I know she is there for I can hear her coughing. Sometimes I even hear her voice, meek and demure, amidst the wheezing. But beyond that, I have never met her nor does the duke speak of her. Perhaps in his life, she is an enigma too.

I find their relationship intriguing. He must love her, for she is his wife. But there seems to be something amiss, as though their union is fractured or one of convenience. He rarely mentions her, not even in quiet, unguarded moments and never a gentle tap on the door or a visit to her bedside to ensure her comfort. He does not seem overjoyed that she has returned to him.

Alas, it is none of my business. I remain faithful in service.

Rose

Emma placed the diary in her lap and chewed her lip pensively.

'What are you thinking?' Matt asked, watching her.

'Just that she became quite close to the duke. She seemed to know he had marital problems.'

'Do you think he's her mystery man?'

'I'm not sure. She writes about him often. Most of July 1918 has been about him.'

'That's probably because they were always together. He occupied her days.'

They had returned to the little room behind the museum and had once again pulled Rose's suitcase from beneath the dusty grey blanket. Inside, exactly where they'd left them the week before, were the stack of five diaries.

They were nearing the end of the first one, and all entries for July so far had pertained to the duke and Rose's flourishing relationship with him. She had written almost every day about this man who enjoyed her company and valued her opinion. In other entries, she spoke of a love so great she was powerless to refuse it, though she never gave name to that love.

It left Emma feeling confused. Were the duke and her mystery man one and the same? Considering that Rose had become pregnant with Gwendoline so quickly, her mystery man had to be someone she knew at that point in time and whom she felt strongly for.

'I guess the only way we're going to know for sure is if we keep reading,' Matt said, as though knowing her thoughts.

'Yes, you're right. I'm being too impatient.' She gave a contrite grin.

'I understand why.'

'I just wish I'd asked my grandmother more. I should have shown interest long before this.'

'You were a kid. Kids aren't interested in stuff like that.'

Their visits together, and there had been quite a few now, had morphed into a routine. They would sit on the hard floor of that tiny back room and read a few pages of Rose's diary, then they would start talking as they cautiously peeled back the layers of each other's personality. At some point, they would remember the task at hand and return to the diary.

Matt didn't seem to mind that it was interrupting his work day and that he would have to make up the hours later. He always seemed happy when she returned to the station.

Emma wasn't sure what was happening between them or even if she was ready for it, but there was something about Matt that always left her feeling as though she were off balance.

It was the same way she'd felt when she'd first met Drew. She'd been awash with grief back then and desperate for distraction, her heart so vulnerable she'd fallen harder and faster than she could have imagined. And although the circumstances had been different that time, it was the same exhilarating feeling that threatened to undo her.

'Do you see any similarities?' Matt asked.

His question brought Emma back to the room. 'Between me and Rose?'

'Yeah,' he said. 'She was your great-grandmother. Does anything stand out in her diary that makes you think you're alike?'

Emma stretched her legs out and leant back on her hands. 'I don't know. It was a different time back then. There were clear rules in her job and in society. What's obvious is that, despite those rules, Rose believed in love. She wore her heart on her sleeve. While she was sensible and modest, she loved fiercely. I guess I was like that once, brave as though I'd never been hurt. And I hadn't been, not back then.'

'Until the accident with your family?'

'And other things,' she said, Drew coming to mind.

'I think it's okay to be afraid. We're all afraid of something.'

'What are you afraid of?'

He shrugged. 'I was in a relationship once and I was cheated on. I guess I'm afraid of that happening again.'

'Oh, Matt, I'm sorry. That's awful.'

'It was a while ago. Turns out she was married for the entire two years we were together. And I had no clue. Pretty stupid, huh?' He shook his head and cast his eyes down to his knees.

'That doesn't make you stupid. That makes her stupid.'

'How can you not know your girlfriend is married? Natalie worked for a bank and had a lot of so-called international business trips. Really, she was just on the other side of Sydney at home with her husband.'

'Well, she sounds like a talented multi-tasker. I have no idea how she found time for all that coming and going.'

'She was a compulsive liar and a cheat. Anyway, it was three years ago. I'm not so angry anymore.' He gave her a sheepish grin.

'I wouldn't blame you if you were. But I'm glad you've found a way past it. Hurt can be crippling.' She knew that better than anyone.

'What was your family like?' he asked and she sensed he was keen to get past the humiliation of his failed relationship.

Emma grinned at the thought of them. 'My parents were both very sweet, though as a teenager, I didn't always think so.'

'They were just there to ruin your life, right?'

'Exactly.' Emma chuckled. 'But as an adult now, I realise how amazing they were. They were kind and loving. I hope I can be like that one day.'

'I think you're all of those things and more,' Matt said.

Their eyes held and they smiled.

'How about your brothers?'

'They were like any pair of seven-year-old boys to a fifteen-year-old sister. Annoying. They drove me mad. They broke my things and hid my clothes. When I had friends over they were a nuisance and too loud when I was trying to study. But it wasn't hard to love them. Even though they were terrible little monsters sometimes, I adored them.'

She didn't choke when she said this. Instead, she smiled nostalgically at the memory—her two baby brothers, forever young in her mind, never growing old. Had they lived, they would be twenty-four, with jobs and girlfriends and a social life that would probably put hers to shame.

'Your family sounded amazing, Em.'

'They were. I just wish I'd told them that more often.'

Matt gave her a sympathetic smile, then his stomach grumbled. 'Oh! Sorry.' He grabbed it with embarrassment. 'I didn't have breakfast this morning. I guess it's nearly lunchtime.'

Emma glanced at her watch. 'Matt, it's two pm. I've kept you in here for three hours. We should pack this away so you can get back to work.'

'I'm not in any hurry.'

'I don't want to get you into trouble.'

'You won't.' He smiled a smile so lovely that Emma felt her breath catch.

'Tell me about your great-grandfather,' she said, leaning back on her hands.

'His name was Jack Cleveland. He worked as a carpenter at the station in the early 1900's.'

'And your great-grandmother?'

'Edith. I'm told she was a nurse here too.'

'So they met here?'

'Apparently. And when they left, they moved to a property in Mount Sheridan in Queensland. Jack didn't leave any records behind, certainly not any diaries or letters, so he's been hard to trace and so has Edith. I haven't been able to find any record of her being on the station at all. They had three children. My grandfather, Henry, was their youngest.' His stomach rumbled again and they both laughed.

They packed away Rose's things, closed the suitcase and returned it beneath the heavy grey blanket. They stretched and left the small room, heading back outside.

The day was bright when they stepped through the museum door and Emma had to hold her hand up to her eyes to shield them.

'Did you want to grab some lunch?' Matt asked.

Lunch with Matt was something Emma could have happily enjoyed, but she felt guilty at the time she'd already asked of him. 'I should let you get back to work. You'll be here all night making up for it.'

'I can think of worse places to be.'

Emma smiled shyly. 'Maybe another time. I can come back on my next day off.'

'Or maybe, if you don't have any plans one night, we could catch up for a drink'. He said this as he jammed his hands into his jeans pockets and shifted awkwardly from one foot to the other.

'You mean, like, outside of the station?'

'Yeah. Or not,' Matt said quickly. 'It was just a thought.'

'No, it was a good thought,' she said.

'Yeah?'

'Totally. I just...' She shook her head. 'It's been a while since I've...'

'Me too.'

'Right.'

They stood by the museum door, Matt with his hands still in his pockets and Emma feeling out of her depth.

'Well, I better go,' she said finally.

'Sure. Should I get your number first?'

'Yes,' she said without hesitating. 'You should.'

Matt laughed. 'Okay.'

He pulled out his phone and she relayed her number to him. He punched it in and saved it. Then she found herself giving him her address too, which seemed to surprise him but he happily added it to his phone.

'So there's this band playing in a pub in Randwick in a few weeks,' he said, shoving the phone back into his pocket. 'My friend is the drummer. And it's not far from your place. I'm not sure if bands are your thing, but maybe we could—'

'I'd love to.'

'Great! So I'll let you know the details and we can go from there.'

'Perfect.'

'Okay.'

He leant against the doorframe, hands in pockets, and the way he smiled at her with those perfectly green hazel eyes, made her stomach flip.

'Well, goodbye then,' she said.

'Bye, Em.'

She started back up the wharf to wait for the shuttle and when she turned back to see if he was still there, he was, watching her with a smile.

Chapter Fourteen

They exchanged texts all week—a casual 'hello' here and a 'how has your day?' there. Emma didn't want to get her hopes up, had been down that road before, but something told her that Matt was feeling a little of what she was.

The last weeks of July were busy. The days were served up blustery and cold and The Coffee Bean churned through a chaotic month. There was something about warm meals and hot coffee, followed by a movie that somehow enticed people out of their homes.

Chloe had hired two new university students but one had already quit and the other was busy with exams, so Emma worked additional shifts to help out. The extra money was a blessing, but the one day off a week she had she spent with Gwendoline and this left little time for Matt and the Q Station.

On a Tuesday morning that dawned bright after a week of rain, Emma woke late after a twelve-hour shift. She showered, dressed, ate a slice of toast then drove the fifteen-minute drive in her cold and spluttering VW to Eastgardens Aged Care.

She stopped at a florist in Pagewood and bought twelve red roses, then found a parking spot on the street beneath an old maple that still had plenty of crunchy brown leaves to dump on her car. She locked her doors and walked across the road to the main entrance.

The facility was busy when she arrived, visitors helping patients take slow, careful steps around the grounds. Emma signed the visitors' book and made her way down towards the north wing of the building. She was almost at Gwendoline's room when she heard someone call out her name.

'Mrs Wilcott!'

Emma turned. The director, Anastasia Thornbury, hurried towards her.

'Hello, Mrs Wilcott.'

Emma didn't bother correcting her. 'Good morning, Ms Thornbury. How are you today?'

Anastasia was impeccably dressed in a grey wool suit and pink blouse, her heels so high Emma wondered how she didn't roll her ankles. Her hair was pinned back tightly, pulling on the corners of her eyes.

'I've been hoping to catch you. Do you have a moment?'

'Sure.'

Emma followed Anastasia back to her office and sat opposite her, the large oak desk between them. Anastasia closed the door and poured Emma a glass of water, setting it down on a coaster.

'Is there a problem?' Emma asked.

'Not at all,' Anastasia said, taking a seat in her leather chair. 'In fact, I've been meaning to commend you. Whatever you've been doing lately during your visits with your grandmother has been working. The last time she wandered from the facility was almost two months ago and... well, we can both agree that's the longest run we've had.'

'Yes, it's certainly a relief.'

'What have you been doing, if you don't mind me asking?'

'I've been visiting the Quarantine Station where she grew up and, with the help of one of the staff members there, we found a suitcase of old diaries belonging to her mother. I've been relaying some of the stories to her from those pages.'

'Remarkable.'

'It was an incredible find and my grandmother seems to be enjoying the things I've been telling her. The entries are from before she was born but I think she's still comforted by them.'

119

'Indeed. We were almost at the stage where we were going to have to ask you to relocate your grandmother. I'm glad for your sake you've turned it around.'

Emma didn't respond. Instead, she fixed a forced smile on her face. Just when she'd thought Ms Thornbury had become tolerable, she was reminded of how tactless she could be.

'Well, I won't hold you up any longer. Keep up the good work.' Anastasia rose and leant across the desk to shake Emma's hand.

Emma left the office and headed back down the north wing of the facility. She found Gwendoline in her room, sitting with *Pride and Prejudice* on her lap, a sliver of sunlight spilling in through the window to light up the coverlet.

'Hey, Grandma,' Emma said, dropping her bag on the chair and placing the bouquet of roses on the bedside table. She leant across and gave Gwendoline's cheek a kiss.

'This is a nice surprise, dear. And you brought me roses.'

'I never forget.'

'Not working today?' Gwendoline said, seeming alert and present.

'It's my day off.'

'You should be doing fun things instead.'

'This is a fun thing,' Emma chided. She saw the book in Gwendoline's hands and frowned. 'I really must get you something new.'

'I like this book.' Gwendoline closed her hands over it, opening the drawer beside her bed and tucking it beneath her underwear. 'It's my favourite and don't you go touching it.'

Emma sighed. 'Okay, let's get you up and out of bed. The day is too beautiful to waste inside.'

She assisted Gwendoline into her robe, helped her put on slippers and grabbed a crocheted blanket, then they walked carefully down the corridor towards the back garden. Gwendoline's steps were a slow shuffle. Emma wondered how she managed to walk as far as she did when she went wandering. Fuelled by a sense of determination, most likely.

They found two chairs by a hyacinth bush that had lost its vivid blue flowers months ago and Emma settled Gwendoline into the seat, tucking the blanket over her lap.

'Are you warm enough? Would you like another blanket?'

Gwendoline swatted her away. 'Stop fussing.'

'You could use a dose of vitamin D.'

'We didn't worry about vitamin D in my day. We were all as healthy as sprouts.'

Emma sat in the seat opposite her grandmother and turned her face up to the sky. For all the cold days and blustering winds, Sydney could still turn on the most glorious winter charm.

The grounds outside were full of visitors sitting with their loved ones, the elderly tucked up beneath blankets in chairs and wheelchairs. There was lots of chatter in the air, mixed with trilling birds and the flow of traffic from nearby Bunnerong Road.

'How is work going?' her grandmother asked.

'Busy at the moment. Chloe is short-staffed so I've been working extra shifts to help her out.'

'You work far too hard.'

'It's good money and it keeps me occupied.'

'I think you should spend more time with friends and less time working in that café.' Gwendoline leant forward and patted Emma's hand. 'A girl like you shouldn't hide herself away.'

'I'm not hiding.'

'It's not who you are. Drew did that to you.'

'I think I changed long before Drew, Grandma.'

'To be fair, perhaps you did.'

Emma tucked a piece of hair behind her ear. 'I haven't been out to the Quarantine Station much lately. I'll have to get back there as soon as work slows down.'

'The Quarantine Station?'

'Yes. Remember I've been telling you about my visits there and about finding Rose's diaries?'

'Rose's diaries?' Gwendoline looked puzzled.

'We found five of them, though we've only gone through the first one so far. She wrote lots of things in them. About her work on the station and the duke and a mystery man she had fallen in love with.'

Gwendoline narrowed her eyes as if recalling something. 'A boy was helping you. A carpenter. Oh, what was his name?'

'Matt.'

Gwendoline beamed. 'Yes, Matt! I like that name.'

'He's just a friend.'

'In my day, if a boy helped you like that he would be more than a friend.'

'*He's a friend*,' Emma said firmly. She ignored the way Gwendoline watched her and ploughed on. 'Anyway, I wanted to ask you something. We've noticed in Rose's diaries that she fell in love with someone soon after starting work at the station, but she won't name who it was.'

Gwendoline sucked in her breath and closed her eyes. 'Oh, yes, Rose did love him. She never stopped.'

'Who, Gran? Who did Rose love?'

'He was a good man.'

Emma perched on the edge of her seat. 'Who was it? Did you know his name? Was it your father?'

'It wasn't allowed, you know.'

'You mean the relationship? Yes, we know. But who was the man?'

When Gwendoline opened her eyes, they were watery and unfocused.

'Grandma, what was your father's name? Is that whose boat you were waiting for by the wharf?'

'It was all to do with the duke, you see.'

Emma straightened. 'The duke?'

'Yes.'

'What does that mean?'

'Love was forbidden on the station.'

'Was Rose in love with the duke? Is that who your father was?'

A nurse shuffled past them, making an exaggerated glance at her watch. 'Gwendoline, what are you still doing out here? Visiting hours are over. It's time for your medicine and afternoon nap.'

Emma looked around the garden. Most of the visitors had disappeared or were helping loved ones to their feet. She hadn't noticed how empty and quiet it had grown. 'Can we have another two minutes please? We're just in the middle of something.'

'Not possible, I'm afraid. Health first,' the nurse sang with annoying mirth.

'Just two more minutes,' Emma pleaded as she watched Gwendoline's eyes. They were still fiercely blue, but confusion had set in again.

'Now, Mrs Wilcott, you know the hours for visiting. They've just finished. Everyone else is following the rules.'

'It's *Ms Wilcott.*'

The nurse looked at Emma as if she had said something utterly ridiculous. 'Come, Gwendoline. I'll help you to your room.' She assisted Gwendoline to her feet as Emma stood too.

She trailed behind them both, biting back her frustration. She'd almost had the name and the missing piece of the puzzle. If it wasn't for the nurse, she might know by now who Rose had been in love with, who Gwendoline's father was and ultimately, who Gwendoline had waited for down by the wharf as a child.

Emma tried not to feel disheartened as she said goodbye to her grandmother, as she smoothed down her white hair and kissed the soft folds of her cheek, as she reminded the nurse to put the roses in water.

After taking her medication and before drifting off to sleep, Gwendoline squeezed her hand gently.

'You're a good girl, Emma,' she whispered as the nurse tut-tutted behind them about visiting hours again. 'Forget about me. Forget about Rose. Go live your life.'

Emma shook her head. 'You are my life, Grandma.'

'Well I shouldn't be.'

Emma held back a sudden surge of emotion and hugged her tightly. She left her grandmother to nap and walked down the corridor, feeling oddly bereft of the warmth she'd felt only minutes earlier in the garden.

Outside, the sunshine still couldn't thaw her. She climbed into her car as the maple shed its dead leaves on her roof and the traffic around the aged care facility continued to flow.

Vividly and without warning, it came to her as she sat behind the wheel—the moment she'd learnt the devastating news of her family's death. She'd been staying at her best friend Tabitha's house for the night and they'd been woken at four am by a phone call from Gwendoline.

Tabitha's mother had come into the bedroom with the phone, gently shaking Emma awake and handing it to her. The look on her face had sent a chill down Emma's spine. Then she'd put the phone to her ear.

Gwendoline's voice across the line had been hoarse. *There's been an accident in France. A plane crash. No survivors. They're gone...*

What took place after that call had been a struggle to remember in its entirety. What Emma did recall was the fierce hug Tabitha pulled her into and Gwendoline coming to collect her an hour later, followed by weeks of numbness as though she were moving in someone else's body.

When the four coffins had been lowered into the ground, reality had set in. Emma's entire world had bottomed out. She quit school, became invisible, blamed the world and hated her grandmother.

The familiarity of her parents, her brothers and the house she'd grown up in were all gone. The backyard she'd played in, the room she'd slept in, the kitchen her mother had cooked in, all sold after a matter of minutes at auction, as though a beautiful young family hadn't once belonged there.

That happy and carefree teenage girl, the one who'd had a pocketful of dreams, would never see her family again, would never hear their voices, would never argue or laugh or cry or go on holiday with them. Instead, she became a stranger to the world.

Emma opened her eyes to the sound of ringing. She realised her cheeks were wet and she shook her head as if to draw a curtain over the memories.

Reaching for her phone, she saw Matt's name. 'Hello.'

'Hey,' he said cheerfully. Then there was a pause. 'Have I got you at a bad time?'

'Not at all.' She steadied herself and dried her cheeks with the back of her hand. 'Just finished visiting my grandmother.'

'Is she all right?'

'She's doing well. She hasn't wandered from the facility since I've been telling her about Rose's diaries. I think we're making progress.'

'That's great!'

'I'll fill you in more when I see you next.'

'That band I was telling you about is playing at the Baggy Green tomorrow night. It's a pub near the Sydney Cricket Ground. Do you know the one?'

'I do. It's not far from my house.'

'They start at nine if you're still keen to go.'

'I am. Should I meet you there?'

'Sure.' There was another pause. 'Em, is everything okay?'

Emma nodded into the phone. 'I think so.' She could feel him reaching out to her from down the line.

'I'll see you tomorrow, then?'

'I'll be there.'

And despite being on the brink of a low that was all too familiar, Emma found herself smiling.

Chapter Fifteen

'So it's a date?'

'It's not a date.'

'He asked you to go see a band with him tonight.' Chloe wiped her hands on her apron and pushed a rogue curl from her face. 'Sounds like a date to me.'

It was three pm. The lunch crowd had diminished and Emma and Chloe were in the kitchen preparing for the next rush. The bench was covered with trays of lasagne, gourmet pies and boxes of pastries that Chloe ordered in daily because she declared the kitchen too small to bake all that food herself. The real reason, Emma suspected, was that Chloe was far more skilled behind a coffee machine than over a stove top.

'I'm not reading too much into it. The band was playing out this way and so he invited me along. As a friend.'

'Don't do that.'

'Do what?'

'Sell yourself short. He likes you. You've spent all that time cozied up together in a little room. I'm not surprised.'

'We haven't been cozied up,' Emma muttered, sealing the lid on a container of salad she'd prepared.

'Call it a date and enjoy yourself. What are you afraid of?'

'It's just been a really long time. Three years.'

Chloe leant against the bench. 'You mean you haven't been out with anyone since Drew?'

Emma shrugged.

Chloe made an exaggerated 'O' with her mouth. 'Wow. I knew things were slow. I didn't realise they were that slow.'

Emma threw a dish towel at her.

The next movie crowd came and went and after seven, the pace slowed. Emma was loading the dishwasher when Chloe entered the kitchen with a pile of plates.

'You should get going or you'll be late,' she said.

Emma took the plates from her and stacked them in the racks. 'Can you manage for the rest of the night?'

'I'll be fine,' Chloe said, pushing her hair back from her face.

'How about I stay until nine? I'll go straight from here.'

'You've been here since seven this morning.'

'So have you.'

'But this place is my baby.'

'I really don't mind.'

'Go. Have a great time. I want to hear all about it tomorrow.'

Emma finished loading the dishwasher, wiped down the benches, arranged salad onto plates ready for serving and stacked clean cups and saucers by the coffee machine. When she'd done as much prep as she could, she hung up her apron, gave Chloe a hug and walked the two blocks home.

Until that evening, Emma hadn't realised just how far removed she'd become from the world, existing inside the bubble of her job, her apartment and the nursing home. She'd lived a shrink-wrapped version of herself, knowing in some small way that it probably wasn't right, but never having the courage to do anything about it.

Now, after years of insulation, she was being thrust back out into society like a baby leaving the womb.

During her shower, she conjured up a million reasons why she should call Matt and cancel—she was tired, she had to work in the morning, she was terrified. And then she had to remind herself, *Matt's just a friend. It's not even a date.* Then she'd panic all over again.

It was the thought of seeing him outside the safety blanket of their research that had her stomach in knots. At the station they had a reason to meet; a common goal—Rose and her diaries. It had always been secure ground. Now he'd asked her out and that safety blanket had fallen away, the boundaries of their relationship cast wider.

Emma took care dressing that night. She brushed her hair until it shone, applied makeup with a careful hand and spritzed herself with a bottle of something florally she'd unearthed from the back of her cupboard. She slipped on a dress, then second-guessed it and pulled on a white cotton blouse, black jeans and boots instead. The mirror told her she looked good, but her mind was over-thinking every detail.

At eight-thirty, she grabbed her purse and was about to call a taxi when there was a knock at the door. She didn't know who it could be, thought it might be pizza delivery for the wrong apartment and opened the door. She was mortified at who she found there.

'Drew!'

'Hey,' he said, with that same charismatic smile she knew well, even though it had been three years since she'd seen him.

They stood staring at each other, he with that disarming smile and she with a rush of nostalgia that almost barrelled her over.

He cleared his throat. 'Are you going to let me in?'

'What? Oh, sorry, yes.' She rearranged her expression. 'Come in.'

Drew stepped around her and into the apartment. He wore an Armani wool coat she recognised and a cologne that took her back to a time when she had fallen so hard for this man she would never quite be the same again. The Marc Jacobs satchel slung around his shoulder was new, as were the black shoes that smelt strongly of leather.

He looked around, taking in Gwendoline's old couch, the plain walls, the threadbare carpet. 'Place looks good. I see it's still a work-in-progress.'

Emma closed the door. 'It will always be a work-in-progress. You left me with nothing, remember?'

He avoided her eyes. 'Well, it looks good anyway. Tabitha and I just moved to a new house in Bellevue Hill. Three levels, eight bedrooms, a pool and gym.'

'I'd heard,' Emma replied. 'How is Tabitha?'

'She's good. Busy with the baby. She goes to mothers' group and yoga group and fitness group. There's a group for everything these days.'

'That's right, you had a baby. What's his name again?'

'Felix. He's an eating, sleeping, pooping machine,' Drew said.

'How lovely.'

'Tabitha's obsessed with him.'

Emma glanced at her watch. 'I don't mean to be rude, but is there a reason you stopped by? I have to be somewhere.'

He looked at her properly then, taking in her outfit. 'Are you meeting someone?'

'Yes.'

'You have a date?'

The shock on his face irritated her. 'So what if I do?'

He looked her up and down again. 'Who with?'

'None of your business. If you don't mind.' She reached for the door handle.

'Actually,' he said, rustling inside his satchel and pulling out a large yellow envelope. 'I have something for you to look over.' He held it out for her take.

Her fingers stilled on the handle as she eyed the envelope. 'What is it?'

'It's divorce papers.'

She closed her eyes, took a breath and opened them again. The envelope was still between them and she nodded resolutely and closed her hand around it.

'I had my lawyer draw them up yesterday. Tabitha's on my case about it. She wants to get engaged.'

'Oh.' Emma said. 'Right, of course.'

'She said to say hello. She misses you.'

Emma raised an eyebrow in response. She walked into the kitchen and flicked on the light. Drew followed. On the kitchen bench she opened the envelope and slid a thin stack of papers out, bound with a bulldog clip and tagged with six 'sign here' stickers.

'You'll find everything is in order. You're welcome to have your lawyer take a look at it if you want.'

Emma flicked through the pages, a quick glance telling her that

Drew's settlement offer was less than adequate. It was hardly surprising but she had nothing left in her to fight it.

'It's for the best, Emma,' Drew said.

'I know. It's just that I haven't heard a word from you in three years and you suddenly drop this on me.'

'There's no point putting it off any longer.'

She set the papers down and searched through the stationary container near the microwave for a pen.

'Let's get this over with then,' she said. She ran her eye over as much text as she could, absorbing and processing.

'How's Gwendoline?' Drew asked.

Emma looked up briefly. 'She's doing okay.'

'How about your job?'

'That's good too.'

He was making small talk as though he couldn't bear the silence. Emma paid him no attention as she read and signed, trying not to feel the significance of the moment.

She felt Drew move closer, could smell the scent of his cologne and the expensive wool of his coat. His hand touched her waist and she looked up from the papers. His face was next to hers, his hand trailing up her back.

'You look good, Emma,' he said, eyes fixed on hers. He smiled, perfect white teeth, a dimple in his cheek. It was the same smile that had melted her heart. Then it had melted her best friends.

'Drew, we shouldn't.'

His hand moved from her back to her cheek. 'Despite everything that's happened, I've missed you.'

'This isn't a good idea.'

'When you opened the door tonight, I couldn't believe how amazing you looked.'

'Don't.'

His lips brushed her neck, his hips pushing her back against the bench. 'Tabitha is so pre-occupied with the baby these days. She won't let me touch her. We haven't had sex in months.'

Emma closed her eyes.

'God, you taste good. I miss having sex with you.' His breath was hot on her skin. 'You always needed me. You needed me so much it was suffocating.'

Emma's eyes flew open. She gulped and slid away from him. 'Okay, that's enough.'

Drew pulled back, looking surprised. 'Baby?'

'Don't call me that. We're not doing this.'

'Doing what?'

She rolled her eyes at him. He really was an obnoxious jerk, one that she had loved fiercely once. One that had put her on a pedestal then had dropped her like a hot potato. One that she realised she no longer felt anything for. His touch had told her so and his kisses too, her body failing to respond. More than anything she'd felt awkward, as though she were being touched by a stranger.

She finished signing the pages, slipped the sheets back into the envelope and held it up for him to take. 'Thanks for stopping by. Now go home to your girlfriend.'

* * *

Emma didn't bother calling a taxi. She ran down the stairs of her apartment block and burst out onto the street. The night was cold and she gulped lungfuls of winter air.

Laughter bubbled up her throat as she walked. Drew had looked so stunned when she'd handed him back the forms and told him to leave.

A leopard never changed its spots. He had cheated on Emma with Tabitha and, over divorce papers, had attempted to cheat on Tabitha with Emma. How many times had he done this with other women? How many times would he do it again?

She was under no illusion that had she been a pitiful mess, begging for him to take her back, he would never have tried to kiss her. He'd only wanted her because she'd moved on. How glad she was that he and his games were no longer her problem to deal with.

She followed Anzac Parade up through Moore Park, grateful for the chance to clear her head and feeling lighter than she had felt in a long time. Who knew that divorcing Drew could be so freeing?

Music was spilling out of the Baggy Green when she arrived. The pub was packed and the band had already started. The noise was deafening as she squeezed between people searching for Matt. When she couldn't find him at the bar or near the stage, she checked the restaurant and beer garden outside, but he wasn't there either.

Confused, she tried calling him, his phone going straight to voice message. Maybe he'd got sick of waiting for her, a glance at her watch confirming she was twenty minutes late. *Why, Drew, of all nights did you choose tonight to want a divorce?*

After another twenty minutes of roaming the pub, satisfied that Matt wasn't there, she walked home. A light drizzle had started to fall and she was cold and wet by the time she stepped through her apartment door.

There was still no reply from him and she changed into pyjamas and climbed into bed, perplexed by the turn of events. He had seemed so keen initially, and yes, she'd been a little late, but surely he wouldn't have just left.

Eventually she fell into a sleep heavy with restless dreams, of Matt asking for a divorce and her not wanting to sign the papers.

* * *

The next morning, Emma texted Matt to ask if he would like to meet her at the Q Station to go through more of Rose's diaries.

On the drive over she felt nervous, aware that something subtle had shifted between them and perhaps not in a good way. He hadn't been at the pub when she'd arrived. He hadn't returned any of her calls or texts. She was anxious to see him, to know what had changed, if anything.

She parked her car in the Q Station carpark and caught the shuttle bus down to the shower blocks. Not even Ted's cheerfulness could shake the gloom that had attached itself to her.

The day was uncharacteristically warm for winter. A bright sun hung in the sky and the water in the cove twinkled as though lit by thousands of tiny gems. At the shower blocks, she hopped off the bus and walked towards the museum.

Matt wasn't waiting for her outside like he usually was. A quick glance around told her he wasn't anywhere on the wharf and she wondered if he'd even gotten her messages.

She stepped inside the museum and saw a girl she recognised sitting at the tour desk. 'Hello,' she said, setting her mobile down on the countertop.

'Oh, hey there.' The girl smiled. 'You're Matt's friend.'

'Yes. I was wondering if you'd seen him today.'

'Not yet but I just came on shift. If you give me a few minutes, I can try to locate him.'

Emma shook her head. 'No, that's fine. Don't go to any trouble. I'll wander around.'

She walked back out into the sunshine and in the direction of the shower blocks. Diverting right, she climbed the steep path up to the Former Hospital and Isolation Precincts. The station was vast and she couldn't even be sure Matt was working that day.

She searched around the old first and third-class hospitals then through isolation. The former buildings there had been converted into guest accommodation and people were on the verandahs drinking champagne and eating from cheese platters.

Emma passed quickly, not wanting to disturb them, following a narrow path through the trees that cut to the back of third class and Asiatics. Peering through windows and along the interconnected maze of verandah walkways, she searched for him.

Navigating a path that stepped down to the former post office, she eventually found him at the corner of the verandah, hammering a replacement board.

'Hey, Matt.'

He looked up, surprised to see her. 'Oh. Hey.' His tone was cool as he returned to hammering the board.

She waited for a pause in the noise then cleared her throat. 'I sent you a couple of texts to let you know I was coming by today.'

He didn't respond.

'Did you get them?'

He stopped and looked up at her. 'Yeah, I got them.'

'Oh.'

'I've been kind of busy. I can't really take time off anymore. If you need help with Rose's diaries, you can talk to the girls at the museum.'

There was an edge to his voice she couldn't quite place. 'I see.'

He went back to hammering as Emma watched him.

'I went to the pub last night. I couldn't find you there,' she said.

'Yeah?'

'I know I was late and I'm sorry. Something came up.'

He gave a bitter laugh. '*Something came up.*'

'Yes, something came up.'

'Like what, your husband?'

Wrong-footed, Emma stammered.

Matt put the hammer down. 'I went to your apartment last night. I thought I'd pick you up. I ran into your husband out the front.'

Emma stared at him, her heart dropping into her stomach.

'He came out as I was searching for your unit number on the intercom. He asked me if I was the guy you were meeting up with, then he told me you were married.' He picked up the hammer again and hit the board so hard, it split. 'Damn it!'

'Matt.'

'I don't want to talk about it.'

'I need to explain.'

'What's there to say? I mean... what is it with you women?'

'You're misunderstanding the situation.'

'I don't think so.'

Emma sighed. 'Drew and I have been separated for a long time. Last night, he came over and we signed the divorce papers. He's a jerk for telling you we were still married.'

'At least someone told me.'

She cast her eyes down. 'I deserve that. I should have said something sooner. I was going to.'

Matt shook his head sadly. 'Emma, you might have had good intentions, but it's the secrets I can't handle. I've been there before.'

'This isn't like Natalie.'

'Feels exactly like it to me.'

Emma swallowed past a lump so large in her throat she thought it would choke her.

'I have to get back to work.' He picked up the hammer and the broken piece of board and gave her a sad look. 'Good luck with everything. I hope it all works out for Gwendoline.'

He started off down the path towards first class and Emma watched him go, his shoulders slumped, the hurt written all over him.

Chapter Sixteen

ROSE 1918

August drew to a close, spelling the end to Rose's first Australian winter.

Spanish Influenza cases were on the rise and the government had signed a decree—mandatory quarantining of every ship that sailed into Port Jackson. The boats arrived daily at the wharf, an endless succession of them, and the hospitals overflowed, tents dotting every spare patch of grass because the wards and verandahs couldn't hold any more patients.

Influenza vaccinations arrived from Europe, enough only for the staff, which they queued for in a long line outside the third-class hospital. It was an unprecedented time in the station's history as the world braced itself for a swift and silent killer.

Despite all this, life in first class continued to grind out a familiar shape for Rose. She tended to the duke from morning until night and, when the station's residents slept, she and Thomas snuck away to the clifftop outside his cottage to sit beneath the stars. They would talk for hours, kissing until their lips were grazed, and sharing their deepest desires, conjuring up a future that seemed, for the moment, too distant to grasp.

It was always with regret that he would look to the sky and declare that the sun would rise soon and it was time to walk her back.

The morning would come again and Rose would resume her duties with the duke as though Thomas and the kisses had merely been a dream. And from there, the days would play out on repeat.

On a day that promised the ushering in of spring, Rose arrived at the kitchen to load the duke's breakfast onto the trolley. Bessie was already at the sink, hands plunged deep into steaming brown water, and Mrs March was berating her for the grease she'd left on the copper pots.

Rose threw her friend a sympathetic look and pushed the trolley to the laundry for fresh linen, then up the hill to the duke's cottage. She climbed the steps with the breakfast tray and knocked on the door. The duke opened it. As always, he seemed delighted at her arrival.

'Rose! I was just thinking of you. Do come in.' He stepped out of the way. 'Are you well this morning?'

She curtseyed before entering the room. 'I am, Your Grace. And you?'

'Splendid.' He watched her place the tray on the table, remove the cloches and set out the spreads. She lined up the cutlery, though he hardly seemed bothered with protocol these days and sometimes even grabbed the knife and fork himself.

'How is the duchess this morning?' she asked, pulling the chair out for him to sit.

'She is no better, no worse,' the duke replied, taking the seat. 'Doctor Holland is in with her now. I rarely go in there, to be honest.'

'Are you worried about contamination?'

'They say it's her asthma now that's making her weak.'

'Why are you still afraid?'

The duke sighed almost sadly. 'I'm not afraid of getting sick. It's just that...'

Rose placed a napkin on the duke's lap and poured his tea. She dropped two cubes of sugar into the cup and stirred through milk.

'She's always been sickly, Rose, for as long as I can remember. Bad lungs. And, as terrible as it sounds, I fear I've become weary of it.'

'Had you known the duchess long before you married?' Rose moved around the table to serve him bacon, poached eggs and sausages.

'Since we were children,' he said, looking up at her with a wistful smile. 'We grew up together. She's my third cousin and a second cousin to Queen Victoria.'

'I see.'

It was not unusual for them to speak freely these days. Rose used to resist the conversation as though Miss Dalton herself were in the room listening. Now, after all these months, it was as natural as if they had known each other their whole lives.

He seemed to crave his interactions with Rose, for his time was otherwise limited to the doctor and nurse, and on rare occasions, the duchess through a closed door. They had become unexpected friends, or at the least, had found a commonality in their co-patriotism.

'I remember as a child she wasn't allowed to play in the gardens or have dirty hands,' the duke went on. 'She would have to stay inside, away from the dust and flowers. Everything made her wheeze.'

'That must have been hard for her as a child.'

He shrugged. 'Yes. My father assured me she would outgrow the sickliness when we were betrothed. I was unsure about the marriage, to be perfectly honest. Cordelia has always been beautiful, but at fourteen, it didn't seem likely she would outgrow her poor health. It's why she's yet to give me an heir. I should never have brought her here. I should have known she'd catch the first sniffle going around.'

As if on cue, Rose heard a raspy, wheezy cough escape from the bedroom behind them and the muffled voice of the doctor saying something that Rose couldn't identify. She could barely hear the duchess at all; her voice meek, almost inaudible.

'Sit with me, Rose,' the duke said, pushing out the chair next to him and motioning for her to sit. Rose hesitated, then lowered herself, placing her hands in her lap. He offered her tea but she declined.

He was a different man from the one she had encountered on her first day of service, when he'd been on a mission to secure more troops for Britain. How impressive he'd been with his many responsibilities and many letters to write. *This quarantine business is ghastly,* she remembered him declaring with self-importance, as though he couldn't bear to have it slow him down.

Rose hadn't seen him at the walnut bureau in weeks, his papers and pen untouched and a fine sprinkling of dust settling over the chair. The duke seemed resigned to the fact that he would be stranded in this foreign land for the unforeseeable future, unable to go anywhere as long as his wife was ill. He spent his days on the verandah, staring out across the station with an almost peaceful and childlike vulnerability.

'She asks about you, you know.'

He was watching her with intense blue eyes, and Rose was brought back to the room. 'The duchess?'

'Yes. She can hear you speaking through the wall.' His voice lowered. 'She's curious about you. She wants to know what you look like. She imagines you're quite beautiful. I daresay she's right.'

Rose shifted uncomfortably in her seat. 'I don't mean to cause her distress.'

He waved a hand. 'I have assured her there's nothing untoward going on between us. You're just the parlourmaid.' But his eyes searched hers with hope.

Rose stood quickly. 'I best be getting on with the morning, Your Grace.'

His face fell. 'Yes, of course. I've held you up long enough.'

She curtseyed and retreated to his bedroom, stripping the linen and carrying the sheets and chamber pot out to the verandah. She moved back and forth across the living room to fit the bed with clean linen, to tidy and dust and beat the pillows outside as the duke ate his breakfast silently and with a vacant expression.

When he finished, she cleared away the tray, bid him good morning and caught his sad little wave before she closed the cottage door behind her.

Rose pushed the serving trolley back along the road towards first class. The landscape of the station had altered in recent months. Tents were popping up everywhere. The population had tripled and she rarely saw Thomas at all during the day, their trips down to the cove long over, even a fleeting moment outside his workshop a thing of the past.

Rose offloaded the duke's linen into the steaming tubs of disinfectant and returned the breakfast tray and trolley to the kitchen. She was joking with Bessie and helping Mrs March prepare the duke's morning tea when a housemaid poked her head through the kitchen doorway.

'I'm looking for Rose Porter.'

'That's me,' Rose said, looking up from the clotted cream she'd been spooning into a dish.

'Miss Dalton wants to see you in her office immediately.'

Rose shared a look with Bessie while Mrs March made a funny noise that sounded much like *what have you done now?*

Rose wiped her hands on her apron, put aside the cream and started up the road towards Miss Dalton's office.

She knocked tentatively on the door.

'Is that you, Rose? Come in.'

She pushed the door open. Miss Dalton was in her usual place behind her desk, a pen in her hand as she signed a document. She put the pen down and waved to the chair opposite her. 'Please take a seat.'

Rose sat, holding her breath, wondering what she could have been called in for this time.

'I'll get straight to the point,' Miss Dalton said. 'The Hospital Precinct is overrun. They do not have enough staff to cope. We'll need to contribute maids from housekeeping to assist the medical team. I've nominated you from first class.'

Rose audibly gulped. 'You're sending me into unhealthy ground?'

'Yes. I realise it's a tall ask, but they need help in the hospitals.'

'I'm not sure I'd be of any use. I have no medical training.'

'I realise that and so does Matron Cromwell. Your duties will include changing bed linen and towels and taking the soiled ones to the laundry. You'll empty chamber pots, deliver meals to patients and perform any other housekeeping tasks the matron requests of you. This will free up the nurses to concentrate on the medical side of things.'

'For how long?'

'Two weeks.'

'Won't the government give us more hospital staff? We're in the middle of a crisis.'

'I wish it were that simple, but the government isn't the problem here. People are hardly lining up to fill our hospital positions because of the risks involved.'

Rose pushed down a lump of fear and gathered her resolve. 'Who will see to the duke?'

'I'll ask Bessie. We have a new third-class scullery maid starting tomorrow. She can help Mrs March in the interim.'

'Bessie will be perfect,' Rose said. 'The duke is lonely. She'll be like a breath of fresh air, something to lift his spirits.'

'How do you know the duke is lonely? You speak out of turn, Rose.'

Rose stumbled. 'No, I just mean it's something I sense. He's not happy.'

'Of course he's not happy. His wife is unwell. He's probably beside himself with worry. But we do not concern ourselves with that. We are in service.'

'Yes, Miss Dalton,' Rose said sheepishly.

Miss Dalton pursed her lips. 'You will report to the first-class hospital at once. Matron Cromwell is expecting you.'

'My first shift starts now?'

'Yes.'

'Should I inform the duke?'

'I'll take care of that.'

Rose nodded, heart pounding a little harder in her chest.

'You will see things at the hospital, Rose,' Miss Dalton said soberly. 'Things that you have never seen before, things that will shock you, that might repeat in your head for a long time. I want you to be aware of that.'

'I understand.'

'And hygiene is important. Wear your mask and scrub your hands often.'

'I will.'

'Matron Cromwell will fill you in on the rest of the requirements.' Miss Dalton stood and held out her hand for Rose to shake as if they were parting ways forever. 'Good luck, Rose Porter.'

* * *

Rose left Miss Dalton's office and walked briskly back down Main Axial Road. She passed the kitchen and the duke's cottage, but didn't stop at either.

She continued as instructed to a place she'd never been before. A place that, from day one, she'd been told to stay away from because of the danger it posed. The Hospital Precinct.

Rose tried to quell the fear rising up her throat, certain that if she stopped to think about the task she'd been assigned she would turn and run back to first class. She passed the morgue and laboratory, bodies lined up along the path draped under sheets ready for autopsy.

She strode by quickly, trying not to breathe, the smell of death and decomposition working its way into her nostrils no matter how fiercely she tried to keep it out. She moved her legs harder, carrying her away from the morgue and deeper into unhealthy ground.

Five minutes later, she reached the Hospital Precinct and circled her way around the doctors and nurse's living quarters, interconnected by similar walkways and verandahs to those in first class. It was there that she collided directly into Thomas.

'Rose!' From behind a surgical mask he looked surprised to see her. He tugged it down. 'What are you doing up here? Are you lost?'

'No. I've been assigned to work in the hospitals.'

'You're going to be *working* up here?'

'I won't be treating patients. I'll just be doing housekeeping.'

'But, Rose...' He glanced around to ensure no one was watching them, then reached for her hand, closing it tightly in his. 'It's not safe up here.'

'I'll be fine,' she said with false bravado. 'What are you doing up here?'

'I work everywhere on the station,' he said, pulling her into the shadow of the building. 'Rose...'

'It'll only be for two weeks.'

'I don't like the idea.'

'It's my job.'

He closed his eyes, took a breath and opened them again. 'Get yourself a mask.'

'I've been inoculated.'

'It doesn't matter.'

'Okay, I will.' She reached up and kissed him and he responded, his lips parting against hers, and she felt a familiar wave of desire wash over her. 'Will you come for me tonight?'

'Of course.'

He held her close and she rested her head on his chest, pausing to inhale the smell of his shirt, wishing she could remain there forever. With great reluctance, she said goodbye and watched as he walked back towards healthy ground.

The first-class hospital was an impressive building, connected to the doctors and nurse's quarters by a direct walkway. The view across Port Jackson to Sydney was lovely, though it was probably the last thing on the minds of the people who occupied this part of the station.

The third-class hospital was a separate building across the way and in between the two lay a sea of tents and makeshift beds that had been set up to cope with the influx of patients.

Rose had never seen such a pitiful sight. People were everywhere, moaning and writhing in pain, clammy with fever, their faces a bluish hue and their coughs laced with blood-stained sputum. It was Spanish Influenza and her hand went instinctively to her mouth, afraid to breathe the same air.

Forcing her eyes away, she found a nurse hurrying from the tents towards the first-class hospital and she hurried after her. 'Excuse me. Can you help me?'

The nurse was young with black hair and vivid green eyes. She pulled down her surgical mask to talk. 'I can try.' Her accent was thick Irish.

'I'm looking for Matron Cromwell. Do you know where I might find her?'

The nurse pointed to the first-class hospital. 'She'll be in there. I'm going inside. I can take you to her if you like.'

'You are most kind. Thank you.'

The nurse began walking again. 'You're not from unhealthy ground. Do you work in accommodation?'

'I'm a parlourmaid in first class.'

'I can tell,' she said, indicating Rose's black uniform and white apron.

'I've been assigned to help in the hospital for two weeks.'

'We'll be glad for the help. I'm Dolly.'

'Rose.'

They climbed the steps of the hospital and Dolly led the way across the verandah and into the building.

The scene was only slightly more orderly inside. Beds were crammed symmetrically against the walls, leaving a walkway down the middle where doctors and nurses bustled. The patients there were in no less pain than outside.

Dolly urged Rose quickly through the middle, past racking coughs, shivering bodies and lungs ravished by Spanish Influenza.

She ushered her through a door and into the next room where the mood was a little less chaotic. They passed through a small closet-like room where medicines and equipment were stored. There were ewers and bowls for hand washing, stacks of towels and bed linen, vials of medication in cabinets, jars of gauze, syringes and steel dishes of all sizes.

Dolly led the way to a closed door and gave it a light knock. She opened it a touch to poke her head through. 'Matron Cromwell, I have Rose for you, from first-class accommodation.' She moved aside for Rose to enter and whispered, 'Good luck,' before slipping away into the ward.

Matron Cromwell stood and moved around the desk to stand in front of Rose. She was heavyset with broad shoulders, grey hair and a serious face. A light moustache graced her upper lip and Rose couldn't help watching it as she spoke. 'You're Rose Porter?'

'I am.'

Matron Cromwell's eyes travelled up and down her. 'Is that a London accent? You're a long way from home.'

'Indeed.'

The matron nodded. 'Very well, let's get started. You'll need to change. You can't go wandering around the wards in a housekeeping uniform.'

She walked across the room to a narrow closet and opened it, extracting a hanger with a long white starched dress and a cap to match. 'I keep a set of clean uniforms in here for visiting staff. You will need to come here and collect a uniform from me daily. Be sure to register the collection in this log.'

She handed the uniform to Rose and held up the log for her to see.

'After each shift, you will take the uniform off and send it with the rest of the laundry to be disinfected in the steam tubs. You must never take your dirty uniform onto healthy ground.'

'I understand.'

'Here's a surgical mask. Wear it at all times. Be vigilant with hygiene. Scrub your hands often. There's an ewer and bowl in the medicine room next door where you can wash up. You may get changed now, and then I'll show you around.'

Rose paused, wondering if she was expected to change in front of the matron or leave the room and change elsewhere. When she realised the older woman wasn't offering any further instruction, Rose untied her apron from the back and slipped it over her head. She undid the clasp at the nape of her neck and slid her housekeeping uniform down, standing in only her petticoat, corset and stockings.

'Have you been inoculated?' Matron Cromwell asked, returning to her desk and picking up a clipboard.

'I have,' said Rose, sliding into the white uniform and pinning the nurse's cap to her hair.

'You should be aware it's no guarantee.'

'I am.'

'You come highly recommended by Miss Dalton.'

'That's kind of her,' Rose said, folding her housekeeping uniform and apron and placing it on a chair next to the closet.

Matron Cromwell looked up. 'Let's get started then. I'm extremely busy.'

She gestured for Rose to follow her to a door behind her desk. 'Through here is the maternity ward,' she explained as they walked. 'We keep the babies down this end of the hospital, well away from the main ward. If you work in the main ward, you are not allowed in maternity, for obvious reasons. Be sure not to forget it.'

Rose heard the gurgle of babies as they stepped into the maternity ward. It was a tiny space, with three cots side by side, a newborn infant in each. One began to cry and the wet nurse stood from her desk and went to it.

'The babies go straight back to their mothers once they're born, but if the mother doesn't survive, they usually end up here for a little while.'

She closed the door to the maternity ward and they traversed back through her office and into the main ward. Passing through the medicine room again, the matron pointed out various items that would be of use to Rose—washing bowl, fresh towels and linen, a hessian bag for soiled material.

They continued into the main ward and Rose was confronted again with the chaos of earlier.

'Your job will be to strip soiled beds and fit them with clean linen. You will collect dirty gauze and towels and take them with the linen to the steam tubs for disinfecting. You will also need to deliver meals to the patients. Many of them are not up to eating, but we offer it anyway. Fluids are important.'

Rose nodded, taking mental notes.

'You are not to medically treat the patients. That is not your job. If a patient needs medical assistance, ask the nursing staff.'

Rose was still following Matron as she rattled off instructions without pause.

'You will be assigned to this hospital, which is first class. Third class is across the way and the tents outside house the soldiers. You will be asked from time to time to go out there too. Any questions?'

She didn't have a chance to reply. Matron Cromwell gestured for Dolly to join them again.

'You will shadow Nurse Dolly today. She will show you the ropes and assign you tasks.' Without taking a breath, Matron Cromwell bid them a prompt good day and left the ward.

Dolly removed her mask to speak. 'All set then, Rose?'

'I think so,' Rose said. Her steady voice belied the nerves she felt.

'I have rounds to do. Best fit your mask and walk with me.'

She followed Nurse Dolly to a bed where a male patient was clutching his stomach in agony beneath the sheets. The sign affixed to the end of his bed stated 'James O'Grady. 22. Cholera'. He was clammy with fever, as white as the sheets and the stench emanating from him was nauseating.

Dolly lifted the top sheet and frowned. 'Rose, we're going to need new bedding here.'

Rose ran to the medicine room and pulled clean linen from the cupboard. James O'Grady cried out as Dolly and a second nurse rolled him onto his side, all dignity gone along with the insides of his bowel. Rose took one look at the state of the sheets and gagged.

'Pull yourself together, Rose Porter,' Dolly said sharply.

Retching, Rose worked quickly to gather up the sheets while James received a wash down. The odour was revolting as she scooped everything into a bundle, moved it to the side and remade the bed. She knew she was pale by the time she'd hurried the dirty sheets away to load into the hessian laundry bags. It was a sight and smell she would never forget.

James O'Grady was one of many. As Dolly did her rounds, Rose followed her, emptying dirty chamber pots, pulling soiled sheets from beds, cleaning up vomit, clearing away strips of gauze and refilling what felt like a thousand cups of water.

At lunchtime, Rose scrubbed her hands down with carbolic soap, refitted her mask and returned to the ward to serve meals to the patients. Most of them looked green at the thought of eating, although it was simple bread and broth. Rose returned most trays to the hospital kitchen untouched.

After lunch, she followed Dolly around again. Patients coughed and moaned at her, tried to grab her arm and some were so unresponsive, Rose couldn't be sure if they were alive or dead.

The children were the hardest to tend to. Their skinny limbs and pale, drawn faces tore at her resolve, as they looked at her with bewilderment, unable to understand what had ravaged their tiny bodies.

The sun was sinking to the west when Rose finally stepped out of the hospital at five o'clock. She was back in her housekeeping uniform, her hands scrubbed and carrying two hessian bags filled with sheets and towels ready for the disinfecting tubs.

She lugged the bags off the verandah steps and sidestepped the sea of tents and patients, stretching all the way to the path that led down to the laundry.

Matron Cromwell was smoking a cigarette on the third-class hospital verandah when she passed. 'Rose Porter.'

'Good evening to you, Matron Cromwell.' She paused in the fading afternoon. 'Nurse Dolly said I could take these bags to the laundry and finish for the evening. I hope that's all right.'

'Yes, that's fine,' Matron Cromwell replied on a current of smoke. 'How was your first day on unhealthy ground?'

'May I be perfectly honest?'

'Please.'

'It was confronting, not like anything I've ever seen before.'

'Not everyone is built for this kind of work, Rose, for watching children die and men drowning in their own lungs. You need an iron stomach and strong resolve.'

'I have a new respect for the medical profession, that's for certain,' Rose said with a smile.

'And we have the very best here. They're like angels; there can be no doubt about that.'

'Indeed.'

'Will you be returning to us tomorrow?'

'Yes, Matron Cromwell, if you will have me.'

There was a hint of a smile. 'And there's that iron resolve. Leave the laundry bags for tonight. I will have someone else take them down. Get some rest. We will see you in the morning at seven o'clock.'

Rose left the laundry bags by the steps of the hospital, bid the matron goodnight and returned to first-class accommodation. It wasn't until she stepped back on healthy ground that she finally released a proper breath.

Chapter Seventeen

When Rose arrived back at her cottage after her first shift at the hospital, she sat down on her bed and closed her eyes. Bessie had yet to return. It was dinner time and she would be serving the duke his meal now; a routine Rose knew well, one that she suddenly longed for as the images of the day played out in her mind.

She saw the ravaged limbs, wheezing chests and feverish skin of the ill, but it was the children with their pallid faces and terrified eyes that refused to leave her. They were utterly vulnerable and at the mercy of God, a frightening place to find themselves.

Rose let out a long breath and settled back against her pillow. Bessie was hours from returning and Thomas would still be working. She had nowhere to be, her mind ticking relentlessly, unable to hush her thoughts.

She reached across to her bedside drawer and found her diary hidden beneath her underwear and petticoats. She would write about it, she decided, just as she wrote about everything else. Getting it out of her head and down on paper was the best hope she had of making it through the next two weeks.

Using the tiny brass key, Rose unlocked the cover and flicked towards the back to the next blank page, only to realise there were none. She had used up all the pages in her beloved diary. Dismayed, she closed it, locked it and hid it well beneath her petticoats again, intent on placing an order for another one with the postmaster the first chance she got.

* * *

At nine o'clock, Rose changed for staff supper and walked down to the kitchen to eat with the other parlourmaids. They were all eager to hear about her experience at the hospital and she filled them in on most things, keeping the more gruesome details for a time when they weren't digesting food. They seemed to enjoy her stories but Rose sensed that they were mostly relieved not to have drawn the short straw.

Over dinner, Bessie looked like the cat that ate the canary. Her temporary promotion to parlourmaid allowed her to sit at the table with everyone else while the new scullery maid scrubbed the pots. The parlourmaids included her in their jokes, and Mrs March wasn't so whip-like with her tongue.

Rose was keen to learn about Bessie's day and as soon as supper was over, they followed the path up the hill to the female staff quarters.

'How's the duke?' she asked eagerly.

Bessie lit a cigarette and blew a stream of smoke out. It swirled then was carried away on the breeze. 'He's okay. I don't think he likes me much.'

'Why do you say that?'

'I'm fairly certain I repulse him.'

Rose laughed. 'Don't be silly. He just takes a while to adjust. He was the same when I replaced Miss Dalton.'

'He actually recoiled when I served him his tea. It's my hands. They're hideous.'

'They will heal,' Rose said, taking the one that wasn't clenching the cigarette to give it an encouraging squeeze.

'Yes and in the meantime, I will just continue to repulse him.'

'Did he talk to you? He's quite an intriguing man once he opens up.'

'He didn't talk to me. He wouldn't even look at me. He just kept asking me when you'll be back.'

Rose squeezed her hand again. 'Tomorrow will be better, I promise.'

'I shouldn't complain. He was just lovely to be around. I couldn't stop staring at him. I've never seen eyes so blue before. He really is the most handsome thing I've ever seen.'

Rose giggled. 'Did you see the duchess?'

'No. She was quiet the whole day. Doctor Holland was in with her during morning tea though.' Bessie flicked her cigarette away. 'What was the hospital *really* like?'

Rose shook her head sadly. 'It was like nothing I could have imagined. So much foul disease and helplessness all in the one place. The medical staff are truly special. I don't think I could do it for more than two weeks, though.'

'Well hang in there as long as you can. I'm thoroughly enjoying serving the duke, even if he hates it!'

* * *

Thomas came for Rose at eleven.

When she was certain Bessie was fast asleep, she pulled on her coat and boots and opened the door. It betrayed her with a creak and Bessie stirred in the bed behind her.

'Rose, where are you going?'

Rose paused by the door. When she turned back, Bessie was sitting up. 'I couldn't sleep. I thought I might take a walk.'

'A walk? It must be nearly midnight.'

'Not quite,' she said as though it mattered.

'Wait there. I'll come to keep you company.'

'No, please, go back to sleep. You have a big day with the duke tomorrow.'

She could feel Bessie's eyes on her in the dark. 'Are you sure?'

'Perfectly.'

It seemed an age before Bessie relented and laid back down in her bed, pulling the covers over herself. Rose let out a trapped breath and crept to the door, closing it softly behind her.

Thomas was waiting for her at the bottom of the steps. 'Is everything okay?'

'Bessie woke. She saw me leaving.'

'Do you think she suspects anything?'

'No, I don't think so.'

They walked quickly and quietly through the trees, hurrying past Asiatics, where the dormitory windows were dark and the outdoor ovens were cooling.

Within minutes, they had reached the path behind the male staff quarters. They scurried through the bush beneath a majestic moon and out onto the clifftop next to Thomas's cottage. As he had become accustomed to doing in the cooler nights, he collected a blanket from his room to wrap around them.

The wind was brisk high up and Rose burrowed beneath the blanket, Thomas's arms circling her. She wondered if this was what it was like to be courted, meeting a boy out on a clifftop, kissing and cuddling beneath the stars.

She hadn't gone out with any of the boys back home. The ones the war hadn't taken had been snapped up quickly by the oversupply of women and, in any case, they'd held no appeal to Rose, much like the butcher's son.

Thomas was different. He was some years older than her, that much she knew, and very grown up. He had a gentle soul, a quiet strength, and in that place of sorrow and death, that strength gave her hope.

Thomas was a man of few words, unlike the duke, who thrived on conversation. They couldn't have been more different. Thomas used his eyes, his hands and his expression to tell Rose how he felt and it wasn't confusing. She didn't have to read his mind or guess. They were always in perfect accord.

Bessie had once said that the isolation could make people go a little crazy. It had made Agnes act with promiscuity fifteen times on her bed with soldiers from the troopship *Canberra*. Perhaps Rose had gone a little crazy too. Perhaps she'd lost her mind. Everything felt intensified in the confines of the station, her feelings for Thomas most of all.

'Are you warm enough?' Thomas asked, holding her close.

'Yes, much better.'

'Spring is coming. The nights will warm soon.'

'I'm not sure I'll be ready for a hot Christmas, though. That will take some time.'

He chuckled and leant down to kiss her and she responded as she always did, with a fierceness that surprised her. They had yet to venture back into his cottage, choosing to sit outside on the cliff where they were less likely to traverse a threshold they dared not cross.

'How was your first day at the hospital?'

She told him about her work with Dolly, the dreadful things she'd had to clean and the frightened children with eyes too large and round for their tiny faces.

Thomas held her a little tighter when she finished talking. 'I'll be happier when the next two weeks are over and you're back in first class.'

'It's gruelling and squeamish work, yes, but I like the idea that I can make a difference.'

'You can make a difference in first class too.'

'I don't think serving the duke his meals counts.'

'You obviously make a difference to him. He likes you. He wants you and you only.' Thomas's jaw twitched.

Rose changed the subject. 'I wrote on the last page of my diary today. I'd like to get a new one. If you could tell me where you purchased it from, I'll place my order with the postmaster tomorrow.'

'I'm glad you've enjoyed the diary,' he said, somewhat happier.

'Oh, I have. It's the most wonderful gift I've ever received.'

'I'm pleased to hear that.' He smiled at her. 'Rose?'

'Yes, Thomas.'

'There's something I've wanted to ask you for a while now.'

'What is it?'

'Well.' He seemed hesitant. 'I'm not sure quite how to say it.'

She sat up on her knees, still swathed in the blanket. 'Tell me.'

'It's just that,' he looked at her with shy eyes, 'I don't think it's any surprise how fond of you I am and, well, you are someone I could see myself with for a long time.'

Rose's breath caught.

'Maybe, on the outside, if I asked you to marry me, you might like to say yes.' He breathed deeply, glad to have come out with it and even in the dark, Rose could see he was blushing.

She touched his cheek. 'I would like that very much, Thomas.'

'I would ask your father's permission at the time, of course.'

'I don't think he would care much what I do.'

'I'm sure he would.'

'He hasn't returned any of my letters.'

They both fell silent, staring out at an ocean that was black beneath a matching sky.

'Do you mean to stay here long?' she asked.

'Maybe until the war is over.' He glanced at her. 'Don't misunderstand me, I'm not afraid of being called up to fight. It's just that, if I leave here now and you come with me, I'll be drafted and you'll be left alone. I couldn't bear that.'

Rose nodded.

'Perhaps the war will end soon,' he said.

'I doubt it. The duke came here to ask for more troops. That doesn't sound like the end to me.'

'Then we will wait a little longer.' He wrapped his arms tightly around her again. 'The world outside is changing. Maybe the world in here will change too.'

'You're far too optimistic.'

He laughed. 'Maybe. But it's not so bad in here. We have everything we need.'

Everything but freedom, she thought.

'I know you're not fond of breaking the rules. Neither am I. If Miss Dalton ever found out, it wouldn't end well for us.'

'I wasn't always a troublemaker, you know,' she said with a frown.

He laughed again. 'Neither was I. And yet you do something to me, Rose. You make me crazy, like I want to break the rules. Like I *need* to break the rules.'

She closed her eyes and melded into him and thought of what a future together would be like outside these walls, with the freedom to grow old, to slip her hand into his and feel him beside her always without the worry of repercussions or condemnation.

'It won't be like this for long, I promise,' he said, as though understanding her thoughts.

She let his words wrap around her and felt his lips in her hair, trying to kiss her worries away.

* * *

Rose arrived at the hospital each morning promptly at seven and left well after the sun went down. During the hours in between, she followed the nurses on their rounds and cleaned up after patients who could no longer control their bodily functions. She delivered meals that were refused and learnt to comfort the ill children whose healthy parents weren't allowed near the hospital.

She was glad to witness the recovery of most patients, though some died and their beds were vacated quicker than Rose could say Spanish Flu. Within minutes, their bodies were taken away to the morgue, their sheets changed and another poor soul was stretchered in to take their place.

Spanish Influenza was indiscriminate, much like a game of Russian roulette. It randomly selected its host with no distinction between the vulnerable or healthy. A seven-year-old child could overcome the virus while a robust man in his twenties succumbed. How vast the world was, how quickly the killer spread to a new host and how insignificant everyone's place seemed to be on the Earth.

It was lunchtime on Rose's seventh day at the hospital and she was sitting out on the grass with Dolly eating a sandwich. It was the first week of September, the sun was golden and warm and spring whispered on the breeze. Yellow-faced honeyeaters foraged in the flowers near where Rose sat, searching for leaves so they could build their delicate cup-shaped nests. Their soft, sweet trill filled the air.

Rose stretched out her legs and bit into her sandwich. 'So where in Ireland are you from?'

'I'm from Balbriggan in North County Dublin. Sailed here three years ago with my four brothers.'

'What made you leave your home?'

'My mother died of consumption when we were little and my father was killed in the war, so I followed my brothers abroad. Our ship was quarantined in 1915 which is how I first came to be here. We weren't ill, though we completed a stay in isolation, then third class. I was so fascinated with life here that I accepted a job in the hospital.'

Rose smiled. 'That's quite a story. What did your brothers think about that?'

'They hated the idea, thought I'd gone mad. But I'm stubborn. When I set my mind to something there's no changing it. We've all gone our separate ways now. One of my brothers is still here in Sydney and the other three went north to Darwin.'

'So why did you work in the hospital and not somewhere in accommodation? It would have been safer.'

'I studied nursing back home and I helped out a little in the Irish army. I don't think I really knew what it meant to work here though, but I've been here three years and I haven't succumbed yet. Maybe it's the luck of the Irish.'

Rose laughed, finishing her sandwich and dusting crumbs from her hands.

'What about you, Rose? That's a Londoner's accent if I ever heard one.'

'I'm from Bethnal Green. I came here to escape an arrangement, if you get my meaning.'

Dolly made a face. 'Oh yes, how awful! Was he repulsive?'

'Not repulsive. He just wasn't for me,' Rose said. 'So I boarded a troopship to Australia, mending soldier's uniforms and helping in the galley in exchange for free passage.'

'You're brave boarding a troopship. They say it's the soldiers who are spreading the flu.'

'Brave or perhaps foolish. The latter, I suspect.'

'When my mother died of tuberculosis, I never thought I'd live another day to see an illness of the lungs that horrid. I guess I was wrong.'

'Will they be able to stop it?'

'They've built a new inhalation chamber down by the shower blocks. They say three hundred soldiers are on their way here now from the Western Front. They'll have to have their throats and lungs sterilised in the chamber before they come up to isolation.'

'How do they sterilise throats and lungs?'

'By pumping zinc sulphate into them. The scientists say it's the cure we've all been waiting for. It'll burn the flu right out of them.'

Rose bit into her apple and spotted Thomas emerging from the side of the doctors and nurses' quarters. He was inspecting the sandstone piers, a tool belt wrapped around his waist. He looked up, saw Rose and waved. She waved back and they shared a smile.

Dolly watched with interest. 'Are you sweet on him?'

Rose coloured. She hadn't meant to be so obvious. 'He's just a friend.'

'You know it's not allowed. If they catch you with him...'

'There's nothing to catch,' Rose said quickly, biting into her apple again.

Dolly nodded slowly. 'Well, I wouldn't blame you if you did fancy him. He's awfully handsome. All the nurses like him. They think he's the best looking lad on the station.'

'I wouldn't know,' Rose said.

Dolly dusted crumbs off her uniform and stood. 'We best get back. Lunch break is almost over. Matron doesn't tolerate tardiness.'

Rose stood too and tossed the apple core into her lunch bag. She followed Dolly back towards the hospital, passing Thomas on the way. He tipped his hat to them both, but Rose knew his smile was for her.

* * *

Rose was washing her hands in the medicine room when the matron entered.

'Miss Porter.'

'Matron Cromwell.'

The matron set a log book down on the bench and opened one of the glass cabinets. She began counting the vials inside. 'Morphine.'

Rose turned, her wet hands still in the bowl. 'Excuse me?'

'Morphine. The doctors and nurses have been known to take a vial or two for their own personal recreation. I count them every day to ensure no sticky fingers have been in the supply cabinet.'

Rose smiled and went back to scrubbing her hands.

'Be careful there, Miss Porter. That soap is five percent carbolic acid. You'll scrub the skin right off your bones.'

'I just finished cleaning up the bowels of a rotavirus patient. '

'Try lavender. It's good for the skin. You should apply it to your hands after every wash. It will protect them from peeling.'

Rose dried her hands on a towel and turned to face the matron. 'Will it repair raw and painful hands, ones that are in scalding water every day?'

The matron turned. 'I didn't realise you were suffering already.'

'It's not for me. A scullery maid in first-class accommodation has poor hands. The wounds are open and they won't heal.'

'Sounds like atopic dermatitis. It's caused by breaks in the skin that become infected.' Matron Cromwell turned, reached back into the cabinet and retrieved a small bottle, setting it down beside Rose. 'Try this instead. Tea tree oil. It's an antiseptic and an anti-inflammatory. It will promote healing. She should apply it three times a day.'

Rose picked up the small bottle and inspected the liquid inside.

'Keeping her hands out of water won't hurt either.'

Rose pocketed the bottle. 'Thank you, Matron Cromwell.'

The matron studied her. 'You have a heart for healing. Did you know that?'

'I'm not sure what that means exactly.'

'It means you care about others. And that's the first step in a medical profession, aside from some formal training, of course. You have to care. Have you ever thought about becoming a nurse?'

Rose shrugged. 'I can't say that I have.'

'I've heard a lot of good things about you from the nursing staff, particularly Nurse Dolly. You seem to be a natural.'

'That's very kind of her.'

'Not kind, just the truth.' Matron Cromwell closed her log book. 'How would you feel about staying on for a few more months at the hospital? Don't feel pressured, but we need good people like you.'

'I'm flattered that you think of me like that.' Rose smiled. 'I'd love to.'

Matron smiled back. 'Very good, Rose. I shall inform Miss Dalton of it.'

* * *

'So you're going to stay on?'

'Yes.'

'For how long?'

'A few more months. Now will you sit still?'

Rose was perched opposite Bessie on her bed with Bessie's hands in her lap. She soaked a piece of gauze in tea tree oil and applied it liberally to the infected skin.

Bessie hissed.

'You *have* to sit still.'

'It stings!'

'Of course it stings, but it will help. And now that you're working with the duke and your hands aren't in water anymore, these sores should heal quickly.'

'Maybe the duke will stop recoiling every time I go near him.'

'He means no offence, I'm sure.'

'He pines for you, you know.' Bessie turned large eyes up to Rose. 'He talks about you every day. He's always asking when you'll be back.'

'A few more months in the hospital and I will be a distant memory to him, especially with these new hands.' She winked at Bessie.

'Had you ever considered nursing?'

'No, not ever. I'd always fancied myself as a seamstress, though those roles have been hard to come by with the war on.' Rose tilted her head. 'Maybe I'll be as good at sewing wounds as I am at fabric.'

'That's ghastly!' Bessie said, laughing. 'Well, you must be doing something right. They say Matron Cromwell is a real dragon. She must like you if she's keeping you on.'

'I've yet to see her breathe fire.' Rose screwed the lid back on the tea tree bottle and balled up the gauze to throw away. 'She's certainly strict, but she has to be. She has two hospitals to run in one of the busiest quarantine stations in the country. That's no small feat.'

There was a knock at the door and Rose climbed off the bed. 'Leave your hands to absorb the oil.' She opened the cottage door and found the young assistant from the post master's office on the verandah.

'Good evening, ma'am.' He tipped his hat. 'Are you Rose Porter?'

'I am.'

'I have a parcel for you from the post office.'

'For me? I haven't ordered anything.' Rose eyed the package in his hand, wrapped in brown paper and bound together by string.

'It has your name on it, ma'am.' He handed it to her and skipped off the steps before she could question him further.

Rose closed the door and took the package to her bed.

Bessie looked up. 'What's that?'

'A parcel for me, apparently.'

'What kind of parcel?'

'I have no idea.'

'Well go on, open it.'

Rose collected a pair of scissors from her sewing kit and cut away the string. Next she tore at the paper until a bundle of books fell into her lap. Diaries. Four of them! Enough to keep her writing for the next year. Her heart soared.

A small card was affixed to the top of one of them that read simply, *To my beloved Rose, keep writing. All my love, TVC.*

'What are they?' Bessie asked, leaning over for a better look.

Rose quickly slipped the note into one of the diaries and shook her head, feigning foolishness. 'Books. They're just books. I placed an order for them months ago and forgot all about it. Silly me!'

'Oh, books.' Bessie looked disappointed.

'Yes, boring old books.' Rose wrapped them back up in the paper, tied them together with the string and slid them into her suitcase. Fastening the locks, she hid them away, along with the love she felt brimming inside her.

She would write, just as he wanted her to. She would pour her heart out to those diaries and tell them of a love so hopeless that it couldn't be, that it might never be the longer the world existed in turmoil. The longer they remained inside the station, cut off from civilisation, with its structure and rules.

A love so hopeless it had the power to fill Rose's heart and break it at the same time.

* * *

Rose grew to enjoy her time at the hospital. It had unexpectedly filled her days with a sense of purpose and achievement, and she found herself bounding up the hill to unhealthy ground well before seven each morning.

She became a familiar face to the staff and patients and was given a growing list of tasks to complete, not just housekeeping and serving meals, but dressing blisters, administering medications and draining fluid from lungs.

She was allowed to hold the children when they cried and sing them to sleep in the evenings and, in the absence of a station priest to administer last rites, she held the hands of the dying as they drew their last breath.

Such was her sense of accomplishment she hardly noticed the time fly by. She had been at the hospital for five weeks when she was collecting urine from a smallpox patient and felt someone touch her arm.

It was Matron Cromwell. 'Miss Dalton has asked to see you urgently,' she said, her expression grim.

'Is everything all right?'

'Please change out of your uniform and leave it in the laundry bag. You are relieved of your hospital duties.'

'Relieved?'

Matron Cromwell patted her arm affectionately. 'It has been a pleasure having you here, Rose. I would have you back in a heartbeat. Thank you for your service.'

Confused, Rose hurriedly scrubbed her hands down and changed out of her uniform and back into her tunic. She slipped into her own shoes and sprinted all the way back to first class.

She was panting when she knocked on Miss Dalton's door and didn't bother to wait for permission to enter before flinging it open and barging in. 'What's going on?'

Miss Dalton looked up in surprise. 'Well, do come in, Rose.'

'Why have I been relieved of the hospital?'

Miss Dalton sighed and pinched the bridge of her nose. 'You better sit down. There's been a development.'

Rose sat in the chair, perched on the edge, breathing hard.

'The duke has requested... no, he has *demanded*, that you return to his service.'

'What?'

'I know.'

'Since when did the passengers start dictating where we work?'

'He's been badgering Bessie about your absence for weeks and when she finally told him you would be gone a few more months, he flew into a rage.'

'But Miss Dalton,' Rose said, leaning forward. 'I'm doing well at the hospital. I'm learning new things and I'm good at them! I'm of use there. Please, can't you reason with him, tell him I'll just be a little longer?'

'If it were any other passenger, I'd do so, believe me. But this is the duke, the first cousin to the king. And unfortunately, he hasn't just submitted the complaint to me. It went all the way to the superinten-dent.' Miss Dalton's face softened. 'I'm sorry, Rose. I know what wonderful work you've been doing at the hospital. Matron Cromwell has been filling me in. She wasn't happy about this reassignment. My ears are still hurting from all the cussing.'

Rose closed her eyes and watched one more thing she loved slip through her grasp.

Miss Dalton gave a small smile. 'As soon as the duke and duchess are on their way, I will reassign you to the hospital. You have my word. But, for now, you will return to first-class accommodation.'

Rose was devastated. 'When?'

'Take the rest of the day off. You can start first thing tomorrow.'

She nodded reluctantly. 'Yes, Miss Dalton.'

Woodenly, she rose from the chair and headed for the door. It wasn't until she was back outside in the sunshine that the first tear of frustration broke through her resolve to slide down her cheek.

Chapter Eighteen

Bessie was overly apologetic when Rose arrived at the kitchen the next morning. 'I'm so sorry, Rose.'

'It's not your fault.'

'I opened my big mouth and ruined everything. You had to leave the hospital and now I'm back here in the kitchen.'

If Rose wasn't feeling so glum, she might have offered some words of absolution, but she could only force up a disheartened smile.

Collecting the duke's tray of breakfast, she loaded it onto the serving trolley, rolled past the laundry to collect fresh linen, then pushed the trolley up the hill to his cottage.

The duke greeted her arrival with a look of anticipation on his face. 'Rose, you've returned to me!' he said, arms outstretched as though she might fall into them.

'Good morning, Your Grace,' she replied morosely, curtseying.

He seemed not to notice her lack of enthusiasm. 'Come on in. I do say you look splendid this morning. It is so nice to have you back!'

He whistled as he helped her set out the plates and remove the cloches. He poured his own tea while she set out the jam and butter. He sat himself down, shook out his own napkin and placed it in his own lap.

'Ah, everything smells amazing. Better than it has in weeks, I can assure you.'

Rose remained silent, laying the cutlery.

'How was the hospital work? Bet you're glad to be back on healthy ground.' He winked at her and sipped his tea.

'I was rather enjoying it actually.'

Her meaning was clear, but he brushed it aside with a wave of his hand. 'Be that as it may, it is much safer for you here in first class.'

Rose didn't respond.

'And they can send that bumbling oaf back to the kitchen. Is she not a full quid, that one? She spilt my tea every morning. And those unsavoury hands!' He gave an exaggerated shudder. 'Turned my stomach every time.'

'Bessie is not a bumbling oaf, Your Grace,' Rose said firmly. 'She's a kind girl who was trying to do her job. There's no need to be rude.'

He gave her a double look and fell silent. Rose knew she had over-stepped the mark, but she was frustrated with the duke's mercurial and self-indulgent nature, and she found herself struggling to contain it.

He was a man used to getting his way and what he wanted was a pretty servant to tend to his every need, irrelevant of the fact that she had become useful in the infirmary where people actually needed her. She was angry and she was taking it out on him even though she knew his patience would only stretch so far.

She straightened her shoulders and took a composing breath. 'I apologise, Your Grace. I spoke out of turn. Forgive me.'

'There is nothing to forgive, Rose. You are quite right. I should not have spoken ill of the fat girl.' He grabbed her hand and held fast to it. 'I'm just glad to have you back. You can't begin to imagine what the past few weeks have been like for me, not knowing if you'd return.'

Rose stared at him as he bent his head to rest it against her hand. It was not the way he was holding her that was alarming—though that in itself was a worry—but rather the way he seemed to be unravelling before her. It had only been five weeks since Rose had seen the duke, but here sat a man she hardly recognised.

The isolation can make people go a little crazy. How true of him as he clung to her hand like a child, caressing it with his cheek, afraid to let her go should she disappear on him a second time. He had been cooped up in the cottage for four months, never venturing further than the porch, cut off from all civilisation save for the parlourmaid who served him his meals and the doctor who tended his wife. And she felt all that pent-up energy fixated on her.

Rose gently extricated her hand from his. 'Perhaps after breakfast, you could go for a walk, Your Grace. The smoking room is quite lively this time of morning.'

His head was still bent, shoulders slumped. 'I don't want to.'

'How about the cove?'

'I don't like sand.'

Rose raised her eyebrows. It was like reasoning with a child. 'Well then, you should eat your food before it gets cold.'

He turned huge blue eyes up to her. 'Can you butter me some toast please?'

She reached for a piece from the rack, buttered it, sliced it in half and set it down in front of him. Then she left and retreated quickly to his bedroom. Once inside, she shut the door and leant against it, closing her eyes and taking a breath. She wasn't sure what she'd just witnessed, but it had been altogether strange.

Eager to leave, she gathered up his bed linen and pillows, piling them by the door ready to transfer to the verandah. She crouched beneath the bed and retrieved his chamber pot, ammonia filling her nostrils.

It was while she was down there, pulling the pot out and trying not to spill the contents, that she heard three gentle knocks against the wall.

Knock, knock, knock.

She froze. She knew the duchess was on the other side, lying in bed, recovering from her bronchial problems, but never had she tried to get Rose's attention before.

Then she heard another set of knocks, like delicate knuckles rapping the plaster.

Knock, knock, knock.

She raised her hand to the wall and knocked back. Three more came in reply. The duchess was making contact.

Slowly, Rose opened the duke's bedroom door and walked back out

165

into the living room. He was no longer at the table, the front door was open and she could see him standing on the verandah drinking his tea.

Rose crept towards the duchess's closed door and knocked.

'Come in,' a soft voice said from inside, as though she'd been expected.

She opened the door and curtseyed. Lying in bed, like a fragile porcelain doll, was a woman with hollow cheeks and long dark hair fanned out around her. And, just like the duke, she had the brightest blue eyes.

The room had a strong odour of onions, several of them laid out to absorb the illness. They were on the dresser, the cupboard, the windowsill and the bedside table.

'Do not linger,' the duchess said, her voice so faint Rose had to strain to hear it.

She closed the door and moved a little closer to the bed. The duchess gave a wheezy cough, struggling for breath.

'Your Grace, let me sit you up. You'll be able to breathe better.'

The duchess nodded and Rose stepped forward, propping up the pillows and assisting her into a sitting position.

'How is that?'

'Better, thank you.' The duchess eyed her. 'So *you* are Rose?'

'Yes, Your Grace.' Rose poured a glass of water and helped her take a sip.

'I recognise your voice,' she said, swallowing with effort. 'You're the lass I hear through the walls, the one with the opinions. The one my husband is so fond of.'

Rose placed the glass back on the side table and clasped her hands together. 'Are you comfortable, Your Grace? Shall I fetch the doctor?'

The duchess coughed thickly again. 'No, no. I'm sick of doctors. Poking and prodding and making me inhale things. Please, sit with me a moment. I'd like to talk.'

Rose pulled up a chair and sat.

'You're from London,' the duchess stated.

'Yes.'

'My husband adores London. He's originally from Knightsbridge, though you probably already knew that.'

Rose didn't acknowledge the implication.

'You are a beautiful thing indeed.' She stared at her. 'Young, healthy, lovely to look at. All the things my husband appreciates. You're not the first pretty lass to catch his eye, nor will you be the last.'

'Your Grace, I assure you—'

The duchess waved her hand to silence her. 'I don't care for your assurances. My husband can be charming. I know that better than anyone.'

'I have no interest in your husband,' Rose said boldly.

The duchess stared at her. 'You're certainly not shy. I can see where the attraction lies——a woman my husband can't tame. He didn't cope well while you were away. He was terribly cruel to the fat girl.

'I heard it all through the walls. I hear everything. That's the only way he and I communicate these days, through the doors and walls. He's too afraid to come in here, too afraid to touch me. We haven't been intimate in a long time.'

Her candour surprised Rose.

'I want to show you something.' She lifted a necklace out from her nightgown and held it up for Rose to see. It was the largest, brightest emerald she had ever laid eyes on; a magnificent green stone, suspended from a delicate gold chain.

'It's exquisite,' Rose said.

'It's an emerald, the birthstone of May, also known as the stone of successful love.' She laughed dryly. 'Successful love. What an irony.'

'It's the loveliest thing I've ever seen.'

'It was my grandmother's, handed down to my mother, then to me. I'm supposed to pass it on to my own daughter, though I fear the window to bear children is drawing to a close.'

'Your illness is a bump in the road, Your Grace. Once you've recovered and returned to England, I'm sure things will be better.'

The duchess laughed mirthlessly. 'I've been sick a long time. I won't ever recover, not fully, just enough to function. My husband visits my bed only when he can't find another. I suppose, like the fat girl with the scabbed hands, I repulse him. There's no desire there, no wild abundant joy at being in each other's company. We're merely strangers, tied to each other by a union neither of us wanted.'

'I'm sure he loves you very much,' Rose said, though the words fell flat.

The duchess arched an eyebrow. 'He wants an heir. That's the only reason he ever visits my bed.' Her voice was sad as she tucked the stone back into her nightgown.

Rose stood from her chair. 'I should take my leave, Your Grace.'

The duchess reached out pale fingers and clutched her wrist. Her grasp was surprisingly firm. 'I want you to remember your place, parlourmaid, and resist my husband. Mark my words, he will try to have you, but I am always listening. And if you indulge him, if you take away my chance to pass my stone on, I will have you sent back to the slums of Bethnal Green quicker than you can blink your pretty eyes.'

Her hand fell and her head lolled to the side, spent from the energy mustered to utter her threats.

Rose, still feeling the duchess's nails in her skin, backed away from the bed and quickly left the room, closing the door behind her.

She was relieved to see the duke on the verandah with Doctor Holland and took the opportunity to step unseen back into his bedroom, rustle up the linen and collect the chamber pot. She passed them as they stepped into the cottage and she stepped out.

Quickly she beat the pillows, emptied the pot and remade the bed. And, grateful that he was still occupied with the doctor, she slipped away and hurried back down to first class with the trolley.

* * *

The duke's cottage became a silent battleground borne from the marital woes of the duke and duchess, and Rose found herself planted firmly in the middle of it.

The duke, with his increasingly childlike behaviour, bounced around like an energetic puppy whenever Rose arrived. But she knew the duchess was listening closely, scrutinising every word from behind the wall, and so she took great steps to ensure her conversations during service were professional. At times, her aloofness seemed to confuse the duke and he became petulant and prone to outbursts that were hardly acceptable for a grown man.

'Rose, what have I done?' he wailed theatrically when she wouldn't participate in discussion. 'Please, sit down and talk to me. We can talk about anything you like. Anything at all!'

'You haven't done anything. Please mind your voice. Your wife is in the next room.'

'Oh don't worry about her. She's too sick to hear anything. Come, have a cup of tea. I've missed you since this morning.'

And so it would go on, day after day, the duke pleading with her to sit and talk with him and Rose resisting.

She blamed herself in many ways. She'd encouraged this behaviour. It had been flattering for a nobleman to want to hear her opinion on matters. Matters of which a woman, one in service particularly, should not have an opinion. And in those early days, his wife had not been listening in the next room and so yes, perhaps Rose *had* forgotten her place. Trying to correct the matter was becoming as difficult as prying boiled sweets from a child's hand.

After some weeks, the duke grew quiet and introspective. He hardly ate and Rose was caught somewhere between moral ethics and the conversational needs of a lonely man.

'There are many things to enjoy outside,' she said encouragingly, one afternoon over tea when he was looking particularly glum. 'You could join the other passengers in the dining room or partake in a game of cricket. Main Axial Road too, is lively during the day.'

His reply was always the same. He didn't want to leave the cottage, didn't feel like socialising. He was choosing to isolate himself, a strange irony given where they were.

With the duchess's health neither better nor worse, he had begun to speak of their return to England; music to Rose's ears. He had her darn some of his shirts and socks and prepare their suitcases for packing. He even perked up a little and was starting to eat again at the thought of going home.

But by the second week of October, the duchess's health declined again.

Rose had arrived back at the cottage for the lunch service and was serving the duke lamb stew when they heard the duchess moaning from behind the wall. They exchanged a look and he nodded for her to check.

Rose knocked on the bedroom door and entered. She saw the duchess on her side, thick coughs racking her small frame and a hand-kerchief in her hand, soaked with bloodied mucus. Her skin was pale and clammy and when Rose placed a hand to her forehead, it was burning.

She retreated quickly back to the living room where the duke was eating his lunch. 'The duchess isn't well. She's running a fever.'

He waved his hand. 'She's always unwell.'

'She's coughing up blood, Your Grace. I'm going to fetch the doctor.' Rose didn't wait for a reply. She dashed out of the cottage and ran along the stretch of road that carried her past the morgue and labo-ratory to the hospital.

Her lungs were screaming by the time she arrived at the perimeter and she was clutching a stitch in her side when she finally found Dolly, who summoned Doctor Holland.

Together they rushed back to the cottage to find the duke waiting outside on the verandah smoking a pipe.

'She's coughing quite thickly and can't catch her breath,' he informed them as they hurried up the steps and into the living room. 'I do say I hope this doesn't place our travel plans in jeopardy. I was hoping to sail on Friday.'

Doctor Holland and Dolly disappeared into the bedroom and closed the door. Rose remained in the living room with the duke as the first signs of worry started to crease his brow.

'We will be able to sail, won't we Rose?'

'I'm not sure, Your Grace. She didn't look well.'

He sat down at the table with slumped shoulders.

'Let me pour you some tea,' she said kindly. 'Mrs March put a slice of lemon cake on the trolley for you to have after lunch. I'm sure it's here somewhere.'

The duke reached out and grabbed her hand. Rose held her breath as he closed his fingers around it and squeezed. 'I just want to go home,' he said in that childlike manner she recognised.

She gave his hand a small squeeze back. 'I know, Your Grace. And you will.' She gave him a reassuring smile. 'Now, let me find you that cake.'

* * *

The duchess wasn't able to sail; she had contracted bacterial pneumonia. The doctor couldn't be certain how she had caught it, only that her illnesses were so chronic they seemed to stretch into one continuous affliction.

'We're giving her oxygen by mask and cinnamon powder in warm milk to reduce the fever,' Doctor Holland told Rose and the duke that evening. 'Some extra onions around the room will help too.'

Rose nodded. She would collect them from Mrs March's kitchen in the morning.

'When will she be well enough to sail?' the duke asked.

'I can't say for certain,' the doctor said. 'She's weak and the journey to England is arduous.'

The duke sighed audibly. 'I will never get out of here.'

Doctor Holland exchanged a look with Rose. 'I'll leave a nurse here overnight and I'll be back tomorrow.'

'Thank you, Doctor,' Rose said.

The following morning, armed with a bag of onions, Rose walked quietly around the duchess's room while she slept and replaced the old ones with the new, adding a few extra. The night nurse had departed already and her replacement was due to arrive with the doctor.

Rose cleaned out the chamber pot and refilled the ewer with water, noticing traces of valerian root by the bed and realising the night nurse must have administered the herb, sending the duchess into a deep sleep.

The duke was quiet that morning and Rose left him to pick at his breakfast while she tended to his room. She was stripping the linen from his bed when she heard movement by the door.

'I'll just be a moment, Your Grace.'

Footsteps approached from behind. She felt the duke's hands rest on her hips then slip around her waist, pulling her in close.

Rose's breath caught in her lungs and she froze. She could feel the duke's breath on her neck. He smelt of tea and tobacco.

His face moved to her hair and he inhaled deeply. 'You smell heavenly, Rose. Just like peonies.'

She spun around. 'What are you doing?'

He moved forward, pinning her against the wall with his body and in that moment, when she felt him against her, she realised his intentions. 'You are the prettiest rose I've ever seen. I just want to touch you.'

'Your Grace!' She pushed him away but he came back again, pressing himself into her. She swallowed hard, trepidation coursing through her.

They were alone in a cottage up on a hill, she and the duke in the dressing room and the duchess next door in a valerian-induced sleep. Rose could scream but would anyone hear her?

'Oh, Rose, it has been so long since I've touched a woman.' He buried his face in her cleavage. 'You are beautiful indeed.'

'Please, Your Grace. Your wife is in the next room.'

'She's fast asleep. She won't hear a thing.' He stooped to place his hand under her uniform and travel it up her thigh, his breath heavy, full of desire. 'Rose, I have wanted you for so long. Do you have any idea what you do to me?' He reached inside her underwear and she cried out in alarm. 'Don't fight it. You will like it all the more if you just let me have you.'

Rose was gripped with paralysing fear as he pushed her onto the bed, falling on top of her with crushing weight. She could feel him struggling with the belt and button of his pants, freeing himself with one hand and pushing her uniform up with the other.

'Stop, Your Grace, please!' She struggled with all her might, but he was strong and she was no match for his strength.

The sound of her sobs were muffled as he lay on top of her, rubbing himself against her legs. Then, with a primitive instinct she didn't realise she possessed, she brought her knee up hard between his thighs.

He let out a howl, clutching his groin and rolling off her in pain. Scrambling to her feet, she tugged her uniform down and ran out of the room. On the verandah, she almost collided with Doctor Holland and Nurse Dolly who both looked astounded at the sight of her; wild hair, apron askew and tears streaming down her face.

She muttered an apology, pushed past them and hurried down the steps.

* * *

Rose burst into the cottage on the cliff. 'Thomas!'

She looked around frantically for him but the cottage was empty. He was still at work.

Sinking to the floor beside his bed, she curled up into a ball. Her arms and face were scratched from racing along the path where branches and shrubs had caught her skin. She pulled her knees to her chest and tried to make herself as small as possible.

Her mind was still racing, trying to process what had just happened, and the very thought of it again made her curl up tighter.

She concentrated her ears on the world beyond the windows. She could hear the water in the harbour heave and sigh, imagined the wide open sky above it and she breathed, in and out, in and out, focusing every fibre of her body on that soft, sedate sound.

She wasn't sure how long she'd sat there for on the floor of Thomas's sanctuary, surrounded by his things, feeling a sliver of security return. Nor was she sure of the exact moment her eyes grew heavy, her pulse calmed and her breathing slowed.

Or the moment she slipped into a turbulent sleep.

* * *

'Rose, wake up.'

Rose opened her eyes slowly, the cottage gathering shape again.

Thomas was kneeling beside her. 'Rose?'

'Thomas!' She sat up and flung her arms around his waist.

He circled her with his own. 'What are you doing here on the floor?'

She could only shake her head, unable to speak.

He pulled away from her and studied the scratches on her arms and face. 'What happened to you?'

'I'm all right.'

'Did someone hurt you?'

She should have told him what the duke had tried to do, but then she would have to explain that she'd encouraged him, that for the past four months she'd been more than a maid, she'd been his friend. Thomas would only march back down there and pummel him flat and then they'd both be in trouble.

So she shook her head again. 'I just needed to get away.'

'From what?' he asked, sitting down next to her. 'Did the duke do something to you? Are you in trouble with Miss Dalton? I've never seen you like this before.'

'Please.' She forced a smile that she was sure didn't convince him. 'Can we just sit here a little longer? I don't want to go back to first class right now.'

'Of course.' He helped her to her feet and she sat on the edge of his bed, conscious suddenly that they were alone together in his cottage.

He must have felt it too for he began to fidget. 'Shall I fetch you a glass of water?'

'Yes, thank you.'

He filled a glass from a jug on the table and handed it to her.

She took a large gulp. 'What time is it?'

Thomas sat on the bed beside her. 'It's two o'clock. I usually come up here for my lunch. I wasn't expecting to find a parlourmaid sleeping on my floor.'

'I'm sorry. I didn't mean to make myself at home.'

'It's quite all right. You could have slept on the bed though.'

She smiled.

'Are you certain you're okay, Rose?'

'Yes.'

'You would tell me if something bad happened, wouldn't you?'

Rose looked down at the glass in her hand and tears filled her eyes. Thomas wrapped his arms around her and she burrowed into him, a vastly different feeling to being pinned beneath the weight of the duke.

Thomas soothed her, made her feel safe. She could have sat there forever in that lovely warm cottage in his arms.

'I won't make you tell me if you don't want to,' he said, kissing the top of her head.

'I don't want to,' she whispered.

'All right.'

It was sometime later when he let her go and climbed to his feet. He made them each a sandwich and cut up an orange to share and once finished, he kissed her gently on the cheek. 'I have to go. I have some jobs to finish around the shower blocks then I'll come back.'

'I'll wait for you.'

He turned the covers down on the bed and fluffed up the pillow. 'Rest and I'll see you soon.'

She climbed under them and curled up into his pillow. It smelt exactly of Thomas——of sandalwood and soap. He kissed her lips so tenderly she barely felt it, then let the door close behind him.

She didn't sleep, but laid there, warm beneath the blankets, breathing him in. As the light in the room changed and prisms of afternoon sun patterned the walls, she collected an apple from the table and let herself out to eat by the cliff.

It was different there by day, though equally as peaceful. White-breasted woodswallows and fairy-wrens regaled her with a chorus in the trees, and an aloof echidna idled by, searching for ants. It felt like a world away from the duke and his roving hands pushing her uniform up.

Thomas returned at five o'clock with freshly-baked bread, cheese, grapes and a bottle of gin. 'I found Bessie by the kitchen. I told her that I saw you walking up to the hospital with a migraine. She said she would inform Miss Dalton so that someone could cover the duke's service. That should take care of them all for a while.'

Rose lit the oil lamp as sunlight dwindled. 'Thank you. I was starting to worry how I was going to explain my absence.'

'I also told Bessie that I'd skipped lunch. Mrs March was in the dining room, so she made me up a bundle.'

'The bread smells delicious.'

Thomas placed the food down on the table and stood before her, touching her cheek. 'I could get used to this, you know. Coming home to you every afternoon. Waking up beside you every morning.' He blushed at his choice of words. 'I mean...'

'I could get used to it too.' She nestled against his touch.

'Have you been enjoying your diaries?'

'More than anything!' Rose said. 'I write in them all the time. I've almost finished the next one. You'll have to tell me where you purchase them from. I couldn't possibly have you buy them at the rate I'm going through them.'

'I would buy you a lifetime supply if it made you happy.'

She lowered her eyelids and smiled. 'A lifetime with you would make me happy.' She wondered if his heart was bursting like hers was.

'Are you feeling better?'

'Yes.'

'Are you still not going to tell me what frightened you earlier?'

She turned away from him, lest he see it written across her face.

'I won't push you to tell me. I'm just glad you came.' He turned her face back to him and bent to kiss her. She responded in a way that surprised her and that she wasn't sure she was capable of after the events of the day. But with Thomas, it felt different. Everything felt different.

His hand drifted from her cheek to her collarbone and when he sucked in his breath, she pulled from him.

'What's the matter?' she asked.

'We should stop, before I can't stop.'

'I don't want to stop,' she said. She pulled him to her again and his lips met hers.

They kissed for a long time, their hands exploring each other's bodies. Eventually, their kisses grew urgent and they stumbled backward towards the bed. Rose could feel that Thomas wanted her and she wanted him too.

'Is this your first time?' he whispered.

She nodded.

'Are you sure you're ready?'

'I'm sure.'

He kissed her again. It felt like feathers on her lips.

'Will it hurt much?' she asked.

'It might at the start. I'll be as gentle as I can.'

She closed her eyes and melded into him. He untied the back of her apron and lifted it above her head. Next he flicked the buttons at the top of her uniform and she slid that and her petticoat down her body so that she was standing in only her corset and stockings.

'Shall I unlace you?'

She nodded and turned around. He untied the ribbon at the bottom, strips of whalebone relenting as he tugged on the threads and she let out a breath, feeling her chest and stomach release. He pulled the corset free and dipped his head to kiss the bare skin on her shoulder. She shivered.

He reached above his head and pulled his shirt off while she rolled her stockings down. Their movements were slow and measured. Thomas was incredibly gentle with her.

Standing naked with their eyes sweeping over each other, Thomas reached for her hand and helped her onto the bed. 'You are so beautiful, Rose. You have skin like satin.'

She blushed in her vulnerability. 'Thomas?'

'Yes.'

'Is this your first time too?'

'No, Rose, it's not my first time. But it is with someone I love.'

Her heart soared at the way he said it. *With someone I love...*

And she let him take her, wholly, unreservedly, breaking every rule possible, there on the bed in his little cottage.

Chapter Nineteen

EMMA 2019

The call came after midnight.

It was the shrill ring of the house phone that woke her, not her mobile, for Emma had placed that down somewhere days ago and couldn't remember where. She sat up in bed, rubbed her eyes and checked the clock beside her bed—twelve-forty am.

Her stomach flipped unpleasantly. Calls that came after midnight could only mean one thing and it was never good. She kicked the covers back, hurried out of bed and into the kitchen, snapping up the house phone.

'Hello?'

'Is this Mrs Wilcott?'

'It's *Ms Wilcott*. Who is this?' But Emma recognised the voice instantly.

'It's Anastasia Thornbury from Eastgardens Aged Care. I'm sorry to bother you so late. Actually, I've been calling your mobile for the past forty minutes with no luck. I found this number on our file and thought I'd give it a try.'

'I lost my mobile a few days ago. I'm not sure where it is. Is my grandmother okay?'

'Mrs Wilcott, she's gone wandering again.'

'What?'

'The night nurse last checked on her at ten-thirty pm. When he walked past her room again just before midnight, he saw her door open and her bed empty. We've called the Mascot Police Station and they've assembled a search team.'

Emma closed her eyes and rested her head against the wall. When she opened them again, she was still standing in the kitchen in her pyjamas, the cordless house phone to her ear, listening to Anastasia Thornbury tell her yet again that her grandmother had gone missing from right under their watch.

'Mrs Wilcott, are you still there?'

'I'm here.'

'Can you come down to the facility?'

'Of course. I'll be right there.'

'Thank you, Mrs Wilcott.'

Emma didn't bother correcting her.

Back in her bedroom, she struggled against exhaustion as she pulled on jeans and a jumper and ran a brush through her hair. Grabbing her bag from the lounge, she rushed to the door and flung it open, slamming straight into Matt.

'Oh God!' she exclaimed, startled. 'You frightened the hell out of me.'

'Sorry,' he said.

'What are you doing here?'

He held up her mobile. 'Rebecca from the museum came to find me yesterday. She said you left this at the tour desk a few days ago. I was going to drop it in your letterbox tomorrow, but then I saw the calls coming through from the nursing home.' He handed the phone to her. 'I thought you'd want to know about them now.'

She took the phone from him. 'You drove all the way here at one in the morning to bring me my phone?'

'The calls looked urgent.'

She smiled. 'Thank you. They were.'

'Is everything okay?'

'My grandmother's gone missing again. I need to get over there now.'

'I'll drive you.'

She locked her apartment door. 'You don't have to do that.'

'I want to.'

She had no time to think about the way they'd ended things, how disappointed he'd been with her and if this meant, in some small way, that she'd been forgiven. She could only relent, conscious of time.

They hurried out to his car and climbed in. He guided them onto Anzac Parade and swiftly into Eastgardens, turning into the quiet tree-lined street of the aged care facility. It was a mild September evening. Winter had come and gone and a gentle breeze blew through the new leaves of the ancient maples above.

They crossed the street and pushed through the glass front doors. Anastasia was waiting for Emma in the foyer and strode to greet her. As always, she looked as though she'd glided out of bed perfectly coiffed. She wore a dusty pink Chanel dress with a matching jacket and large pearl earrings. Her bobbed hair was sleek and glossy, unlike Emma's hair, which hung in hurriedly-brushed strands around her face.

'So good of you to come quickly, Mrs Wilcott,' Anastasia said, thrusting out her hand and shaking Emma's. 'Is this your husband?'

Emma caught the slight stiffening of Matt's spine. 'I'm no longer married. This is my friend, Matt.'

Anastasia was already walking away. 'Let's talk in my office.'

They reached her office and once seated, she offered them water, tea and coffee. They declined.

'Have they found my grandmother?' Emma asked.

'Not yet, Mrs Wilcott.'

'How did this happen again?'

'Well, as I mentioned on the phone, the night nurse did his rounds and Gwendoline was in her bed seemingly asleep at ten-thirty pm. Closer to midnight, he walked past her room again, noticed her door open and her bed empty. He raised the alarm straight away. He's terribly upset over the matter.'

'*He's* upset? What about my grandmother who's missing again? How is she able to wander out without anyone noticing?'

Anastasia's bright red lips curled. 'I'm sure we can all agree, Mrs Wilcott, that your grandmother can be as slippery as an eel when she wants to be.'

Emma's jaw clenched. 'Where are they searching? Are they checking the ports and bays? She seems to be drawn to the water each time.'

'I'm sure they are. We have an ambulance on standby ready to go to her once she's found.'

'It's almost one-thirty in the morning. She's been out there for two hours already, if not more.'

'I don't think it's fair to blame the police now,' Anastasia said coolly. 'They're doing everything they can.'

'It's not the police I'm blaming.'

Anastasia scoffed. 'As I said before, Mrs Wilcott, your grandmother can be as slippery as an eel.'

'My grandmother is a hundred years old, Ms Thornbury,' Emma snapped. 'She's not as slippery as an eel or as cunning as a cat. She's an old lady with an ailing mind and she's in your care. And time and time again, despite the money I pour into this place, you let her walk right out the front door!'

Matt touched her arm. 'Em.'

'No! This is not the first time they've let her do this and I doubt it will be the last. Every time it happens they blame her, they blame me, they blame everyone but themselves.' Emma stood. 'If you let my grandmother walk out of here one more time, Ms Thornbury, I'll relocate her, then I'll make sure everyone knows exactly what kind of establishment you run.'

Anastasia's hand flew to her chest.

'And one more thing,' Emma said. 'My name is *Ms Wilcott*, not Mrs Wilcott. I'm not sure how many times I have to tell you that. Have the courtesy to address me properly.'

She stalked out of the office.

* * *

Matt found Emma sitting out the front on a garden bench. He lowered himself beside her and reached for her hand. 'You're trembling.'

'I'm so bloody angry!'

'I can tell.'

She looked at him and despite how furious she was, they burst out laughing. 'I'm sorry you had to see that.'

'It's all right,' he said. 'She needed to hear it.'

Emma let out a breath. 'She is just so frustrating to deal with. For years my grandmother has been wandering and for years I've let that wretched woman blame her for it. Gran doesn't hatch escape plans. She wanders because her mind is failing.'

'Are you really going to move Gwendoline from here?' He hadn't let go of her hand and Emma didn't want him to.

'I'd prefer not to. She's settled and a big move like that could be disruptive. But if this facility can't find a way to keep one elderly lady from going on midnight walks, then I'll have to. I don't even know if she'll come home tonight.' The words caught in her throat.

Matt squeezed her hand. 'She'll come home.'

'I thought telling her about Rose and her life on the station was helping. And maybe it was for a while. She seemed to settle, she wasn't wandering. I'm not sure what went wrong.'

'She has dementia, Em. Like you said, her mind is failing. The diaries were never going to be the one thing that stopped her. This place needs to do their part too. It won't be the last time Gwendoline chases her memories.'

Despite all that had happened between them, Emma was grateful he was there. She leant her head against his shoulder, exhausted and worried. He stroked her hair with his free hand.

They stayed like that for a while, enough time for Emma's tears to come and go, for her to doze briefly and wake again, for dawn to kiss the sky and for Matt to tell her that he was glad he'd come.

At five am, Anastasia came out to tell them they could sit in her office but Matt declined and Emma was so overcome with anxiety she couldn't speak. There was still no word from the police and at seven am, with the sun winking over Sydney, Emma went in search of a bathroom.

She was at the front doors when Anastasia came hurrying out. 'They've found her!'

Emma's knees went weak. 'Where?'

'Port Botany. She must have walked over an hour to get there. They found her sitting on the edge of the wharf at Bumbora Point, just staring out. She told them she was waiting for the boat.'

Emma and Matt exchanged a glance.

'The ambulance is with her now. Soon they'll transport her to Prince of Wales Hospital.'

'Is she injured?'

'I don't believe so. Just some mild hypothermia and dehydration.'

Emma clutched her chest. 'Thank God.'

'I'll call the hospital and get the details of your grandmother's arrival.'

Emma, still furious with the facility, gave her a cold, curt nod. It didn't go unnoticed, for Anastasia Thornbury seemed to shrink a little before scurrying back inside.

* * *

Matt parked the car outside Emma's apartment and walked her to her front door. It was almost midday and they both smiled at each other, exhausted.

'Thanks for hanging out with me last night and this morning. It meant a lot,' Emma said, searching her bag for her house key.

'No problem. I'm just glad Gwendoline's okay.'

'I think she'll be fine. She's a fighter.' Emma found the key and turned it in the lock. Hesitating, she said, 'Do you want to come in? I could make you a coffee or you could crash on the lounge for a couple of hours. I don't like the idea of you driving home tired.'

'Coffee sounds great.'

Emma smiled and opened the door. 'Don't mind the mess. I left in a hurry last night.' She dropped her bag on the lounge and led the way into the kitchen. 'So I should warn you, I'm an instant coffee girl at home; no barista or machine here, I'm afraid.' She pulled out cups, sugar, milk and a jar of Moccona and lined them on the bench.

'I don't mind instant coffee, actually.'

'Liar,' she said, filling the kettle and switching it on.

He laughed.

'I did have a nice machine once. Unfortunately, when Drew and I separated, I left with only a suitcase of clothes. Everything in this apartment belongs to my grandmother. He gave me nothing. Drew can be shrewd.' Emma stopped and glanced at Matt. 'I'm sorry. Is it weird that I'm talking about him?'

Matt shrugged. 'It's not weird. He just sounds like a jerk.'

Emma chuckled. 'He is.'

'But then again, I was a jerk too.'

'You weren't. I should have been honest with you the day you told me about Natalie. I wanted to but I lost my nerve. I didn't want to scare you off. And I guess it's been a long time since I've considered myself married. Not that that's an excuse.' She collected a spoon from the drawer, holding it above the sugar. 'I'm the one who should be sorry.'

Matt moved towards her, took the spoon from her and set it down. With both hands he brought her face to his and kissed her.

She hadn't realised just how much she'd wanted him to do that until it was happening. And it was delicious. All her senses were trained on his lips and on his hands as they moved from her face, down her arms, finding their way beneath her jumper to rest on her bare skin.

When he pulled away, she was breathless. 'Does that mean I'm forgiven?'

He laughed, that wonderfully deep laugh that made her stomach somersault. 'There's nothing to forgive.'

He leant in and kissed her again and this time, Emma's whole body fired to life, like a distant but familiar friend she'd thought gone.

Coffee and exhaustion forgotten, she grabbed his hand and led him boldly to her bedroom. With hands and lips on each other, they scrambled out of their clothes and fell onto her bed. Any modesty she might have felt at being out of practice had been left behind in the kitchen. She wanted him as keenly as he seemed to want her.

It was thirty minutes later when they finally separated, sweat cooling on their skin. As their breathing slowed, Matt's fingertips moved down her back, across her hips, along her thighs and back up around the curve of her waist.

It was refreshing to know a lover who took the time to appreciate her body, to want to drink it in with his eyes and hands, unlike Drew who had always been so self-absorbed in the bedroom. Despite the sleep deprivation, Matt had tasted, kissed and explored her, and it had driven her to act full of hunger and without inhibition.

The traffic pulsed to some unknown hour outside and the walls grew dim in her bedroom. Wrapped tightly in Matt's arms, exhaustion came quickly and they slept like the dead.

* * *

When Emma woke, it was dark outside and the street lamps were on, lighting up the edges around her window shades.

Matt stirred next to her, hair ruffled from sleep. He opened one eye, then the other and smiled. 'Hello there.'

'Hello,' she said, tugging the covers up around herself, suddenly self-conscious.

But he flung an arm around her and pulled her in close and the awkwardness vanished.

'I wonder what time it is.'

'Time for food. I'm starving,' he said into her hair.

'This is probably a good time to tell you that I live on café leftovers. I don't use my oven.'

He laughed. 'I could duck out and get us some food.'

'I would love that.'

He rolled out of bed and found his jeans on the floor. He pulled them on and slid his jumper over his head, leaning back across the bed to kiss her. 'I'll see you in a bit.'

She heard him pull the front door shut and listened to his car as it grumbled to life on the street. When she rolled over to check the time on the clock next to her bed, she was stunned to see it was ten pm. They had slept the day away.

Emma yawned and stretched. She felt pleasurably whole and satisfied, like something long dead had returned to life. Then, realising that a man was probably going to stay the night, she climbed out of bed, dressed and rushed around the apartment tidying up, emptying the fridge of old leftovers and taking the garbage down to the bins outside. When she was done, she ran a shower, washed her hair and dressed in clean clothes.

It wasn't until after midnight, well past the time when Emma feared Matt might not return, that she heard his car outside and a few minutes later, a knock at the door. She opened it for him and he grinned at her, holding up a plastic bag and a small bundle wrapped in a grey blanket.

'I got us Chinese food from the Cross. It was the only place still open.'

Emma couldn't wipe the smile off her face as she took the bag from him. 'I wasn't sure you were coming back.'

'Sorry,' he said, walking in. 'I made a detour and didn't want to call or text in case you'd gone back to sleep.'

'We slept all afternoon. I doubt I'll be sleeping for a while.' She eyed the bundle wrapped in the blanket. 'What's that?'

'This is what I detoured for.' He set the bundle down on the coffee table and peeled back the blanket, revealing four tan hardcover books inside. Rose's diaries!

Emma squealed. 'You brought Rose's diaries here?'

'I did. I drove to the Q Station to get them. I thought we could do some reading tonight, since we're both wide awake.'

'Is the Q Station open at this time of night?'

'Twenty-four hours a day.'

'But are you allowed to just take these?'

He looked sheepish. 'Not really. I could lose my job if anyone knew. So we have to be careful with them and I'll have to put them back as soon as we're finished.'

'We'll be super careful.' She held up the bag. 'Hungry?'

'Starving.'

She took the food into the kitchen and heaped rice, dumplings and beef into bowls. When she carried them into the living room, Matt was holding one of the diaries up.

'This is the second diary we were reading a few weeks ago.'

Emma sat next to him and handed him a bowl.

He took a few bites of a dumpling, then put it to one side, opening the cover. 'Ready?'

'Ready.'

And with bowls of greasy Chinese food, they went back to 1918.

Chapter Twenty

1 5th September, 1918
Forgive me, dearest diary,
I have not written to you in weeks. It was not my intention to neglect you. *On the contrary, I've missed our time together. Although I have been preoccupied, the real reason I couldn't write is that I ran out of diary pages. My love, my wonderfully kind and generous love, the one of whom you know I speak of, has bought me four new diaries! They arrived today. The postmaster's assistant brought them to me.*

Of course, I had to hide them from dear Bessie. I don't believe she is a keen reader, but I have to be careful all the same. Zealous eyes can lead to secrets exposed and I must protect the one thing I hold dear in this place; the one person that tethers me to the ground and catapults me to the sky all at the same time.

So much has happened since we last spoke. I've been working at the hospital for the past two weeks, assisting with housekeeping duties and it has been extremely rewarding. Matron Cromwell sees potential in me and has asked me to stay! I seem to have found a place where I truly belong.

The hospital has become, ironically, a tonic for my soul. Bessie thinks the work is ghastly and she is right. At times, it can be. It's not for the faint-hearted and it chips at my soul when we lose the children, though I don't think Bessie intends to talk me out of it. She's enjoying her service to the duke, even if the enjoyment is not always reciprocated.

The weather is warming, dear diary, as we stride into spring. They say the warmth brings relief to the ill. For their sake, I hope so, as more boats arrive, delivering passengers down with this wretched influenza, and sometimes I think our station will truly burst at the seams.

Until next time,
Rose

They read page after page of Rose's diaries, spread out across the coffee table, the words whispering tales from a century before.

'I'm intrigued about who this man was.' Emma settled back into the lounge, massaging her neck. 'He bought her all these diaries. Do you think he and the duke are the same person?'

'I doubt it. I get the impression she liked being away from the duke when she was at the hospital.'

'Or was she just being clever in writing it that way so no one would suspect a thing?'

'I think you're reading too much into it.'

'I probably am.' Emma sighed. 'I guess at this point I just hoped I'd have more to go on. We're still no closer to knowing why my grandmother wanders at night. I fear we may never know.'

'What does she say about the duke? Surely she would have mentioned if he was her father.'

'The only time she ever mentioned him was last week when I visited her. Her exact words were "it was all to do with the duke".'

'What was to do with the duke?'

'I have no idea. After that, I couldn't get a straight answer from her.'

'And so it goes, round and round in circles.' Matt sank back into the lounge next to her. He rested his hand on her thigh and she liked the way it felt there; an almost comfortable possessiveness that stirred something inside.

'I like hanging out with you,' he said with a slow smile.

'You do?'

'Yeah. It's comfortable and uncomplicated.'

'It's just me.'

'I like *just you*,' he said.

She leant across the lounge, cupped his face in her hands and kissed him. He responded, his hand travelling from her thigh up to her waist, moving beneath her top to settle on her bare back.

She looped her arms around his neck, pulling him down on top of her and he gave a small groan. The late hour and Rose's diaries were quickly forgotten. She gulped him in like oxygen, every inch of him as clothes were quickly flung to the floor.

When they made love, Emma knew exactly how Rose must have felt. How the kind and gentle man in her life had tethered her to the ground and sent her catapulting all at the same time. A hundred years later, Emma felt it too, with a man she had accidentally stumbled across on a station that was tied to the core of her being.

Was it a coincidence or was it fate? Was it Rose reaching out across the threads of time to guide Emma and bestow a little wisdom?

Afterwards, they climbed into bed and Matt held Emma close, planting soft kisses along her neck. The clock on her bedside table blinked three-thirty am.

'Are you tired?' Matt asked softly.

She burrowed deeper against him. 'I'm not sure. I feel almost jetlagged.'

'Same. My body doesn't know what it wants to do.'

'Your body knew a few minutes ago,' she said cheekily.

He laughed out loud. 'That's the effect you have on me.'

She pulled his arms tighter around her.

'Why didn't it work?' he said into her neck.

'What's that?'

'Your marriage to Drew.'

Emma turned to face him. She traced a fingertip down his arm, tanned from the sun. 'For lots of reasons, but the final straw was the affair. He cheated on me with my best friend.'

Matt's eyebrows went up. 'Wow.'

Her fingers met his and their hands locked. She could feel the rough callouses on his skin——carpenter's hands. Strong, rugged. She liked it.

189

'Drew and I weren't a good match from the start. Our relationship was fraught with problems.

'I'd met him a few years after my parents died. I was in the worst possible headspace, living with Gran, still grieving, hating the world. He lifted me so high on a pedestal I lost sight of the ground. That's what Drew does, you see, he conquers people. I was a challenge, a thing to be rescued.'

'Sounds like a nice guy.'

'That's the problem. I thought he was. He was like my saviour. He made me see the world again, gave me something to live for.

'We dated for several years and then he asked me to marry him. I said yes, even when deep down I knew we weren't a good fit. I was never myself around him, always trying too hard. But I gave it a go because apart from my grandmother, Drew was the only other thing I loved and I couldn't have survived another loss. So I clung. I clung to him so damn hard I suffocated him.

'The first cracks started to appear a year after we married. We were living together in Rose Bay and Gran was diagnosed with stage three dementia; a mild cognitive decline. She had difficulty concentrating and she'd gotten lost a few times on the way to the shops.

'The doctors said she wasn't able to live on her own anymore because her condition would deteriorate. Drew wanted her admitted to an aged care facility but I wanted her to stay with us. The other option was to pay for a full-time caregiver to live with her, but that was expensive and Drew didn't like the idea of our money being used for that. Eventually, he relented and Gran moved in with us.

'He struggled having her in the house. He felt that his space had been invaded. I guess it was a lot to ask of him when we had only just gotten married, but I reasoned that if it were his parents or grandparents, I would have happily welcomed them into our lives.'

'I think most people would have.'

'Not Drew. He resented the intrusion. He spent less time at home, went out more. I hardly saw him and that made me more fearful, not only because I knew he was pulling away from me, but because I was worried something terrible would happen to him. That he'd get hit by a car or stabbed by a drunk. I was so terrified of him dying that I clung to him more. And that pushed him further away.

'Then one afternoon I came home from a doctor's appointment with Gran to find him in our bed with my best friend, Tabitha.'

'What did you do?'

'I can't even remember those initial few seconds. I think I retched on the carpet then I left. I took Gran and we went to sit in the park for a few hours. She was so upset for me. She felt responsible, but it wasn't her fault.

'I've known Tabitha my whole life. She was my best friend. She was there the night I was told my family were killed, was the first one to hold me, to understand my shock, to expect nothing from me because she was just a kid herself. And after all that, she slept with my husband in my bed.' Emma shook her head. Just when she thought she didn't care anymore, she realised that no amount of time or healing would ever make her forget the humiliation and betrayal.

Matt squeezed her hand a little tighter. 'I'm sorry, Em.'

'Don't be. It turned out to be a blessing in disguise. After we left the park, I took Gran home and decided I would talk to Drew and maybe we could still salvage our relationship. I was prepared to forgive him. But when we got home, Drew had changed the locks and mine and Gran's suitcases were on the front step.

'I tried calling him, tried calling Tabitha. Neither of them would answer. With my marriage obviously over, I took Gran to a hotel and a few weeks later, we found this rental here in Kensington. We relocated her furniture from storage and I've been here ever since.'

'Drew's a jerk.'

'So you can see why I didn't want to tell you about him. There's nothing there anymore. We should have gotten divorced years ago but we haven't been in contact and it was just forgotten about. I've considered myself single for a long time and he's moved on too. Tabitha and Drew have a baby now and they're getting engaged.'

'I get it, Em. I do. And I shouldn't have acted the way I did down by the post office. It just reminded me of Natalie and... well, I don't always think straight when it comes to what she did.'

'I'm sorry she hurt you. You didn't deserve that.'

'She loved me in her own way I suppose, but what's the point if you belong to someone else?'

He held her tighter in his arms and she smiled at the feeling of security it gave her. They both had baggage, they'd both been hurt terribly, but in some weird and wonderful way, they'd found each other.

Emma knew it was too early to know what this was, but in that moment, it felt good, and she knew that was all she could ask for.

'What made you decide to place Gwendoline in the nursing home?'

'I started working at The Coffee Bean to support us and that meant she was left home alone for hours at a time. She'd forget to turn the stove off or leave the bath running. She would wander from the apartment and I'd come home from work and wouldn't be able to find her.

'Anyone going through that mind-altering state would feel fearful and isolated. She was terrified, didn't know what was happening to her. I learnt as much as I could, but I couldn't be here twenty-four-seven to watch her and that was the difficult part.

'I persisted as long as I could but, in the end, I had to make a decision. Placing her in permanent care was the hardest thing I've ever had to do and not a day goes by that I don't feel guilty for it.'

'You're so hard on yourself all the time. You did the only thing you could do.'

'When my family died, Gran took me in. She put up with all my teenage bullshit——she dealt with the tears, the tantrums, the drinking, the stealing. I put her through hell and she loved me unconditionally. I couldn't do the same for her. I couldn't cope with her ailing mind. I just put her in a home.'

'You didn't *just* put her in a home. The circumstances were completely different.'

'I'm not so sure they were.'

They fell silent as Matt nestled into her neck and she could feel his rough jaw against her skin. She admired his tolerance. She had bared the ugliest parts of her soul to him and he was still there, holding her, not running for the door.

'Do you know what I wish for?' she asked.

'What?'

'I wish for my mum back. Just to have one more day with her. I would ask her so many things. She would have known what to do about Drew and Tabitha and how to handle Gran's illness. She was a practical lady, classy and smart as hell.' Emma wiped a tear away that had leaked onto her cheek. 'I miss her every day. I miss them all.'

Matt didn't say anything, but as she closed her eyes and sleep finally took hold, she felt his powerful arms around her and all the sadness, like a second layer of skin, melted away. It would come back, there was no doubt, but for the first time in a long time, Emma almost felt whole again.

Chapter Twenty-One

Not even the rising sun could stir them the next morning and they slept soundly until eleven.

When they woke, they made love again, showered then devoured toast and instant coffee like they'd never eaten before. At midday, Anastasia Thornbury called to advise that Gwendoline would be transferred back to the aged care facility at three pm if they wanted to visit her.

By some stroke of luck, Emma and Matt both had the day off and with a few hours to spare before Emma would leave for Eastgardens, they curled up beneath a blanket on the lounge to trawl through more of Rose's diaries.

Clouds had gathered outside, turning the blue sky leaden, and fat drops of rain began to spatter against the glass. Matt found the diary they'd last been reading from and turned to the next page.

In the neat cursive style they were becoming used to, Rose described in greater detail her time at the hospital and the patients she'd met and treated. She seemed to have found a passion for what most people would have thought a gruesome task.

The next few entries caught their attention. After five weeks of working at the hospital, in late September 1918, Rose was summoned back to first class by Miss Dalton. She wrote of the duke's unreasonable demands that she return to his service, and her vexation that a decision like that could be made so easily at the behest of a passenger.

Upon working for the duke again, she met the duchess, still in poor health but who had mustered the strength to warn Rose away from her husband.

Matt placed the diary down. 'That's interesting.'

'The duchess believed there was something improper between them.'

'It doesn't necessarily mean there was.'

'Or that we can rule it out entirely,' Emma countered. 'It's not a stretch to consider he might have been her mystery man.'

Matt still looked unconvinced and picked up the diary again. His eyes skimmed quickly over the next page and a sound escaped him. 'I think I found something.'

25th September, 1918

Oh diary! What a day it has been. What a wonderfully thrilling and terrifying day. I have so much to tell you, most of which I know will embarrass you, so I apologise in advance.

You know of whom I speak——the love of my life, the one that fills my heart with a joy so abundant I want to scream it from the rooftops!

We have shared an intimacy that I did not realise was possible between a man and a woman. An intimacy so incredibly passionate that it makes me shiver just to think of it again.

We did not intend for it to happen; quite the contrary. Just this morning, service at the duke's cottage turned out to be one of the most horrifying of my life. The duke has been unwell in the mind. I fear the isolation and the duchess's health complications have sent him mad. He thought it appropriate to attempt to take what was not his.

I will never forget that moment on his bed, with his hands near my sacred places. I thought I would be ruined. And yet, surprisingly, it is possible to find strength when backed into a corner. His ego will not be the only thing bruised today.

I fled from his cottage and I went to my love. So tender were his words and so gentle was his touch that the awfulness of the morning faded and I was helpless to resist. I gave him my flower.

My heart is so full right now, dearest diary, I fear it will burst! This must be what love feels like. Not a single minute idles by when I don't think of him. I crave his arms, his voice, his bed.

Oh diary, I must be making you blush, for I certainly am! I will embarrass you no more. I will lock these words away and they will forever be our secret.

For now, Rose

Matt put the diary down and turned to Emma. 'I think that confirms it. The duke wasn't her mystery man.'

'No. In fact, it seems like the duke attacked her and she fought him off. Which means Gran's father must be someone else.'

'Probably the man she went straight to afterwards and lost her virginity with.'

'The man she loved.'

Matt smoothed his hand over his jaw. 'Does that also mean we can rule out the duke as the one Gwendoline might have been waiting for by the wharf?'

'I guess so,' Emma said thoughtfully. 'He doesn't seem to fit into the equation anymore.' And yet, even as she said it, she heard Gwendoline's words. *It was all to do with the duke, you see.*

'So we're back to square one,' Matt said. 'We don't know who Rose's mystery man was, who Gwendoline's father was, who she was waiting for by the wharf and why they left the station suddenly in 1926.'

'Still so many questions.'

Matt sighed.

'I'm going to go back through Gran's boxes in storage. There has to be a photo album with a picture of her father in it or a birth certificate with his name, at least.'

'Have you not seen anything like that before?'

'Not that I recall. When they left the station they didn't take much with them except for one suitcase. I also think Gran was a bit of a wild child, not unlike me at that age.' She smiled ruefully. 'She ran away from home when she was a teenager. I'm not sure that she kept in touch with her family after that. It will make her father harder to trace.'

She glanced at her watch. 'I'm going to have to leave for Eastgardens shortly. Gran will be arriving soon.'

'If you want company, I could come along for the drive.'

'Really? I don't want to bore you with another trip to the nursing home.'

He leaned across to kiss her on the lips; one, two, three, four of them. 'Being with you is anything but boring.'

* * *

Later that afternoon, Matt reversed the car into a parking spot on the quiet tree-lined street in Eastgardens and they climbed out. The rain had eased to a sprinkle and the sky was multi-coloured as sunshine spilled through the clouds.

They crossed the street and pushed through the front doors. Anastasia Thornbury hurried over to them and pumped Emma's hand keenly, in a warm and most un-Anastasia like way.

'Ms Wilcott, it's so wonderful to see you. Your grandmother has arrived and she's in her room waiting for you.'

'Thank you, Ms Thornbury. Did her transfer go okay?'

'Perfect. I oversaw the details myself. I even had roses waiting for her in her room. She does like roses, doesn't she? I was told she does.'

Emma exchanged a look with Matt.

'You'll also be happy to know that we're revising our patient care policy. We'll be introducing new measures, like locking the front doors at eight pm and installing security cameras at all the exit points which will be monitored by our new security team.'

'That's great,' Emma said. She flashed Anastasia a smile.

The woman looked slack with relief. 'Let me know if you need anything at all, Ms Wilcott. I'll let you get to your grandmother now. She'll be happy to see you.'

Emma signed the visitor book and she and Matt headed down the corridor to the north wing.

When they were out of earshot, Matt leant in. 'Wonder what brought that on.'

'I suspect the police have been questioning Gran's disappearances too,' Emma said. 'Either that or the media paid her a visit. I doubt Gran's the first patient to have wandered from here.'

Gwendoline was sitting up in bed when they arrived. Jane Austen's *Pride and Prejudice* was resting on her lap.

When they entered the room, Emma tut-tutted over the book and Gwendoline snapped it up, shoving it quickly to the bottom of her bedside drawer.

'I'm stopping by the bookstore to get you a new book,' Emma said, stooping to kiss Gwendoline's cheek.

'I don't want a new book,' Gwendoline said petulantly. 'I like the one I have.'

'Wouldn't you like a new story?'

'Don't touch my book.'

Emma sat on the edge of the bed and smiled. She wasn't going to argue. She was just happy to have her back safe. 'How are you feeling, Grandma?'

'They took me to the hospital yesterday. Did you know that? I came back today.'

'Yes. Do you recall going for a walk two nights ago?'

Gwendoline looked perplexed. 'A walk?'

'Yes, you went for a walk,' Emma explained gently, not wanting to frighten her.

'Did I go anywhere nice?'

'Bumbora Point. You were sitting on the wharf. Do you remember who you were looking for?' Emma could see her trying to search the far corners of her brain for the answers.

'I don't know anyone at that place. Where is it?'

'Port Botany,' Emma said.

'They took me to the hospital yesterday. Did you know that?'

Quietly despairing, Emma patted Gwendoline's hand. 'Yes, Grandma. I knew that.' She turned to Matt. 'I want you to meet someone. This is my friend from the Quarantine Station, Matt.'

Matt stepped forward and held out his hand for Gwendoline to shake. 'It's nice to meet you. I've heard so much about you from Emma.'

Gwendoline gave a sharp intake of breath and gestured towards her bedside table. 'My glasses, Emma dear. Quick, get my glasses.'

Emma found the glasses. She handed them to Gwendoline, who pushed them onto her nose and leant forward to take Matt's hand.

'It's not possible.' She studied him closely. 'You look just like him.'

'Like who?' Emma asked.

'You could be the same person.'

Emma looked at Matt. 'Do you know what she's talking about?'

Matt shrugged. 'I'm not sure.'

Emma looked from Gwendoline to Matt and back again. 'Okay, Gran,' she said, prying Matt's hand from her grip. 'You're still worn out. Just settle back there on your pillow and I'll get you a glass of water.'

Gwendoline relented and lay back, closing her eyes.

'Sorry about that,' Emma said, smoothing the bed covers down, tucking Gwendoline in firmly. 'She gets a bit confused.'

'I understand.' He turned to the bedside table and picked up the framed photograph. 'Is this your family?'

Emma moved beside him. 'Yes, that's them.' She took the frame, wiping dust from the glass with her sleeve and handing it back to him. 'That's my mum, Catherine, and my dad, John. And that's Max and Liam. The terrible twins!' she added with a laugh. 'They'd just turned six and lost their two front teeth when that photo was taken.'

'They look like fun kids.'

'They were. They'd be all grown up now with jobs and girlfriends had they lived.' She turned away as emotion shook her voice.

'You look a lot like your mum. You have the same eyes.'

'Do you think so?'

'Absolutely,' he said. 'You have a beautiful family.'

'I wish you could have met them. They would have liked you.'

'I would have liked them too.' He returned the frame to the table and touched the roses in the vase. 'Anastasia said Gwendoline loves roses.'

'She loves them because of Rose.'

'And yet as a teenager she ran away from her and never kept in touch. Why?'

Emma looked across at Gwendoline, who had fallen asleep and was snoring softly. She looked childlike in the bed, swamped by the covers, her tiny body too small for them. 'I'm not sure. I've never asked.'

They left Gwendoline to sleep and Emma and Matt climbed back into his car and drove to the storage facility to search through Gwendoline's belongings again.

Unsurprisingly, they turned up nothing that represented her time at the Quarantine Station or answered the questions that still confounded them. There were no photographs or letters, birth certificates or health records, nothing that could tie Gwendoline to anyone or anything.

They packed the items back into boxes. Matt rolled the storage door down and Emma locked it with the key.

'I didn't expect to turn up anything new,' she said with a sigh as they headed back to the carpark. 'I've been through those boxes hundreds of times. I would have remembered seeing something significant.'

'Did your mum ever talk about her grandparents? Did she mention Rose or Rose's husband?'

'She never talked about her grandfather, but we sometimes spoke of Rose.'

'What about the boat and the wharf?'

'If my mother knew about this mysterious boat and who might be sailing on it, she never said anything to me.'

They climbed into Matt's car and he navigated them onto Anzac Parade and back to Kensington as the sun bled into the horizon. He parked the car out the front of Emma's apartment block.

'Would you like to come up?' Emma asked.

He responded with the kind of kiss that told her yes, the kind that would probably always give her butterflies whenever she thought of it.

She tucked her hand into his and they walked up the steps to her apartment.

Chapter Twenty-Two

ROSE 1918

Beneath an indigo sky, Thomas guided Rose back along the path towards the station.

He held fast to her hand, and she to his, as if the sanctity of their love for each other depended on it. They had spent the afternoon in his bed, exploring one another, Rose viewing the naked male anatomy for the first time and marvelling at how beautiful and strong it was.

She thought she'd known Thomas's touch by heart——the way he held her hand or circled her waist with his arms. Never had she realised that a closeness beyond that could exist between a man and a woman.

As the afternoon slid into dusk, they acknowledged with regret that she had to return to first class before her absence was questioned.

Just before the path opened onto the male staff quarters, Thomas held her close and whispered into her hair. 'Was your first time all that you thought it would be?'

'Everything and more.' The place between her thighs told her so as they ached with a pain and pleasure she had never thought possible.

'I'm so glad.'

'Can I come back tomorrow night?' she asked, turning her eyes up to him.

'I will come for you at eleven. Wait up for me.'

'I couldn't possibly sleep.'

He kissed her so deeply and unreservedly that she wanted to run back down the path with him to his cottage and never return. The entire night and day until she saw him next would be an agonising wait.

'You should go, Rose, before Miss Dalton and the others start searching for you.' He let go of her and she reluctantly crept through the shadows back towards the station.

She found the road and, in the growing darkness, walked briskly until she reached her cottage. She had barely made it through the door when she heard Bessie climbing the verandah steps behind her.

'Oh Rose, you're back.' She hurried to give her a hug. 'I saw Mr Van Cleeve earlier. He said you were ill and off to the hospital. Are you not well?'

Rose hid her face in Bessie's shoulder as it reddened with guilt. She rarely told lies, but since she'd arrived, it felt like they were all she'd been telling. 'I was sick to the stomach but I'm much better now.'

Bessie pulled back with a perplexed look. 'Sick to the stomach? That's odd. Mr Van Cleeve said you had a migraine. Anyway, you look better. Was it something you ate?'

'I'm not sure.'

Bessie plonked down on her bed. 'Mrs March threw away two pints of sour milk this morning. Perhaps you drank from those by accident.'

'Perhaps.' Rose turned away to hide her guilt and lit the candles in the lantern. 'Who took care of the duke today?'

'I did. He was awfully quiet through lunch and dinner. He didn't ask for you like he normally does. Maybe my new hands are helping.' She studied them in the dim light and seemed pleased with their progress.

Rose sat on her bed and watched the flickering shadow from the candle flames crawl up the walls.

'Will you be well enough for service tomorrow?'

'I think so.' The last thing she wanted to do was face the duke, to be in the same room with him and serve his meals, but to request another position would mean she would have to tell Miss Dalton why and she doubted that conversation would go in her favour.

'Well, the duchess has recovered a little. Her fever broke this evening and her lungs have cleared.'

'Oh that's wonderful to hear,' Rose said brightening.

'The doctor was there while the duke was eating his dinner. He told us the news. The duke perked up a little then and was a bit friendlier to me. He said my hands looked nice. The tea tree oil is helping.'

'Show them to me.'

Bessie stood and thrust her hands out for Rose to see.

'Indeed. They are healing. The skin is smoother and you have no more open wounds.'

'They started itching a little yesterday, for the hot sink doesn't help, but I just apply the oil whenever I can.' Bessie yawned and untied her apron, slipping her uniform down. 'I'm going to bed. It's been a long day.' She pulled on her shift and climbed in, burrowing deep under the covers.

Rose undressed also and as she unlaced her corset, she thought of Thomas doing the same thing only hours earlier, how gentle he'd been as he'd picked at each loop, how terrifying and freeing it had felt to stand before him in little more than her bare skin.

'You have a strange smile on your face,' Bessie said sleepily. 'Are you sure you're well?'

Rose slipped her shift on. 'I think I'm just tired. Goodnight, Bessie.'

'Goodnight, Rose.'

But Rose wasn't tired. She listened for Bessie's snores on the other side of the room and when she finally heard them, she reached for the diary in her bedside drawer and unlocked it.

For the next hour, against the circle of candlelight, she told her diary all that had happened that day, from the duke's improper advances in the morning to the afternoon she'd spent with Thomas in his cottage. Of the way his hands had roamed her body and the kisses that had made her head swim. Of the way she'd hungrily kissed him back, surprising even herself with how much she had wanted him. Of the way they had lost all good sense, there on the edge of the cliff.

* * *

The next morning, Rose awoke with anxiety gnawing at her stomach. She had heard Bessie leave sometime before dawn to fire up the ovens, and she was grateful for a moment to herself to collect her thoughts.

While she was still giddy with the secret knowledge that she was more womanly than before, it was tainted by the prospect of facing the duke again. She couldn't be sure how he would react. Would he lash out at her or be remorseful? Would he seek to do it again? Would he blame her for it and tell Miss Dalton she'd been the instigator?

All of these possibilities twisted inside her as she washed, dressed and headed to the kitchen. The parlourmaids were setting up the dining room when she arrived, and Mrs March was pulling loaves of bread out of the oven.

'Oh, feeling better, are we?' she said as though she couldn't believe Rose had been sick.

'Much better, thank you,' Rose murmured, setting up the duke's trolley.

'No one else has fallen ill, so don't you go blaming my cooking.'

'I wouldn't dream of it, Mrs March.'

Bessie threw Rose a grin as she pushed the cart out of the kitchen. She collected clean linen along the way and headed up the hill to the duke's cottage. At the door, her heart hammered in her throat as she gave it a knock.

The duke appeared with a stunned look on his face. He opened the door for her and she curtseyed before carrying in his tray and setting it down on the table.

'Good morning,' he muttered.

She nodded politely.

'I didn't expect to see you. Where's the fat girl?'

'Bessie is in the kitchen today, Your Grace.'

'I see.'

Rose fell silent again as she laid out his breakfast and cutlery. She poured his tea and pulled out the chair for him. When he took the seat, she placed the napkin on his lap and rested the newspaper at his elbow. They remained that way, locked in a silent standoff, neither talking.

'I'll tend to your room now,' she said, turning away.

He grabbed her wrist and she snatched it back as though he had burnt her.

'Rose, I...'

She couldn't meet his eye, no matter how remorsefully he was watching her.

'I want to apologise for my behaviour yesterday.' He hung his head. 'I acted appallingly. I'm sorry.'

Tears welled in her eyes as she fought to push them down.

'I'm just so lonely all the time. And you are lovely; the only one I can talk to. Can we still be friends?'

She shook her head.

'Rose, please.'

'I'm sorry.' She curtseyed and left him at the breakfast table.

Thinking of Thomas was the only thing that got her through breakfast, morning tea and lunch. By afternoon tea, the duke had stopped begging for her forgiveness and had turned sullen. They had reached borderline civility as she served his meals and tended to his housekeeping.

She hadn't realised how exhausting it could be, how much energy it took to prop up a wall between them and to keep him at arm's length. She was his maid, not his friend; a line she'd foolishly crossed some time ago and which had almost cost her dearly.

At dinnertime, while she was serving him roast chicken, he asked about Bessie. 'Maybe that nice kitchen girl could bring my meals tomorrow.'

Rose was unperturbed. 'If that's your preference, place the request with Miss Dalton and she will see to it.'

He gave a nod as if that's what he would do, but the next day and the day after that, Rose waited. No notice was forthcoming about the reassignment of roles.

* * *

Rain thrummed the roof of Thomas's cottage as a thunderstorm brewed somewhere out at sea. Rose lay on her back among the covers, Thomas beside her, his breath slowing, their legs entwined.

'Do you get tired during the day, my love?'

'Not at all,' she lied.

'I've been keeping you up late at night.'

'Yes but I like it,' she said wickedly.

Thomas laughed; a lovely, languorous sound amidst the falling rain.

They had been meeting in secret every night in his cottage for the past six weeks and every night, just before dawn, Rose would scurry back to her quarters in the dark, making it there as Bessie stirred awake. This made her tired during the day, sometimes with little more than a few hours' sleep to see her through, but by the time dinner came around, she was fuelled again by the urge to see him.

Rose rolled onto her side, pulled his face to hers and kissed him. He kissed her back, his hands sliding slowly up her spine, making her shiver with every stroke of her vertebra. He pulled her in close, pinning her pleasurably against him.

'One day we'll leave here, my Rose,' he said. 'I'll save lots of money for us, we'll marry and we can live together as husband and wife. You'll be the last person I see at night and the first person I wake to in the morning. Nothing would make me happier.'

She climbed on top of him and traced her hands across his chest and stomach. 'And where will you take me to live, Mr Van Cleeve?'

'I'll take you to North Queensland.'

'Is that where you're from?'

'No, I'm from Adelaide in the south, but I've always liked the idea of Queensland,' he said.

'Is it far from here?'

'It's quite further north, near the top end of Australia.'

'And what's there?'

'Well, if we move to Cairns or Port Douglas, there's warm weather, white sandy beaches and palm trees.'

'Oh!'

'Or we could go further inland to Edmonton or Mount Sheridan where there's farming land.'

'Will there be animals and lots of room for our children to grow?' she asked.

'All of it and more.'

They both smiled.

'Thomas?'

'Yes.'

'Let's leave now.' Her own boldness surprised her.

He raised his eyebrows. 'Now?'

'Well, you know. Soon. Tomorrow or the next day.'

'Rose...'

'We could move to Queensland. We wouldn't have to worry about the rules anymore, or the fear of getting caught or sneaking around after dark.'

'It's not that simple, my love.'

'But it can be.'

He sighed. 'I don't think this is something we should rush. We'll leave soon, I promise. I only want to save a little more for the purchase of a house. I never want us to have to struggle or for you to go without.'

'I don't need much.'

'But that's not good enough for me. I want you to have everything.' He looked crestfallen at the prospect that he'd upset her. 'Have I made you sad?'

'No, my love, of course not.'

She dipped her head to kiss him, to try to show him how much she loved him for the kind and generous person he was. She tried not to feel disappointed, only lucky to know a man who wanted nothing but the best for her.

They made love for the third time that evening and she forced the uncertainties from her mind. She concentrated only on the present—the soft rain spattering against the tin roof and the pleasing sensation of her body beneath his.

Just before dawn broke, the rain moved on and Thomas walked her back to first class. Rose bid him goodnight on the road and hurried back to her quarters. She just made it inside the door when Bessie rolled over in her bed.

'Rose, is that you?'

'I didn't mean to wake you. I thought I heard a noise outside.'

'What time is it?'

'Not quite dawn. Go back to sleep.'

Bessie rolled over and when she was silent again, Rose let out a breath. She would have to be more careful next time. She would have to leave Thomas's cottage earlier to avoid getting caught.

But it was hard. She had so little time with him as it was and with no end in sight to the rules that bound them, they would have to make do with precious stolen hours.

It was well after Bessie left for the kitchen that Rose finally fell into a troubled sleep.

* * *

The following morning, Rose overslept. When she awoke, the sun was high and she scrambled to wash and dress, hurrying down to the first-class kitchen. Breakfast had already started and the dining room was full of passengers as parlourmaids ran back and forth pushing trolleys of food and drinks.

'Where have you been?' Mrs March crossed her arms over her ample bosom and frowned when Rose walked in.

'I slept in. I'm sorry.'

She scoffed. 'Sick one minute, late the next. Go on, then. The duke's breakfast is getting cold.'

Rose quickly loaded the trolley, feeling Bessie's eyes on her the entire time. She threw her a small smile and shoved the trolley out the door.

At the duke's cottage, she knocked and waited for him to greet her or grant permission to enter. He did neither, only grumbling at her from the bureau. She let herself in, curtseyed and took the tray to the table.

She served his breakfast, set out the spreads and toast and poured his tea. He still hadn't bid her good morning so she excused herself to tend to his room.

He had been acting like that for weeks now, treating her as he had once treated Bessie, refusing to acknowledge her except to throw her looks of disdain. Rose didn't mind. The quicker he and the duchess were on their way, the quicker she could return to the hospital and put the last few months behind her.

She changed his linen and carried his chamber pot out to the verandah. After rinsing it in the garden, she dried it and placed it back in his room.

While she was assembling his pillows on the bed, she heard a familiar set of knocks against the wall. Rose placed her ear to it and again the knocks came. It was the duchess trying to get her attention.

Having finished his breakfast, the duke had ventured out onto the verandah with his pipe and tea. She quickly stepped out of his room and slipped unseen into the duchess's, closing the door behind her.

The room no longer reeked of the pungent aroma of onions; each one of them now removed. The duchess looked healthier, propped up on a pillow with a veil of shiny hair and brilliant blue eyes. Sitting on top of her nightgown was the spectacular green emerald on the gold chain.

'Your Grace,' Rose said, curtsying. 'Can I get you some breakfast?'

'Take a seat, Rose Porter.'

Rose sat in the chair closest to the bed and folded her hands in her lap. 'You're looking well today.'

'I'm much better now. The warm weather is helping.'

'It's glorious outside. Perhaps I could move you to a chair on the verandah so you can enjoy the fresh air.'

The duchess leant forward and snatched at Rose's wrist so violently that Rose gasped. 'I warned you, parlourmaid, to stay away from my husband.'

Rose winced as the woman's nails dug into her skin with a vice-like grip.

'I know he's been intimate with someone! I know he lies with another woman. I can smell it on him.'

'Your Grace, you're hurting me.'

'It's the same perfume you wear. Peonies. He reeks of it.'

'Your Grace, I assure you, I have not been intimate with your husband.' *Not by choice, anyway,* she wanted to add.

'Then why does he have you on his skin? Why do his clothes smell of you, harlot?' She thrust Rose's arm away in disgust and turned away. To the wall, she said, 'He has been coming in here of late. All I can smell is you.'

She turned back to Rose and there was such vehemence in her voice and such loathing in her eyes it made Rose shrink into the chair. 'I am to give him his heir, parlourmaid. Not you! I have the emerald to pass down. You keep away from him.'

Rose was so shocked, all she could do was let her mouth gape open.

'Get out! I don't ever want to see you again.'

Rose leapt from the chair and quickly left the room. The nail marks were still visible on her arm as she darted out the door, past the duke on the verandah and down the steps. She didn't bother clearing away the breakfast tray. She would come back for it at morning tea.

Her mind whirred with a thousand questions as she pushed the trolley down the hill to first class.

Was someone on the station being intimate with the duke? *Someone who smelt of peonies?*

It was the same perfume Rose wore every day, but why would he smell of it? Why would it be all over his clothes and skin? Rose and the duke never touched; they'd barely been civil in weeks. It hardly seemed possible that the scent could have come from her.

And yet, if not from her, then whom?

Rose had her suspicions but the match was so unlikely. She would never have placed the two in the same room together, let alone intimate in the same bed. All she knew was the day would drag before she got the chance to find out.

Chapter Twenty-Three

It was well after nine when Rose heard Bessie's shoes on the verandah outside. The door opened and moonlight spilled into the room.

Bessie gave a start when she saw Rose sitting on the bed. 'Oh, God!' she exclaimed, clutching her chest. 'You gave me a fright. What are you doing here in the dark?'

Rose stared at her.

'Are you all right? We missed you at dinner.' Bessie lit the oil lamp and stooped to peer into Rose's face. 'Are you ill again?'

'Tell me you haven't been,' Rose said.

Bessie straightened. 'Haven't been what?'

'Wearing my perfume then sleeping with the duke.'

Bessie opened her mouth to speak then closed it. She turned, reached for her cigarettes on the bedside table and lit one. She exhaled a plume of smoke and sat on her bed.

'Do you not have anything to say?' Rose pressed with thinly veiled disappointment.

'Well, which part are you angry at? That I wore your perfume or that I slept with him?'

'For goodness' sake!'

'It's not like you can talk, Rose. You've been sneaking off to bed with the carpenter. Don't think I haven't seen you.'

It was Rose's turn to fumble for words.

'I worked it out ages ago, that night when I woke and you were sneaking out. You said you were going for a walk, but I mean, really, a walk? In the cold? At eleven at night? You didn't come back for hours and I knew you were up to something. I followed you one time, and I saw you disappear into the bush with him.'

Rose closed her eyes for a moment then opened them again. 'How long have you known?'

'For weeks,' Bessie said.

'Why didn't you say anything?'

'Because you're my friend and I would never pry like that. Your business is your own.'

Rose climbed off her bed and went to sit beside Bessie. Bessie stubbed her cigarette on the window sill, opened the window and flicked it out.

'I'm sorry,' Rose said, reaching for her hand. 'I didn't mean to pry.'

'But you did.'

'I know. And I've been no better.'

Bessie's face softened.

'How long have you and the duke...?'

'About six weeks. It started a few days after you were unwell with your stomach upset. Do you remember?'

How could Rose forget? It was the day the duke had forced himself on her and the afternoon she'd first made love to Thomas. It was the day that had changed everything for her.

'I was passing by his cottage one afternoon and he called me over to the verandah. He asked if I'd come by at midnight with a glass of warm milk as he was having trouble sleeping. So I did. That night I took him the milk and well, it turns out it wasn't milk he was after.' Bessie smiled sheepishly.

'So after Thomas and I leave at eleven each night, you sneak out too, at midnight?'

'Yes. But I never take as long as you. The duke is quick and I don't

212

have as far to walk. I always hear you come in before dawn. You spend a lot of time with the carpenter.'

Rose dropped her gaze to Bessie's hands. They were soft and smooth, the tea tree oil having done its job. 'The duke must like your new hands.'

'He does. And he likes your perfume.'

Rose looked up. Even in the dim light, she saw Bessie's cheeks burn.

'I didn't mean to steal from you. Honestly. It's just that when you were working in the hospital, he told me that he missed your scent. So I thought...' She shrugged. 'A spray here and there wouldn't hurt. It makes him happy.'

'Bessie, the duke is married,' Rose said. 'The duchess knows someone has been intimate with him. She can smell the peony on his clothes. She thinks it's me.'

Bessie looked horrified. 'Did you get into trouble? Are you going to be fired?'

'I don't know. She threatened to have me sent back to Bethnal Green last time. I don't know what she'll do now. But Bessie, if you're caught, Miss Dalton will fire you without pay or references.'

'I won't be caught. And if I am, the duke will protect me. He told me that he and the duchess aren't intimate anymore, that he's falling in love with me. When he leaves for England, he's going to take me with him. I'll be employed as the duchess's lady maid so that we can still be together every night. They don't share a bed, you know. All that sickliness repulses him.'

'I don't think he's well in the mind,' Rose said gently. 'The isolation is affecting him. You shouldn't trust what he says.'

'Are you jealous?' Bessie narrowed her eyes. 'Because I don't think that's fair. You have your carpenter.'

Rose sighed. 'I'm not jealous. I'm worried for you.'

Bessie's expression softened. 'You don't have to be. I'm happy, Rose, the happiest I've ever been. The duke wants me at Somersby Castle with him. He's promised me new clothes and a huge bedroom. He said he might even introduce me to the king. And the duchess need not know a thing. It's perfect.'

Rose didn't know what to say. How could she make Bessie see that none of this was perfect? Taking a scullery maid home to Somersby Castle to pose as the duchess's lady maid would fool no one, least of all the duchess herself. She would see right through the façade.

'Tell me about Mr Van Cleeve,' Bessie said, lying back on her bed.

Rose lay down on the narrow sliver of space beside her so that their shoulders were touching. They both stared up at the ceiling. 'Well, he's gentle and caring and he has a wonderful heart. He's a little older than me, by six years, I think.'

'Is he your first?'

Rose flushed. 'Yes.'

'The duke isn't my first,' Bessie said confidently. 'My first was the teacher who lived next door to us in Leura. He was twice my age.'

'We plan to marry.'

'Oh that's sweet,' Bessie said. 'Did he ask you?'

'Well, not properly, but we talk of it all the time.'

'I always did think Mr Van Cleeve was a lovely chap. A bit quiet for me, but lovely all the same. The duke isn't gentle at all. It's always over very quickly. I don't mind. I'm sure the more time we spend together, the gentler he will be.'

'Does the duchess not hear you?'

'He puts valerian root in her milk before bed. She doesn't hear a thing.'

They talked well into the evening about Thomas and the duke. They spoke until they were free of their burdens and there were no secrets left.

Despite her misgivings about Bessie's affair, Rose found it difficult to chastise. She'd been breaking the rules since the first day, falling for Thomas—an attraction that should have been quelled but was allowed to flourish as if the rules didn't apply to her. Who was she to judge?

At eleven, Thomas came for her.

'Take your uniform and stay with him the night,' Bessie said as Rose pulled her boots on. 'There's no need to rush back here. You can go straight to the kitchen in the morning at sun up and no one will know.'

Rose considered the idea as she tightened the laces.

'Go on,' Bessie urged. 'I'll cover for you. Now that we have similar secrets, we can look out for each other.'

Rose relented with a smile. 'Okay, I'll stay the night.' She collected her uniform, clean undergarments, hairbrush and diary and placed them into an empty pillowcase. She left her perfume on the bedside table, unsure she would ever wear it again.

'Rose,' Bessie said as Rose moved towards the door.

'Yes.'

'I'm so happy for you.'

'Thank you, Bessie.'

'Are you happy for me?'

Rose hesitated. 'I am.' But even as she said it, she wasn't sure it was the truth.

* * *

'So Bessie knows about us?'

'Apparently for some time.'

'Will she say anything?' Thomas looked worried.

'I can trust her.'

'And she's sleeping with the duke?'

'Yes.'

Thomas let out a low whistle as he opened the door to his cottage and they stepped inside. 'Does the duchess know?'

'She knows he's been with another woman. Bessie's been wearing my peony perfume. The duchess can smell it on him. She thinks it's me.'

Thomas's face grew dark.

'I promise you it's not.'

'No, I didn't...' He turned away with a look of vague weariness. 'I don't think you've been intimate with him, obviously. I just don't want you to get involved. He's trouble. We'll all be better off once he and his wife are gone.'

Rose knew what he was saying. Even though she hadn't told him about that awful morning in the duke's bedroom and what he had almost done to her, Thomas was no fool. He sensed something had happened, something that had frightened her, and he knew it had to do with the duke.

'He's promised to take Bessie to Somersby Castle with him when he

215

leaves. He will employ her as the duchess's lady's maid so they can still be together.'

'Is that so?' His face was perfectly still.

'Do you think he will?'

'I don't know what goes through that man's head.'

'I worry for Bessie. I feel uneasy about it all.'

'Maybe the duke does love her,' he said fairly. 'Maybe he intends to do the right thing. We can't tell from the outside what goes on between two people.'

'Something's not right.'

'Be that as it may, but I don't want to spend our night talking of them.' He took the pillowcase from her hand, placed it on the bed and slid his arms around her waist.

She sank into his embrace. 'What *would* you like to do?'

'I can think of many things, Rose, perhaps all too unsavoury for your innocence.'

She laughed. 'I'm not as innocent as you think.'

He ran a hand down her neck and across her collarbone, his touch so delicate it made her shiver. 'But that's what I like about you. You're brave and strong-willed and yet completely vulnerable.'

'I don't know that that's entirely true.'

'Just know that it makes me want you in ways I can't even describe.'

A bubbling happiness welled up inside her. 'And yet the rules tell us we're wrong.'

'It's the rules that are wrong, Rose.'

Seized by something wildly sensual, she kissed him, feeling his heart beat hard against her chest. She pulled him towards her onto the bed and they rushed to remove clothes and shoes, her petticoat and stockings.

It wasn't long before he was moving against her and she had never felt anything as natural as this—Thomas's skin pressed on hers, so close she thought she would disappear into him. It was like stepping off a cliff; free-falling and uninhibited.

Afterwards, he slept a deep, solid sleep. She watched the gentle rise and fall of his chest, his face handsome in repose and it dawned on her. This man was her everything. He was her love, her oxygen, her night and day. And where there was love as addictive as this, there was always further to fall. She was falling as hard and fast as she could ever have thought possible and it terrified her.

She ran her hands over the contours of his face; the straight nose and strong jaw, across skin kissed by the sun and lashes so long they curled at the ends. *You are beautiful,* she thought. *Strong and beautiful and mine.*

She rested her head beside his, pulled his arm around her and fell into a sea of scattered dreams.

* * *

Rose was up long before a velvet dawn graced the sky.

She lit the lantern and curled up beside Thomas with her diary. She had written two pages, her pen scratching against the paper when Thomas stirred beside her, his hand settling on her thigh.

'Hello there,' he said, opening his eyes.

'Hello.'

'Did you sleep well?'

'I did.'

'You didn't for long; just a few hours.'

It was true and she felt exhausted for it, but her mind would hardly settle. 'I'm all right. A little tired.'

'You were tired last night too.' He reached for the diary and put it to one side. 'Come, my Rose. You need to sleep. There's still a few hours before you're due in the kitchen.'

She burrowed down into the blankets beside him and rested her head against his chest. She heard the light thud of his heartbeat against her temple.

'I'm glad you're staying the night,' he said softly into her hair. 'No time-watching, no rushing off before dawn.'

'I wish it could be like this all the time,' she said.

'It will be. One day, I promise.'

'Have you ever been in love, Thomas?'

'Before you, no. You're my first love, Rose.' He smiled. 'You caught me quite by surprise, actually. That day when I found you in my workshop and you bumped your head on the underside of the bench. I wanted to burst out with laughter. It was the cutest thing.'

She swatted him.

'I don't think I've ever stopped thinking about you since that day. And I don't know much about love, but I know enough to know this feels different to anything I've felt before.'

Rose understood what he was saying. It was exactly how she felt, as though she was existing in an elusive dream, suspended in reality. It was terrifying and thrilling, the future tainted with uncertainty while brimming with promise. She had so few answers, felt the station and its rules squeezing her; trapped and freed all at the same time.

She gave herself up to fatigue and drifted to sleep in his arms. When dawn broke and the sun smudged the horizon, they woke, made love and he eventually let her go so she could dress for work. It was a glimpse of what life could be like if they just hung on long enough.

Chapter Twenty-Four

Bessie was already in the kitchen when Rose arrived at six. She threw Rose a wink and Rose smiled back.

The duke's breakfast was still on the stove so Mrs March ushered Rose across the road to help set up the dining room with the other parlourmaids. When she returned, the greasy smell of bacon and fried eggs hit her like an avalanche and her stomach turned.

'What's the matter?' Mrs March barked, jabbing her hands onto her hips. 'Something wrong with my food?'

'No. Just tired,' Rose muttered.

Mrs March thrust a teapot into Rose's hands. 'Go to bed earlier then. Now get the duke's food onto the trolley before it spoils.'

Rose did as she was told, pushing the trolley out of the kitchen, past the laundry for fresh linen and up the hill to the duke's cottage. He was sitting at the bureau writing a letter when she arrived. He looked up and waved his hand absentmindedly for her to begin setting the table.

She carried in the tray and set it down. She laid out his toast and teapot, the spreads and cutlery, watching the back of him as he leant forward to write.

It occurred to her now that there were other reasons why their relationship was strained. It was not solely because of the incident that had taken place in his bedroom weeks earlier, but rather his focus had been diverted elsewhere. He'd found an outlet for all that pent-up mental and sexual frustration and it was no longer directed at her.

'Breakfast is ready, Your Grace,' she said, hands clasped in front of her.

'Thank you,' he said formally.

He set down the pen and joined her at the table while she held the chair out for him.

'Will that be all, Your Grace?'

'That will be all.'

'I'll tend to your room now.'

'Rose,' he said.

'Yes.'

'The duchess is recovering. We may be able to travel soon. I'll confirm with the doctor then you may prepare the suitcases.'

'Very well,' Rose said. 'Will there be two travelling or *three*?' The words were out before she could stop them.

He met her eyes but it was impossible to tell what he was thinking. 'That will be all.'

She gave him a stiff curtsey and retreated to his room. The linen caught the brunt of her disapproval as she ripped it from the bed, bundling it up to take outside. On the verandah, she beat the pillows and placed the dirty linen on the bottom shelf of the trolley, catching a whiff of peony as she did so.

Returning to the room with the pillows and fresh linen, she bent to collect his chamber pot and the strong smell of ammonia collided with her so intensely, her stomach heaved and she ran with the pot outside. With seconds to spare, she made it to the railing and vomited violently into the garden below.

The duke was outside in an instant. 'Rose? Goodness, are you okay? Give me that.' He took the offending chamber pot and placed it down the other end of the verandah, far from her.

'I'm terribly sorry, Your Grace. I don't know what came over me.' She wiped saliva from her mouth.

'It's perfectly fine. Come back inside.' He guided her into the living room and sat her down at the breakfast table, kneeling in front of her.

The smell of bacon turned her stomach again and she put her fingers to her mouth.

'Rose, you're as white as a sheet. Let me get you some water.' He poured her a glass from the jug on the table. 'Have you had anything to eat? You might be hungry. I'll fix you dry toast.'

Rose took the water but shook her head to the food. 'No, thank you. Please, I'm embarrassed.'

'There's no need to be. Just sit for a moment.'

Her skin had grown clammy and she was flushing from her head to her toes with humiliation. She sipped the water, cold against her raw throat.

'Have you been feeling ill lately? The stomach flu perhaps.'

'I've been lacking sleep. I'm sure that's all it is.'

He nodded. 'Perhaps you should take the rest of the day off. I can speak to Miss Dalton on your behalf.'

She shook her head. 'That won't be necessary. I'm fine, really. The water is helping.'

He was still looking worriedly at her.

'I should finish your bedroom, Your Grace.'

'Don't worry about my bedroom.'

'But the sheets. Your bed needs to be made.'

'I can do it. Stay here and get some colour back in your cheeks.'

Rose knew that if Miss Dalton, or anyone else for that matter, had walked in at that precise moment and seen a parlourmaid drinking at the breakfast table while the Duke of Northbury made his own bed, they would have dropped dead from the horror.

Rose forced herself to climb to her feet, take several deep breaths and walk into the duke's bedroom. 'Your Grace.'

'Now, Rose, I've got this,' he said defiantly, struggling to spread the sheet out on the mattress. 'I just need to pull it a little here and...'

'Please, let me.' She took the sheet from his hands. 'I'm feeling much better.'

He searched her with intense blue eyes. 'Are you sure?'

'Yes.'

He stepped to the side and watched her as she laid the sheet down and tucked the edges beneath the mattress. She spread the top sheet out next followed by the coverlet and the pillows.

After some time, the duke said softly, 'I'm sorry for what I did to you in here.'

Rose stopped.

'I wasn't myself. I mean, it's not something I've ever done before, forcing myself on a lady.'

She gave him a small, conciliatory nod and continued fitting the bed.

'She's a nice girl, the kitchen maid. It's surprising how much I enjoy her company. She's just from the scullery after all, but she makes me laugh.' His cheeks grew crimson and he turned away quickly, clearing his throat. 'Well, if you're feeling better then, I'll take my leave.' He bowed slightly and turned for the door.

'The duchess thinks it's me,' she called out.

He paused in the doorway and sighed resolutely. 'Indeed she does.'

'I don't want to lose my job.'

'You won't lose your job, Rose. I'll speak to her.'

Rose nodded gratefully. The duke gave her a small smile and left the room.

* * *

'They passed the decree yesterday. All arriving vessels are subject to mandatory quarantine because of Spanish Flu. Five boats arrived today and they say there are four more waiting outside the Heads.' Thomas sliced a piece of cheese and ate it off the knife. 'I spent all day pitching tents. The unhealthy ground has completely transformed. You wouldn't recognise it if you saw it now.'

Rose nibbled a plain cracker at the little table in Thomas's cottage. It was almost midnight and they were having a late supper. Bessie had sent them off with a small basket of food and a flask of gin.

'They say we're at almost twenty-five hundred passengers, even though we only have capacity for half of that. The situation has gotten so bad here they're sending the police force to patrol the station's perimeter to ensure patients don't try to leave. The soldiers say the flu is running rampant in Europe, far worse than here.'

Rose yawned deeply and popped a hand over her mouth. 'Forgive me, Thomas. I didn't mean to be so rude.'

'Oh, Rose,' Thomas said, putting the knife down. 'You can barely keep your eyes open. And you've been listening to me waffle on for almost an hour. Come, change into your shift and lie down.'

'No, please, finish your story.'

'Don't worry about my story. You need to sleep. The late nights and early mornings are getting to you, I can tell.'

'I am quite tired,' she admitted, letting him help her up and onto the bed. As he assisted her out of her tunic and into her shift, she told him how she'd become ill at the duke's cottage earlier that morning. 'I was about to clean out his chamber pot and I couldn't hold it back. I was sick all over the front garden.'

'Was it something you ate?'

'I don't think so.'

'You haven't been near the hospital have you? There's been a small cholera outbreak.'

'I've been inoculated, but no, I haven't.'

He helped her beneath the covers and she laid her head on his pillow, breathing in the scent of him. It was about the only thing she could stomach.

Thomas stroked her hair and she closed her eyes, feeling monumental exhaustion wash over her.

'Promise me you'll see the matron if you still feel unwell tomorrow.'

'I will,' she said sleepily.

He brought her hand to his mouth and kissed it. 'I don't like to see you like this. It worries me.'

'I'll be fine in the morning. Will you wake me so I'm not late for work?'

'I will wake you, my love.'

She drifted away after that, lulled to sleep by the soporific sound of the sea.

* * *

The next morning, Thomas shook her gently awake and she opened her eyes to a peach sunrise tiptoeing across the cottage floor. She dragged herself up, washed and dressed for work, and Thomas encouraged her to eat some crackers from Bessie's basket. Her stomach still churned and she told herself that if she didn't inhale while serving food or while changing the chamber pot, she could keep the contents of her stomach down.

The duchess called her into her room during the lunch service and asked for a pot of tea and a scone. Her skin looked rosier and her eyes brighter, further signs of convalescence at long last. Her tone was softer too, in comparison with their previous encounter, when she'd referred to Rose as a harlot and had left the scars of her nails in her wrist.

Rose could only deduce that the duke had spoken with her, clearing her of any wrongdoing, but how he had explained away the peony on his clothes she couldn't be sure. For now, her job seemed safe and she was relieved not to be in hot water with Miss Dalton.

The day dragged and four o'clock finally came where she had the longest gap in service, between afternoon tea and dinner. Thomas wasn't in his workshop and Bessie was busy at the sinks under the steely watch of Mrs March. Rose climbed the hill to the female staff quarters and let herself into her cottage.

She stole a brief nap, wrote in her diary then glanced at the growing pile of clothes and undergarments next to her bed that needed laundering. There had been barely any time to get her washing done. Between service with the duke and nights spent with Thomas, she felt like she existed in an endless tailspin.

She sat on the edge of the bed and began to sort through the pile, putting her intimate items—petticoats, corsets, underwear and stockings—aside to wash separately while the rest of her dresses and uniforms could go to the laundry.

It wasn't until she'd finished sorting her clothes that she realised it had been some time since she'd had to wash her bleeding cloths. The room ground to a sickening halt and something cold reached into her bones as she stretched her memory back. Four weeks... Six weeks... Eight weeks. How long had it been?

Rose rushed to her bedside table and pulled opened the bottom drawer. Down beneath the pairs of gloves and rolls of stockings lay a wad of clean bleeding cloths. She stared at them. They stared back. And it occurred to her.

She couldn't remember the last time she'd bled.

Chapter Twenty-Five

EMMA 2019

'That smells wonderful!'

Matt beamed as he stirred gravy in the pan. 'Roast chicken is about the only thing I do well. Everything else you eat at your own risk.'

Emma laughed. 'You're one up on me. I burn water.'

He turned the heat down and checked the chicken resting in the tray. 'This should be ready to carve soon.'

Emma climbed down off the stool and moved around to the cupboards and draws, collecting cutlery, plates and napkins. Her knowledge of his kitchen was improving with each new visit and visits were become increasingly frequent.

They had fallen into a bubble of spending their free days together, lying around in bed, drinking coffee or eating at the cafés along Manly's Corso.

They spent long hours reading Rose's diaries and the amount of stolen treasures they'd acquired from the station, in moments of temporary madness, now littered his coffee table. It was against station policy to take archives off site without permission, but they couldn't help themselves. Rose had slipped deep under their skin. How addictive it had become to leap into her diary pages and transport themselves to her world.

And at the end of the day, it was for Gwendoline. Emma never lost sight of that. Eastgardens Aged Care had improved their patient security but without the wanderings, Gwendoline had become increasingly frustrated and prone to greater slips from reality. The doctors told Emma that her condition was worsening, but Emma felt it was more than that. It was the station her grandmother longed for; memories she chased but couldn't catch hold of, something from her past that she was trying to get back to.

Matt served chicken and salad onto plates while Emma poured the wine. They ate at his dining table and talked about their day in a rhythm so natural that it still surprised her. It was almost *too* effortless; an inexplicable perfection that she had to remind herself not to try to understand but rather to just let be.

They finished eating, stacked the dishwasher and carried their wines to the coffee table. Sprawled across the table top were Rose's diaries; the puzzle pieces of a mystery they were still trying to solve.

They had read the first four cover to cover—June 1918 to October 1918. Settling against the couch, they sipped their wine and Matt retrieved the last diary, placing it in his lap. He turned to the first page and after just a few words Emma sensed they'd finally stumbled across something significant; something they'd been waiting to read for months.

13th October, 1918

I write to you today, dear diary, as the carrier of a burdensome secret, one that has stolen the ground from underneath me. I do not consider myself a naïve girl, uneducated or lacking in sense, but I was naïve about this.

We ignored the rules, we pushed the boundaries, we gave in to our indulgences. How selfish lovers can be. Now I bear the weight of that selfishness. I have carried this secret for weeks now and I cannot begin to tell you how heavy it is, crushing me inside.

Every day I am ill to the stomach and exhaustion pervades my body. I cannot stand the smell of food, nor the taste, and can barely hold down a few sips of water. Hiding this from everyone has become almost as weari-

some as the sickness itself. But I cannot tell them what I've done, this sorry state of affairs I've fallen into.

In any other scenario, I would think this a miracle. I would be over-joyed at the changes to my body, irrelevant of how laborious they have become. I would welcome the strange stretching and tugging inside my stomach and the way my breasts have swelled. I would look forward to the next nine months with anticipation of the blessed new arrival.

But how can I? I'm terrified! I can't tell anyone the truth. I haven't even told my beloved. He would never look at me the same way again for I've ruined everything for us. We'll both be fired and kicked off the station at a time when the outside world is as destitute as the Western Front.

What am I to do? There will come a time when I will no longer be able to hide it. And God help me when that time comes.

Rose

Matt placed the diary down on his lap and let out a breath. 'I'm guessing Rose has fallen pregnant with Gwendoline.'

'Yes,' Emma replied. 'She doesn't say it explicitly but it's obvious. And she's terrified.'

'She mustn't have been thinking straight either. She took a risk writing these words. It could have gotten her fired if they'd fallen into the wrong hands.'

Emma took the diary from Matt's lap and ran her fingertips over the words. The fear and panic was jumping off them. *You must have been so scared*, she thought of her great-grandmother.

'She kept it a secret from her lover,' Matt said.

'Though I'm not sure why. I always got the impression he was a nice man, whoever he was. He would have understood.'

'Times were different back then. A woman falling pregnant out of wedlock was not viewed upon favourably. Society thought of them as whores and most were spirited off to homes for unmarried mothers until they gave birth and their child was adopted out. Rose had a lot to be concerned about, including rejection by her lover.'

'She was worried they would both lose their jobs. It clears up one aspect at least. Her lover was definitely an employee.'

'And the rules were clear for employees back then,' Matt said. 'The station was no place to raise a family. There was no school and they didn't have funding to feed extra mouths. Rose would have been dismissed instantly for falling pregnant.'

'Yet something transpired in her favour because she gave birth to my grandmother and remained on the station for another seven years. And Gran has always maintained that the *three* of them left in 1926. Not two, *three*. I'm assuming the third person was her father.'

'Who we now know wasn't a passenger. He worked there.'

'We need to know who she fell pregnant to and who Gran was waiting for by the wharf. That person arriving on a boat.'

'It could have been anyone.' Matt chewed his lip. 'Her father is the missing link.'

'I'm certain he's not the duke. He didn't work there and Rose would have hinted at it by now.'

Matt reached for the diary and turned to the next page, ready to read again, but it was blank. He flicked through the remaining pages and found nothing. 'This is the last entry. She wrote one page and didn't write anything else.'

Emma leant across him for a better look. 'Did we leave any diaries at the station, ones that we haven't read yet?'

'There were five in total. This was the last one.'

'How are we going to know what happened to Rose?'

'I don't know.'

Emma pursed her lips determinedly. 'I'll visit Gwendoline tomorrow before work and speak to her again. But I hate to admit it, without the wanderings, she's become despondent, like we've taken something away from her. She hardly eats and when she talks it's just confusion.'

Matt reached out and stroked her bare shoulder, a gesture that still threw her with force and she realised again, with that simple touch, just how much she was falling for him.

He sat up and reached for a photograph they'd taken from Rose's suitcase, a black and white shot of two young women. It was Rose and Bessie Briar, taken in August 1918, according to the inscription on the back. They were smiling brightly into the camera, Rose in her black housekeeping uniform and Bessie in a brown dress and apron, a bonnet taming a tumble of fair curls.

'This was taken out the front of the first-class kitchen,' Matt said. 'I recognise the building.'

Emma stared at the photograph, searching it for clues, wondering who might have taken it. Rose was incredibly beautiful, with thick dark hair twisted away in a knot at the nape of her neck. She had a warm smile, slender shoulders and was clutching her friend's arm as if they had been struggling to contain their laughter when the camera clicked.

The moment of joy was more candid than one might expect of an early twentieth-century photograph, when serious expressions were customary. It was obvious she'd felt comfortable in that immediate circle of three—herself, Bessie and the mystery person behind the lens; her lover, perhaps, whomever that was.

'What I wouldn't give to step inside this photograph back to 1918 to ask her what happened,' Emma said. 'Who did she fall pregnant to? Who was Gwendoline's father? And what made them run suddenly in 1926?'

'It's all linked.'

'Yes. And I hate to admit it because it makes everything more complicated, but the duke is part of it. We can't discount him.'

'I have an idea.'

Emma looked up.

'It's a little crazy but I think it could help.'

'What?'

'We should take Gwendoline to the Quarantine Station.'

Emma frowned slightly.

'Hear me out,' he said quickly. 'I think it would be good for her to be back in the place she's been trying to find. We could take her to the wharf. It might trigger memories and get her talking. She has the answers in her head, we just have to get them out.'

Emma was unsure if she loved or hated the idea. 'I don't know, Matt.'

'We can take it as slow as we need to.'

'It's a lot of walking.'

He raised an eyebrow. 'She goes on night walks all the way to Foreshore Road.'

Emma punched him. 'You know what I mean. I don't think she's physically up to it.'

'The shuttle bus will be there. I'll speak to Ted. He'll be happy to drive us around. And the team will love it. We never get people like Gwendoline coming by anymore. Most of her generation are gone.'

Emma sighed. The idea was plausible, she just worried about pushing her grandmother beyond her limits. But what if this was Gwendoline's last chance to see the station, her last chance to make peace with her memories and to help Emma understand them? What if tomorrow Gwendoline was gone and Emma was left with a pile of puzzle pieces and the knowledge that she had failed at helping her grandmother sort through them?

If that were the case, the idea made sense.

'I suppose I could speak to the nursing home. Though their security policy is pretty strict now.'

'We can only ask.'

'Okay,' Emma said with a smile. 'Let's do it.'

He pulled her into him and hugged her. She closed her eyes, melding into his chest. His shirt smelt quintessentially male, like cologne and soap.

'When's your next day off?' he asked, moving a strand of hair from her eyes.

'Tuesday.'

'Perfect. Tuesdays are quiet. It won't overwhelm her with too many people.'

'Do you have Tuesday off?'

'No, but I can still take you both around.'

She smiled at him and squeezed his hand. 'Thank you. It means a lot that you're doing this. It always has.'

'At first the mystery got me, but then you got me, Em.'

His hazel eyes caught the dining room light, flecks of green and gold. She leant forward to kiss him, the feel of him on her lips sending her stomach somersaulting. He responded with such need that it took little more than a moment for clothes to be shed and 1918 was temporarily shelved.

Chapter Twenty-Six

Anastasia Thornbury had qualms about releasing Gwendoline for the day. Their new patient care policy allowed for day release but only under exceptional circumstances. According to Anastasia, a visit to the Q Station could hardly be deemed exceptional but, after some convincing, and after Emma signed a waiver, she relented.

On the following Tuesday, a morning that augured a warm spring day, Emma collected her grandmother from her room, bundled her into the car and drove her north to the Q Station.

As they followed the flow of traffic along the Sydney Harbour Bridge, Emma explained where they were going and her grandmother responded, first with an audible intake of breath, then a small cry of nervous glee that made Emma smile.

They arrived at the Q Station carpark and she swung into a spot. Matt emerged from the reception building to greet them, opening the car door to help Gwendoline out. 'It's nice to see you again,' he said.

Gwendoline peered intently at his face. 'Have we met before?'

'Yes, at Eastgardens, though only briefly.'

'You remind me of someone,' she said, reaching out to touch his cheek with her fingers. 'Goodness me, you're just like him. You have his hazel eyes.'

Emma saw the unease on Matt's face. She stepped in, took Gwendoline's hand and offered him a smile. 'I'm sorry. She has a habit of doing that.'

Matt smiled back, but his troubled look remained.

Emma looped her arm through Gwendoline's and together with Matt, they took sure and steady steps towards reception.

Once inside, Emma was surprised at how many people were waiting for them. She saw the receptionist, Joan, the tour ladies from the museum and Ted, the shuttle bus driver, along with a few faces she didn't recognise, including a man in a suit who stepped forward to greet them.

'I'm Anthony, the station director,' he said, shaking Emma's hand. 'We are so pleased to have your grandmother visit us. When Matt told us about her story, we wanted to be here personally to greet her. We don't get visits from people like Gwendoline anymore.'

'Thank you,' Emma said. 'That's very kind.'

'And this is for you, Gwendoline,' Joan said, bending down to pass her a small posy of red roses. 'We heard these were your favourite.'

'Thank you, dear,' Gwendoline said, taking the roses and attention in her stride. 'They are indeed.'

'We have so much to learn about your time here,' Rebecca from the museum said. 'We'd love to include some of yours and Rose's experiences in our tours.'

There were lots of nodding heads and eager faces.

'I'm sure you have much to see today,' Anthony said, clapping his hands together. 'Why don't you make a start and we can arrange a time later to meet with you both. The shuttle bus is yours for the day.'

'And there's a packed lunch in there too,' added Joan proudly.

They took turns shaking Gwendoline's hand as she moved along the line like station royalty, eyes bright and speech intelligible, smiling, chatting and handing back the flowers to place in water until she returned. The station, like the fountain of youth, seemed a temporary cure for Gwendoline's ailments.

Outside by the shuttle, Emma helped her up the steps and into a seat. She reached for Matt as he moved down the aisle to take the seat behind them.

'Thank you for arranging all that,' she said, touching his hand.

Matt smiled. 'Hope it wasn't too much excitement for her.'

'Are you kidding? She loved it.'

Ted closed the door and the bus rumbled to life. 'Where's our first stop today?'

'The wharf, please,' Emma said decisively, wanting to get straight down to business.

Ted navigated away from the reception building and along Wharf Road, rolling past first and second classes and eventually coming to rest on the gravelly road outside the shower blocks.

They helped Gwendoline down from the bus as the sun burned fiercely and the water in the cove shone like crystals.

Gwendoline took a few steps along the gravel and turned in a slow circle, taking in the shower blocks, the autoclaves, the former boiler room—now a restaurant and café—the museum and wharf.

'Yes, yes,' she said quietly. 'Oh, how I remember this.' A small smile spread across her lips. 'After passengers had their health and status classified, they came here to the showers for a scrub down. Their luggage was transported on these tracks. They called it the funicular railway.' She turned again, pointing her finger. 'Autoclaves for luggage fumigation. The boiler room. The inhalation chamber. It all looks so different and yet in some ways, it hasn't changed at all.'

'Did you used to come down here as a child?' Emma asked.

'I did,' Gwendoline said. 'I used to play all around here. I'd sit by the boiler room with the other children and watch the women go in and out of the showers. We were allowed to do that, you see, play anywhere we liked, except the hospital and isolation. But that never stopped us.' She chuckled at some private thought. 'We used to sneak in and out of there all the time.'

'Did you play at the beach?'

Gwendoline turned and squinted in the direction of the cove. 'Yes, with my mother. She adored the cove. She always said it was the place she fell in love.'

'With your father?' Matt asked.

'Well, that's another story.'

'Can you tell us?' Emma pressed.

'She didn't want me to know. She worried constantly, you see. But I eventually found out what happened.'

Matt and Emma exchanged a look.

'I waited and waited for that boat to come.'

Emma's anticipation peaked. 'Yes, which boat, Grandma? Who was on the boat? Who were you waiting for?'

Gwendoline made a small sound as a trickle of sweat slid from her temple down her face. 'Goodness, that sun is warm.' Her shoulders went slack and Emma gripped her elbow.

'Let's get you out of the heat.' She guided her towards the shade of the autoclave building and retrieved a bottle of water from her bag.

Gwendoline took slow, shaky sips. 'Thank you, Catherine. That's better.'

Emma ignored the slip. 'Shall we take a walk to the wharf?'

'Yes, let's do that.'

With Emma on one side and Matt on the other, they led Gwendoline towards the museum and wharf. The sun was on them again as soon as they left the shade of the autoclave.

'We used to jump off here at high tide all the time,' Gwendoline said, pointing towards the end of the wharf. 'Straight into the water! Oh, it was such fun.'

'Did you see many boats come, Grandma?' Emma said, trying to steer them back on track.

'Yes, though from what I recall, they slowed down a little after 1924. The Spanish Influenza threat was over by then and medical research had improved. The boats still came with the sick, don't get me wrong. But we weren't bursting at the seams.' She gazed towards the end of the wharf. 'Those poor souls. They were completely ravaged by the time they walked off those ships. Sometimes death was kinder.'

'Was there any particular boat you liked to come down here and wait for?' Emma urged.

Gwendoline turned to her. 'As a matter of fact, yes,' she said, as though it was the first time she'd been asked the question. 'I used to come down here all the time to wait for it. The big naval ship, the one with the Union Jack flag.'

'The Union Jack flag?'

'It was a lovely boat.'

'Did it have anything to do with the duke?' She suddenly wanted to shake the answers out of her grandmother.

'The duke?' Gwendoline said thoughtfully, as though she could sense the answers close but couldn't quite reach them. 'What do you know of the duke, dear?'

'Not enough. Tell me!'

'Emma,' Matt said.

'What?'

'Calm down.'

'I'm calm!'

He gave her a look. 'We need to get your grandmother out of this heat.'

Emma bit down on her lip, flushing at her bad behaviour. 'Of course. You're right. Come, Grandma. Let's get back on the bus where it's cooler.'

They guided Gwendoline towards the bus, Emma berating herself for letting her impatience bubble over. It wasn't Gwendoline's fault that she couldn't remember. Her mind was deteriorating and these events had taken place almost a century ago. It just seemed that whenever Emma was close to some kind of answer, it was snatched out of her hands before she could grasp it.

Back on the bus in the air-conditioning, they started to cool. Gwendoline looked tired but insisted she wanted to keep going. She stared out the window as they bumped back up Wharf Road towards the former female staff quarters.

'This is where I believe you lived, Grandma,' Emma said, helping Gwendoline down from the bus where a cluster of cottages could be seen through the trees.

'This is all guest accommodation now,' Matt said, 'so it probably looks a little different from when you lived here with Rose.'

'Did you know Rose's friend, Bessie Briar?' Emma asked.

'Bessie Briar. Yes, I'd never met her but I knew her name. I saw it often in stone.'

Emma looked at Matt. 'In stone?'

'Maybe she died.'

'I also didn't live here in these cottages,' Gwendoline said.

Emma gave her a double look. 'What do you mean you didn't live here in these cottages?'

'I didn't live in these cottages.'

Emma frowned. 'But this is where Rose lived, at the female staff quarters. We read so in her diaries. She shared lodgings with Bessie Briar.'

'She may have done so at one stage, Emma dear, but for as long as I can remember I lived in another cottage with her. I didn't live here.'

Emma frowned. It was like connecting one piece of the puzzle only to have another piece removed. 'Okay, so where *did* you live?'

Gwendoline looked around at the cluster of trees. Emma could see her brain trying to work it out. 'Third class. The male staff quarters.'

'You lived in the male staff quarters?'

Gwendoline shook her head and closed her eyes. 'No, no, not in the male quarters, but near there. Oh, my useless brain.'

Emma threw her arm around her and held her close. She felt shameful for pushing her again. 'Let's go back to the bus. We can have a rest and a cold drink.' She guided her to the waiting shuttle and helped her back up the steps.

Once Gwendoline was seated, Emma turned to Matt. 'I think we should take her home. It's hot and she's had enough.'

Matt walked to the back of the shuttle and pulled a cooler bag from a seat. 'Joan packed us lunch. What if we eat and then Ted drives us around for a bit? We could take a look around third class and the former male staff quarters. Gwendoline wouldn't have to leave the bus.'

Emma looked from the cooler bag to her grandmother, who was staring vacantly out the window. 'Okay. Maybe just one more hour, then I'd like to get her back to Eastgardens.'

'Sure.' Matt passed her the bag and he moved to the front of the bus to confer with Ted.

Emma unzipped the bag and pulled out neatly wrapped sandwiches, fruit, slices of vanilla cake and bottles of juice and water. She sat beside Gwendoline and they ate in silence, her grandmother still staring out the window.

After lunch, the bus rumbled to life again and Gwendoline turned to Emma.

'I'm sorry I have trouble remembering. I know how interested you are.'

'It's fine, Grandma. I didn't mean to push you.'

'Your young man is lovely,' she said softly. 'What's his name again?'

'Matt.'

Gwendoline looked out the window. 'He looks exactly like him.'

Emma was about to ask like who when Matt came shuffling down the aisle. 'Ted's going to drive us up to third class. After that, we'll take you back to the car.'

'Okay.'

Lunch perked Gwendoline up. On the drive to third class, she pointed at the window at things that triggered her memory. When they passed the post office peeking through the trees, she burst into a story with complete lucidity.

'If you were from third class doing a transaction at the counter and someone from first class entered, you had to drop everything, leave the post office and allow them to enter and complete their business. Only once they left were you allowed back in to finish. It was a terrible bother if it happened four or five times in a row.'

Emma's mouth fell open and Matt laughed.

'Segregation,' he explained. 'I'd heard of that happening in the post office. Third class and Asiatics weren't allowed in the same room as first class.'

'They took that sort of thing very seriously in those days,' Gwendoline said.

The bus rolled past the former Asiatic dormitories and the outdoor dining rooms.

'Those poor little Chinamen,' she said, face up against the glass, coherent, as if time itself were hurtling her back. 'They would shiver through winter having to eat outside with their bowls of rice. They were the lowest of all classes. Terrible children we were. We would poke fun at their bamboo coolies and pointy beards.'

The third-class accommodation and dining room rushed by and the bus pulled up along a cluster of trees at the end of the Former Third Class Precinct.

'Male staff quarters,' Ted announced cheerfully.

Gwendoline was already rising.

'Are you sure?' Emma said, grabbing her elbow. 'We can just watch from the window.'

Gwendoline gave her a look. 'I don't want to watch from the window. I want to walk.'

They stepped down from the bus as a breeze whipped through the headland. The wind rattled the eucalypts, filling the air with the medicinal smell of their leaves.

Through the trees, Emma spotted a cluster of cottages and Matt explained that they were the former male staff quarters and, like the female quarters, they'd all been converted to guest accommodation.

'Is this where you lived with Rose?' Emma asked.

Gwendoline peered through the trees. She took one step, then another and suddenly her legs were moving with surprising vitality. She led them around broad-leaved paperbarks and Port Jackson figs, past the cottages and to the rear where the perimeter of the station lay; a border of snow white flannel flowers and beyond it, thick bush.

'I lived in there,' she said, pointing towards the trees.

Emma was perplexed. 'You lived in the bush?'

'Not in the bush. I lived in a cottage through there.'

Emma looked at Matt. 'Are there any more cottages out there?'

He shook his head. 'Not that I know of.'

'Grandma,' Emma said gently. 'Perhaps you're mistaken. There's nothing out there but bushland.'

Gwendoline shook her head defiantly. 'I grew up in a cottage through those trees. There was a path that used to take us straight to the cliff on the other side. I lived there with my mother and father until we left in 1926.'

Matt scoured the ground. 'I can't see any path. Maybe it's grown over.'

'Gran, Rose was a first-class housekeeper. She would have lived in the female staff quarters back up near first class. I don't think there's another cottage out here.'

'There is and I grew up in it,' Gwendoline insisted. 'And my mother wasn't a housekeeper.'

'What was she then?'

'A nurse.'

Emma heard Matt gulp audibly behind her. From the corner of her eye she saw him sway. 'Are you okay?' she asked. 'You don't look well.'

He averted his eyes. 'I... I just...' He swallowed several times before speaking. 'Gwendoline, did you say Rose became a nurse?'

'Yes she was a nurse.'

'She didn't just help out in the hospital from time to time? She actually became a nurse?'

'And I thought my hearing was bad,' Gwendoline remarked. 'Yes, dear. She was a nurse until the day she died.'

Matt went white. 'Yes, she was.'

'Matt, what's wrong?' Emma asked.

He shook his head and ran a hand through his hair. 'I just remembered. I have some work I need to get done before I finish today. Is it okay if I leave you with Ted and he'll take you back to the car?'

'Seriously?'

'Yeah.'

'What's going on?'

'Nothing, I just...' He was still pale. 'I've got a heap of stuff to do. I'm sorry. I have to go.'

'Do you want to come to my house after work? We can order some food.'

'I can't.'

'Why?'

'I've got to go, Em.'

She reached out to kiss him goodbye but he turned his face and gave her a small, awkward peck on the cheek. He apologised to Gwendoline and hurried away from them, back through the trees and male staff cottages to third class, until he disappeared completely.

Chapter Twenty-Seven

On the drive back to Eastgardens while Gwendoline slept, Emma was alone with her thoughts. Worried, shifting, rattled thoughts that circled her brain relentlessly.

When she reached the aged care facility and delivered Gwendoline safely back to her room, she tried calling Matt, but his phone went to voicemail. She texted him once, twice then a third time but with no response.

She had a gnawing feeling in the pit of her stomach that he was avoiding her but she didn't know why.

Something had transpired down by the male staff cottages, when Gwendoline had revealed that Rose had given up her housekeeping role to become a full-time nurse on the station. Matt had reacted strongly to this and it had stirred up a fragment of a memory for Emma too, but she couldn't recall why. She and Matt had ploughed through an enormous amount of content in the past weeks and frankly, those pieces were becoming a jumble to reconstruct.

Over the next few days, Matt steadfastly refused to answer her calls and Emma wondered what this mystery had cost her. He wasn't talking to her, Gwendoline was more unsettled than ever and Emma had opened a Pandora's Box to a world that seemed to want to be left alone.

Clearly the people of 1918 didn't want their secrets revealed, otherwise they would have left a trail of breadcrumbs easier to navigate, rather than a pile of diaries, an old suitcase in the back of a museum and a mysterious cottage that *possibly* existed, according to a one-hundred-year-old woman with early-stage dementia. And how the duke fit into it was possibly the greatest mystery of all.

Gwendoline had said she was waiting for the boat with a Union Jack flag. Had she been waiting for the duke? Had he been so in love with Rose that he couldn't keep away? But why would Gwendoline have been waiting for him? And who was her father, the kind and gentle man Rose had fallen pregnant to? What had become of him? What had become of them all?

After three days of agonising silence, Emma's phone rang. She'd stayed back one night at The Coffee Bean to descale the coffee machine when she saw Matt's name light up the screen.

'I know you're wondering what's going on,' he said simply when she answered.

It was an understatement and she kept quiet for fear she would say something regrettable.

'I had some things to sort out.'

'You've been ignoring me.'

There was silence down the line, a small sigh, then, 'Can you meet me at the Q Station tomorrow? There's something I have to show you.'

'Like what?'

'Can you come?'

'I finish work at two. I can come after that.'

'I'll see you then. And Em?'

'Yes.'

'I'm sorry.'

* * *

The next afternoon, Emma turned her car into the Q Station carpark and walked across to reception where Matt was waiting for her. He didn't reach out to take her hand or kiss her.

'Thanks for coming,' he said with crisp politeness.

She didn't know what to say. He looked uncomfortable and tired like he hadn't slept. 'Is everything okay? I don't know what's happened in the last few days, but you've got me worried. Did I do something?'

He didn't offer any reassurances. He just stared at the ground and her heart dropped into her stomach.

'Ted's waiting in the shuttle,' he said. 'He'll drop us near third class.'

'Why third class?'

'There's something you need to see.'

They climbed into the bus and Ted greeted them cheerfully. They sat on opposite seats in silence, Emma staring blankly out the window as the familiar sights of the station rolled by, careful not to look at Matt in case she burst into a torrent of frustration. She was over the games and the heartbreak, had had enough of it to last her a lifetime and yet here she was again with life refusing to be anything but complicated.

Ted dropped them in third class at the former male staff quarters.

Emma watched him pull away and rumble back down the road. 'Isn't he going to wait for us?'

Matt was already walking. 'We're going to be a while.'

Emma jogged to catch up. 'Why did you bring me back here?'

'Because I have something to show you.'

'What?'

'There's so much to this story we don't know yet. We haven't even begun to scratch the surface.'

'Matt! Stop talking in riddles and tell me what's going on.'

They had reached the back of the male staff quarters and he led her to an opening in the bush, close to where they had stood with Gwendoline only days earlier.

'I came back here yesterday to look around again and I found the remnants of an old path. It was overgrown but I could just see it. I spent all day cutting my way through it.'

'And?'

'About a hundred yards to the east, the path emerges onto a clearing; a clifftop that overlooks Sydney Harbour.'

Emma stared at him.

'Em, there's a cottage up there.'

'Just like Gwendoline said?'

'Yes. I looked through the windows. I could make out beds and furniture. I think a family used to live there.'

'A family who left in 1926?'

'Possibly.'

Emma released a breath. 'Gwendoline wasn't confused. She knew exactly what she was saying.'

'It's the cottage she lived in with her parents.'

'Can you take me there?'

Matt reached for her hand but then seemed to think better of it. He indicated for her to follow and they started down the path he had cleared the day before.

It was still wildly overgrown. Saplings and thick weeds had sprung up to push and weave their way across the track. Tiny furry animals scurried away at the sound of their approach and the smell of sunshine wattle and eucalyptus infused the air. A kookaburra gave a discordant laugh somewhere in the treetops and beyond the solitary tempo of the bush, Emma was distinctly aware of civilisation—ferry horns on the harbour and the chug of a seaplane.

They walked for five minutes while Matt led the way, pushing branches aside to allow Emma clear passage. The afternoon sun was hot, bearing down on them so fiercely she felt sweat gathering on her brow.

Finally, after climbing over, dodging and sidestepping a thousand branches, she found herself at the top of a cliff overlooking Sydney Harbour. A splay of bright blue ocean swept below her, dotted with ferries and tilting yachts. Across the water, on headlands lined with colourful mansions were Vaucluse, Rose Bay and Double Bay.

'Wow,' she said.

'It's some view, isn't it?'

'It must be the best of the station.' She felt Matt beside her and wanted to reach out and touch him, to share in the beauty together, but something told her he would pull away if she tried.

He beckoned for her to follow and she turned to see a ramshackle old cottage behind them. Climbers had attempted to claim it long ago, long fingers of tendrils, broad-leafed and tenacious, clinging to the weatherboards.

'The windows are still intact,' Matt explained, 'which is a miracle really, for all the storms this cliff would have endured over time.'

'Why wasn't anyone aware this place was out here?'

'I went through the archive room again. I pulled all the files for 1926 and 1927. In the 1927 records, I found plans to renovate it, then there was a bulldozing proposal. But the station changed management hands around that time and a lot of the old staff left. I guess it fell through the cracks.'

Emma stepped up to a window and placed her face against the glass. Through the thick grime, she could just make out a room beyond, the shape of two beds, a small round table and wardrobe, the remnants of a family that had once lived there. She had a profuse urge to see more.

'Can we get inside?' she asked.

'I don't have a key. I'd have to break open the door.'

'Let's do it,' she said, pushing back from the window.

Matt joined her at the door. Brown paint was peeling and the once-shiny brass handle corroded. He gave the handle a firm jiggle and, when he seemed satisfied that the door wasn't going to oblige, he followed through with two hard shoves with his shoulder.

There was a splitting sound, the lock snapped off and the door flung open. Dust motes spiralled through the air as splinters from the door-jamb flung across the room.

'Watch your step,' Matt said, rubbing his shoulder.

Emma stepped across the threshold. It was a completely different feel from the outside looking in. The air was cool, the smell pungent like rotting floorboards and animals droppings. She felt the room exhale as though it had been closed up and forgotten about for far too long.

She took a few more steps towards the middle and shrieked. A rat scurried from a corner, darting across the floor near her feet and under a bed. The cornices were caked thick with opaque spider webs and the furniture and floor were covered in a dense layer of dust.

Emma's gaze was drawn to the beds first. There was a double bed with a nurse's uniform and cap draped across the end of it and black shoes at the foot. On a single bed were the remnants of stuffed animals, long ago ripped apart and nibbled at by rats and bandicoots.

There was a dusty children's book on the pillow. The corners of the pages had also been gnawed at. Emma picked it up and blew at the cover. *Peter Pan in Kensington Gardens.* She turned it over in her hands and smiled, realising this must have been Gwendoline's, given to her possibly by Rose. There was something decidedly English about it and all around her, despite the condition of the old cottage, with its age and decay, she felt the presence of her grandmother and great-grandmother.

She heard Matt move and looked up. He was inspecting a door at the back of the cottage. 'It looks like a bathroom was added on back here. I can see extension work that wasn't part of the original structure.'

'Gwendoline's father must have put the bathroom in when Rose and Gwendoline moved here.'

Matt fell silent and Emma moved to the kitchenette. In the sink were dishes, any crumbs or scraps long ago eaten by furry intruders. The kitchen table was a clutter of objects—a dusty abacus, the remains of an old school book and a dry bowl and ewer.

There was something pervasively silent about it all which made Emma open a narrow wardrobe as quietly as a thief, careful not to disturb the unspoken balance.

Gently flicking through the hangers, she saw clothes from another era—men's collared shirts, women's skirts and blouses, a child's coat and dresses. All of them smelt strongly of mould and were moth-eaten.

She pushed the clothes along the railing and found a large leather trunk resting on the floor of the wardrobe.

She bent to take a closer look. It must have been a beautiful navy blue once with tan borders and leather handles. The initials *RP* and *TVC* were stamped into the leather.

'Look what I found.' She heaved the large trunk all the way across the floor, leaving a trail through the dust behind her. 'It belongs to Rose and someone with the initials TVC.'

Matt came to her side and bent down to inspect it.

'I wonder who TVC was,' she mused.

He traced his fingers across the initials then straightened beside her. 'Thomas Van Cleeve.'

'Who?'

'Thomas Van Cleeve. He was Rose's lover and Gwendoline's father.'

'How do you know that?'

'Because he went by another name as well. Jack Cleveland.'

She looked at him, unsure if he was joking. 'Jack Cleveland? But that's your...'

'Can we sit and talk? There's something important I need to tell you.'

Emma moved to the single bed and sat. Iron springs groaned as Matt sat beside her. Something like dread dropped into the pit of her stomach.

'There's been a lot going on the past three days and I haven't known how to tell you any of it.' He scratched his head and his jaw, closed his eyes, then opened them again. He looked unbearably tired. 'I went to see my grandfather Henry, to ask him some questions. It was something that Gwendoline said the other day that got me thinking. Maybe I always wondered, just a little, if it were possible. But it seemed so far-fetched that I didn't really give it too much thought.'

Emma watched him closely, feeling an awful truth coming.

'She said that Rose had become a nurse. And not just one that helped out occasionally between housekeeping duties. She became a nurse in the Hospital Precinct. And it made me wonder.'

'About?'

'My great-grandmother, Edith. She was a nurse.'

'So?'

'She was a nurse here at the station. And she was a nurse until the day she died, just as Gwendoline put it.'

Emma felt the room spin like vertigo and she clutched the edge of the bed to anchor herself.

'My grandfather filled in some of the blanks. He found a copy of his father's birth certificate when he died. His real name was Thomas Van Cleeve. He met his wife, Edith, here at the station in 1918. They became lovers. According to him, Thomas often referred to Edith as "his rose". Everyone thought it was just an affectionate pet name he had for her.

'My grandfather told me of an older sister he had, one he's never spoken of before. I certainly didn't know she existed. I think it's been a painful topic for him. She ran away from their North Queensland home when she was a teenager. He was only four but he remembers they never saw or heard from her again. He thinks her name was Gwendoline, but they always called her Ginny.

'From what Henry knows of their time at the station, Thomas, Rose and Gwendoline left in 1926. They moved to a farm in Mount Sheridan in North Queensland and changed their surname from Van Cleeve to Cleveland. Rose also changed her name to Edith. They had three more children, my grandfather being one of them.'

'Matt, stop please,' Emma said, shaking her head.

'Rose and Edith are the same person, Em. Rose's lover was the station carpenter, Thomas Van Cleeve. She gave birth to Gwendoline and lived in this cottage until they left in 1926. Something made them run from here, something that frightened them enough to want to make them change their names and disappear.'

'I said please stop.'

'Your great-grandparents are my great-grandparents. Your grand-mother is my grandfather's sister. Your mother Catherine is my mum's first cousin.'

'Matt, stop!'

'We're related, Em.' The anguish of it was all over his face. 'We're second cousins.'

Gwendoline's words rang in her ears. *He looks exactly like him...* She had seen it. Matt looked like Thomas Van Cleeve. Emma choked back a sob and stood, hurrying for the door. The cottage was suddenly too small and too judgemental of what they'd done. *Rose, Thomas, Gwendoline, Henry, Catherine.*

Outside in the daylight, Emma thought she might heave. She forced it back, not wanting to stop, desperate to get away.

Matt was behind her, grabbing her arm. 'Em, wait!'

She wheeled around. 'You son of a bitch! You knew!'

'I didn't know.'

'You said you knew!' she said, flinging her fists at his chest. 'You knew we were related and you let it happen. You let us have sex. You let me fall for you!'

'I didn't know,' he said again. 'I mean, I wondered, but I never thought it could be possible. Obviously I didn't think it was possible or I wouldn't have let it get this far.'

'Oh God, what have we done?' Emma said, clasping her hands over her mouth to stifle the shame. 'We're cousins.'

'We weren't to know.'

'Leave me alone.'

'At least let me walk you back.'

'I said leave me alone.'

Emma stalked down the path, branches flying at her face and snagging her clothes.

'Em, for God's sake wait!'

'Don't touch me,' she said when he reached for her again.

She ran from him, leaving him alone on the path looking as ashamed and bewildered as she felt.

Chapter Twenty-Eight

ROSE 1918

On a warm spring day that had buds bursting into bloom, Miss Dalton came racing down the main road of first class and into the kitchen, startling everyone inside as they cleaned up after the lunch service. 'It has ended!'

Mrs March gave her a wary glance. 'What's ended?'

'The war!'

Mrs March gasped. 'What do you mean?'

'It's over. I just got confirmation on the telephone from the superintendent. The Germans agreed to an armistice. The Allies have won.'

There was a cheer from within the kitchen, the parlourmaids throwing dishtowels into the air and hugging each other. It spelt victory, peace, an end to human folly and torment, a return of husbands and sons, alive or otherwise.

'We need champagne,' Miss Dalton yelled above the cheering. 'And lots of it. Fill the glasses. We'll pass them around first class.'

'It's only two o'clock,' Mrs March said.

'Oh, Mrs March, let your hair down a little. The war has ended.'

Mrs March harrumphed. 'Don't fill the glasses all the way. Champagne is not cheap!'

Rose and the other parlourmaids began to pop corks off the bottles as Mrs March begrudgingly slid out crates of it from her larder. The mood in the kitchen had become one of joy, but Rose was finding it difficult to concentrate.

For weeks she had existed as if moving through molasses. She had become unrelentingly sick, heaving and gagging on the slightest smells. Her breasts were swollen, her mind muddled and the once bright future she'd gleaned with Thomas was now as sludgy as the trenches of the Western Front.

By her own calculations, her pregnancy was at approximately eleven weeks. Her body was changing at a pace that frightened her. She hadn't yet told Thomas. She hadn't been able to conjure up the words to explain. The station was not a place to raise babies. It would result in instant dismissal as was the case with poor Agnes.

And Thomas had made it clear he wasn't ready to leave yet.

* * *

News of the war's end spread like wildfire. The station laid down its own troubles like guns on the battlefield to celebrate. All the classes were jubilant; isolation and the hospital too. Their cheers could be heard on the breeze and up the funicular railway from the wharf. Champagne corks popped, people cried, opinions and debates waged. The men's smoking room was abuzz with political discussion.

Rose was so ill with morning sickness, she could barely climb out of bed. Having fabricated countless excuses already for her nausea, she decided to seek advice.

After breakfast service with the duke, she followed the path down past the morgue and laboratory to the Hospital Precinct. It had been months since she'd visited, noticing the new barbed wire fence that had been erected to separate the unhealthy ground from the healthy. Spanish Flu had shown no signs of slowing; on the contrary, cases were rising with every new boatload that docked. The end of the war had sparked a chain of outbreaks as thousands of soldiers carried it home with them.

She spoke to a guard by the gate, who, after some convincing, allowed her to pass, and she stepped around the tents and moaning bodies to find the steps to the first-class hospital.

Dolly was surprised to see her, but indicated that Matron was in her office when Rose enquired.

Rose knocked on the door and heard the matron's voice inside. 'Come in.'

She opened the door and the matron stood with a smile. 'Rose Porter, how nice to see you.'

'Good day, Matron.'

'To what do I owe this pleasure?'

Rose took a deep breath. 'I've been having stomach issues. Is there something you can prescribe for me?'

'What kind of stomach issues?'

She knew the matron was no fool. 'Nausea,' she said weakly.

Matron Cromwell looked down her nose at her.

'I'm with child,' she blurted, then burst into a flood of tears.

The matron pursed her lips and moved around the desk to close her office door. She returned to Rose, gesturing her to take a seat while she leant against her desk.

'Please don't tell Miss Dalton,' Rose said, between gulps of air.

The matron was quiet for a long time.

'You're going to tell Miss Dalton, aren't you?'

'I'm not going to tell anyone. But goodness, how on earth did you get yourself into this?'

Rose cried harder.

The matron fell quiet again, passing Rose a handkerchief, and once she had gained control, the matron spoke. 'Who's the father?'

'The carpenter, Mr Van Cleeve,' Rose said. 'We're in love.'

'Does Mr Van Cleeve know about the child?'

Rose shook her head shamefully.

'Why haven't you told him?'

'Because I'm worried how he will take it.'

'Mr Van Cleeve seems like a reasonable man. Have you discussed marriage?'

'Yes, but he may not wish to marry me now. Even if he did, the rules are clear. We cannot raise a child on the station. We'd both be kicked out.'

'I think it best you tell him what's happening.'

Rose shook her head adamantly.

Matron Cromwell sighed. 'Very well. Explain your symptoms.'

'Nausea, vomiting, exhaustion, tenderness in my breasts. I feel a strange tugging in my lower stomach, like stretching.'

'When did you last bleed?'

'Eleven weeks ago.'

The matron nodded. 'It does sound like the first trimester of pregnancy.'

'Is there a test I can take to be sure?'

'You can submit a urine sample to the laboratory and they will try to analyse for abnormalities, but it's a guessing game. Women usually listen to their own bodies to know for certain.'

Rose welled up again, planting her face into the handkerchief.

'Do you know anything about contraception, Rose? About the female body and reproduction? Has anyone taught you?'

'My mother spoke of it on occasion.'

'Pregnancy can be a surprise occurrence if you're not careful.'

'I've been a fool.'

'And Mr Van Cleeve too. You mustn't bear all the blame.'

Rose sniffed. 'The nausea is horrendous. The slightest smells make me vomit.'

'It's to be expected.'

'Will I feel this way the whole time?'

'It should subside in a few weeks and you'll feel better. If you're unlucky, it will remain for the entire pregnancy.'

'I'm worried about drawing attention. I'm constantly ill.'

'Try boiling ginger in tea. It will settle your stomach. Mask with a dash of honey to get it down. It has an awful taste.'

Rose mustered a small smile.

The matron pushed off from the desk and walked to the cupboard. She opened the door, rummaged inside and withdrew a corset. She walked back to Rose and handed it to her.

'It's a maternity corset,' she explained, holding it up to demonstrate. 'It has no boning and laces at the front instead of the back. As you swell, release the lacing, like so. Refrain from wearing it too tight.'

Rose took the odd-shaped corset and examined it. Without the boning, the material was fashioned courser and stiffer to provide shape, the laces longer to allow more release, the bodice cut high for swelling breasts, all in an attempt to hide one's terrible secret.

'Thank you, Matron.'

'I'd like you to come back to see me in two weeks so I can give you an examination in your second trimester.'

Rose sighed heavily. 'Then what am I to do?'

'Hide this pregnancy for as long as you can. And I urge you to speak with Mr Van Cleeve.'

'And then?'

'Make preparations for the inevitable. Once you give birth to your child, you will not be allowed to remain on the station.'

* * *

Later that evening, Thomas came to fetch her and they walked back to his cottage. The night air was warm, a reluctant breeze lifting her hair and dropping it again. The moon was spectacularly bright, balancing in a clear, black sky. For the entire way, Rose thought of the maternity corset hidden beneath her bed with her suitcase pushed up against it. She hadn't had the nerve to pluck it out, put it on and lace it up.

Make preparations for the inevitable. Matron's words had sounded in her head all afternoon.

'Rose?'

She started, realising they were already at his door.

'Is everything all right? You were quiet the whole way.'

'I'm sorry. Just tired, I guess.'

'Let's get you into bed.'

Thomas opened the cottage door and let them in. While he lit the candles in the lantern, Rose went to the bed and dropped her pillowcase of belongings onto the coverlet.

'I can't stay, I'm afraid,' he said. 'I have to get down to the wharf. Three troopships entered the Heads earlier. It's all hands on deck to process the soldiers and get them into the inhalation chambers.'

'Where will we put them?'

'The accommodation and hospitals are full. We'll head further up the headland at first light to clear bush for more tents.'

'They've fought a long and bloody war only to have to come home and sleep in the bush with the snakes,' she said grimly.

'We can't release them back out into the population without time in quarantine.'

Rose bent to unlace her shoes. When it was time to remove her dress, she turned her back to Thomas as she had become accustomed to doing so he wouldn't notice the bloat of her stomach, and slipped off her tunic, petticoat and stockings.

She hadn't quite gotten her shift on when she felt his arms slip around her naked waist. She stiffened imperceptibly, but he didn't seem to notice.

'I wish I could stay with you, my love,' he said, kissing the back of her neck. 'I'd give anything to lie beside you right now.'

'I wish you could too,' she said, turning to face him.

'Are you sure everything's all right?'

She pulled her eyes away from him. They were like a doorway into her soul where it was all there on display for him to reach in and see. To know her shameful secret and what she had done to their future. 'Yes, I'm all right.'

'Would you tell me if something was wrong?'

Her breath caught. It was on the tip of her tongue. *Tell him.* 'You should get back to the wharf.'

She heard him sigh as she turned and slipped on her shift.

He pulled back the covers for her and she climbed beneath them. 'Get some sleep. I'll see you in a few hours.'

'I love you, Thomas.'

He reached down and kissed her. 'I love you, too.'

He left the cottage and through the window, Rose watched him disappear down the path and into the darkness. It was some time later that she finally wept herself to sleep.

Chapter Twenty-Nine

Rose woke the next morning to the sound of Thomas pouring water from the ewer into the bowl.

'Good morning,' she said, feeling nausea sweep over her as it did every morning.

'Good morning, my Rose.' He washed his face and hands, then dried them with a towel.

'What time is it?' she asked.

He walked to the bed and bent to kiss her. 'Not quite dawn.'

'Are you leaving already?'

'I have to get back down to the wharf. There's much to do.' He pulled on a clean shirt and pants. 'You're not due to rise for another two hours. Stay in bed and sleep.'

She watched him as he ran a comb through his hair and a hand over his jaw, assessing the stubble. 'I can run a blade over that tonight, if you like.'

He smiled. 'Thank you, my love.'

'Thomas,' she said sitting up in bed.

'Yes.'

'The war is over.'

'It is.'

She took a deep breath, choosing her words carefully. 'How would you feel about leaving?'

'The station?'

'Yes.'

He glanced at her for a long time before replying. 'May I be perfectly honest?'

'Please.'

'I'm not comfortable with the idea yet.'

Rose's heart sank. 'Oh.'

He sat on the bed beside her and took her hand. 'That's not the answer you were looking for, was it?'

She shrugged, feeling emotional suddenly. 'You said we could leave soon. That's what you said months ago.'

'Yes, but the war is over now and there are thousands of men returning from the front, thousands more men looking for work. I wouldn't be able to secure a job on the outside, let alone accommodation for us.

'Here, we have everything we need. We're saving our wages and putting all that we can away. We'll have enough money for Queensland soon, but not yet.' He shook his head resolutely. 'If we leave now, it would be to our own detriment.'

Rose blinked the tears away.

'I don't want us to have to struggle. I want us to be comfortable and to have children knowing we can provide for them. I don't want to live day to day, wondering when our next meal will be. That's not the life I want for you.'

'I told you I don't need much.'

He watched her with intrigue, his eyes boring into her soul. She had to look away, uncomfortable under a gaze so full of questions.

'No, you're right.' She forced a smile. 'We should stay. It was just a thought.'

He looked towards the window at the changing sky. 'I have to go, but let's talk more when I'm back later.' He brought her hand to his lips and kissed it.

When he left for the wharf, Rose didn't fall back to sleep. She laid awake turning panicked thoughts over and over in her mind. She turned them over until the sky coloured and the sun rose on Sydney.

* * *

Unable to sleep or stomach the ginger tea Matron Cromwell had suggested, Rose washed and dressed for work. She avoided the nause-ating smells of Mrs March's cooking by helping set up the dining room then, unable to put it off any longer, she crossed the road to the kitchen, barely inhaling as she loaded the duke's breakfast trolley.

As the sun climbed over the towering eucalypts, she pushed the cart up the hill and climbed the steps to the duke's cottage, knocking on the door. To her surprise, it wasn't he who opened it, but the duchess, dressed and out of bed.

'Good morning, Rose,' she said demurely. 'Do come in.'

Rose curtseyed, carried in the breakfast tray and set it down on the table. For weeks, Mrs March had been preparing meals for two, with the duchess taking a tray in her room while the duke dined at the table. And, until recently, for reasons owing to isolation, only the nurses had been allowed to tend to the duchess's housekeeping. Now, Rose tended to both bedrooms.

This was the first time since they'd arrived at the station that the duchess was not buried beneath a pile of covers with sallow skin and dishevelled hair, but regally tall in a slate grey dress, hair swept into a bun and eyes shining as deeply blue as her husbands. She had a touch of makeup on——rouge on her cheeks and a hint of red on her lips.

The duke was at the walnut bureau writing and he stood when he saw Rose. 'Ah, good morning. Time for a spot of breakfast, I see. Marvellous.'

Rose set the table, laying out the spreads and teapot, lining up the cutlery and plates. The duke pulled out the chair for the duchess to sit. Rose noticed the large emerald stone resting on her neckline against collarbones that no longer protruded skeletally from her skin.

'You're looking well, Your Grace,' she said, laying their napkins and pouring tea.

'Thank you,' the duchess said. 'I'm feeling better. Perhaps some toast and jam.'

'Certainly.'

'I'll have the sausages, eggs and potatoes,' the duke said cheerily. 'I'm ravenous! I've been working up quite an appetite lately.'

The duchess shot him a scathing look.

Feeling a marital war about to erupt, Rose served their breakfast, curtsied and retreated quickly to his bedroom. She pulled sheets from the duke's bed, noting as she did each morning that, despite the duchess's improving health, they were still residing in separate bedrooms.

When she gathered the pillows to beat outside, she caught a familiar whiff of peony, so strong it was as if Bessie had been lying there only moments before.

She suspected the duke was still drugging his wife to sleep, for how else could such acts take place in the room just next door to her? Still, she was no fool. She knew something was amiss, if her husband's *ravenous appetite* was anything to go by.

Either way, Rose couldn't concern herself with their affairs. She had her own troubles to deal with. And now that the war had ended and the duchess was well again, she prayed there would be no reason for them to stay.

* * *

Rose skipped the staff dinner, too ill to eat, deciding to stay in her room and nap. At nine-thirty she heard Bessie's shoes on the verandah and the door creak open.

Bessie walked in, plonking herself down on her bed with a noisy squeak of the springs. 'Argh, what a day.'

'How was dinner?' Rose drew herself up into a sitting position.

'The same as always. You haven't been to one in a while. You skip lunch too. Are you unwell?'

'I'm just weary. All those late nights.'

'Well, I brought you something.' She sat up, reached into her apron pocket and produced a bundle wrapped in cloth and tied with string. She tossed it across to Rose. 'Yorkshire pudding and an egg custard.'

'Thank you.' Rose placed it on her bedside table for later.

'I understand about the exhaustion. I could do with a full night's sleep. The duke is insatiable.'

'The duchess is up and out of bed,' Rose said. 'She was looking well today. Has he spoken of their plans to depart?'

'I expect they will leave soon, but he will take me with him.'

Rose leant forward. 'I know he says that to you, but how can you be sure?'

'Because I am.'

'The duchess knows he's being unfaithful. She'll never allow you to go with them. I don't want you to be disappointed.'

'He won't leave me, not now.'

Rose straightened. 'What do you mean "not now"?'

Bessie looked sheepish in the lantern light. 'Not now I'm carrying his child.'

Rose heard her own sharp intake of breath. '*Bessie Briar.*'

'Don't look so shocked, Rose.'

'I don't mean to. I just...' She was speechless, but she could hardly chastise. Had she not gone and done the same thing? Was she not sitting there in that room in the same state—unmarried, pregnant and having broken a thousand rules?

All she could think to do was sit beside Bessie on the bed and give her a hug. She folded her arms around her friend and they sat there for a long time. That's when Rose told Bessie of her own circumstance. Eleven weeks pregnant, horrendously ill and with a maternity corset hidden under her bed.

'Have you not also been unwell?' Rose asked, surprised that anyone could experience the first trimester of pregnancy and not look and feel as poorly as she.

'Once or twice I've felt a bit peaky, but mostly I'm just tired.'

'I feel terrible all the time. Just thinking of food makes me vomit. Is it normal to feel so sick?'

Bessie shrugged. 'I have no idea. I've never been pregnant before.'

'How far along are you?'

'I think I'm thirteen weeks. I can't believe this! We're going to have our babies at the same time.' Her blonde curls bounced with her sudden jubilation. 'Have you told Mr Van Cleeve?'

'No, I...' Rose looked down at her lap. 'I haven't been able to find the words.'

'What are you frightened of?'

'That he won't want me anymore. That I'll be fired and he won't want to leave with me.'

Bessie squeezed her hand sympathetically. 'I don't think Mr Van Cleeve would do that to you.'

'I've asked him twice if we could leave, but he says he wants to stay.'

'Yes but have you given him all the facts?'

Rose shrugged sadly.

'Once you do, I'm sure he will know what's best,' Bessie said. 'And if not, then you and the baby will have a home at Somersby Castle with me and the duke.'

'Have you told him?'

'Yes. He's thrilled. He said finally he'll have an heir. I mean, it's not ideal. Obviously I'm not his wife, so the baby will be illegitimate and not blueblood, but life doesn't always go to plan. And if he waits for her, then he'll be waiting forever and he'll have no child to carry on his name or legacy.'

Rose grabbed hold of Bessie's hands tightly. 'He will never leave her, Bessie,' she said kindly. 'He's under obligation to stay with her. The royals don't divorce. He can't marry you.'

'I don't care for marriage and I don't care if he stays with her. What I care for is ensuring our child has everything he or she could possibly need in life—a good home, a meal on the table, clothes on its back, an education. I want my child not to be privileged or entitled, but to have the basics, to be comfortable and loved.'

Her words made Rose want to cry. Fiercely maternal and protective, they were the words of a mother who had already formed a bond with her unborn child.

Her hand went to her stomach. It was the same feelings she'd been trying to resist because then her pregnancy, and all it brought with it, would be a tangible thing and not just a dream she might actually wake from.

'How do you know he will be true to his word?' she asked. 'And not disingenuous.'

Bessie smiled. 'Because he loves me. And I love him. We make each other happy.'

Rose sighed glumly.

'Don't look so worried for me. So we'll never be married and I'll never share his bed entirely. I'll always be his mistress, but I don't mind. I'm not beautiful like you, or educated or desired, so I have to take what life gives me. And it has given me this wonderful opportunity.'

'I would hardly call myself educated. I lack sense, I assure you.'

Bessie reached for her hand. 'Don't be hard on yourself.'

Rose stood and went to her bed, dropping to her knees to reach beneath it. She pushed aside her suitcase and her fingers closed over the maternity corset pressed against the wall.

'Here, take this,' she said, handing it to Bessie.

'What is it?'

'The maternity corset I told you about. The matron gave it to me. It will hide the swelling of your stomach so that no one will notice you're with child.'

'You've told the matron?'

'I have. She's going to examine me in a couple of weeks, once I'm properly into the next trimester.'

'What's a trimester?'

'The different stages of pregnancy. There are three. I'm about to start the second and you already have. You should arrange an appointment with her.'

Bessie shook her head adamantly. 'I won't need an examination. I feel fine.'

'I think you should go. The matron will understand. She'll help you.'

'I don't need an examination and I don't need that,' she said, pointing to the corset. 'I won't be having my baby here so I have nothing to worry about.'

Rose frowned.

'And you have nothing to worry about either. You'll leave with Mr Van Cleeve before the baby is born or you'll come with me to England to have it.'

'Bessie...'

'Keep it,' Bessie said, folding her hands around the corset and placing it in Rose's lap. 'You're smaller than me. You might start to show soon. I'm a lot bigger. No one will know the difference between a pregnant stomach and too much roast beef.' She laughed, but it sounded hollow and sad.

Rose looked down at the corset. 'Are you scared?'

'A little.'

'All of it scares me—the pregnancy, the birth, raising the child. I don't know the first thing about it.'

'You know more than you think.'

'I'm not ready.'

Bessie threw an arm around her shoulders. 'You *are* ready. And you're not alone. We'll do this together as best friends should. Don't worry, Rose. Everything will work out. I promise.'

Chapter Thirty

B y the beginning of December, three weeks after the war ended, Rose started to feel better. As each day progressed she could keep down more food, tolerate more smells and last the hours on her feet without feeling utterly exhausted.

Another strange sensation took hold of her body, something akin to energy, as though the weariness were melting away with the cool mornings. She saw this reflected in Bessie as well who looked less tired and whose skin was starting to glow.

Rose visited the matron for her first examination at the hospital. The matron had her lie on a bed in the maternity ward where she examined her privately.

She prodded her stomach, pushed her legs up to inspect her internally, which Rose found dreadfully unpleasant, and asked her a multitude of questions about cramping, bleeding, nausea and her diet.

Matron enquired again if she'd told Thomas.

'I haven't,' Rose said, climbing down from the bed and adjusting her undergarments and dress. 'But I will soon.'

'I think you should,' the matron said as she made notes on a clipboard. 'This pregnancy won't slow down and if you are still intimate with each other, he will notice soon.'

The matron was right. She could only hide her growing stomach and breasts for so long before he would see the changes.

'And I noticed you're wearing the corset.'

'Yes, every day. Thank you for loaning it to me.' Rose ran her hand over the shape of it beneath her dress. 'What can I expect from this next trimester?'

'You should feel increased energy and appetite. Your areolas will darken and your stomach and breasts will continue to grow. You'll gain weight, grow thicker hair and your skin will brighten.'

'Wow. Such changes,' Rose said wearily.

'It's nothing that your body won't know how to handle. I fear it's your mind that is struggling to catch up.'

'Should every pregnant woman have an examination?'

'Yes, it's recommended.' The matron looked up from her clipboard. 'Why do you ask? There isn't another pregnant parlourmaid on site is there?'

Rose turned quickly away. 'I was just curious.'

But the matron continued to stare at her anyway.

* * *

After lunch service, Miss Dalton appeared in the first-class kitchen, flustered like she'd just completed a sprint around the station.

'Gather around everyone,' she said breathlessly. 'I have important news.'

Rose, Bessie, Mrs March and the parlourmaids gathered in a circle in the centre of the kitchen.

'I was informed a moment ago by the Duke of Northbury that he and his wife, the duchess, will remain on the station for the foreseeable future.'

'The foreseeable future. What does that mean?' Mrs March barked.

'It means there has been a development with her health and they will be staying.'

'I heard from the hospital that she's with child,' blurted a parlourmaid.

Rose heard Bessie's sharp intake of breath as an excited murmur rippled around the circle.

'Must you be so crass?' Miss Dalton said sternly.

The parlourmaid shrugged.

'Is it true, then?' Mrs March asked. 'Are they staying because she's having a baby?'

'Since the cat is out of the bag,' she shot the offending parlourmaid a look, 'yes. I have been informed that, due to her delicate state, they will remain on the station until the heir is born. Once that occurs, they will return to England.'

Another murmur rippled through the group.

'So they're going to stay here for free while we wait on them hand and foot?' Mrs March looked outraged. 'I didn't realise we were a hotel.'

'The duke assures me we will be well compensated for the trouble. The superintendent has agreed to the arrangement.'

'I saw the duchess on the verandah yesterday. She didn't look delicate to me.'

'Mrs March, it's not our place to pass opinion on such matters. The duke wants to stay and so they are staying.'

'We can't get rid of them,' Mrs March muttered.

'I'll pretend I didn't hear that.'

'How far along is she?' Bessie asked quietly.

The group turned to look at her.

'What a thing to ask! That's none of your business,' Miss Dalton said sharply, but Mrs March was also looking at her expectantly and so she relented. 'I believe she is sixteen weeks.'

'She's got six months to go. They'll be here until May next year!' Mrs March complained.

'Yes Alice, they will be. And I expect everyone to give them privacy for the duration of that time,' Miss Dalton said. 'Rose, you are the only one allowed contact with them. You will continue in your usual duties. See to it that the duchess has everything she needs.'

'Yes, Miss Dalton.'

The group disbanded and while Mrs March complained to Miss Dalton about missing bags of flour in her latest delivery, Rose followed

Bessie outside, who lit a cigarette on the kitchen step and puffed heavily on it.

'Are you okay?' she asked, touching her friend's arm.

'Of course. Why wouldn't I be?' Bessie said nonchalantly, though Rose could tell the news of the duchess's pregnancy had hit her like a dose of Spanish Flu.

'Do you want to talk about it?'

'There's nothing to talk about.'

'She's sixteen weeks, the same as you.'

Bessie pulled back on her cigarette and blew out a stream of smoke, her eyes fixed on the road.

Rose nodded. 'All right. I will leave you be, then.' She turned to step back into the kitchen.

Bessie reached for her hand with an anguished look. 'He was intimate with me then he was intimate with her.'

'Yes.'

'He told me she was too delicate to lie with. That she repulsed him. That he loved only me.'

'I know.'

'It doesn't change anything.'

'It changes everything.'

Bessie dragged deeply on her cigarette, tossed it to the ground then crushed it with her shoe. 'She's giving him a legitimate blueblood heir.'

'And she's staying on the station to give birth. Bessie, that means you'll have to give birth here too.'

Bessie grew pale.

'Talk to the duke. Make him state his intentions. He *must* take you and the baby with him back to England in May.'

'I'm sure he will.'

'Make him tell you. I'd feel better if he said it.'

'How terribly funny,' Bessie said wryly. 'Come May, the duke will have two new babies.' She looked anything but amused as she said it.

'I'm so sorry.'

Bessie waved her hand. 'Don't be sorry. I have faith. The duke will take me and our baby back to Somersby Castle as planned. He will never cast us out. He gave me his word.' But her smile was strained as she stepped back into the kitchen.

Rose stood on the step and turned her face to the sky, feeling the sun on her skin. Two babies due in May, both fathered by the duke. She contemplated how angry the duchess was going to be when she found out about Bessie's baby, what an awkward boat ride it would be back to England for them and that the duke was perhaps the luckiest, or unluckiest, fellow in the world.

* * *

Thomas came for Rose at eleven. She was silent on the walk back to his cottage, still turning over the news of the day.

When they walked through the door, Thomas reached for her hand and squeezed it. 'Are you okay, my Rose? You've been awfully quiet tonight.'

She smiled apologetically. 'I don't mean to be.'

'Did you hear about the duchess?' he asked as she laid her pillowcase of belongings on the bed and sorted through it for her shift.

'I did. But how did you hear of it?'

'I heard it from the autoclave boys, who heard it from isolation.'

'And how did isolation hear about it?'

'From first-class housekeeping.'

'And we heard it from the hospital.'

'Spreads like wildfire in a place like this.' He sat on the edge of the bed and pulled her into him. 'So I guess they're staying?'

'Until she has the child in May, yes.'

'Is that what's been bothering you tonight?'

Rose hadn't yet told Thomas about Bessie's pregnancy. She hadn't even told him of her own. So to his question, she simply shrugged. 'Yes, but not for reasons you're aware.'

He gave her a strange look and she knew she had to tell him of the child growing inside her, that it was no longer her secret to keep. She undid the button at the nape of her neck and while he watched her, she slipped her dress down. Next she let her petticoat slide from her body and pushed down her underwear and stockings, while Thomas's eyes roamed over her.

'You are so beautiful, my Rose,' he said, leaning forward to kiss her collarbones and neck.

'Thomas, there's something I need to tell you.' Her voice shook.

'What is it?' He looked up at her with such adoration she had to force herself to continue, to risk never seeing that look from him again. To risk losing him forever and being thrust out into the world with an illegitimate infant and not the faintest idea how to survive.

Bravely, she reached for his hand and rested it on her stomach, holding his gaze with her own so that, after a moment, realisation dawned and he looked down at her abdomen. His fingers traced the skin around her navel, across the swell that was starting to protrude from her hips, and his eyes widened.

'Rose?'

'Yes.'

'You're pregnant?'

'I am.'

He looked completely astounded and for a minute, for one agonisingly long minute, he just stared at her. Rose gulped when he glanced down at her stomach again, holding onto her hips, just staring.

'You're pregnant,' he said again.

'Yes.'

His mouth fell open but no sound came out.

'Say something,' she said.

'I'm sorry, I... How far along are you?'

'I'm fourteen weeks. Matron says I'm in the second trimester.'

'She knows?'

'She's been taking care of me.'

'How did you find out?'

'I missed my monthly flow.'

He blushed and scratched his head. 'Yes, of course. So the exhaustion and feeling poorly...?'

'Morning sickness.'

He sat back and she moved away, giving him space to digest it. She saw him swallow, his Adam's apple bobbing, the air around them charged.

'Why didn't you tell me sooner?'

She reached for her shift and dropped it over her head and shoulders, pulling it down over her stomach. 'I was afraid.'

'Of what?'

'That you wouldn't want me anymore.' Her voice was so meek she wasn't sure it had left her lips.

'How could you think that?'

'Because I know how much you want to stay on the station, but this baby changes everything. I can't stay here.'

He nodded as though a second wave of realisation hit him. 'No, I suppose you can't.'

'Are you mad?'

He pulled her to his lap and she sat, letting him wrap his arms around her waist. 'Of course I'm not mad. I'm still absorbing it, but I'm not mad.' He kissed her and she felt her body respond, leaning into him. His hand slid under her shift to rest on her stomach. 'I just wish you had told me sooner.'

She burrowed into his neck and he held her tight. 'Where do we go from here?'

'I'm not sure. You're already starting to show. I don't know how much longer you can hide it.'

'Matron gave me a maternity corset to wear during the day. I should be able to get through most of my pregnancy without anyone noticing.'

'Are you thinking of having the baby here?'

She sat upright. 'Yes. Initially, I wanted to leave but at least here I'll have the matron to help me deliver. I think it's the best place to be.'

'And afterwards?'

'I'll be fired,' she said.

He nodded. 'Then that will be our plan. We'll save as much as we can in the next six months, deliver the baby here then leave together.'

'You'll come with me?'

'Of course I'll come with you.' He stroked her stomach again. 'That's my child in there. Wherever the two of you will be is where I'll be.'

She threw her arms around his neck and squeezed him so tightly he coughed. 'I love you!'

'I love you too, my Rose.' He kissed her lips, her neck, her breasts, sliding the shift off her body in one swift motion. He stood her up so he could inspect the new curves of her hips again, tracing them with his fingers and she could see the wonder on his face. He touched her, kissed her, made her sigh with pleasure.

Then his fingers went lower and lower until she gasped and could stand it no longer. She pushed him back onto the bed, unbuckled his trousers and straddled him, loving him all the more for the man he was —brave, honest, a gentleman, unlike anyone she had ever known. And she showed him just how much he meant to her, just how much he meant to the tiny life growing inside her.

* * *

An hour later, they lay with limbs entwined and sweat drying on their bodies. Thomas laced his fingers through hers, pressing her hand to his lips. It was well after midnight though neither was tired.

'The female body is a wonder,' he said. 'It knows how to create this little person in your stomach with tiny fingers and toes, a heart and a brain. It's incredible.'

'And it has let me know every day for the past fourteen weeks just how hard it's been working.' She could laugh at the morning sickness now, no longer feeling quite so awful.

'And to think there's only two weeks between you and the duchess. There's every chance you'll deliver at the same time.'

Rose sat up so she could see him better. 'There's something else I should tell you.'

'Uh oh,' he said, sitting up too. 'I'm not sure I can handle any more surprises today.'

'Well, it's after midnight, so technically it's a new day and a new surprise.'

He laughed heartily. 'All right, tell me then, my Rose. What new surprise do you have for me?'

'Bessie is pregnant.'

'I wasn't expecting that.'

'To the duke.'

Thomas looked horrified. 'Oh, dear lord.'

'Indeed.'

'Does he know?'

'Bessie told him. She's sixteen weeks, the same as the duchess. He got them both pregnant at the same time.'

Thomas looked gobsmacked.

'The duke is expecting two children in May.'

'But Bessie won't deliver a true heir. The duchess has the blueblood. What are his intentions for Bessie's child?'

'She still believes he will take her and the baby with him to Somersby Castle.'

'For her sake, I hope he will.' Thomas drew her closer into him. Rose could feel the gentle, reassuring thud of his heartbeat against her back, his soft and steady breath on her neck.

She closed her eyes, feeling lighter than she had in weeks, a great weariness lifting from her shoulders. Thomas wasn't going to leave her. He still wanted her. And most of all, he wanted their child.

As she drifted to sleep, cocooned in his arms, she heard him speak the words, 'I can't wait any longer to ask you. Will you marry me, Rose?'

To which she replied, 'Yes.'

Chapter Thirty-One

EMMA 1918

The weeks following Matt's revelation at Rose and Thomas's cottage, Emma launched herself into distraction like a newfound friend. She buried herself in triple shifts at The Coffee Bean and endless visits to see Gwendoline at the nursing home.

The key was to ensure she never slowed down long enough to fully absorb what she and Matt had done. She became good at this during the day but at night, alone inside her empty apartment, the shame of it set in again and she felt her stomach flip unpleasantly. There was that and the great gaping hole Matt had left in her life, because despite it all, she'd known a wonderful man that she missed.

But they were related. Matt's great-grandfather, Jack Cleveland was her great-grandfather. Matt's great-grandmother, Edith Cleveland—also known as Rose Porter—was her great-grandmother too. She and Matt were bound by blood, sprouted from the same family tree. And they'd had sex. Lots of it! She'd fallen in love with her second cousin.

Every time she thought of it, the shame washed over her again and it stayed there until she could successfully distract herself. All the preconceived notions she'd had of a future with Matt had been washed away. It was much like anything in Emma's life. Nothing ever remained tacked together for long, eventually falling apart.

On a dry and hot November day that left the leaves looking tired,

Emma was piling blueberry muffins onto a cake stand. The lunch rush had passed and except for a few late diners, the café was empty.

Chloe was next to her, refilling the coffee machine with beans. 'Why don't you take off early today?' she said over the bag. 'You've been here since six am.'

'I'll stay until closing.'

'You've been doing triple shifts for the past three weeks.'

'It's no problem,' Emma said. She disappeared through the door into the kitchen before Chloe could question her again.

But Chloe was hot on her heels, following her in. 'Okay, I'm not asking anymore. I'm telling. Go home and get some rest.'

'I'm doing the same shifts as you. What's the problem?'

'I own this place,' Chloe said. 'I'm supposed to pull the long hours, and I have student staff who I can roster on.'

Emma lugged a crate filled with bread onto the counter and unpacked it.

Chloe leant against the fridge and gave her a look. 'Well?'

'I need to get in there,' she said, pointing to the fridge door.

'What's going on with you?'

'Nothing.' She hadn't told Chloe about her family ties with Matt. She didn't want anyone to know. Ever.

'You've been acting strange the last few weeks. Kind of angry.'

'I'm not angry.'

'Moody then.'

'I'm fine.'

Chloe moved out of the way and Emma extracted containers of salad and packs of cold meat from the fridge. She placed them on the counter, opened them and began constructing focaccias and wraps for the pre-movie dinner rush.

'Did something happen with Matt?'

At the mention of his name, Emma slapped cheese, tomato and salami on a piece of focaccia with such vengeance that she put a hole through it.

'We're not going to have anything to serve if you keep destroying the bread like that,' Chloe said with an eyebrow raised.

'I'm sorry.' Emma took a breath. 'We're not together anymore.'

'What happened?'

'We're just...' *Related*. 'It's hard to explain.'

'Try me.'

'I don't want to get into it right now.'

Chloe gave her a sympathetic pat on the arm. 'That sucks. You guys were a nice fit. You really bonded over Rose's story.'

'Oh yes, there was a lot of bonding,' Emma said dryly.

'How's Gwendoline?'

'She's okay. The nurses have caught her at the front door at midnight on a few occasions trying to get out. They have a locked-door policy now after eight pm.'

'Good!'

'Yes, but she's agitated. I thought taking her to the station would help, but it's only intensified her need to follow her memories. And after everything we found and all the diaries we trawled through, I'm still no closer to knowing who she was waiting for down by the wharf all those years ago.'

And since she'd discovered who Matt was to her, their research had ground to a halt. They'd exhausted Rose's diaries and Emma was desperate to find more, but she would never set foot on the station to search, no matter how badly she wanted to, for fear of bumping into Matt.

'So what's next?'

Emma shrugged. 'Maybe it's time to let it go.'

'But all that research, all the hours you put into it. You were so close.'

Yes, but it had cost her dearly. She'd turned over too many rocks, ones that should have been left firmly in place. Ones that she wished she'd never looked under.

Chloe gave her a kind smile. 'How about I make you a coffee? You can finish up the sandwiches then I want you to go home and get some rest.'

Emma made to protest but Chloe stopped her. 'That's an order.'

* * *

Emma left The Coffee Bean and walked the short distance home to her apartment through crowds of Wednesday night revellers. She let herself in and kicked off her shoes, hearing the sound of their laughter drift up through her windows. She hadn't wanted to admit it, but working long hours on continuous cycle had left her drained. So drained, she'd forgotten to bring a plate of food home and there was nothing but mouldy bread and an old tin of tuna in her cupboard.

She dropped her bag onto the coffee table and fell into a heap on the lounge, reaching for the remote. Her stomach growled as she flicked through the channels. The six o'clock news was on and some game shows, nothing of any interest.

She considered driving over to see Gwendoline or maybe just climbing into her car and heading south to nowhere, but then she'd be alone inside her head for too many hours and the thought of that unnerved her.

Her phone tinged unexpectedly, for Emma's phone never made noise anymore, and she brought her bag to her lap to rummage through it. When she plucked it out, the screen was lit—one new text from Matt.

Emma stared at his name for a long time. There had been no contact since that day in the cottage when he'd told her all that his grandfather had said. Why would he contact her now and what could he possibly have to say?

Ignoring the text, she placed the phone down and returned to the news. It continued to ting at her, reminding her that Matt's message was still unseen, until she snatched it up, opened the message without reading it and deleted it.

* * *

The next morning at eight, as Emma finished loading takeaway coffees into a cardboard tray for a frazzled-looking secretary, her phone tinged in her back pocket. She glanced at it and saw that it was Matt again.

Once the secretary had left, she retreated to the kitchen to look at it properly. Why was he dragging the pain out? Hadn't enough hurt been inflicted? Unless he was feeling as she was, confused and ashamed, and the contact was an attempt to assuage, not just his own guilt, but hers too.

She shook her head. It didn't matter. She could never look at him again knowing they'd been deeply intimate while cut of the same cloth. Knowing that she'd felt so strongly for someone who was so obviously off limits. She did what she had done the night before and deleted the message without reading it.

Later in the day, after the lunch rush was over and Emma was slicing quiche for the dinner service, Matt called. She bumped it, shoving the phone into her jeans.

He rang again as she was walking home and she bumped that call too, putting the phone on silent. Too tired to eat the salad roll Chloe had sent home with her, she showered and fell into bed. When she woke the next morning, there were two more missed calls.

* * *

Three days past and Emma didn't hear from Matt again. She was relieved, falling back into her quiet life in her little Kensington apartment where she moved between work and Gwendoline. As lonely as that could be, it was safe in its predictability.

On a busy Friday afternoon, Chloe came rushing into the kitchen holding her mobile. Cheeks flushed, she groaned. 'The milk isn't coming!'

Emma looked up from slicing tomatoes. 'What do you mean it's not coming?' They had been waiting since seven am for the usual morning delivery, but the truck had broken down somewhere near Summer Hill and the milk had yet to arrive.

'They said they can't get another truck out here today. I'm down to my last bottle of milk.'

Emma untied her apron and slipped it over her head. 'I'll go to the supermarket and grab some.'

'Oh, would you? You're a gem!'

'No problem.'

'Can you grab twenty bottles? A mix of full cream, skim, soy and almond. That should see us through until tomorrow morning. Here,

277

take my car.' Chloe handed Emma her keys. 'There's money in the register. I'll finish up in here while you're gone.'

Emma found Chloe's silver Toyota Yaris parked in the lane behind the café. She started it up and pulled out onto the street, following the flow of traffic until she reached the Woolworths in Randwick.

She loaded the trolley with milk, paid and packed it all into the boot of the car.

When she returned to the café, Chloe was waiting for her with a troubled expression.

'I got the milk,' Emma said, holding up the first lot of bottles she'd brought in.

'You had a visitor.'

Emma placed them down on the counter. 'A visitor?'

'Yes. He came in while you were gone.'

'Who was it?' But she already knew.

'Matt.'

'I better bring those other bottles in.'

'He left a message asking if you could ring him. He looked disappointed that you weren't here.' Chloe stared at her. 'I don't know what happened between the two of you, but he seems like a nice guy.'

'It's complicated, Chlo.'

'Breakups usually are.'

'It's so much more complicated than you could imagine.'

'You should call him.'

Emma shook her head. 'I don't have time to think about it now. I have to get the milk in.'

She didn't call Matt back later that night or the next day. Numerous times she had the phone in her hand, willing herself to dial his number, but her fingers stalled on the buttons, bringing her back to the same conclusion—what was left to say?

Two days after his first visit, Emma was clearing the tables after the lunch service when Matt stepped in.

Her breath caught at the sight of him. He was still so handsome to her, despite all the reasons why he shouldn't be. He wore jeans and a white shirt pushed up at the sleeves and she was drawn immediately to his eyes. *Thomas's eyes.* Hazel with flecks of green and gold.

'Em.'

She ignored him but he came closer to her and touched her wrist.

'Emma.'

'You shouldn't be here, Matt.'

'I had to see you.' He followed her to the counter and waited there while she disappeared into the kitchen to offload the plates.

When she returned, he was waiting for her. Chloe had moved discreetly away to clear the rest of the tables.

'Is there somewhere we can talk?' he asked.

'There's nothing left to say.'

'There's a lot left to say.'

'Matt, please. This is hard enough.'

A moment passed before he spoke again. 'I found some things in the archive room at the station. I was digging around in boxes last week and came across them. That's why I've been calling you.'

'What kinds of things?'

'Old log books from 1919 with some interesting entries.'

'That's the year Gwendoline was born.'

'Yes. I think you should take a look.'

'I'm not sure that's a good idea.'

'I miss you,' he said, the words rushing out in a way that seemed to surprise even him. 'Sorry, I know I'm not supposed to say that.'

She dropped her gaze, looking down at the countertop.

'Anyway, I'll be at the museum tomorrow morning from eight if you change your mind.'

He left the café and Emma retreated to the kitchen so that Chloe wouldn't see her tears.

Chapter Thirty-Two

F ive minutes out from the Q Station and Emma was still making up her mind whether to go through with it.

Seeing Matt the day before at The Coffee Bean had been disconcerting. She'd barely slept a wink, racking her brain over whether she should meet him.

He said he'd found old log books pertaining to their search and she was certain he had, but the thought of being around him again, solving Gwendoline's mystery together, threw her back to a time when their relationship had been simpler.

She'd called Chloe that morning asking for the day off, hoping with fingers crossed behind her back, that Chloe would say no and the decision would be out of her hands. But of course, Chloe said yes.

Emma navigated her car up around the headland, past the Manly Hospital and through the sandstone arch to the station. She parked her car in the carpark and walked towards the reception building.

Ted was parked in his usual spot, reading the paper and drinking a can of Sprite behind the wheel.

'Hey, Emma,' he called out from the window. 'Here to see Matt?'

'Hi, Ted. Yes. Can you give me a lift down to the museum?'

'Sure. Hop in.'

She boarded the bus and took a seat. Ted started up the engine, turned the bus around and rolled along Wharf Road, down towards the water. He parked on the gravel out the front of the shower blocks and Emma stepped down into warm air, fragrant with banksia and bottlebrush.

Thanking Ted, she turned and walked towards the museum, heart pounding.

She didn't see Matt at first. He was inside the doorway, lost in shadow, but then he emerged into the sunlight and Emma's heart beat faster.

'Hey,' he said when she got closer. 'I'm glad you came.' He grazed her cheek with a soft kiss.

'I wasn't sure I was going to.'

He nodded. 'Come through to the archive room. I'll show you what I found.'

Emma followed Matt through the museum to the archive room located at the back. He fished out a set of keys from his pocket, turned one in the lock and let them into the room. Emma felt the same blast of cold air hit her cheeks as last time.

Matt flicked on the light, closed the door behind them and signed them in. They washed their hands at the sink and he led her to a stack of brown, acid-free boxes.

Pulling the top one off the pile and placing it on the floor, he indicated that Emma sit, and she found a spot on the floor and crossed her legs. He sat beside her, the box in front of them.

'Ever since that day at Rose and Thomas's cottage, I've felt a bit lost,' he said candidly. 'I've been coming back here to search through files and boxes. I'm not sure why. Maybe to make sense of it all.'

The look on his face broke her heart. It was clear she hadn't been the only one suffering.

'Anyway, I came across this.' He pulled out a small, thin notebook and handed it to her.

'Another diary?'

'Not quite. It's a notebook belonging to a Doctor Holland. He kept personal notes in it relating to patient examinations. All the entries are dated 1919.'

Emma flicked open the cover and scanned through the pages.

Doctor Holland's writing was scrawly, almost unintelligible, but after careful scrutinising, Emma found an entry dated tenth April, 1919.

'"Bessie Briar, female, twenty-years of age. Thirty-four weeks gestation. Housekeeping. First Class."' Emma looked up in shock. 'Bessie Briar was pregnant?'

'It looks that way. But check out the next page.'

Emma flipped the page over. '"April eleventh, 1919. Lady Cordelia, Duchess of Northbury. Female, twenty-eight years of age. Thirty-four weeks gestation. Passenger. First Class." Bessie and the duchess were both eight months pregnant?'

'And if I calculate from Rose's last diary entry on the thirtieth October, 1918, that would place her at eight months pregnant in April 1919 too,' Matt said.

Emma was stunned. 'All three of them were due to deliver their babies in May.'

'Take a look at what the doctor noted during each of his examinations.'

Emma turned back to Bessie Briar's page and read aloud. '"Patient is thirty-four weeks pregnant, requiring examination due to false pains of labour. Patient is otherwise in good physical condition, carrying excessive weight. Foetal heartbeat noted strong and foetus engaged for delivery. Patient was nervous about examination." What does that mean?'

'It could relate to her anxiety about being pregnant on the station. She might have been scared that the doctor would tell someone.'

'And it appears she was having Braxton Hicks contractions and thought she was going into labour,' Emma said.

'I wonder who the father was.'

Emma turned the page to read about the duchess's examination with Doctor Holland. '"Patient is thirty-four weeks pregnant, undergoing routine weekly examination. Patient seems in good physical condition and at ideal weight. Lungs appear healthy with no obvious respiratory complications, though patient complains of being tired and out of breath. Foetal heartbeat noted strong and foetus engaged for delivery. Patient is in good state of mind."'

'A little different from Bessie's report.'

'Yes,' Emma said. 'The duchess's state of mind was positive. She was privileged enough to have weekly examinations and had less to fear of the experience. Is there anything in here for Rose?' She flicked through the pages.

'I couldn't find anything. Perhaps she was being treated by another doctor or maybe she hadn't had an examination yet. But I did find this.' Out of the box he pulled a large, square hardcover book, thick with yellowed pages. He handed it to her.

'What's this one?'

'The First Class Hospital Registration Book. It's where they logged all patient admissions and discharges for 1919. This hospital also had a small maternity ward behind the matron's office. It was kept separate from the main ward for disease control.'

'And what am I looking for in this?'

'There's a maternity section at the back that states which babies were born in which month—the date, name, parents, class, weight, gender et cetera.'

Emma flicked to the back and found April 1919 which then jumped straight to June 1919. 'There's no page for May.'

'That's right. Someone ripped it out.'

'How can you be sure?'

'Because look at January and February. There were no babies born during those months but the pages still exist. And yet a month like May, when we know three babies were due to be born, is missing.'

Emma spread the book apart and sure enough, embedded in the binding was the jagged edge of the residual page. 'You're right. I can see it. May was ripped out. But why?'

'Maybe something happened in that maternity ward that needed to remain hidden.'

Emma glanced at the acid-free box. 'Have you gone through the entire box? Could the page be in there somewhere?'

'I went through the whole thing. It's full of more hospital log books but from different years. More doctor's notebooks, also from different years. I couldn't find the May page anywhere.'

'So we have a missing page.' Emma closed the book, exasperated. 'This story just gets more convoluted.'

'It's like peeling back one layer to find three more.'

'And it brings us no closer to finding out who my grandmother was waiting for by the wharf.'

They fell silent, sitting side by side on the floor in the small archive room with the air-conditioner humming persistently in the background.

'How have you been?' Matt asked eventually.

'Fine. No, not really,' Emma said ruefully. 'I've been struggling with what we did.'

'Me too.'

'Matt, did you know the whole time but let it happen anyway?'

'No. I didn't know. It only started to click in the reception carpark when Gwendoline said I looked like *him*, that I had his hazel eyes. I had no idea who she meant, but it was obviously someone from both our pasts. Then I pieced it together properly when she said Rose became a full-time nurse in the hospital.'

'Just like Edith.'

'Yes.'

'But in the cottage you said you'd always wondered, just a little, if it were possible.'

'Yeah, as a far-fetched idea. As in hey, wouldn't it be funny if my great-grandparents were your great-grandparents. But...' He shook his head. 'I never thought it was actually possible. I would never have let things continue between us if I'd known.'

'Did you ever get the chance to meet Rose or Thomas when you were younger?'

'Thomas died in 1973 from pancreatic cancer before I was born. Rose died in her sleep a year later. She just slipped away. They say she died of a broken heart.'

'I wish I could have known them.'

'From what I've been told, they were good people. Rose was headstrong and fiercely protective of her family, particularly Gwendoline. From what I know of Thomas, he was a kind and gentle man, and a damn good carpenter.'

'You're Thomas's great-grandson in every way.'

Matt blushed as he played with his shoelace. 'I haven't told my grandfather about Gwendoline yet.'

Emma looked at him.

'He's eighty-eight. I'm not sure I want to dredge all that up for him again. He was close to her. She was his big sister and when she ran away, it devastated him.'

'So he has no idea she's still alive?'

'They never kept in contact. I don't know whether to say anything.'

Emma let out a frustrated sigh. 'There's so much to this story we still don't understand. Why would Thomas and Rose pack up suddenly and flee in 1926? Did it have something to do with the boat my grandmother was waiting for? Is that why they changed their names? Were they running from someone?'

'The answers are here on the station. We just need to find them,' Matt said.

'Are they? Because I feel like we keep hitting dead ends.'

'We're making progress.'

'We're chasing ghosts.'

They fell quiet, avoiding eye contact, until Emma broke the silence. 'I better go.' She stood, packed the books back into the acid-free box and closed the lid.

Matt stood too. 'I was thinking of taking a walk out to Thomas and Rose's cottage tomorrow to have another look around. Did you want to come?'

She gave him a sad smile. 'I don't think that's a good idea.'

'Just as friends.'

'I can't be your friend, Matt.' She thought she saw his heart crack a little and she turned away. 'It's for the best.'

He didn't say anything as he picked up the box and stacked it on top of the others. He followed Emma outside, back into the daylight.

'So where to from here?' he asked, hands jammed into his pockets as though that might fend off the awkwardness.

'This is goodbye, I guess.'

He nodded.

'Thanks for everything.'

He didn't respond.

She gave him her bravest smile and turned away before he could see her eyes fill and the crack in her resolve. Before he could see just how much she wanted to run back to him, no matter how wrong it was.

Chapter Thirty-Three

ROSE 1918

Christmas Eve was hot and humid. It was a first for Rose, not used to moving through such stagnant heat or better still, trying to sleep through it while four months pregnant.

She spent the evening with Thomas in his cottage, the windows thrown open trying to catch the breeze off the water. They ate cold roast beef, potatoes and Christmas pudding purloined from Mrs March's larder. They drank glasses of eggnog followed by gin until they were giddy. After dinner, Thomas suggested they open presents.

'I hope you didn't spend too much,' Rose said as she climbed onto the bed.

'Just a little of our savings,' he said, winking.

While he was busy at the wardrobe, she slipped her hands beneath the bed and pulled out three wrapped presents she'd hidden under there earlier.

Thomas joined her on the coverlet with similarly wrapped gifts.

'I'll go first,' she said, handing hers to him. 'Merry Christmas, my love.'

His face lit up as he accepted the packages and tore the red paper from each, revealing inside a new leather tool bag, a bottle of single malt whiskey and a model-build kit for a 96th Aero Squadron Fighter plane, an exact replica of the one that had fought over the Western Front.

'Oh, Rose.' He looked genuinely delighted with each of them. 'You are so kind. I love them.'

'And I love you.' She leant across the bed to kiss him.

'Now it's my turn,' he said. There were four gifts in total and he handed her the first three.

She tore the wrapping off each. Inside were a new set of diaries with matching keys and fountain pens, a simple gold necklace in a velvet pouch and Jane Austen's *Pride and Prejudice*. Never had she received an abundance of such thoughtful gifts and her heart swelled.

Thomas had the fourth gift in his hand, a small black velvet box, which he held out to her. It wasn't wrapped and Rose's breath caught.

'This, my darling, is something I've been wanting to give to you for some time now.' He looked nervous as he said it. 'May I open it for you?'

'Please,' she said breathlessly.

He tilted the box and opened the lid. Inside, on a white satin bed was a small diamond engagement ring. 'Rose, you would make me the happiest man in the world if you would be my wife.'

She threw her arms around his neck and kissed him. 'Of course I will be your wife. Nothing would make me happier!' She looked down at the ring and touched the tiny diamonds with her fingertips. 'It's glorious, Thomas.'

'I'm glad you like it.'

'However did you get it?'

'I ordered it from Hardy Brothers in Melbourne. It arrived a few days ago. I had to beg with my life for it not to be put through the autoclaves.'

'Hardy Brothers?' Rose looked at the exquisite ring, diamonds catching the lamp light. 'They're a reputable jeweller. This must have cost a lot of money.'

'It was worth it, my love.'

She kissed him again, slowly, tenderly, her heart bursting with joy. Thomas prised the ring from the box and slipped it onto her finger. It fit perfectly as though it had been made for her.

'It's so beautiful. What a shame I won't be able to leave it here,' she said, inspecting the ring, her happiness tinged briefly with reality. 'I could never let the others see it.'

He held up the plain gold necklace he'd given her earlier. 'Will you settle for wearing it around your neck, hidden beneath your dress?'

Rose smiled. Ever was he practical. 'I will. It would stay close to my heart.'

She slipped the ring off her finger and threaded it onto the gold chain. Thomas fixed it around her neck and she could feel the cool metal of the ring against her skin. They were edging closer to their dream, a glimmer of a future she could almost touch. The tips of her fingers were upon it.

They cleared away the presents and fell back into bed, kicking off the sheets and making love until the stars dulled and the sky grew pale.

Afterwards, they lay awake and Thomas, as always, grew enthralled with her stomach. Rose had begun to feel the tiniest ripples inside, like a stone being skimmed across calm water. It was nothing that Thomas could feel from the outside yet, just the private internal correspondence between a mother and her unborn baby.

Christmas Day offered no reprieve for Rose. While Thomas and many of the ground's staff had been granted all or part of the day off, Rose woke early as usual, washed and dressed for service with the duke and duchess.

The royals had been invited to the dining room to enjoy celebrations with the other first-class passengers. There was going to be a visit from Santa and a great fruit tower which Mrs March had been agonising over since dawn. But they had declined, preferring to take their meals in their cottage, which meant Rose had to work a full day in service.

The morning dawned hot and still. Even the bush lacked the sounds of wildlife. Sweat appeared instantly on Rose's brow when she stepped out of Thomas's cottage and set down the path towards the station.

Sometimes, when she closed her eyes, she thought of London. She could see the frost rising from people's breath, the layers of threadbare hats and coats, the frigid air as it sparkled with snow. It made her heart ache in hope that London had recovered from the war, that the new year would bring peace and prosperity and that her family were warm and fed, wherever they may be.

Rose arrived at the kitchen as the early sun beat fiercely down. The parlourmaids were already in the dining room setting up for breakfast. She bid Mrs March and Bessie good morning, loaded the serving trolley, collected fresh linen along the way and set on up the hill to the duke and duchess's residence.

She was pouring their tea when a knock came at the door. Rose placed down the teapot and went to answer it, finding Miss Dalton on the verandah.

'Ah, Miss Dalton,' the duke said from his seat. 'Do come in.'

'Merry Christmas, Your Grace. I apologise for the intrusion over breakfast,' Miss Dalton said, 'but that important telephone call you were waiting on has come through. You can take it in my office.'

'Yes, thank you.' He placed his napkin on the table and rose from his seat. 'If you will excuse me. I won't be long,' he told Rose and the duchess.

He left and Rose placed the cloche over his breakfast plate to keep it warm.

'He's organising some additional funding for the station in gratitude for your hospitality,' the duchess said, sipping her tea.

'That's very kind. It will be most welcome.'

'If it were up to me, we'd already be on a boat sailing home.' The duchess smiled wryly. 'Alas, this place has gotten under his skin. He likes it here, for whatever reason.'

Rose remained silent as she laid out the toast and spreads for the duchess. She noticed again the incredible green emerald sitting on her ivory décolletage; a rare and precious stone, flawed throughout with natural fissures. It was much like the duchess herself—a tower of strength, yet so delicate she could almost break.

The duchess caught Rose's eye and looked down at the stone. 'My unborn child means everything to me. While I cannot guarantee a girl to pass my emerald to, an heir at least will make my husband happy.'

'He's the happiest I've seen him in a long time, Your Grace.'

'And yet, is it I alone that am making him happy?'

Rose forced her face into a blank expression.

'Who is she?' the duchess asked.

'Who do you mean, Your Grace?'

'Who is the other woman my husband lies with?'

Rose opened her mouth but couldn't find the words to speak.

'I know he sleeps with another. I know he puts valerian root in my milk before bed. I know there is no way to avoid drinking it, for he sits with me until it is down. I know they are intimate in his room for if I put my face to his sheets the next morning, I can smell the peonies. And yet it's a smell you don't wear anymore, so I know it's not you. Tell me, Rose, who is she?'

Rose gulped.

'Is it Nurse Dolly from the hospital? She's been here a few times with the doctor and I see the way my husband stares at her.'

'It's not Nurse Dolly, Your Grace.'

'Then tell me,' the duchess said through gritted teeth. 'Tell me who he lies with! Tell me who is keeping us here!'

She shook her head. 'I don't know, Your Grace.' Of course it was a lie for what else could she say? To give up Bessie would place her and her baby in terrible trouble.

'You are keeping it from me.'

'I don't know anything.'

The duchess closed her eyes and took a breath. 'Protect her if you must, but I will find out.'

Rose bowed her head.

The duchess waved her away. 'Just go.'

Rose curtsied and retreated to the bedrooms, leaving the duchess to stare blankly into her tea.

* * *

Christmas came and went in a swirl of sticky heat. On New Year's Eve, the staff were allowed to gather on the wharf and in the cove to watch the fireworks explode. Champagne was passed around and cigarettes were smoked, the staff exuberant as the sky lit up; one year farewelled, another arrived.

Rose sat with Bessie and the other parlourmaids under Miss Dalton's watchful eye while Thomas sat with the luggage boys from the autoclave.

January leeched into February and Spanish Influenza spread world-wide, aided by troop movements. It broke the station containment lines, infecting the Sydney populous as the world faced its worse pandemic since the black plague.

Despite all this, in their own private sanctuary high up on the cliff, Rose made plans with Thomas for the future. She was six months pregnant with a growing stomach that she hid behind her maternity corset during the day. At night, after fourteen hours on her feet and pushing the trolley up and down the hill in the scorching heat, she would slip the corset off, feeling her stomach release.

She had grown fiercely protective of her unborn child in ways she couldn't put into words. She saw those same feelings reflected in Thomas whenever he placed his cheek to her stomach to feel their child move beneath it. She even saw it in Bessie, catching her in moments of contemplation, a soft smile on her face, a hand on her stomach.

In early March, as the weather started to cool again, heralding the arrival of autumn, Rose was lying in bed while Thomas cleaned up after supper.

'You didn't eat much, my Rose,' he said, dusting crumbs off the table.

Rose shifted on the mattress. 'I feel uncomfortable.'

Thomas sat on the edge of the bed and reached for her hand. 'Uncomfortable because baby elbows and knees are digging into you?'

'More like an intense backache.'

He gave her a worried look.

'Don't fret, my love. I've had it all day. The matron said I would feel aches and pains like this.'

Thomas dimmed the oil lamp and climbed into bed, holding her close. After some time, she felt his breath slow and noticed the moment he dropped off to sleep.

She lay next to him trying to get comfortable but an hour later, the pain had moved from her back to her abdomen—a tightening sensation across her middle which made her stomach turn rock hard. It took her breath away and she rolled over and gently shook Thomas.

He woke looking dazed. 'Are you okay?'

'It hurts.'

He sat up. 'What hurts?'

'My stomach, my back. Everywhere.'

'Should I warm some towels for you?'

The pain intensified and she couldn't reply.

'Rose, you don't look well. Tell me what to do.'

'I don't know.'

'Did the matron say if this was normal?'

'She said I might experience false labour pains but not to worry.' She lay back down on the bed and Thomas placed a hand on her stomach, gently stroking it. After several deep breaths, the pain released its grip on her.

Thomas watched her closely, eyes never straying. 'Are you still suffering?'

'It's not as bad now. It comes and goes.'

He looked relieved. 'Try to get some sleep and at first light, I'll walk you down to the hospital.'

She nodded and closed her eyes, but she couldn't sleep. Ten minutes later, the intense pain was back and she gripped Thomas's shoulder tightly. 'Something's wrong. I don't think it's meant to feel like this.'

He climbed out of bed and relit the oil lamp. 'Come, get dressed. I'll take you to the matron now.'

'It's two in the morning.'

'I don't care.'

Rose gulped, mortified. 'Oh dear, I think I've soiled myself.'

He cast the lamp light over the bed and let out a gasp. 'Rose, my darling, don't look.'

But it was too late. She glanced down and saw a dark red patch on the front of her shift, saw its stickiness seeping through the sheets to the mattress. She let out a groan as the pain ripped through her again, across her stomach and down her back and legs.

She couldn't remember much after that. So acute was the pain, she was only vaguely aware of Thomas collecting her in his arms and hurrying out the door.

He trotted down the path with her, Rose catching glimpses of the moon in the sky as she curled up in his arms in agony, praying that her baby would be okay, knowing that it was far too soon to deliver at seven months.

They reached the perimeter of the Hospital Precinct and Thomas hurried past a stunned guard who didn't try to stop them. He carried her past the tents and confused looks of the patients, his arms straining under her weight. He carried her straight to the nurses and doctors' quarters.

Placing her down on the verandah, he rapped sharply on the matron's door.

The matron answered, struggling into a robe. 'Mr Van Cleeve. It's two in the morning.'

'Help us!' he cried.

Rose was on her knees doubled over in pain. She heard them talking, the matron asking what had happened and Thomas saying *she's in pain, there's blood, the baby's coming!*

In one swift motion, Thomas collected her again in his arms and the matron told him to go via the back door into the maternity ward and she would call for the doctor.

Rose was placed on a bed, a light turned on in her eyes. Thomas was next to her but was shooed away by the matron.

'Thomas!' she called out, feeling his hand leave hers.

'You have to go, Mr Van Cleeve. Doctor Holland and I will take care of this.'

She heard Thomas protest, heard the matron insist, felt the doctor push her shift up and then spread her legs. She struggled against him, swore at him and cried out in agony.

'Hold her legs down, Matron!'

'Rose, please stay calm!'

'Get the restraints for goodness' sake. Hold her down!'

But she didn't feel the restraints around her ankles. Instead she felt something sharp sting her arm, cold fluid filling her body, then time slipped. She faded with it and blacked out.

* * *

Rose heard the voices long before she was aware of her own consciousness. Eyes closed, vision black, but voices in the room.

'Did you get the entire placenta, Doctor?'

'I believe so.'

There was shuffling, the sound of instruments hitting a steel dish, a sharp smell of alcohol in the air.

'Thomas.' Rose could hear her own garbled speech as though through someone else's ears. Her throat was parched. She felt a hand on her arm.

'There now, child. Just rest.' It was the matron's voice.

Rose felt tugging between her legs, then she was being wiped with something wet. The intense pain in her body was gone, replaced with cramping. Her stomach! Her hands reached up and grabbed where her swollen abdomen should have been but found a deflated mound instead.

'My baby!' she said, forcing her eyes open and trying to sit up. 'Where's my baby?'

There was a soothing hand on her forehead and gentle force on her shoulder, encouraging her back down. 'Just lie still and sleep. You need to rest.'

Rose couldn't hang on any longer. Everything tilted again.

* * *

When Rose awoke, the sky outside was indigo and the sun was falling steadily towards the horizon.

She looked around the room. She was alone in the small maternity ward at the back of the hospital. There were no nurses or doctors around and she couldn't see the matron.

Swallowing through a dry mouth, she recalled the pain she had felt in the early hours of the morning, the way Thomas had carried her fifteen minutes without halting, all the way to the Hospital Precinct.

She vaguely recalled being placed on the bed, Thomas being ushered from her side, the sharp, cold steel in her arm injecting a sedative so strong it must have knocked her out for the entire day.

Her hand fluttered to her stomach, but she found nothing there but lumpy flesh, a gaping emptiness. Where was her baby?

There was shuffling in the matron's office next door, then she materialised through a doorway into the maternity ward. 'Rose Porter, you're awake.'

Doctor Holland followed, carrying a small notebook.

Rose struggled onto her elbows. 'Where's my baby?'

'There now, Rose, lay back down,' Matron Cromwell soothed.

'Where's my baby?' Rose asked again, panicked.

Matron Cromwell and Doctor Holland exchanged a look.

'Rose,' the matron said, 'you went into premature labour. Your baby was already with the angels when born.'

An incomprehensible sound escaped her.

Matron Cromwell sat on the edge of the bed and took her in her arms, holding her as she sobbed. 'I am deeply sorry, Rose,' she said rocking her.

Doctor Holland cleared his throat and opened his notebook to write. Matron Cromwell put her hand out to stop him.

'I don't think Rose's procedure needs to go into your book.'

His eyebrows shot up. 'Matron?'

'Rose is from first-class housekeeping. You understand the predicament, Doctor.'

He looked from Rose to the matron and back again.

'We ask for your discretion please.'

He threw them both a disapproving look, slammed his notebook shut and left the maternity ward.

Matron dragged a chair to Rose's bedside and sat. She held tightly to her hand as Rose crumbled again. 'There, my child,' she sang gently. 'It will all be okay.'

Rose sobbed until she had cried herself dry, until the intensity of her grief gave way to something numb and disbelieving.

'These things happen,' Matron Cromwell said. 'There was nothing that could be done. Your baby was not meant for this world.'

She looked into Matron's eyes. 'Who says my baby wasn't meant for this world?'

'It's God's way.'

Rose made a small scoffing sound. 'Was it a boy or a girl?'

'It was a boy. Tiny little thing he was.'

'Can I hold him?'

'No.'

'Can I name him?'

'I don't advise it.'

'*Please* let me name him.'

The matron patted her hair but didn't respond.

'Where's Thomas?'

'He has left to fetch you fresh clothes and undergarments. I will send word to Miss Dalton that you are ill in hospital with cholera. That should buy you a few days' peace.'

'Does Thomas know?'

The matron nodded. 'He has been keeping vigil on the steps outside.'

Rose closed her eyes succumbing to a fresh wave of tears. The shock of it overwhelmed her, like she'd been thrown from a great height, hitting the ground at full speed.

When the sun had slid to the other side of the world, Matron Cromwell helped her out of bed. With a wet cloth, she washed Rose down, ridding her legs, stomach and back of the blood that had dried hours before. They removed her shift and Matron Cromwell sent it to the incinerator to be burned, giving her a hospital gown to wear.

She climbed back into bed but couldn't sleep. The noises from the main ward and the tents outside filtered in—patients moaning in agony, begging for help. For once, she felt nothing for them, just a profuse sense of loss for her child, the one she'd felt moving inside her only the day before.

How could a child be with her one minute then slip so easily from her womb the next? What had she done wrong? Had she worked too hard, stayed on her feet too long, worn her corset too tight? Had her sins amounted to such that God felt the need to punish her so brutally?

When the station had retreated into slumber, Thomas came for her. Matron Cromwell took the dress he proffered and helped Rose slip into it. She waited on the hospital steps while Thomas and the matron conversed behind her. She could hear Thomas's pleading voice, but knew nothing of what they were saying. She only wanted the ground to open up and swallow her.

Thomas took her hand and they walked back to his cottage where she was to spend the next few days. They spoke little, clinging to the shadows, Rose walking gingerly from the procedure, a reminder that the past eighteen hours had not been a nightmare.

Her baby was no longer inside her. Her loved and precious child, robbed of the chance to experience anything in this world, was gone. And Rose, robbed of her chance to meet him, to hold him, to breathe him in, to hear his gurgles and soothe his cries. A bond severed in the blink of an eye.

The cottage loomed solemnly when they reached the end of the path. Moonlight spilt across the cliff and out onto the harbour, illuminating the water in an otherworldly glow.

Thomas let them in the door and once inside, she heard him release the heaviest sigh, one that told her just how much his world had come crashing down too. She went to him and they held each other, standing there for the longest time.

Tears sliding.

Shoulders quivering.

Hearts breaking.

Chapter Thirty-Four

When Rose opened her eyes, it was to the sound of the breeze billowing through the curtains and the fairy-wrens whistling a sad tune outside. The sun hung high in the sky, the room bright as though daybreak had arrived long ago.

Her hand went automatically to her stomach again, bereft of the hard bump she'd been nurturing over the past seven months. Nothing remained but an empty womb and she wondered if she would ever recover. Physically, perhaps, but not her soul. The piece of her that died in the maternity ward could never be made whole again.

She rolled over and discovered the spot next to her was empty. On the small table beside the bed was a glass stained white. Thomas had fixed her warm milk the night before, laced with valerian root, sending her to sleep. But rest had not come without nightmares—the pain, the blood, the syringe plunging deep into her arm, then waking to be told her baby had died.

She closed her eyes against the memory, willing the hollowness away, the vast black feelings of insurmountable despair.

The door opened and Thomas walked in, closing it behind him.

'You're awake.' He washed dirty hands in the bowl, dried them then came to sit beside her on the bed.

'What time is it?'

'After midday. I didn't want to wake you.'

She studied the neckline of his shirt, soaked in a circle of sweat. 'What have you been doing?'

'Come, my Rose. I'll help you dress, then there's something I want you to see.'

The sunshine was blinding when she stepped outside, the day so beautiful it felt like an insult to her bleakness. Thomas took her arm and led her to a patch of sandy earth behind the cottage. There was a shovel on the ground and a small, narrow hole had been dug.

Her breath caught and her body went slack against him. Lying beside it was the tiniest wooden coffin she'd ever seen, open, with a small wrapped bundle inside.

'He deserves a proper burial,' Thomas said.

Rose's eyes filled, her shoulders shook. She took a step forward, then another until she was kneeling beside the coffin on the ground.

'I begged the matron to let us have him. She allowed me to collect him this morning. He's wrapped tightly. She doesn't recommend we open the coverings.'

'Can I hold him?'

Thomas stepped aside to allow her.

Rose took her baby boy in her arms. She didn't heed the matron's warnings, peeling back the coverings slightly to kiss the crown of his head, to feel his soft, cold skin against her cheek, to pray for a breath, a flutter of those translucent eyelashes. Her tears dripped onto him, soaking the layers of cloth he was wrapped in.

'You are so beautiful,' she whispered, holding him close to her breast, marvelling at the tiny creature in her arms. 'How I would have loved to have seen you grow.'

She sat out there for a long time, cradling him as the sun moved across the sky and midday became afternoon.

Thomas didn't leave her side, but after some hours, squeezed her shoulder gently. 'It's time to let him go.'

She nodded, pressing her lips to his skin and holding them there. 'Goodbye my angel.'

He took the baby boy and held him close, kissing the top of his head. 'Would you like to name him?'

'Oh, yes.'

'What shall we call him?'

'Alexander Thomas Van Cleeve.'

Thomas let out an anguished sob. 'Then that shall be his name.'

He gently placed Alexander back into the coffin and secured the lid, nailing it in place with a hammer. Rose traced her fingers along the wood, whispering a prayer to a god she would never understand and probably never forgive, before Thomas lowered Alexander into the ground.

'My heart is fractured,' she said, staring at the tiny box in the earth.

He reached for her hand. 'I know, my love.'

'It hurts like physical pain.'

'Like you might die of a broken heart?'

'Yes. I am broken.'

* * *

A snowflake suspended on the breeze, neither floating nor grounded, was how Rose felt following the loss of Alexander. Thomas carved the name *Alexander Thomas Van Cleeve* onto a headstone, along with birth and death dates, which were joltingly the same, before erecting the stone in the ground by the mound of earth.

Rose remained in his cottage for four days, her fabricated case of cholera making the gossip rounds in first-class accommodation, buying her time to grieve, as Matron Cromwell had intended. It was just as well, for she could barely muster the energy to do anything more than sit by the window staring out at the ocean or lie in the sun by Alexander's grave.

She passed the hours reading to him, while her stomach contracted and her breasts produced milk for an infant who would never suckle. Saplings had begun to spring from the mound as the bushland around the cliff came to claim him, but Rose didn't mind. There was something comfortingly organic about having Alexander out there, that if he couldn't be in her arms, the next best thing was here amongst the wilderness, behind the cottage. Better than in the hospital awaiting disposal, with no one to love and visit him.

Four days after Rose gave birth, she returned to the female staff quarters to resume work. It was with mixed emotions that she climbed the steps to the lodgings she shared with Bessie; glad for the distraction work might bring but still reeling from a loss so great she wasn't sure how she would ever smile again, how she would ever think happy thoughts or talk about inconsequential things.

Bessie was waiting inside for her, having snuck away after the lunch service. She'd made and laid a native Australian wreath of bottlebrush, wattle, banksia leaves and kangaroo paw on Rose's bed. Rose saw the wreath and silent tears slid down her cheeks as Bessie collected her in her arms and held her.

'Your stomach is almost flat again,' she said when they were seated on her bed and Rose had calmed.

'Yes.'

'How did it all happen?'

'I'd been feeling back pain the entire day, then at night it moved to my stomach; the most excruciating agony I've ever felt, like someone was squeezing me in a clamp. Then the blood came.'

Bessie reached for Rose's hand and held it firmly in her own.

'Thomas carried me all the way to the hospital. I don't remember much.' She shook her head. 'The pain was so awful I think I passed out several times.'

'Did the baby come fast?'

'I believe so. They gave me a heavy sedative. I wasn't awake for the birth.'

'I'm sorry you had to go through that,' Bessie said, throwing her arm around Rose and pulling her close. She stroked her hair maternally. 'Thomas stopped by the kitchen to tell me what happened. I thought he would break apart right there in front of me.'

'He's been so strong, stronger than I've been.'

'You had a little boy. Alexander Thomas.'

'Yes. He was beautiful. We buried him behind the cottage. I don't think I can ever leave here knowing he's there.' She felt Bessie nod and she lifted her head to look at her. 'Are you well?'

'I'm feeling heavy and the baby gives me no peace. It's an active little thing.' Bessie coloured slightly, resting a hand on her stomach. 'I'm sorry. The last thing you want to do is hear about my baby.'

'Of course I want to,' Rose said, but her eyes welled all the same. 'You have two months to go. Are you excited?'

'After what you just went through, I'm petrified.'

'Is it still the duke's intention to take you and the baby to England?'

'Yes. Nothing has changed, except the weight I've gained.' She laughed lightly and Rose revelled in the sound of something positive. 'Nobody has guessed I'm pregnant. Mrs March keeps telling me I'm fat and to stay out of the larder, but I don't believe she thinks it's anything more than a hearty appetite.'

'You should wear the maternity corset.'

Bessie waved her hand. 'There isn't long to go now and I'm hardly showing. Then the baby will be born and I'll be on my way to England.'

They fell silent, then Bessie changed the subject.

'So, according to everyone in first class, you're recovering from cholera. Miss Dalton said you can start back tomorrow. You can stay here for the remainder of the day and rest. I'll bring you dinner later.'

'Thank you.'

'I should warn you, though, Mrs March was particularly offended at the idea that her cooking might have made you sick. So be prepared. Tomorrow morning, you may not be her favourite person.'

* * *

The suggestion of winter arrived with a blast of cold May air. Frosty winds blew in from the south, rattling the tall gums and shaking the window panes. Spanish Influenza still raged in all corners of the globe; a great medical cataclysm.

Life in first class returned to a somewhat routine state for Rose. After the death of Alexander, she resumed her service to the duke and duchess, though she wasn't sure anything would ever feel completely normal again.

Matron Cromwell counselled her on the need for contraception and to officialise her union with Thomas through marriage. Of course, the latter was difficult, for Rose was tied to the station now and marriage was not an option for them.

The duchess's stomach continued to swell in approach of her May delivery and on her petite frame, she looked ethereally lovely, like a perfect little porcelain doll. Rose witnessed too, her abundant joy at the prospect that in a few short weeks, if she gave birth to a baby girl, she would be able to pass down her beloved emerald.

How the duke coped with the two impending arrivals, Rose wasn't sure, particularly as his wife knew nothing of his lover's pregnancy. He seemed unusually relaxed given the circumstance. He continued to pronounce his intentions to Bessie while lying with her each night, and in Rose's company, he would gush infinite amounts of affection over his wife and their unborn heir. It was all rather confusing to Rose, not that it mattered. She had other things on her mind.

She learnt to live with the grief of losing her son, but the pain hadn't abated an inch, and she still felt the overwhelming urge to rush back to his grave each evening after the staff dinner. She would often find Thomas out there too, wiping a tear or touching the headstone. She knew, in those moments of watching him, that she wasn't alone in her darkness.

At the end of staff dinner one cool May evening, Rose and Bessie stepped out of the kitchen and wandered up the path towards their lodgings. Bessie had been quiet at the table, barely touching her food.

'I feel strange,' she said when Rose asked her if something was wrong.

'In what way?'

'My stomach has grown tight, like it's clenching.'

'How long have you been feeling like this?'

'Most of the day.'

'You're still two weeks from your due time. Do you think it could be the false labour pains again?' Rose had encouraged Bessie to visit Matron Cromwell and Doctor Holland in April when she'd felt tightening in her stomach and had become concerned she was losing her baby. Matron Cromwell had assured her that she was experiencing false contractions, which were perfectly normal. She had also assured Bessie, with a look of reproach, that her pregnancy would remain secret until she gave birth.

'It could be, though this time it feels stronger.'

'You might have overdone it today. Let's get you to bed.'

Bessie stopped and clutched her stomach, her eyes wide in panic. 'Oh, Rose, it's really starting to hurt.'

'Okay take deep breaths, nice and slow.' Her voice was the epitome of calm but Rose felt the first hints of panic too. If this baby was coming, she had no idea what to do; vivid images of her own labour rushing back to her. All she knew was that she had to get Bessie off the side of the road and back to their room before anyone saw her.

Bessie panted a little then righted herself and Rose assisted her slowly up the hill.

They reached the steps to their cottage and she grabbed Bessie's hand. 'Wait here. I'll collect a shift and undergarments for you then I'll take you to Matron Cromwell.'

Bessie held back. In the dark, Rose could see the terror on her face. 'It's all right. I think the baby might be coming, but you have nothing to worry about,' she said as buoyantly as she could.

'I don't want to have my baby in the hospital. I want to have it here.'

'You should go to the hospital.'

'Can you send for the duke? Tell him I need him. I don't want to do this alone.'

Rose squeezed her hand. 'You're not alone. I'm here with you. And I'm not sure it's a good idea to send for him right now. The duchess will still be awake.'

'He'll come. I know he will.' Bessie was starting to fret.

Rose wasn't sure what to do. She doubted the duke would welcome the intrusion at this hour. She knew for a fact the duchess would not. And, given her own experience, she didn't want to delay medical help for Bessie if indeed these were the first signs of labour.

Torn between decisions, she helped Bessie into the cottage, into her shift and under the covers.

'Are you comfortable?' she asked, perching on the edge of the bed.

'No, but I'm thankful you're here.' Her eyes were large and round in the dark. 'Will you deliver my baby for me? You worked in the hospital. You know about these things.'

'Not about delivering babies.' And truthfully, she didn't know if she would ever be able to witness a birth or hold another infant again and not feel overcome by grief.

'I'm scared.'

'You're doing wonderfully.'

'Will you stay beside me?'

'I won't go anywhere.'

She lit the oil lamp, turned it down low and sat on the edge of Bessie's bed. Every twenty minutes Bessie winced and clutched at her stomach, and Rose knew these to be valid contractions. Matron Cromwell had taught her about the onset of labour, that it could be a long process and how to time the pains. She'd already made the decision that when they reached ten minutes apart she would run for the doctor.

'Tell me a nice story,' Bessie said.

Rose turned her eyes upward in thought. 'Well, I'm getting better at weaving those lovely native wreaths you taught me to make.'

'That's wonderful,' Bessie said, then grimaced through a contraction.

Rose held her hand, trying to distract her. 'Yes, I pick bottlebrush, wattle, kangaroo paw and the green leaves from banksia plants. Every week I thread and weave a new wreath to place on Alexander's grave. His spot is so peaceful out there, behind the cottage, that I often lose hours sitting with him.'

'I'm yet to visit his special spot.'

'You must come one time. We will make a wreath together.'

At eleven, Thomas arrived and Rose met him on the verandah.

'I'm fairly certain Bessie's in labour,' she told him.

She saw his eyes cloud over and knew he was revisiting painful memories. 'Is there anything I can do?'

'Her contractions are fifteen minutes apart. I'll need to send for the doctor when they get to ten, but I'm worried about leaving her here alone.'

'She's not going to have the baby in the hospital?'

'She wants to have it here.'

He nodded. 'I'll call in on the matron now and let her know. Then I'll come back.'

Rose reached for his hand and he leant down and kissed her. He left her on the verandah, disappearing down the hill through the trees.

Rose returned to Bessie's bedside as she let out a howl and curled herself into a ball.

'Rose,' she whispered hoarsely. 'I think I've soiled myself.'

Thinking of the blood in Thomas's bed only months earlier, Rose ripped back the covers and patted her hands along the sheets. It wasn't blood she found, but a thin, clear liquid and she knew Bessie's waters had broken.

Thirty minutes later, there were footsteps on the verandah and Rose opened the door to let the matron and doctor in. She turned up the oil lamp, light growing diffuse as Matron Cromwell sat beside Bessie on the bed.

Rose could see Bessie's white face, her clammy forehead, and the way she was struggling with each contraction that gripped her.

'Have you been timing the pains, Rose?' Matron Cromwell asked.

'I think they're at three minutes apart now. Her water has broken.'

Matron nodded. 'Can you fetch some clean towels and a bowl of hot water?'

'I'll have to run to the kitchen to heat the water.'

Doctor Holland grumbled. 'No time. We'll make do.'

Rose collected as many towels as she could find, filled a bowl of water from the ewer and left it beside Bessie's bed. The doctor opened his medical bag, producing shiny forceps, a scalpel and leather straps to restrain Bessie's legs. A sharp smell of alcohol filled the room.

Rose was ordered to leave and she and Thomas sat out on the verandah, holding each other as they listened to Bessie's whimpers, which eventually gave way to the harrowing grunts of labour.

Then, after one excruciating scream and a moment of silence, they heard it—the beautiful but displeased cries of a newborn baby.

Chapter Thirty-Five

'I'm terribly disappointed in you both,' Miss Dalton said, standing at the foot of Bessie's bed with her arms crossed. She wore a frown that made Rose want to shrink into the floor, but Bessie sat up confidently in bed, holding her new baby daughter in her arms with a contented grin.

The child slept peacefully, unaware of the chaos she had caused hours earlier, when Bessie had gone into labour and Matron Cromwell and Doctor Holland had been called to deliver the baby.

The labour had gone smoothly, Matron Cromwell had told Rose and Thomas out on the verandah later, as the sky began to colour, ushering in a new day. But the noise and commotion had caused the other parlourmaids to wake and Miss Dalton to be promptly informed that a baby had been born in the female staff quarters.

Now, with the sun high in the sky and Bessie and child washed and resting, Miss Dalton had arrived to deliver the inevitable news.

'The rules are clear, Miss Briar, and you have broken many of them. You partook in improper relations with a male on the station and gave birth to his child. You are hereby relieved of your position as scullery maid effective immediately. You will be given a day to recover, gather your belongings and leave the station with your baby. Without pay or references.'

'I won't need pay or references,' Bessie said boldly. 'I will be leaving with the baby's father in two weeks.'

'And who might that be?'

'The Duke of Northbury.'

Miss Dalton gasped, her hand flying to the necklaces at her throat. 'The Duke of Northbury? Oh, dear lord!'

'He'll be taking me and the baby with him to England. As soon as the duchess gives birth, we will set sail.'

'Goodness me.' Miss Dalton, pale with shock, sat on the edge of the bed. 'Bessie Briar, how could you? Oh, the scandal!'

'He loves me,' Bessie said defensively, holding her child close.

'He's the first cousin to the king with a royal heir due in two weeks! This cannot get out. We must contain it. We will be the laughing stock of the Commonwealth.'

Miss Dalton took a deep breath and stood. Her voice was resolute. 'I'm afraid, Bessie, this doesn't change a thing. You still broke the rules. Pack your belongings and leave the station tomorrow.' She nodded curtly and left the cottage.

Rose followed her out onto the verandah where she caught Miss Dalton in a rare, unguarded moment, taking gulps of air.

'I'm disappointed in Bessie,' she said quietly, 'but most of all I'm disappointed in you, Rose. You kept this a secret from me for many months. You're one of my best housekeepers. I expected more from you.'

Rose couldn't meet Miss Dalton's eyes lest she see all the other things she'd been keeping from her, Bessie's pregnancy the least of all.

She looked out across the female staff quarters. Women were on their balconies smoking, eyes and ears trained on them, hoping to catch snippets of their conversation for gossip.

'Will you really make Bessie leave tomorrow?'

'She has to go. She broke the rules.'

'Bessie has worked hard here. Can't we extend her some goodwill in return?'

'If I extend favours to Bessie then I have to extend them to everyone.'

'But the duke is leaving soon. He'll take Bessie and the baby with him. Please, can't they both stay until then? I'll help her with the child. They'll be no trouble, I promise.'

Miss Dalton sighed.

'The duke may not take kindly to the head of housekeeping casting his child out onto the street,' Rose added bravely.

Miss Dalton threw her a look. 'If the duke wishes to impregnate my staff, then he must deal with the consequences too,' she snapped. Her hand flew to her chest and she closed her eyes. 'Forgive me, Rose. I didn't mean that. It's been a stressful morning.'

Rose touched her arm. 'I understand.'

Miss Dalton gave her a small smile. 'Very well. Bessie and her baby can remain here until the duke and duchess sail and not a day longer. I hope for her sake he honours his intentions.'

Rose let out a relieved breath.

'Speak to the matron and have her prepare some nappies, blankets and a hospital crib. There should be some infant's clothes lying around too. Bessie is to remain in this cottage with no visitors. She is not to flash that child around. It will only encourage the other maids.'

Miss Dalton regained her fortitude and stepped down from the verandah, disappearing into the trees, the whispers of the other female housekeepers trailing her.

Rose went back inside and perched herself on the edge of Bessie's bed. The child was still sleeping, Bessie staring at her with unreserved adoration.

'She's perfect,' Rose said softly. 'Like a tiny little bud.'

'Would you like to hold her?'

Rose hesitated. 'Maybe another time.'

Bessie nodded. 'Of course.'

They fell silent, watching the little infant peaceful in her mother's arms.

'Have you thought of a name?' Rose asked.

'I have. I'd like to call her Gwendoline Anne, after my mother.'

'It's a beautiful name.'

'I'm going to ask the duke to give her a title; Lady Gwendoline. And even though she's not entirely blueblood, she's still the rightful heir to the Duke of Northbury's estate. She was born first.'

'I don't think it counts if she's illegitimate.' Rose bit her lip. 'I'm sorry. That came out wrong.'

Bessie gazed down at her child. 'No, I suppose you're right. Gwendoline is illegitimate. I shouldn't concern myself if she's the heir or not. It will be enough that she has a loving home to grow up in.' A look of concern crossed her face momentarily. 'The duke hasn't come to visit her yet. You did pass along the message at breakfast, didn't you?'

'I slipped him the note, yes.'

'Did he say anything?'

'He read it discreetly. The duchess was at the table too. I'm sure he'll speak to me about it at lunch.' She patted her arm encouragingly.

'Yes. I suppose it wouldn't be wise for him to come to me here.'

'Not with all the housekeepers out on their verandahs. They're itching to know who the father is.'

But when Rose saw the duke at lunch, he didn't mention the note about Bessie giving birth, and she had to wait for the duchess to leave the room for a few minutes before she could enquire about it.

'Oh yes, I did read that. Did it all go swimmingly?' he asked, sipping his tea.

'Yes, Your Grace. You have a healthy new baby girl. Gwendoline Anne,' Rose whispered.

'Jolly good,' he whispered back. 'Do they need anything?'

'Just you, Your Grace. They're both looking forward to seeing you.'

'Lovely. Tell Miss Briar I'll make the arrangements to visit soon.'

* * *

Blankets, nappies, infant gowns, soap and a crib arrived from the hospital the next day. Bessie almost cried with relief when she saw it all, for she'd been managing without the essentials for the past twenty-four hours.

In between the lunch and dinner shift, Rose helped her line the crib with blankets and wash the baby in warm soapy water. Together they struggled through assembling the first nappy, the cloth falling off no matter how many pins they fastened.

Gwendoline was a delightful baby who moved through the motions of sleeping, crying and feeding in precisely that order. Rose marvelled at the array of little sounds she made, the squeaks and grunts, gurgles and cries. And when she opened her eyes, they locked firmly on her mother with such precision that at times Rose had to turn away for fear the grief she still felt for Alexander would spill over.

Five days passed and the duke had yet to pay Gwendoline a visit. Before the breakfast shift one morning, Rose stopped to check in on Bessie on her way to the kitchen.

'What do you think is taking him so long?' Bessie asked, kneeling by her bed to change Gwendoline's nappy.

'I imagine he's waiting for the right moment. It would be hard for him to leave with the duchess there. And coming here in broad daylight would only attract attention.'

'Maybe I should go to him.'

'He'll come, don't worry.'

'Can you say something to him today? Tell him how beautiful she is. We just want to see him.'

'Of course I will.'

Then Bessie burst into tears. Rose threw her arms around her.

'I'm sorry,' she cried. 'I'm a wretched mess.'

'You're a new mother and you're exhausted.'

'I just want him to see her. If he did, then he'd fall in love with her too.'

Gwendoline cooed in reply.

'Let's just change the subject,' Bessie said, sniffing. She stood and returned Gwendoline to the crib. 'What's been happening in the kitchen?'

'They've brought the third-class scullery maid in. She's petrified of Mrs March. I daresay the poor girl is anxious to get back.'

'Do they gossip about me much?' Bessie cast her a sideways glance.

'Not at all,' Rose said. It wasn't the truth. She often walked into the kitchen catching Mrs March and the other parlourmaids huddled together in gossip. They always fell silent when she entered and Rose never hung around long, eager to escape an inquisition.

Later that afternoon, at the duke's cottage, she tried to speak to him about Bessie and Gwendoline but there was no opportunity, nor did lunch or dinner present any. The duchess remained in the room with them the entire time, and Rose resolved to try again the following morning.

When she arrived back at her lodgings after dinner with a plate of food for Bessie, the room was empty. Alarm bells rang in Rose's head. Bessie wasn't meant to leave the room.

It was possible she'd taken a brief walk to settle the baby, though something told her exactly where she'd gone.

Rose lit the oil lamp and sat on her bed to await their return.

At ten o'clock, Rose heard footsteps on the verandah and the anguished cries of a hungry baby. She flung open the door and Bessie stumbled in. Gwendoline wasn't the only one crying.

'Goodness, what happened? Where have you been?' Rose asked, taking the baby from Bessie and pacing around the room to calm her.

Bessie was trying to speak through great hiccupping sobs. 'I went to his cottage. He told me to go away. The duchess is in labour. He wouldn't even look at our baby.' The words rushed out of her in a flood. Gwendoline wailed incessantly.

'Why would you go there when you were told not to?'

'Because he hasn't seen his child!'

Rose pursed her lips. 'I need you to get a hold of yourself now and feed the baby. She's very distressed. Then we can talk.'

'I tried to get him to take her. He pulled away, like we were diseased.'

'Bessie, please!'

Gwendoline's cries were so loud and shrill Rose thought they must have been heard from the autoclaves.

Bessie took the child, sat on the edge of the bed, fixed Gwendoline's mouth to her breast and allowed the baby to suckle. Gwendoline was soothed in an instant.

'That's better,' Rose said, touching her temples. 'Now I can hear myself think.'

'Why wouldn't he take her?' Bessie asked. 'His own child.'

Rose sat beside her. 'I don't know. You say the duchess is in labour?'

'That's what he said. When I knocked on his door, he came out but didn't seem pleased to see us. Through the door I could hear the doctor and nurse. I could hear the duchess in discomfort.'

'She was a little quiet at dinner. I guess the labour came on shortly after that.'

'My timing wasn't good, I admit, but he's had all week to come and see us. Why hasn't he?'

Rose couldn't think of anything to say. If he was free to share his bed with Bessie every night at midnight, surely he could spare some time to see his new baby. The alarm bells sounded in her head again.

'What am I to do?' Bessie asked, her voice full of angst.

'Perhaps he just needs more time. He has two births to deal with now.'

'What if he doesn't take us with him? Gwendoline and I will be forced out onto the street.'

'I won't let that happen,' Rose insisted.

'It's not up to you,' Bessie said, her eyes welling again. 'You heard Miss Dalton. I'm to leave with no pay or references.'

For the second time that night, Rose couldn't think of anything to say.

* * *

Lady Eloise Cordelia Jane Asquith was born six days after her half-sibling, Gwendoline, on a cool and blustery May morning. News spread quickly of the birth, some hailing it an exciting royal event, others excited for other reasons, such as the prospect that the cumbersome duke and duchess might finally be on their way.

For Bessie, however, the news sent her into decline. Disconsolate, moody and prone to teary outbursts, she confessed to Rose that she'd grown fearful for her future, unsure whether the duke had any intention of taking her, for he had yet to show interest in Gwendoline.

News of the duke showing off Lady Eloise in the first-class dining room, dressed in a royal gown with the heavy green emerald displayed around her neck sent Bessie spiralling further.

'He doesn't even like the dining room!' she cried when she heard.

Rose became so concerned that she spoke privately with Miss Dalton.

'She fears he will no longer take her and the baby to England with him.'

Miss Dalton raised an eyebrow. 'Well, I'm hardly surprised it has come to this. She brought it on herself, I'm afraid.'

'Please, can't she be allowed to remain here with the baby? I'll help her. They'll be no trouble.'

'Out of the question,' Miss Dalton said.

'Then can they be given the means to survive on the outside? Clothes, money, accommodation, good references.'

'Rose, the rules have always been clear. Bessie Briar chose to break them. And if the repercussions were good for Agnes all those months ago, then I'm afraid they're good for Bessie.'

* * *

A week after Lady Eloise was born, Rose returned to the female staff quarters after lunch service. She had a few hours to spare before she was to return for the dinner shift.

When she climbed the steps and opened the door to her cottage, she was confronted with a foul smell and Bessie lying in bed staring out the window.

'Bessie Briar,' she chastised. 'When was the last time you changed little Gwendoline's nappy?'

Bessie turned to look at her and Rose could see she'd been crying. She collected the infant in her arms and placed her down on Bessie's bed, collecting a wet towel, pins and a clean nappy cloth.

'What time is it?' Bessie asked.

'It's after lunch. Can I bring you something to eat?'

Bessie turned to look back out the window. 'I'm not hungry.'

Rose pulled the soiled nappy away from Gwendoline, wiped her down with the wet towel and fastened a clean one to her bottom. 'Her skin is raw. They call it nappy rash. I'll fetch some corn starch from the kitchen tonight. That should heal it, but you'll have to be more diligent with her hygiene.'

'All right,' Bessie replied. 'You would have made a good mother, Rose.'

Rose returned Gwendoline to the crib. 'Well, it wasn't meant to be.'

'Alexander would have been lucky to have you.'

'I'm the one who would have been lucky.' Rose bent to tickle Gwendoline under the chin. 'You're fattening up, little one.'

Gwendoline gurgled at her.

'How are you feeling today?' she asked Bessie, sitting beside her on the bed.

'I went to see him again this morning,' she said, her gaze fixed on the trees outside. 'I took Gwendoline with me. He wouldn't hold her, wouldn't even look at her. He just told me I was being intolerable, that I should know my place and exercise patience.'

'I saw the duchess today at breakfast. The labour was hard on her and she's unfit to sail at the moment. Perhaps that's all he means. He just needs your patience to sort it all out.'

Bessie turned to her and the look in her eyes was of crushing defeat. 'You're defending him.'

'I'm not.'

'Either that or you're trying to make me feel better. You and I both know he has no intention of taking us with him.'

Rose looked down at her hands.

'I just want my baby to have a chance at life. I don't expect gowns and tiaras and jewels, although all of that would be nice. I just want her to have a chance.'

The way Bessie spoke tore at Rose's heart. It was the desire of every parent surely, to want to give their child the basics, to never want them to struggle, to be given the opportunities that they themselves never had.

'If I leave here without pay or references, we'll be on the street without a penny to our name. I doubt even a church or shelter would take us in. Those places are always overrun with expectant mothers.'

'What about adoption?' Rose suggested, though just saying it rang uncomfortably in her own ears.

'I won't do it.'

She reached for Bessie's hand. 'I wouldn't either.'

Bessie turned again to the window and was quiet for the rest of the afternoon.

* * *

Two days later, after lunch service, Rose went to check on Bessie and baby Gwendoline. She rounded the corner of first class and climbed the hill up to the female staff quarters.

When she arrived, parlourmaids and housekeepers were gathered on their verandahs and a dull hush fell over them as she walked by. She could feel their eyes on her, pointing and whispering.

When she reached her cottage, she saw a group huddled on the verandah—Miss Dalton, Matron Cromwell, Doctor Holland and a man in a suit whom she guessed must be the superintendent. They were conversing sombrely around the open door, their voices low and expressions dark.

Rose climbed the steps, but Matron Cromwell moved her large body in front of the doorway to prevent her from going in. 'Rose, stop.'

'What's happened?' She looked past the matron's bulk into the room. She could hear the baby crying, could see a chair overturned and a note on her bed. But it was the sight of the plump, lifeless body hanging from the rafters that brought her to her knees.

Chapter Thirty-Six

EMMA 2019

Three weeks after Emma said goodbye to Matt on the wharf outside the museum, he called. She felt the phone vibrate, saw his name flash across the screen and she sighed.

It was nine pm on a Saturday night and it couldn't have come at a worse time. She was in her pyjamas, eating a cold slice of quiche from The Coffee Bean, watching bad TV and listening to the jeers of the football crowd beneath her window as they moved from the stadium to the pubs.

It was a feeling she had only just gotten used to again, that one of solitude and ineptness, of being alone, her phone silent and her inbox empty. Matt's call, so out of the blue, threatened to undo the carbon copy of normalcy she'd begun to tack together.

She let the call go to voicemail. After a minute, her phone tinged, letting her know a message had been left. Despite all self-reasoning, she dialled her voicemail service and her heart leapt involuntarily at the sound of his voice—warm, gravelly, still as desirable as she remembered it.

'Hi, Em. It's me.' He sounded nervous, clearing his throat. 'I know you probably don't want to hear from me right now but I've found something you're going to want to see. I've found a lot of things, actually. Meet me tomorrow at Rose and Thomas's cottage around three. If I don't see you there, I'll understand.'

Emma placed her phone down and stared at it. Her shift tomorrow ended at three, but she knew Chloe wouldn't mind her leaving early. The question was, should she? Did Emma want to go down that path again? It had been hard enough three weeks before, sitting beside him on the floor of the archive room, wanting to put her arms around him but knowing she couldn't. Could she dredge it all up again, prolong the inevitable in that they just weren't meant to be?

Still, the next morning, as is the way with intrigue, it got the better of her. She was curious as to what he'd found. *Something you're going to want to see*, he'd said, and with such conviction that it caused Emma to wonder about it the entire day.

With Chloe's blessing, she left her shift at two and headed north towards Manly.

Under sultry, grey skies she passed the Manly Hospital, drove beneath the sandstone arch and followed the road to the reception carpark. Ted was waiting in his usual spot out the front reading the newspaper when she climbed aboard.

'Hey there, Emma,' he said cheerily. 'Matt said you might be coming.'

'Hi, Ted. Can I get a ride to third class?'

'You sure can.' He placed the paper down and started up the shuttle.

They rumbled down Entrance Road, veering left onto Cottage Road. Ted halted the bus at the former male staff quarters near third class, and Emma climbed down onto the grass.

'Get Matt to radio me if you need a lift back. I don't know how much longer this weather's going to hold out.' He indicated towards dark, brooding skies.

'Thanks, Ted,' Emma said, waving goodbye as he closed the door and swung the bus away. She skirted the former staff cottages, as euca-lypts rattled in the wind and fallen gumnuts crunched under her shoes. She saw Matt waiting for her by the concealed path.

'Hey,' he called out.

'Hi,' she replied, reaching him.

'I wasn't sure if you were going to come.'

'I wasn't sure myself. Chloe gave me an early mark.'

He nodded. 'Well, we better get moving. I'm not sure how long we've got before this storm hits.'

'What did you find?' she asked as they followed the path towards the cliff edge, dodging branches.

'A lot of things. We weren't there long enough last time to have a good look. And I understand why,' he said, glancing back at her apologetically.

'Are you going to give me any hints?'

'It's better if you see for yourself.'

They emerged out onto the clearing, waves crashing against the escarpment below. The wind was starting to whistle and black clouds from the west charged towards them. Thunder rumbled down the harbour.

Matt, having fixed the door from the last time he'd broken through it, turned the handle. It squeaked open and Emma stepped inside.

The temperament in the cottage had changed as though something of significance had been unearthed. The navy blue trunk she'd pulled from the wardrobe last time was now open and she glimpsed what looked like more of Rose's diaries sitting on top of old blankets and clothing.

Over on the table, Matt had set aside the bowl and ewer, abacus and other items and had wiped the surface clean. Lying there now was a gas lantern, torch, his drink bottle and phone, a backpack and an apple core.

'You didn't spend the night here, did you?' she asked, raising an eyebrow at him.

He laughed. 'No, but I've been here since early this morning. I was here all day yesterday too.'

Emma turned back to the trunk and pointed to the small brown books, all with the same matching clasp. 'Are those more of Rose's diaries?'

'Yes,' Matt said. He reached into the trunk and retrieved one of them. He seemed to know exactly which one to select and Emma realised he'd already read them.

The room had grown dim, the sun slowly being swallowed by storm clouds and Matt lit the gas lantern at the table, indicating that Emma should take a seat.

'I found this entry when I was going through the diaries.' He opened it to the first page and placed it under the circle of lantern light. 'It's something you need to see.'

Emma glanced down at the diary and began to read.

5th March, 1919

My heart is broken, shattered into tiny pieces, beyond hope of ever healing.

I gave birth yesterday. I delivered a beautiful baby boy who was already with the angels when he appeared, who had the breath stolen from him before he could open his eyes.

To my beloved little Alexander Thomas, today we laid you to rest in a coffin built by your father, in a hole dug by the same. I held you in my arms and kissed your delicate crown. I heard your cries on the wind and the sweet sounds you would have made had you lived. I heard them all and it's all my heart will ever know for I never got the chance to be your mother in the flesh. For that I will always grieve.

I will never forget the feel of you in my arms or against my cheek. I will always see your reflection in the windowpane, forever an imprint on my heart; your pure soul entwined with mine as mother and child should be.

Goodbye, my darling child. May you rest in peace.

Rose

Emma leaned back in the chair and let out a breath. The diary entry had been brief but it spoke volumes. More than that, it changed everything. 'Rose gave birth to a baby boy and he died.'

'Yes, a stillborn. I found the grave outside behind the cottage. There's a headstone. It's covered mostly with creepers and weeds now but I cleared enough of it to see the inscription. It belongs to her son, Alexander Thomas Van Cleeve, my great uncle.'

'So Thomas and Rose didn't give birth to Gwendoline. They gave birth to a boy and he died.'

Matt watched her closely.

'That must mean Gwendoline isn't Rose and Thomas's biological child.'

'Right.'

'And that must mean we're not...'

'Related.'

Emma couldn't help it. Her eyes flooded with tears and she wiped them away, feeling embarrassed. 'I'm sorry. I'm just so relieved!'

Matt sat in the chair beside her. 'I felt the same when I read it and put two and two together.'

'It's interesting why this diary wasn't with the others in her suitcase behind the archive room. It could have saved us a whole lot of anxiety.'

'She must have written about the birth then hid it here in the cottage to protect it from prying eyes.'

Emma chewed her lip thoughtfully. 'So Rose and Thomas's first-born died, but is there any chance they had another child soon after and that could have been Gwendoline? Maybe her birth dates got mixed up. How else could Gwendoline have come into their care?'

'She's definitely not their child. There's something else you need to see.' He took the diary and flicked through the pages to an entry dated the twenty-second of May, 1919. 'Read this one.'

Emma took the diary and her eyes swept over the page as Rose wrote about the suicide of her best friend, Bessie Briar, who had left behind an infant daughter called Gwendoline Anne.

It was another harrowing account and she could feel Rose's grief in the sad loop of her letters; an outpouring of complete and utter devastation. When she turned the page, a folded piece of paper caught in the binding slipped out and dropped onto the table.

Thin and fragile with age, she carefully unfolded it.

I know you will care for her as I cannot.
I know you will give her all that she deserves.
Do not be sad, dear Rose, as I know you will be.

Gwendoline will have a better life with you.
She will grow to know you and Thomas as her parents.
Give her the castle I never could.
Your dearest friend, in life and death.
Bessie.

'Gwendoline was Bessie Briar's child,' Emma said, stunned. The tiny hairs on her arms prickled. 'My great-grandmother wasn't Rose. It was Bessie.'

'Yes. And not only did Rose have to contend with the loss of her child, a couple of months later she lost her best friend.' Matt leant back in his chair. 'After I read the diary entry and suicide note, I remembered something Gwendoline had said, that she recalled seeing Bessie Briar's name on stone.

'I took a walk down to the cemeteries that still exist on site. It took me a couple of hours, but I found Bessie's grave. There isn't much on her headstone, just her name and date of death.'

'So Rose and Thomas must have cared for Gwendoline after Bessie died and raised her as their own. By some turn of events they were allowed to remain on the station with her and live together in this cottage.' Emma glanced again at Bessie's note. '"Give her the castle I never could."'

'The duke was Gwendoline's father.'

Emma's eyes widened. 'How can you be sure?'

'I read through the entire diary. Rose names him as the father. She talks about how he promised Bessie he would take her and the baby back to England with him.

'But when his wife, the duchess, had their child, his intentions changed. Bessie became fearful for her future. She either had to sail for England with the duke, which was looking more unlikely, or she'd be fired without pay or references. It was post-wartime and she was a single, unmarried mother. The prospects weren't good.'

'So my great-grandfather is the Duke of Northbury?'

'Puts a different spin on things.'

As if to agree, the weather unleashed an almighty crack of thunder outside and Matt stood to peer out the window.

'It doesn't look good out there. We should head back.'

Emma slipped Bessie's note back inside the diary and stood, placing the diary with the others in the trunk and closing the lid. Matt waited for her by the door with his backpack and the extinguished gas lantern.

When they opened it, they were greeted with a sizzle of lightning that lit up the sky and a downpour of torrential rain so heavy and cold, it brought with it pellets of hail.

'Quick, back inside,' Matt said.

They hurried back into the cottage and closed the door, Emma shaking water off her shirt and hair.

'We're not going anywhere in that,' he said.

'How long will it hang around for?'

'It could set in for the rest of the afternoon. We might as well get comfortable.'

The clouds outside were black, chasing the daylight away. Matt relit the gas lantern and checked that the torch worked. He handed it to Emma and she took the opportunity to walk around, casting the beam of light over furniture and belongings, taking the time to appreciate it all properly as she hadn't been able to the first time.

She ran her hands along Rose's nurse uniform, over the remnants of Gwendoline's half-eaten toys and a model WWI aeroplane that she guessed had been constructed by Thomas, everything coated in a thick veil of time.

A strange mix of emotions ran through her. These two wonderfully kind and caring people, who she thought had been her great-grandparents, weren't at all. Two other people were—the Duke of Northbury and his lover, Bessie Briar.

It made Emma wonder just how much Gwendoline had known. Had she been aware that Rose and Thomas weren't her biological parents? Was that the reason for her teenage rebellion? Could it have been the duke she'd been waiting for down by the wharf as a young child, hopeful that one day her real father would return for her?

It had to have been a pipedream at best. The duke would have been long gone by then, having sailed home already to his castle with his wife and Lady Eloise. But if that was the case, who were Rose and Thomas running from in 1926 and why did they change their names? There were still so many questions unanswered.

She cast the torch beam across an open doorway and into another room as thunder clapped overhead, rattling the windowpanes. The rain was relentless, drumming the roof.

'This is the bathroom I showed you last time,' Matt said, appearing at her side.

Emma swept the light across the room. She saw a small porcelain bathtub, a shelf lined with cobwebbed bottles, three hooks on the wall with towels hanging and an empty chamber pot in the corner.

'It's like they just got up one day and walked out,' Emma said.

'Maybe the duke sent for Gwendoline and Rose didn't want to give her up so they fled.'

'I doubt it. He wouldn't have come back for her. He sounded like a jerk to be honest.'

Matt moved close beside her, their hands brushing, a silence settling between them.

'I've been struggling the last couple of months,' he said openly.

'Me too.'

'And I'm not sure what this means for us now, Em, but I'm hopeful.'

She smiled at him in the dark. 'I'm hopeful too.'

His arms reached for her hips, drawing her in. She turned, tossed the torch onto the bed and let him embrace her, her head falling onto his shoulder. She was exhausted, the emotion of the past weeks and the long hours she'd worked to escape her own thoughts, taking its toll. They stood there for a while, holding each other.

'I'm dying to take your clothes off right now,' he whispered into her ear, 'but I don't know how clean the bed is.'

She laughed out loud. No matter what happened from here, gone was the gloom hovering above them.

Matt let her go and returned to the table. He picked up his phone to check the time. 'It's five o'clock. Are you hungry?'

'A little.'

While he rummaged around in his backpack, Emma glanced out the window. The storm had cleared out to sea but another was brewing in the south. Thunder rumbled and the rain continued to fall steadily. They would be stuck in the cottage for some hours.

'Muesli bar, banana or salt and vinegar chips?'

Emma turned to look at the food he'd laid out on the table. 'The chips.'

He grabbed the packet and opened it. They crunched hungrily, standing in the dark room, watching the flickering lantern light and listening to the rain pound the roof.

'What else was in the trunk?' she asked.

Matt dusted his hands of salt. 'Apart from the diaries, just some old blankets and ladies and children's clothing. I haven't been through the whole thing yet.'

Emma balled up the empty chip packet. 'Should we look through it together since we have time to kill?'

Matt kissed her his answer. They knelt beside the trunk and Emma opened the lid. Scattered across the top were the diaries Matt had already read and layers of folded blankets and clothing.

'These diaries end with Bessie's death,' Matt said.

'What's underneath here?' Emma asked, peeking beneath the blankets.

'I didn't get that far.'

She lifted the pile of blankets and clothes and found beneath them more diaries, with similar brown hardcovers and tiny metal lock clasps. 'Wow, there are so many. Rose was quite the writer.'

Matt brought the lantern down to the floor and cast the light over them.

Tucked away in the pile of diaries was a larger page folded over. Emma recognised the yellowing paper instantly for she'd seen it before in the First Class Hospital Registration Book. Matt leant in with the lantern as she unfolded it and laid it out on her lap. *May 1919—First Class Maternity Ward.* It was the missing May page.

There were just two baby names listed there—Gwendoline Anne Briar and Eloise Cordelia Jane Asquith.

'It looks like at some point in May both babies were admitted to the maternity ward. Not sure why someone would rip the page out,' Matt said.

'Maybe the duke didn't want any affiliation with Gwendoline,' Emma said.

'But why is the page hidden in here? Why wouldn't the duke have it or have seen to it that it was destroyed?'

'I'm not sure.'

Matt reached for the piles of diaries, stretching open the covers a little so that the hidden keys fell out.

'You've gotten good at that,' she said, smiling.

'I've read enough of them by now to know where she hid the keys.' He unlocked each one, placing the lantern light over the pages, flicking through them, like he was in search of something particular.

'What are you looking for?'

'Bessie died on the twenty-second of May, 1919. I'm looking for Rose's entries dated from that day onwards. If we know Rose as well as I think we do, she's going to tell us exactly what happened and why someone would want to hide that maternity page.'

His fingers traced the tops of the diary pages, across the dates, working backwards from July 1919 and June 1919. Then he tapped one suddenly. 'Got it. Twenty-fourth of May, 1919.'

24th May, 1919

The hospital fire took everyone by surprise. It was midnight; sirens wailing, flames licking the sky like the fires of hell. The station was in a panic. People were everywhere, fleeing the wards, the verandahs, the tents outside as the blaze tore through.

I had come from the cemetery, laying flowers on my dear friend's grave, not long after burying her; her tombstone still wet with my tears. She didn't deserve this of the duke. He had failed her, pledging promises he could not keep, driving her to fear a life so bleak that death seemed like the only option. I have never felt hatred towards someone before, but I feel it now. It's black and hostile; all-consuming. I fear it will stay with me for some time to come.

When I saw the flames from the cemetery, I knew something was wrong. It was only when I got closer to unhealthy ground that I realised what was happening. The first-class hospital was alight and little Gwendoline was inside, where she'd been sent after her mother's death to be cared for by the wet nurse.

The hospital was already engulfed when I arrived. People flooded out of the perimeter as I fought my way in. The doctors and nurses were pouring buckets of water onto the flames, sick troops doing the same, but it was to no avail.

I saw the matron running out of the hospital and down the steps holding two infants, one of them I knew would be Gwendoline. She came to me, told me to take the children. I took them both in my arms and asked her who the other child belonged to. She said it was Lady Eloise, that she was spending time in the ward whilst the duchess fought off another bronchial infection.

I looked at both babies, so alike in features, half-sisters, fathered by the same man. Then the matron held out a gold necklace with a large emerald stone, the exact one I had seen the duchess wear many times.

She told me it had slipped off Lady Eloise. Her eyes flickered between each child as she said it. She hesitated, then she placed the necklace around one of the baby's necks and ran to help the other patients.

The duke and duchess were upon me. The duchess was screaming 'give me my baby,' so I handed over the baby that wore the emerald necklace.

But in all the chaos and with the children so alike, I cannot say for certain which baby was hers.

Rose

Emma finished reading and looked up at Matt, her eyes wide. 'There was a baby swap.'

'We don't know that for certain.'

'I think we do. Rose was pretty clear about it.' Emma leant back in her chair. 'Oh my God, this all makes sense now. The matron put the emerald on the wrong baby. She put it on Gwendoline. Rose then handed Gwendoline to the duchess. The duke and duchess mistakenly took Gwendoline home to England, and Lady Eloise was raised on the station by Rose and Thomas. Lady Eloise is my grandmother, and she

327

was waiting by the wharf all those years ago for her family to come back for her. '

'I don't think we can assume all that.'

'No, you don't understand,' Emma said, the words rushing out of her like rapids. 'That's exactly what happened. I know it because Emma isn't my real birth name. It's not the name on my certificate. It's just what people call me.'

Matt was staring at her as if she'd gone mad. 'What are you talking about?'

'Gwendoline must have known she was Lady Eloise. And my mother, Catherine, must have known, for why else would they call me that name?'

'What name?'

'*Emerald*. My birth name is Emerald.'

Chapter Thirty-Seven

ROSE 1919

Dawn broke. What should have been a clear and crisp autumn morning burned black with smoke. It spewed into the sky as the fire truck arrived, pumping water onto flames that glowed brighter than the rising sun. The first-class hospital was unsalvageable—a charred ruin.

But it wasn't the blaze Rose watched. It was the infants she rocked in her arms, one wearing a precious emerald heirloom placed around her neck by Matron Cromwell. The babies' similarities were extraordinary; both had fair hair and grey eyes, both had gained a little weight since birth. But it was a question she dared not ask herself. Who was wearing the emerald?

Clouded by grief and a night that would be burned in her memory forever—the loss of the first-class hospital—she couldn't be sure if her eyes were playing tricks on her. She stared at them both, stared until it occurred to her, just for a split second, that maybe the matron had made a grave error. That she'd put the emerald on the wrong child.

'Give me my baby!'

Rose swivelled and found the duke and duchess rushing upon her, the duchess coughing and wheezing but holding out her hands to take one of the infants. 'Where's my child? Where's Eloise?'

Rose hesitated, unsure what to do.

'Where's the emerald?'

'It's here,' Rose said, indicating the stone that sat around the child's neck.

'Oh, thank God. She's okay. And the stone is okay.' The duchess took the baby into her arms and held her close while throwing the duke a scathing look. 'I told you I didn't want Eloise brought to the hospital. I wanted a private wet nurse. We could have lost her.' She stalked away.

The duke sighed soberly. 'Thank you, Rose. We are forever in your debt.'

'It was the matron who brought them out to safety.'

'Nevertheless, we are eternally grateful.' He gave the sleeping infant in Rose's arms a sweeping glance. 'Is that...?'

'Yes, it's Bessie Briar's child.'

He peered at the baby so closely Rose began to feel uncomfortable beneath his gaze. Could he tell which baby she was holding? Could he distinguish the features between the two? Her insides were screaming at her to say something, to voice her doubts, but what if she was wrong? What if she caused unnecessary panic? Miss Dalton would never forgive her.

The duke righted himself and cleared his throat. 'I'd heard about the child's mother. Terrible shame.'

'Yes. The child has become orphaned.'

He nodded.

Rose clutched his shirt sleeve and looked pleadingly at him. 'Your Grace, can you not find it in your heart to take Gwendoline with you? She will end up a ward of the state otherwise.'

He hesitated then snatched his arm away. 'What are you suggesting?'

'That you take both your daughters with you to Somersby Castle.'

'How dare you?'

'Please, Your Grace. She's a lovely child and Eloise's half-sister. You can raise them together.'

The duke looked shocked at her impudence. 'Good God, you have some nerve, Rose.' He straightened his shoulders and gave the child a dubious look. 'I don't know this child nor did I ever know her mother.'

He stormed off after his wife.

* * *

The fire could not have come at a worse time. The Hospital Precinct was already overrun with Spanish Influenza cases. Now, with the main hospital a smouldering scar on the hill, there was just the smaller third-class hospital left, overflowing with hundreds of patients, with tents covering every inch of ground space to accommodate the ill.

Two days later, while the station tried to recover from its prodigious loss, Rose climbed the steps to Miss Dalton's office and knocked on the door.

'Come in.'

Rose opened the door and stepped inside.

Miss Dalton seemed surprised to see her. 'Hello, Rose. Take a seat. Is everything all right?'

Rose sat and placed her hands in her lap. 'I'd like to speak to you about Bessie Briar's infant.'

'What about her? Is she unwell?'

'She's doing fine. She's been staying in the wet nurse's quarters until a permanent solution becomes available.'

'That's probably not a bad idea. The third-class hospital is hardly a place for a baby.' Miss Dalton pursed her lips. 'And I don't suppose the duke and duchess plan to take the child with them?'

'No.'

She nodded grimly. 'I can't say I'm surprised. I did think Miss Briar was being a tad optimistic with the idea. In any case, thank you for reminding me. I'll telephone the local church and see if they can come and collect the child tomorrow.'

'About that,' Rose said, sitting forward. 'I have a suggestion.'

Miss Dalton looked up from the note she was writing herself. 'A suggestion?'

'Yes. I'd like to keep little Gwendoline here at the station.'

Miss Dalton blinked. 'Excuse me?'

'I'd like to keep her here and raise her as my own.'

Miss Dalton laughed. 'Well, that's preposterous. We don't allow children to be raised here. You know that.'

'I also know that Bessie died to protect her child. That she felt there

331

was no other option than to take her own life because of the pressure this station put her under.'

Rose knew she was speaking out of turn but ever since the hospital fire, she had spent countless hours staring at Gwendoline, studying every line and curve of her face, trying to tell which baby she was. It was remarkable how alike the two were. But without knowing for certain, she couldn't let this child leave the station.

Miss Dalton's back stiffened. 'Careful, Miss Porter. If I didn't know you any better, I'd assume you were blaming *me* for Bessie Briar's suicide.'

'I apologise, Miss Dalton. I meant no disrespect. But Bessie was a dear friend and a good employee who worked tirelessly here. Her child should not have to suffer for the mistakes made by her parents. Will you sleep well at night knowing you're going to give a newborn infant away to the state?'

Miss Dalton sighed wearily as though she no longer had the energy to fight. 'What is it you are asking me exactly?'

'I want to raise Gwendoline here. I'll clothe and school her myself. I'll tend to her when she's unwell and you can deduct money from my wages for any expenses incurred. I expect no assistance and nothing for free, only your blessing for her to remain on the station.'

'And where do you propose to raise her? Right under the noses of the other female housekeepers? One whiff of this and they'll all be falling pregnant. It will catch on quicker than Spanish Flu.'

'I don't intend to live with Gwendoline in the female quarters. In fact, I could never go back to that room again. Not since...' Rose trailed off and looked down at her hands.

Miss Dalton watched her closely. 'Where will you go?'

'There's a cottage out by the cliff behind the male staff quarters. I'll raise her there.'

'From what I understand that's the carpenter's cottage.' When Rose didn't respond, Miss Dalton's eyebrows went up in disbelief. 'Oh Rose, not you too.'

'We'll share shifts,' Rose continued. 'When I'm working, he'll stay with Gwendoline and when he's at work, I'll be with her.'

Miss Dalton shook her head with barely concealed disappointment.

'And after the duke and duchess leave, I'm going to request a transfer back to the hospital where I can do shift work. We won't be your problem at all.'

'Rose, if you and Mr Van Cleeve have engaged in copulation then you have broken the rules too. And that means instant dismissal without pay or references.'

'But Miss Dalton...'

'You both have until the end of the day to pack your things and leave. You can take the Briar infant with you.'

'Please, you're being unreasonable.'

'I don't believe so.'

Rose breathed. 'I'm sorry I disobeyed you. I am, but can this station afford to lose a scullery maid, a parlourmaid, its only carpenter and the first-class hospital all in a matter of days? Please,' she begged, 'give me the chance to prove to you that this can work. That I can raise Gwendoline here and it won't cause any problems with the other housemaids.'

'Goodness, Rose, you're not even married. It's distasteful.'

'We intend to be.'

Miss Dalton massaged her forehead with her fingertips. She looked worn from the influenza crisis, from the overflow of passengers and the constant demands of an overrun station. 'What you are asking of me is monumental. It goes against everything I stand for.'

'I know.'

'It could change life on the station as we know it, throw order into chaos. It could start something that there would be no coming back from.' Miss Dalton sighed. 'And I just don't know if we're ready for that.'

* * *

The May sun was pale in the sky when Rose stepped out of Miss Dalton's office an hour later.

Emotionally drained from a lengthy debate, she walked down Main Axial Road, past children playing quoits and the chatter of women in the sewing room. She passed the kitchen where parlourmaids were carrying trolleys of plates and cups from the dining room after lunch service.

Out of habit Rose stopped, poked her head through the doorway and trained her gaze on the sinks to say hello to the bubbly, plump girl who normally stood there, elbows deep in greasy water and with a head full of golden curls beneath her bonnet. But then she remembered with a jolt of despair, like she was learning it for the first time, that Bessie was gone.

At the top of the hill, she wiped fresh tears from her cheeks and turned away from first class, heading towards the Hospital Precinct. Outside the morgue she ran into Thomas. She was so relieved to see him she had to fight the impulse to throw her arms around him.

'How did your meeting go with Miss Dalton?' he asked.

'I thought she was going to have us both fired. It took some convincing, but she's going to let us trial it for a month.'

'You mean we're allowed to stay? With Gwendoline?'

'Yes.' Rose couldn't wipe the grin from her face.

'That's incredible,' he said, grinning too. 'But you know if she had asked us to leave, it would have been all right. We would have made it work.'

'I know. But I'm not ready to leave Alexander yet,' she said. 'This is where we belong for now, the four of us.'

'The four of us,' he agreed. 'So your move to my place is official? No more sneaking out at night?'

'Yes. I'll collect Gwendoline from the wet nurse tonight and bring her over. But if we are to live together, Miss Dalton has insisted we marry as soon as possible.'

'I agree but there isn't a priest on site.'

'She will try to arrange day release for us so we can travel into the city to have it officialised.'

Thomas smiled ruefully. 'Hardly the ceremony I had in mind, but if it means we can live together, then we should do it. What about your things in the old room?'

Rose shook her head sadly. 'I can't go back there, not after what I saw. I asked Miss Dalton to pack my suitcase and store it somewhere. I'll collect it another time. There isn't much there, just some old diaries, clothes and Bessie's belongings.'

Despite being out in public, Thomas reached for her hand and squeezed it. 'Would you like to take a walk down to the cove? We haven't been there for some time and I have an hour free.'

'I can't,' she said regretfully. 'There's someone I need to see first.'

'Is everything all right?'

She wished she knew the answer to that.

* * *

Rose found Matron Cromwell in the medicine room of the third-class hospital, counting morphine vials in the cabinet. She closed the door and leant against the opposite bench to watch her.

The matron didn't look up. Her lips moved as she murmured numbers from them before writing on her inventory sheet.

'Which child did you put the emerald on?'

Matron Cromwell paused, hand suspended in the cabinet.

Rose waited for an answer, but when one wasn't forthcoming, she crossed her arms. 'Matron?'

Matron Cromwell turned around. She looked tired and her heavy bulk seemed to droop under Rose's questioning gaze. 'I wondered when you'd come by with that question.'

'Well?'

'I don't know.'

Rose closed her eyes, breathed, then opened them again. 'Was there anything that made you choose one child over the other?'

The matron put down the inventory sheet and leant against the bench. They stood facing each other, an incomprehensible nightmare laid out between them.

'When I collected them both from their cribs in the maternity ward, the room was full of smoke and I couldn't see well. I'd realised the emerald had slipped from Lady Eloise's neck when I trod on it on my way out. When I picked it up, I looked at each infant, but I didn't know who it had come from.

'Outside with you, in that split second, I thought I chose the correct

335

child. But the more I think about it, the more I'm unsure.' Matron Cromwell furrowed her brow. 'It was chaotic, there were people everywhere and my eyes and lungs were burning. And those infants, so alike. How can I be absolutely certain?'

'So what should we do?'

Matron Cromwell straightened. 'There's nothing we can do.'

'We might have swapped the babies, Matron. We have to do something.'

'Keep your voice down,' Matron Cromwell hissed. 'And we do nothing. We don't even know if an error was made. Can you imagine if we marched up to the duke and duchess and told them we might have *accidentally* swapped the king's second cousin with an illegitimate bastard?'

Rose cringed. 'Please don't call Gwendoline that.'

'Be reasonable. What's done is done. We should never speak of it again.'

'But Matron, the wrong child could be sent to Somersby Castle. That could meddle with royal bloodlines.'

Matron Cromwell almost smiled. 'Well if that's the case, so be it. Bessie Briar got the last laugh.'

* * *

A week later, as the last of the autumn leaves fell, the Duke and Duchess of Northbury left the shores of Sydney, setting sail for England.

They took with them a baby girl.

Chapter Thirty-Eight

Sometime around midnight, the rain moved out to sea, leaving behind an argent moon that lit the way. Matt led them from Rose and Thomas's cottage back to the former male staff quarters, stepping across muddy puddles and past dripping branches that wet their faces.

'I'll radio Ted and see if he's still around to pick us up,' Matt said, his backpack slung over one shoulder and his other hand closed around Emma's.

'It's after midnight. Wouldn't he have left already?'

'There were two ghost tours booked.' Matt glanced at his watch. 'We might still catch him.'

'I'm happy to walk.' Despite the earlier rain, the evening had grown pleasant, the air heady with wet eucalyptus and wattle.

'It's a long way.'

'I have good company.' She smiled at him.

For nine hours they'd been confined to the cottage while the rain fell. They'd spent that time pouring over the last of Rose's diaries. Rose had documented her life as a new mother throughout the early 1920s, the highs and lows she and Thomas experienced, along with the joy of marrying and Gwendoline's probation period coming to an end, with an invitation from Miss Dalton to stay.

This decision appeared to have sparked a chain reaction. The station had come to the realisation that inviting families to live on the site wasn't going to throw order into chaos, but rather open the door to a plethora of qualified staff who wouldn't previously have been able to apply under the 'no children' rule. The station adapted, throwing itself into a new age.

Rose explained the love she and Thomas felt for the little child they were raising. She had developed an inquisitive nature and a demure manner; a beautiful young soul whom they adored with all their hearts.

Notably absent were any diaries from 1926, the year they had fled the station.

'If they still exist, I know where I might find them,' Matt had said.

Now, as they walked, he squeezed her hand. 'How do you feel about everything? We've uncovered a lot in the last few weeks.'

'Well, I like the fact that you and I aren't related.'

'I like that part too,' he said, his smile wide in the dark.

'I also think that even though Rose wasn't my biological great-grandmother, she's always been a part of my life through Gran. And so I will always think of her as mine.'

'That's a good way to look at it.'

'What I'm unsure about is how much my mother and father knew.'

'Given your name, it seems likely they knew the whole story.'

'And I think that's what upsets me the most. Everyone knew about this. Gwendoline, my mother, my father. They must have known the babies were swapped, for why else would they have called me Emerald? It's not exactly a common name. And yet, no one thought to tell me about it.'

'Maybe they always planned to but never got the chance.'

Emma nodded sadly.

They reached Cottage Road and began the long walk back to Reception. A swarm of bats circled overhead, beating their wings against the night.

'It's incredible to think that something as inconsequential as placing an emerald on a child had the power to change so much,' Matt said.

'And yet it did.'

'Do you know what this means, Em? Gwendoline is the real Lady

Eloise, the true daughter of the Duke and Duchess of Northbury. She's a second cousin to the king. That means your mother, Catherine, was the duke's granddaughter and the king's third cousin. You'd probably be permitted a title and land rights under the British Crown.'

Emma cast him a look. 'That all sounds very serious and probably hard to establish.'

'And you'd have to stir up a lot of old ghosts to get to the bottom of it. But Bessie Briar's child and her descendants may not have any legal claim to the titles they would have inherited. As for the land, we could be talking about castles, estates; acres and acres of Crown land that you and Gwendoline would be entitled to.'

Emma breathed deeply. So many truths had been absorbed that night, so many still to come. She was barely digesting all that she'd learnt and it would be some time before she could get her head around titles and land rights and castles.

She recalled the photograph of Rose and Bessie laughing outside the first class kitchen, realising again that neither of those women were biologically linked to her. That in itself was extraordinary. 'I wonder what the duke and duchess look like. If they have my brown hair and blue eyes. If my mother looked anything like them.'

'We could Google a photo.'

'I need to see my grandmother,' Emma said suddenly.

'What? Now?'

'I have to. Knowing what we know, she could probably fill in the blanks.'

'It's almost one in the morning. They're never going to let you wake her up and start a conversation.'

Emma glanced at her watch. 'I guess it is a bit late.'

They arrived back at reception. The station was deserted in that place of ghosts, where the past roamed freely after dark, whispering secrets from the shadows. In the carpark, Matt and Emma's cars were the only two still there. Even Ted's bus stood locked and solitary outside the reception door.

'Stay at my house tonight,' Matt said. 'We can visit Gwendoline together in the morning.'

Emma leant her body into his. 'And does this stay come with breakfast?'

'It comes with all sorts of things,' he replied, kissing her.

'A bed without rats or dust?'

'A very clean and comfortable bed, as a matter of fact.'

She kissed him in return, slowly, sensually, knowing that the ten-minute drive to his house would be the longest of her life.

* * *

They barely made it through his front door when clothes were flung from their bodies. Nor did they make it to his bed, landing somewhere in the hall between the bathroom and kitchen.

It was as if all the turmoil of the past weeks had bubbled over with the sweet knowledge that what they had was able to be explored, that they weren't bound by history or blood ties. They were absolutely, unequivocally allowed to let this happen.

On the cool timber boards of his Fairlight home, she gave him every-thing she had with complete abandonment and she was fairly certain she woke the neighbours in the next street with her orgasm, but she didn't care.

Never had she felt more alive, ready to take on the next day and the day after that. After years of living a solitary life, of robotically moving through the motions and never taking a gamble, she was ready for this almighty leap of faith.

Later, they relocated to the shower where Emma washed her hair then they washed each other, laughing like teenagers. Matt ran his hands over her body, suds sliding down to be swallowed by the drain. He pulled her into him, kissed the insides of her wrists, her collarbone, her neck, her lips.

Emma couldn't think of a more perfect moment in her life until she heard his voice soft and low in her ear. 'I'm crazy about you, Emma Wilcott.'

Her stomach danced at his words as she beamed from ear to ear.

Because she was crazy about him too.

Chapter Thirty-Nine

GWENDOLINE 1926

The boat arrived on a crisp autumn day.

Gwendoline had been running in the cove with her friends, kicking up sand, dipping her toes in the water as it lapped calmly against the shore. The air filled with their laughter as they chased each other, all the kids that belonged to working parents on the station—housekeepers, doctors, nurses and groundsmen.

Growing up on the station was a constant adventure and all that Gwendoline had ever known. She had lots of friends and an abundance of space to roam.

Her mother, Rose, completed two hours of home-schooling with her each morning before she set off for her hospital shift and after that, the rest of the day was Gwendoline's to explore.

And while they weren't ever permitted to leave the station, weekends with her mother and her father, Thomas, were never dull. There were picnics in the cove and fishing out in the bay with her father. They made wreaths to lay on Bessie's grave, who Gwendoline understood was her real mother who died when she was an infant. They laid wreaths on Alexander's grave too; Rose's son, who'd died at birth seven years before.

They lived in a cottage, high on a cliff, with the harbour sprawled around them like a carpet of sapphires. On clear days, Gwendoline could see all the way across to South Head. She could see the Macquarie Lighthouse and yachts bobbing in the water.

So small was she high up on that cliff that she often wondered about the world beyond the station. What lives were people living across the water? What were children like her doing?

Sometimes, like the tiniest whisper in her ear, she had the oddest sensation that she didn't belong there, that perhaps she was in the wrong place.

Gwendoline was the first to see the boat arrive that morning. She pointed it out to her friends and it was met with cries of glee, for fewer boats arrived these days.

It anchored out in the bay, a magnificent naval ship with the words *HMS Renown* on the hull and a flag with a large Union Jack flapping from the bow. Gwendoline and the other children watched as a rowboat was sent out to collect a single passenger. This was intriguing, for usually all passengers disembarked. The rowboat collected just one man.

'Gwendoline, lunch.'

Gwendoline turned, squinting against the sun, and saw her mother standing at the top of the cove calling for her. A slender hand shaded her eyes, blocking the sun as she too, stared out at the anchored ship with the coat of arms and Union Jack flag.

Rose stepped down onto the sand, hurrying towards her as the man in the rowboat reached the wharf. He climbed out and straightened his tailor-made tweed suit and hat. He had no luggage with him, just a piece of paper flapping in the breeze as he walked along the wooden planks.

'Children, head back now and wash up before lunch,' Rose said quickly.

The instruction was met with groans, but they dispersed obediently as Gwendoline remained where she was, watching her mother with interest. Her face had grown tight, a frown appearing on her lips.

The man had seen them and he stepped down onto the sand, approaching briskly. Rose moved Gwendoline behind her.

'Hello there, ma'am,' he said pleasantly, removing his hat and holding out his hand to shake hers politely. 'I'm Mr Williams, personal assistant to His Royal Highness, the Duke of Northbury, first cousin to the king.'

'Mrs Van Cleeve.'

'It's lovely to meet you, Mrs Van Cleeve. Where may I find,' he consulted a piece of paper, 'a Miss Dalton, Head of Housekeeping?'

'Miss Dalton is no longer here. She left the station in 1920.'

He consulted his paper again. 'How about a Matron Cromwell?'

'She passed in 1922 from tuberculosis.'

'Ah.' He nodded. 'That's a terrible shame. I'm here in an official capacity. Can you point me in the direction of the superintendent?'

Rose's eyes narrowed slightly. 'The superintendent is off-site today. And we don't allow the public to walk freely throughout the station. Perhaps you can relay your business through me.'

The man hesitated.

'I'm a sister at the hospital. Quite senior,' she added.

He looked around, eyes sweeping the cove. There was no one else on the beach. He sighed. 'Very well. I come on behalf of the duke and duchess. They resided here for twelve months from 1918 to 1919. In fact, they had a child here, young Lady Eloise.'

Gwendoline noticed how pale her mother had become. 'I vaguely recall them,' she replied.

'Jolly good. So you were around during that time?'

'I was.'

Mr Williams' eyes fell on Gwendoline, who was peeking out from behind her mother's uniform. 'And who do we have here?' He bent down to meet her at eye level. 'What's your name, little one?'

'Gwendoline Van Cleeve.'

'And how old are you?'

'Seven.'

'Seven? Interesting.' Mr Williams' eyebrows went up. 'What lovely dark hair you have, Gwendoline. And those eyes, bluer than the ocean.'

Rose pushed Gwendoline behind her again. 'You've come a long way, Mr Williams. What is it we can do for you?'

'I'll be frank. The duke and duchess are concerned that on the night of a hospital fire in May 1919, their baby infant, Lady Eloise, was accidentally swapped with another child.'

Rose gasped. 'Why would they think such a thing?'

'I'm not going to beat around the bush, Mrs Van Cleeve. Little

Eloise is a delightful child, highly spirited and extremely outspoken, with dark brown eyes and a head full of golden curls. And while Lady Cordelia adores her, she has voiced her doubts to her husband and he shares the same concern. They do not believe the child is theirs.'

'Well, that's quite an assumption to make,' Rose said, her voice quivering slightly. 'Perhaps the child's hair will darken and her eye colour will change.'

'She's seven years old. I doubt there will be significant change now. It's beside the point. The duke has spoken to me in confidence. He believes the child they are raising belonged to a scullery maid by the name of Bessie Briar, one that he fathered in 1918.'

Gwendoline had been listening languorously to the conversation but her ears pricked up at the mention of Bessie's name. What was the man saying? That the girl he called Lady Eloise, with the dark eyes and golden curls, was Bessie's real daughter.

'I was there the night of the fire, Mr Williams. I held both infants in my arms.'

'So you were there? *You* handed the baby to Lady Cordelia?'

Rose's spine straightened. 'I did.'

'And you are certain you gave them the correct child?'

Gwendoline saw her mother hesitate. 'I am.'

'Intriguing.'

Rose chewed her lip. 'What would happen if, in the unlikely event, a mistake *did* occur?'

Mr Williams smiled encouragingly at her. 'Well, I would take the correct child with me back to England, the exchange would be made at Somersby Castle and the incorrect child would be shipped back here.'

'Like a business transaction? They're just children, Mr Williams.'

'It's the best way.'

Gwendoline was sure her mother swayed. Her hands were trembling, even as she kept them clutched tightly together in front of her. 'I'm awfully sorry, but you've come a long way for nothing.'

Mr Williams pursed his lips.

'If you will excuse me now, I must get my daughter cleaned up for lunch.'

'Of course.' He returned his hat to his head. 'I'll be sailing to

Melbourne to conduct some other business. I shall return in two weeks. Perhaps during that time you will recall a little more. It would save me the trouble of meeting with the superintendent.'

'Perhaps.'

'It was nice to meet you, Gwendoline Van Cleeve,' Mr Williams said, holding out his hand for Gwendoline to shake.

She shook it. 'Nice to meet you too.'

'I will see you again soon. Maybe we can take a little trip to England together.' He bowed his head slightly in farewell and began to walk away.

'Is she well?' Rose called out.

Mr Williams turned around.

'The blonde child. Is she happy?'

'Very much so,' Mr Williams said with a smile. 'Despite the circumstances, she is adored by the duchess.'

'And the duke?'

'He is rather taken with her.'

Rose smiled. 'Thank you, Mr Williams.'

'I will return in two weeks. I trust by then you will come to the right decision.'

* * *

Later that night, as Gwendoline was being tucked into bed by her mother, she asked her again who the mysterious man from the boat was. She had tried asking her on their way up to lunch, but Rose had been vague, then she'd gone back to work at the hospital.

While her father was collecting wood outside for the oven, Gwendoline turned her eyes to her mother. 'Who was he, Mama?'

Rose tucked the covers in firmly around Gwendoline and sat on the edge of the bed. 'He was a man from England who came to ask some questions.'

'About what?'

'That's rather a long story, my darling.'

'Can you tell me?'

'Not tonight.'

'Tomorrow, then?'

Her mother sighed. 'I don't think so. Perhaps when you're older.'

'Why?'

'Because it's nothing for you to worry about right now.'

Gwendoline didn't understand what her mother was saying, only that her face seemed sad in the lamplight. 'Mama?'

'Yes.'

'When Mr Williams returns, is he going to take me away?'

Her mother shook her head resolutely. 'No. Absolutely not. He will not be taking you anywhere.'

'But why does he want to?'

Her mother was quiet for a long time. 'Sometimes, mistakes are made. And people will come along to try to fix those mistakes. But they can be beyond fixing. Some things are better left alone.'

Gwendoline screwed up her face. 'I don't know what you mean.'

'It's getting late. We will speak of it another time.'

The door opened and her father walked in carrying logs for the oven. 'What are you still doing awake, little miss?'

'A man on a boat came from England today,' Gwendoline said. 'He said he wants to take me away.'

Her father's face paled as he shot Rose a look.

'I'll explain later,' she said to him. She smoothed the bed covers with her hands, then kissed Gwendoline's cheek. 'Time for bed, my darling. Goodnight.'

'Goodnight, Mama. Goodnight Papa.' Gwendoline rolled over in bed as her mother dimmed the oil lamps and her parents' voices softened to whispers.

As she drifted on a current of sleep, she heard them take their conversation outside, the door closing softly behind them. She thought she heard her father say, 'I knew this day would come,' followed by her mother's anguished reply, 'I can't lose her, Thomas. I won't let them,' whatever that meant.

As she listened to their muffled voices, images of the boat and Mr Williams and his smart suit and hat skated beneath her eyelids. She was filled suddenly with a number of questions she wanted to ask upon his return—who was he? What was he doing here? Why did he want to take her to England? And who were the Duke and Duchess of Northbury?

It took some time but she eventually slid into a sea of dreams, not before she vowed to wait by the wharf every day for Mr Williams to return.

Gwendoline waited by the wharf for the next five days, but she was never given the chance to see Mr Williams or his boat again. On the sixth day, in the dead of night, with one suitcase between the three of them, Thomas, Rose and Gwendoline left the station and never returned.

Chapter Forty

EMMA 2019

T he next morning, Emma and Matt ate breakfast, dressed and climbed into his car. Before heading south to Eastgardens, they made a detour to an old brick house in Fairlight, not far from Matt's.

He swung into the driveway and switched off the ignition. 'Want to come in?'

Emma chewed her lip. 'I'll wait here. Your grandfather has had enough surprises lately without Gwendoline's granddaughter walking through his door.'

Matt leant over and kissed her. 'I won't be long. He thinks he knows which one we're looking for.'

She watched him climb out of the car and trot up the front steps to the door. He let himself in, disappearing into the house.

Emma leant back against the seat and closed her eyes. They'd hardly slept the night before. Curled up in Matt's bed, they'd research until the early hours of the morning all they could about the Duke and Duchess of Northbury and their daughter, Lady Eloise, who they suspected was the real Gwendoline.

But there was still one missing piece of the puzzle. Rose's 1926 diaries. If they knew her at all, she would have documented her final days at the station, confirming their theory in full. The entries must have been incriminating, for there had been no sign of any such diaries in her trunk in the cottage on the cliff. They could only conclude that she'd taken it with them when they'd fled.

When Matt spoke to his grandfather earlier that morning, Henry recalled having boxes of his mother's diaries stored away in his garage, for she had continued to write for many years. Better yet, he recalled one in particular that his mother was fond of keeping close.

'I could never find the key for it though,' he had told Matt over the phone, 'so I can't tell you what's in it.'

Matt returned ten minutes later, holding a tan hardcover book in his hand. Emma recognised it instantly.

'Is that it?' she asked, sitting up.

'I believe so.' Matt slipped behind the wheel and closed the car door. 'It wasn't with her other diaries. It was in with her personal effects—birth certificate, passport, driver's licence.'

'If it's as telling as we think it is, it's a wonder she didn't destroy it.'

'I don't think Rose was ever capable of destroying her words.'

Matt didn't start the ignition straight away. Instead, he spread the covers of the diary and, as they expected, out dropped the key. They spent the next thirty minutes parked in Henry's driveway reading from Rose's diary. In her own words, she detailed her final anxious days at the station.

An hour later, they arrived at Eastgardens and parked the car across from the aged care facility. It was a warm December Tuesday, the sun bright in a brilliant blue sky.

Carrying a bouquet of roses, Emma signed the visitors' book and led the way down the north corridor towards Gwendoline's room.

Her grandmother was sitting up in her bed with the covers pulled to her waist. She was staring absentmindedly out the window, looking so peaceful in thought that Emma loathed disturbing her.

'Hi Grandma.' She leant across the bed to kiss Gwendoline's velvety cheek.

She looked surprised to see her. 'Catherine, dear.'

'It's Emma, Grandma. Catherine's not here.'

Gwendoline shook her head at the mishap. 'Oh yes, how silly of me. Hello, Emma. You brought me roses.'

'Yes, for *our* Rose.' Emma filled a vase with water and arranged the roses in it, then perched herself on the edge of the bed while Matt pulled up a chair next to her. 'Do you remember my friend, Matt?'

Gwendoline leant forward and squinted, studying Matt's face. 'I remember those eyes. Hazel, just like his.'

'You mean Thomas, your father? Matt is his great-grandson.'

Gwendoline looked delighted. 'Really? Is that so? Oh, I can see the similarities. Your eyes, your face, your build. Yes, the resemblance is quite extraordinary.'

'Tell us about Thomas.'

'He was such a kind man, a good man. And my mother, Rose, was a beautiful lady too.'

'You also knew them as Jack and Edith Cleveland.'

Gwendoline fixed her gaze on Emma, squinting again, as though trying to make sense of what she'd just said. 'Yes. You are quite right. Jack and Edith.'

'They changed their names after they left the station with you in 1926, didn't they? After Mr Williams' first visit,' Emma prodded gently. 'They were hiding from him.'

Gwendoline smiled. 'Goodness, how do you know all that?'

Emma exchanged a look with Matt. 'There are a lot of things we know now, Grandma. Like how an emerald stone meant for Lady Eloise was accidentally placed on another child called Gwendoline. This child set sail for England with the Duke and Duchess of Northbury and the real Lady Eloise was left behind, raised on the station by Thomas and Rose. And we know,' Emma said carefully, 'that that child was you. You're Lady Eloise.'

Gwendoline fell silent as she turned her head to gaze out the window. Emma was unsure if she'd offloaded too much information too soon, if Gwendoline would experience a sudden rush of painful memories that might overwhelm her.

She was silent for such a long time that Emma reached for her hand. 'Grandma, I'm sorry. Did I upset you?'

Gwendoline swallowed and turned back to her. 'No dear, I just... I have these memories in my old brain and sometimes I can't string them together. It's like a mouse has been nibbling on them. They're full of holes.'

'Take your time. We'll get you some water,' Emma said.

Matt stood and poured a glass from the jug on the table. He handed it to Emma who passed it to Gwendoline. She took small sips like a child then leant back against her pillow, closing her eyes.

When she opened them again, she fixed them on Emma with surprising lucidity. 'You are right. A mishap occurred in 1919 when two babies were accidentally swapped on the night of the hospital fire. The duke and duchess were handed a baby that wasn't theirs and they took that baby back to England with them. The real Eloise stayed behind at the station, raised by Thomas and Rose. That child was me.'

'When did you find out?' Emma asked.

'I always knew that Rose and Thomas were not my parents. Rose had maintained that Bessie Briar was my real mother. I suppose she said that because it was the easier story to tell. That was until Mr Williams arrived one day.'

'What did he say?'

'From what I recall, he informed Rose that the duke and duchess were concerned they'd been given the wrong child. He seemed interested in me and told me he'd come back for me two weeks later. I asked my mother about it later that night, but she was evasive.'

'Was she scared?'

'Probably terrified. Thomas too. The child they loved was about to be taken from them. But I was curious. The more they kept from me, the more I craved to know.'

'And that's who you were waiting for by the wharf? The man on the boat—Mr Williams.'

Her grandmother nodded with a small smile. 'Yes, every day I waited for him to return. I had so many questions to ask him, ones that Rose refused to answer.

'I used to lie in bed at night listening to her and my father whisper outside the cottage. I couldn't always hear what they were saying, but I suppose now they were hatching their getaway plan. They had already lost one child to a stillbirth. They had no intention of letting Mr Williams take another.'

351

Emma opened her handbag on the floor beside her chair and retrieved the last diary Rose ever wrote in at the station. 'We've been reading Rose's diaries. You might recall I told you about them.'

'Rose wrote in diaries? How lovely.'

'Would you like me to read from the entry she wrote the day after Mr Williams arrived? It might help put things into perspective.'

'Yes please. I'd like that very much.'

Emma flipped through the pages until she found the entry dated the fourteenth of April 1926, the day after Mr Williams arrived and changed their lives forever.

14th April, 1926

The boat arrived yesterday, the one that we knew would eventually come but prayed we would never see. It brought Mr Williams to our door, a man in the employ of Somersby Castle, sent to get to the bottom of that night, the one I replay over and over in my head until it makes me weary.

Not that I am in any doubt as to what occurred. Not now. It became apparent to me when she reached two, when her hair darkened and her eyes turned blue, brighter than any sky, and I knew the Gwendoline we had was not Bessie Briar's daughter.

Perhaps I always knew. Perhaps I knew the moment Matron Cromwell slipped the emerald onto Gwendoline's neck, an instinct I chose to ignore, like the tiniest inkling that something was amiss. I ignored it because I never had anything more to go on.

But Mr Williams knew it too. He knew it the moment he laid eyes on her, so similar in features to his employers. It won't be long before he reports his suspicions back to Somersby Castle. That moment down on the cove filled me with ice, like a cold, hard stab of dread to my heart for what had been done and what was yet to come.

I worry most for Gwendoline. She has spent the entire day by the wharf and I suspect she is awaiting Mr Williams' return. She asked me about his visit and what it meant. I did not have the strength or the courage to tell her. For what could I have said? That she was swapped. That she was left behind and another took her place. That they are looking for her now.

How can two children living their lives, loved by their parents, simply be exchanged like a business deal? How does one explain such a process to a young mind?

To exchange them now seems like a cruel joke. To send them to a new country with new parents and an unfamiliar way of living, so vastly different from anything they've ever known. Swapping the children back will not fix the issue but perhaps in the long run, make it worse.

And perhaps deep down, I am entirely selfish. I cannot let her go. She is our child and I love her as I do Alexander. That makes the decision difficult, the lines between right and wrong blurred. So help me, I have to protect both girls for I am the only one who can do that, even if the decision I make will be judged by God.

I'm doing it for them and for us all.

Rose

Emma closed the diary and laid it on her lap. Matt leant forward on his elbows next to her, looking utterly absorbed again in Rose's words.

Gwendoline was still lying back against her pillow, her eyes closed and for a moment, Emma thought she'd fallen asleep.

Then her eyes fluttered open and she smiled. 'Did my mother write that?'

'Yes,' Emma said. 'Rose wrote a lot of diary entries. She has books and books of them stored at the station, from 1918 through to 1926. She also wrote many more during her time in North Queensland. Today we discovered boxes of them still exist.'

'She writes with such honesty.'

'All her entries are like this——raw and poignant.'

'That was my mother,' Gwendoline said fondly. 'She wore her heart on her sleeve.'

'I'm sure the station would allow us to have them if we asked. I could read them all to you. They really are quite lovely.'

'We can put in a request to Anthony, the station director. It shouldn't be a problem,' Matt said.

'Does it help you to understand why Rose and Thomas made the decisions they did?' Emma asked her grandmother. 'To leave the station before Mr Williams returned, to change their names and flee with you to North Queensland in the hope of losing him? They loved you as if you were their own child. The idea of sending you away broke their hearts.'

Gwendoline looked out the window again. 'I understand now but I didn't always. As I got older, I put two and two together. The realisation began to manifest into something else entirely—a bitterness, a longing to know the tapestry from which I'd been woven.

'I felt lost and I called them hurtful things. I told them they'd lied to me, stolen me, that the life they'd given me was terrible in comparison with the English one I could have had. They called me Ginny and I shouted that my name was Gwendoline or Eloise, that I wasn't even a Cleveland. Oh, I was a rebellious teenager.' Her cheeks coloured. Even though decades separated the now and then, she still looked guilty as if no time had passed.

'I remember saying horrible things to you once,' Emma said, sheepish too.

Gwendoline patted her hand forgivingly. 'You didn't choose to leave your family, though. They were taken from you. I ran away from mine when I was sixteen. I left them all behind and I never saw them again. It is still one of my greatest regrets.'

'You ran to Sydney and met Grandpa. Some good came from it, at least.'

Gwendoline grimaced. 'That's not quite what happened, as I recall. I went somewhere else first.' She pointed to her bedside table. 'Open the drawer and fetch me my book, would you, dear?'

Emma leant across and opened the drawer of the bedside table. Resting on top of Gwendoline's underwear was Jane Austen's *Pride and Prejudice*, the book her grandmother had been reading on repeat.

She frowned. 'I really need to get you a new book, Grandma. I'll do it today. I'll go to the bookstore.'

'The book is just fine,' Gwendoline said. 'In fact, my mother gave it to me.'

Emma lifted it out of the drawer and handed it to her. She didn't take it, instead gestured for Emma to open it.

Emma flipped open the front cover and a single photograph slipped out. It was black and white, a shot of a man and woman standing with two teenage girls, one fair with golden curls, the other darker, more alike the two adults. The darker of the girls was shaking the hand of the male and curtsying.

Emma stared at the photograph. As she realised what it was telling her, she looked up at her grandmother. 'You went to England?'

Gwendoline nodded.

'You ran away from home and went to England to find them.'

'I stole money from my parents for passage on a ship, something I'm not proud of. But yes, I went to Northern England and I found them.'

'Grandma that's...'

'Silly, I know.'

'I was going to say extremely brave,' Emma said. 'What happened?'

'A new medical college was opening and they were greeting the public on the grounds; the duke, duchess and Lady Eloise. I pushed my way to the front of the crowd to get a better look at them. Because two women had been accepted into the college, the newspaper photographer was asking women to come forward and meet the royals. He asked if I'd like to have my photo taken with them. Of course I said yes. I told myself, when I meet them, if there's even the slightest glimmer of recognition in their eyes, if they should hold my gaze a moment too long, I would tell them who I was.'

Emma held her breath. 'And did they?'

Gwendoline shook her head sadly. 'They didn't recognise me at all. The greeting was over in a matter of seconds and I was hurried along.'

'I'm so sorry.'

'And what about the real Gwendoline?' Matt asked.

'She looked like a delightful girl, pretty with her golden curls, laughing and smiling. She said hello to me. She was very nice and I saw the emerald around her neck which I admit jolted me.

'Then I thought to myself, what am I even doing here? Who am I to intervene after all these years? Who am I to throw her life into chaos when she knows no better? It wasn't her fault. It was the life fate gave her. They all looked so happy, so complete and I was the odd one out again.'

'Oh, Grandma,' Emma said, looking down at the photograph again and feeling hopelessly sorry for the dark-haired, blue-eyed girl who shook the duke's hand with such hope, desperate for a sign that she hadn't been forgotten. 'Why didn't you ever tell me any of this? Why didn't Mum tell me?'

'We planned to when you were older,' Gwendoline said wistfully. 'But then life changed. Your parents and brothers went to France and they never came home. And you had so much to deal with on your young shoulders that the past was no longer as important as the future.'

Then came Drew and his affair with Tabitha, the breakdown of Emma's marriage and the onset of her grandmother's dementia, and she understood what Gwendoline was saying. It had been one heartbreak after another. There had never been a right time to explain it.

Emma looked down again at the photograph in her hand. The duchess was facing the camera and Emma studied her features at length——the thick dark hair, the curve of her lips, the striking eyes. She saw her mother in this woman, right down to the slender frame and demure smile.

'They had the bluest eyes,' Gwendoline said. 'Eyes like the ocean. Eyes like mine and yours.'

'And like my mother's.'

Gwendoline blinked her affirmation.

'This is the photo that's been causing your wanderings,' Emma chastised gently. 'You haven't been reading *Pride and Prejudice* over and over again. You've been using it to store your photograph.'

'What do you mean?' Gwendoline said, her eyes clouding over in that familiar way they did when she was about to lose her grip on the present. It was incredible how she could recall events from eight decades ago like it was yesterday, but events of the past months evaporated as though they'd never happened.

'It doesn't matter,' Emma said, patting her hand. 'It's all in the past now.' She placed the photograph back in the book and returned it to the drawer, ready for when her grandmother's memories would lead her there. 'What did you do after you met the duke and duchess, Grandma?'

Gwendoline looked tired, her eyes glazed, her head sinking into her shoulders from the effort she'd expended to revisit the past. 'I had not a penny left and was stranded in the north of England. I used my return train ticket to get back to London then I snuck onto a ship bound for Sydney.'

'You were a stowaway?' Emma almost laughed.

'I was. And I met your grandfather on that ship. We married eight weeks later, when we sailed into Sydney. After some years we had Catherine and the rest is history.'

'Why didn't you go home to North Queensland or at least tell your family where you were?'

Gwendoline looked down at her lap. She seemed small in her single bed, swallowed by the covers, by time and regrets. 'I'd stolen money from my parents, went to England against their wishes and came back with my tail between my legs. I couldn't have faced them again. I was humiliated.'

Emma glanced at Matt. 'We know someone who would love to see you again.'

'My grandfather, Henry, is still alive,' Matt said. 'I haven't told him about you yet, but I know he's always wondered about you.'

A tear leaked from the corner of Gwendoline's eye and slid down her cheek. 'You're Henry's grandson?' she said, voice quivering.

'I am,' Matt said.

She smiled through her tears. 'He was my favourite,' and that was all her emotion would allow her to say.

Emma stood and retrieved a tissue. She handed it to her grandmother, who blew her nose and wiped her tears. 'I'm sorry we upset you.'

Gwendoline smiled. 'Happy tears, my dear. It's lovely to know Henry is well.'

'We did some research on the duke and duchess, and Lady Eloise too. Would you like me to tell you about them?'

Gwendoline nodded, clutching the balled up tissue in her hand.

'The Duchess of Northbury passed away first in 1943 at the age of fifty-five. She died of lung complications. That's all the article would say. The duke died next in 1987 at the age of, get this, one hundred. It must run in the family. He left a sizeable fortune and estate to his only heir.

'Lady Eloise, your half-sister, lived to the ripe age of ninety-seven.

She died three years ago, passing peacefully in her sleep. She had two children, a boy and a girl, both with lovely golden curls.'

Gwendoline nodded. 'I see.'

Emma sat again on the edge of the bed. 'So I guess we should decide what we're going to do about this. How far do you want to take it, Grandma? We'd be entitled to land, maybe even a title. And the emerald belongs to you. You're the rightful owner. You have the opportunity now to right the wrongs.'

Gwendoline sighed sadly and patted Emma's hand. 'Finding my real parents was never about emeralds or castles. It was about finding myself and where I'd come from.' She smiled. 'Besides, I'm too old for all that now. What's done is done. I can't change the past and I made my peace with that a long time ago.'

Emma nodded understandingly.

'But you have that opportunity, Emerald,' Gwendoline said. 'You can go to the royal family with all this information and state your case. That emerald is not mine. It belongs to you. You're the rightful heir now. And that life, if you want it, is there for you.'

Emma glanced across at Matt, who was watching her closely. She thought of her grandmother, her job at The Coffee Bean, her humble little Kensington apartment and the wonderful man this unexpected mystery had brought to her.

She didn't know what the future held or how it would shape her life but it no longer seemed a daunting concept. Every end had a new beginning. She was open to it, arms outstretched.

She reached for Matt's hand and smiled. 'I'm not sure I want all that, Grandma. I think I have everything I need right here.'

Chapter Forty-One

T he sand between Emma's toes felt cool, as did the water lapping gently against the shore. The cove was deeply peaceful as she stared out across the bay towards Fairlight and Dobroyd Head.

Matt was beside her, a solid and calming presence in her life, never swaying or faltering, as she imagined Thomas would have been for his Rose.

And she could see them together, Thomas and Rose, sitting in this very cove a hundred years before, running their fingers through the sand, as a romance blossomed into an enduring love; the kind that would go on to withstand loss and heartache.

She could see Gwendoline and Rose standing here too, conversing with Mr Williams as he attempted to reverse an error that was made, when two infants were inadvertently swapped one blazing night in 1919.

Over the past week, Emma had thought long and hard about what to do. The power was in her hands. Did she try to right the wrongs? Did she go to England and fight for her grandmother's identity and the emerald?

In the end, she decided to let sleeping ghosts lie. No good could come from shaking up a monarchy, from stripping people of titles and exposing errors of judgement. And for what gain? Some secrets were better left buried.

Emma watched Gwendoline dip her toes in the water. She seemed lost in her memories of a childhood spent on this sand, of swimming in the cove and rowing fishing boats out into the bay with her father. Of picnics on the beach and watching ships come and go.

'My mother's here with Henry,' Matt said, glancing at his phone. 'Should we head up to the café now?'

'Yes, let's do that.' Emma reached for Gwendoline's arm and explained that Henry had arrived.

'Oh, goodness.' Gwendoline looked suddenly uncertain.

'Don't be nervous,' Emma reassured her. 'He's going to be so happy to see you.'

She guided Gwendoline up towards the grass area to dust off their feet and slip their shoes back on. Emma knew how her grandmother must be feeling. She was nervous too, not just for Gwendoline and Henry, but for meeting Matt's mother for the first time. Matt was close to his parents, and Emma worried about failing somehow in his mother's eyes or the reunion being a disaster.

They slid into their shoes and Emma assisted Gwendoline up the grass to the café where tables were spread out under white umbrellas. It was summer and the day was warm, a light breeze ruffling the water in the bay.

Emma helped Gwendoline into a chair and Matt stepped into the café, returning with glasses and a jug of water. As he poured, Emma heard the squeak of Ted's brakes outside the shower blocks.

'That'll be Mum and Pop,' Matt said and Emma could tell he was anxious too.

A slender woman with auburn hair and eyes the colour of Matt's rounded the corner, an elderly man shuffling unassisted at her side.

Matt went to them. 'Mum, Pop.' He hugged them both.

Emma placed her hand on Gwendoline's shoulder and could feel her tremble slightly beneath her fingers. 'You're doing great, Gran.'

Matt led his mother and Henry to the table. The sprightly eighty-eight-year-old looked just as unsure as Gwendoline and when she rose unsteadily to greet him, he held out his arms to her.

'Ginny,' he said, squinting to study her. 'Is that really you?'

'Henry,' she replied, moving closer to him. Her fingertips hovered over his face, over laugh lines and wrinkles as though there was a need to bridge the years. 'Why, it's been far too long.'

'Over eighty years.'

'Good lord. And yet look at you—you're still my baby brother.'

He chuckled. He was taller than her, with a full head of white hair, a friendly face and the kindest hazel eyes.

He took a seat beside her and they clutched hands, reuniting at long last. 'I have so much to ask you, Ginny.'

'I know, Henry. I know.'

With eight decades to catch up on, Emma, Matt and his mother shifted to the side to allow them space.

'I'm Sandra,' Matt's mother said, thrusting out her hand for Emma to shake. When she did, Sandra pulled her into a hug.

'It's lovely to meet you, sweetheart. Matt's told us all about you.'

The embrace was so warm, so motherly, that Emma almost forgot she was being held by a stranger. It had been years since she'd felt an embrace like that and she closed her eyes, almost unaware when Sandra pulled away.

'Thank you for organising this. Dad was beside himself when Matt told him he'd found Gwendoline. He treasured her when they were children. We're just so excited to have the two of you in our lives.' Sandra's hazel eyes lit up as she said it. 'Grandpa Jack and Grandma Edith would have loved this. Well, Thomas and Rose, as you know them.'

'It was quite the mystery to piece together, but I'm glad we persisted,' Emma said, smiling at Matt. He smiled broadly in return.

'Matt's filled us in on everything. It's an impressive story.'

'Bringing the two families together was the best part.'

Sandra nodded. 'Why don't you both come over for dinner next week? Bring Gwendoline if you can. Dad will be there.'

'We'd love to.'

'And we have those boxes of Grandma Edith's diaries sitting in Dad's garage. We never knew where the keys were to open any of them. Matt tells us you both have a little trick for that.'

'We might have,' Emma said with a smile.

'We'd love for you both to have them.'

Emma drew breath. 'The diaries? All of them?'

'Grandma Edith would have wanted that.'

Emma and Matt exchanged a look and it was clear this was news to him too. 'What an incredible gift. Thank you.'

Sandra hugged them both and went to sit with Henry and Gwendoline at the table.

Matt took Emma's hand, leading her back out onto the sand. The sun was drifting towards the west, taking the blue sky with it. Wispy clouds were scribbled with peach and the station glowed like fire behind them.

'Mum really likes you,' he said as he slipped his arm around her shoulders, pulling her in close.

'And I like her. She's a lovely lady.' Emma nestled against him.

He kissed her forehead then her lips as their feet sunk into the sand and the waves broke gently around their ankles. 'You've changed my whole world, Em. I'm so glad I found you wandering around isolation that day.'

'If I remember correctly, I found you.'

'You should visit the station without a map more often.'

She threw her head back and laughed. She had come to the Quarantine Station to uncover Gwendoline's past and somehow, she had found her own future.

Surrounded by the ghosts of yesterday, entwined in all manner of ways, they walked these sands beside her——Thomas and Rose, Bessie and Eloise, the duke and duchess. Her parents were there too——John and Catherine, and her twin brothers, Max and Liam. Each had left their mark on history. Each had helped to shape her in some way.

She tucked them away in the safety of her heart, a better person for knowing them, for following their journeys and experiencing their heartbreak. Rose's diaries had brought the past to life, but for Emma, it was time to stop looking back, to move forward and embrace the future.

She leant her head on Matt's shoulder and knew she wouldn't have to do it alone. Not anymore. They had each other and the future seemed brighter than it ever had.

Author's Note

One of my favourite things about writing a novel is the ability to explore fascinating locations. The Q Station, on Manly's North Head, has long been a place of intrigue for me. It is a wealth of historical information and a fundamental part of Sydney's childhood.

While I have taken great care to respect all facets of this, I did have to tweak some facts to bring this novel to life, such as the strict rules relating to staff relations. These rules in the book forced Thomas and Rose to develop a relationship in secret. It should be known that families, in real life, were allowed to live on the Quarantine Station. There was no rule preventing this. However, it is true that staff members were not permitted to come and go freely due to the risk of contaminating the Sydney populous.

Class segregation is accurately portrayed in the novel. First and second classes were regarded highly over third and Asiatics. The memory Gwendoline recounts of third-class passenger transactions being suspended in the post office if a first-class passenger entered is not only slightly amusing, but correct.

Also accurately portrayed is the procedure Nurse Dolly explains for ridding Spanish Influenza from sufferers by placing them in an inhalation chamber together to inhale a zinc sulphate solution. This was thought to rid the throat and nasal passages of the influenza bacteria.

They did not realise at the time that influenza was viral and that the procedure caused the virus to spread further. This procedure was first carried out in 1919 in the disinfecting blocks in the Wharf Precinct. However, in the story, Dolly describes the procedure to Rose in 1918.

It is also worth mentioning that the first ship to be quarantined under the pneumonic influenza decree was the passenger liner *RMS Niagra* in October 1918. However, in the novel, the liner carrying the Duke and Duchess of Northbury was the first to be quarantined in June 1918 and was not part of any decree.

I'd like to highlight a few key places in the book that I created from imagination——Thomas's secluded cottage on the clifftop does not exist and the locations of the staff quarters have been altered to suit the plot. Matron Cromwell's office, the maternity ward, the extra rooms behind the museum and the standalone cottage that housed the Duke and Duchess of Northbury are also fictional, but all other precincts are accurately described to the best of my knowledge. The Coffee Bean and Eastgardens Aged Care are fictional too.

In the novel, the baby swap happens during the hospital fire of 1919. In reality, this fire occurred in February 2002 when, sadly, the original 1883 hospital burnt to the ground due to faulty electrical wiring. I have altered this event by eighty-three years to suit the storyline.

It is unclear if the term 'parlourmaid' or 'scullery maid' were used in the early twentieth century to describe housekeeping roles on the station. I was unable to find anything concrete to suggest either way. The lovely tour guide at the Q Station thought it would be fine to play my author card here and refer to the roles as I saw fit.

The Q Station, on the site of Sydney's former Quarantine Station, was a great source of inspiration in writing this novel, and it was easy for me to select this location then build the story around it. It was a pleasure to spend much of my investigative time there and if you like disappearing through the doors of time, then I highly recommend a visit to this site.

www.qstation.com.au

Sources

I consulted many sources while writing this novel, both written and in person. The complete list is too long to include but here are some of the useful ones.

The tour staff at the Q Station were a treasure trove of historical information during my visits. Also referred to in my research was the book *From Quarantine Station to Q Station* which can be purchased from the Q Station, and *Sydney Then and Now* by Caroline Mackaness.

The following websites were invaluable and certainly worth a mention; first and foremost www.qstation.com.au. It is also, incidentally, the website Emma consults in chapter two when first making the decision to visit.

The website recordsearch.naa.gov.au had lots of old documents, supply forms and log books from the Quarantine Station that I found helpful when constructing the scenes in the archive room with Matt and Emma.

I also found www.archives.gov useful in understanding the correct way to handle archived documents and www.etiquettescholar.com (plus various online video tutorials) for guidance on how to set a formal table.

Essential in researching the Great War and its relationship to the Spanish Influenza pandemic were www.firstworldwar.com and www.history.com, and I found a plethora of information on www.

dementiacarecentral.com which helped in developing Gwendoline's cognitive decline. Also particularly useful was www. historyofvaccines.org to understand the timeline of certain vaccinations.

While I completed a significant amount of research for this novel any anomalies, where not intentional, are entirely my own.

Acknowledgments

My family, as always, were instrumental in helping me bring this story to life. A heartfelt thank you to Brett, Eve and Connor for exercising an enormous amount of patience throughout this process. I could never have done any of this without your love and support.

To my editor, Lynne Stringer, I continue to learn and become a better writer as a result of your guidance. You challenge me and spot the flaws I don't always spot. I have met some wonderful friends in the book world and you are, without a doubt, one of them.

Thank you always to my girls, Bianca Nash, Liz Butler, Jo Libreri and Natasha Booth. You keep me sane and that's no small feat.

Heartfelt gratitude to my parents, Carmen Montebello, and Joe and Michelle Montebello for spreading the word and being genuinely interested.

To all the reviewers and bloggers; you are tireless in your efforts to promote authors. I applaud you. Thank you for taking the time to read this too.

To my designer, Kris Dallas, who continues to make beautiful covers and other things for me, and to the staff at the Q Station who answered all my questions, no matter how silly they were. You keep the history of the station alive and will always have a visitor in me.

Lastly, to my readers who have made it to the end of another book. I sincerely hope it transported you. Thank you for all your kind words of encouragement. I have listened to, read and appreciated every single one of them.

ALSO BY MICHELLE MONTEBELLO

The Lost Letters of Playfair Street

The Forever Place

Beautiful, Fragile

The Quarantine Station

***

SEASONS OF BELLE

The Summer of Everything (1)

To Autumn, With Love (2)

The Colour of Winter (3)

The Spring Farewell (4)

The Lost Letters
of
PLAYFAIR STREET

MICHELLE MONTEBELLO

THE LOST LETTERS OF PLAYFAIR STREET

A lover's game. A chest of clues.
Come find me. I'll be waiting...

1929: On the night of her engagement to austere banker Floyd Clark, Charlotte Greene meets enigmatic Sydney Harbour Bridge engineer, Alexander Young.

Their encounter is brief, but their attraction is instant.

Alex invites Charlotte to play a game with him, one of daring clues and secret meeting places. She accepts and they embark on a thrilling lover's chase across the city.

But with her arranged marriage to Floyd looming, will she have the strength to let Alex go?

Present Day: Paige Westwood is helping her boss establish a publishing company in his newly purchased Playfair Street house in The Rocks, Sydney.

In the attic, she discovers a chest of old clues that are designed to lead the reader on a journey across the city.

Paige contacts the former owner, Ryan Greene, who explains the clues may have belonged to his great-aunt Charlotte, who once lived in the house, but who mysteriously disappeared in 1929.

Together, they follow Charlotte and Alex's clues to unravel a fascinating tale of lies and intrigue, of two lovers bound by hope, but also by deceit.

Can they solve the mystery of Charlotte's disappearance or has all hope been lost to the past?

Book Club Questions

1. Rose and Emma narrate the story. If you could have another character's viewpoint, who would you like to hear from?

2. Which timeline interested you the most? The present day, as Emma and Matt pieced together the mysteries of the past, or 1918, when Rose and Thomas lived on the station?

3. Compared with modern day standards, do you think the Quarantine Station adopted good health and quarantine practices (consider fumigation, isolation, inhalation chambers and disinfecting showers)? Can you draw any similarities with today's practices?

4. Do you think Rose should have returned Lady Eloise to her rightful parents (the Duke and Duchess) in exchange for the real Gwendoline (Bessie's child)? Why do you think she chose not to?

5. It took many years for Emma to learn the truth about her ancestry. Should Gwendoline and Catherine have told her earlier? Or were they right to withhold the information? How would the monarchy, the media and the world have reacted if the news had been made public?

6. Out the front of the burning hospital, Rose had an opportunity to tell the Duke that a potential baby swap may have occurred. Do you agree with her decision to remain silent? Do you think Matron Cromwell should have formally raised it at some point?

7. To save Gwendoline from a life on the streets, Bessie committed suicide. What other options may have been available to her? Do you think she should have attempted life outside the station with her daughter or considered adoption?

8. What character did you enjoy the most and why?

9. Which scene in *The Quarantine Station* affected you the most? What emotions did it evoke?

10. Did you learn anything new from the book? Were you aware of the Quarantine Station in Sydney or of its history? Are you aware of similar stations in your own town or country?

About the Author

Michelle Montebello is a writer from Sydney, Australia where she lives with her family. She is the internationally bestselling author of *The Quarantine Station, The Lost Letters of Playfair Street, The Forever Place* and *Beautiful, Fragile*.

Her books have won numerous awards. *The Quarantine Station* was a finalist in the 2021 International Book Awards for Best Historical Fiction. *The Lost Letters of Playfair Street* won the 2020 Australian Romance Readers Association Awards for Favourite Contemporary Romance and Favourite Australian-Set Romance.

Michelle has been shortlisted three times for ARRA Australian Author of the Year.

For more of Michelle's book news, subscribe to her newsletter at www. michellemontebello.com.au.